WITH YOU

"With you, I am who I want to be."

Jensen Kristyne

messy modern press
P.O. BOX #226
Farmersville, TX 75442

Copyright © 2020 by Jensen Kristyne

With You is a work of fiction. Any references to historical events, real people, or real places are used fictitiously. Names, characters, places, and incidents are products of the author's imagination, and any resemblance to actual events or places or persons, living or dead, is entirely coincidental.

First Messy Modern Press paperback edition December 2020

For more information, please contact Messy Modern Press at
Business@messymodernpress.com
Cover design by Natasha MacKenzie

The Cataloging-in-Publication Data is on file at Library of Congress.
Control Number: 2020922306

ISBN: 978-1-7360998-0-3 (paperback)
ISNB: 978-1-7360998-1-0 (ebook)

www.messymodernpress.com

10 9 8 7 6 5 4 3 2 1

To all my readers from the start, my family, and my friends. I wouldn't have made it here without you. You mean the world to me.

five years ago

MASON

At the top of Break Point Hill, there's a massive field that sits open, directly beside a ledge. It overlooks our entire town of Elm Brook, and at the base of it lies a small pond that wraps the length of one side. To the locals who live here, it's known as the Drop-Off because of its one-hundred-and-ten-foot drop from the top of the hill's ledge to the water below. It's the go-to place for rowdy teens looking to blow off some steam, drink, and mess around. And as for my friends and me, it's our favorite weekly hang out—Saturday night parties at the D.O.

"Just calm down. . . do you really think Luca is dumb enough to try anything with the two of us here?" I ask my best friend, trying to keep my tone as calm as possible, while I shift uncomfortably in my hoodie.

Fuck it's cold.

Why are we here again?

"Come on, Theo, why don't we head back to the bonfire and see if—"

"No thanks. I'm good."

Okay . . . or we could just stay here, I guess.

If I'm being honest with myself I saw the warning signs building from the moment Luca first arrived. Theo's always hated him, and the fact that he's been so open in his pursuit of Brielle tonight doesn't help. He's oddly protective when it comes to my sister, which I normally wouldn't mind—only tonight I have other things on my mind . . .problems that don't involve my sister's love life.

I slump back against a tree and kick my leg up.

"Dude, why do you even care? She's *my* sister, and if Luca makes her happy then I'm happy for her. She deserves—"

"Exactly, she's *your* sister and the guys had his fucking hands on her all night." Theo pushes off of the massive stone he's been sitting on and tosses his gum off the cliff. I watch it fly out the twenty feet or so, before it drops and disappears into the night sky. "If I were you, I'd tell him he needs to back the fuck off!"

"Oh, for the love of—come on, man. We've talked about this."

Turning toward the clearing where the rest of our group sits, talking and drinking about nothing in particular, I can see the cute, brown-haired girl, Becks, with the pretty golden eyes and feisty mouth, as she tilts her head and stares in our direction. God, I hope I get the chance to kiss her tonight. Last weekend I chickened out.

"Talked? Talked about what?" Theo's voice perks up.

The not so subtle change in his tone snaps me out of my inner thoughts. I watch as he takes a step toward the clearing, when a blonde mess begins working her way around the opposite side of the pit. She stumbles but catches herself—the roaring flames of the bonfire highlight her familiar features.

I look at Theo, then slide my eyes to my drunk-ass sister. Why the hell does he look annoyingly mesmerized by her?

"Brielle, man!" I groan and shove his shoulder. "We've talked about Brielle!"

Half laughing, Theo rubs his chin like he always does when he's weighing his options. He continues to observe her, when Luca calls out her name. The sound of his voice sparks something to flash behind Theo's eyes.

Wait. Is he . . .?

Theo shakes his head when he catches me glaring. "Just chill out, would ya? Nothing's changed. We both know Luca is the perfect guy for her."

I nod and look back at my sister, who's currently walking like she's just landed on the moon. Oh for fuck's sake! The girl's only had . . .what . . .three wine coolers? How the hell is she such a lightweight?

I turn when I hear Theo let out a breath, as he shoves a hand through his hair.

"I just want her to be happy." His words are flat and broken. "I won't let Luca disrespect her. He needs to realize how lucky he is."

I open my mouth to answer him, then shut it, just as Brielle comes tumbling through the tree line.

"What's the deal?" she asks, but because she's drunk, she yells. "I thought only girls went to the bathroom together?"

Theo smiles, shaking his head. The apparent shift in his mood rubs me the wrong way.

He motions for her to turn around. "Go back to the clearing, Brielle. The tree line isn't safe."

"What?" She rolls her eyes as if she's remembering something. "Oh, I get it. . . Jessica isn't here to distract you tonight, so you're taking it out on the rest of us? Is that it?"

What? Distract him?

Oh shit!

I cut my eyes to Theo, then quickly look back at my brave-ass little sister. I almost forgot she'd walked up on the two of them making out last weekend. Theo's been fuming the entire week because of that little incident. He hates being interrupted, especially when the person doing the interrupting is Brielle.

Damn. She has no shame.

"Seriously, go."

"No."

"Brielle . . ."

Brielle squints and squares her shoulders with Theo's. She hesitates for a moment before she moves to walk further into the tree line, which unintentionally places her closer to the ledge.

Ah fuck. This isn't going to end well. All I need is her drunk ass falling off the cliff; how would I explain that to Mom and Dad?

I open my mouth to yell at Brielle to come back, when I see Theo reach out and grasp her arm. She turns and glares at him. The vision of the two of them together, like two burning stars on the verge of a stellar collision.

"What the hell, Theo!" She spits out.

I watch as Theo leans in close to her, to the point where only a couple of inches now separate them.

"Please, just . . . don't." His voice is low, pleading.

Why do I feel like a creeper, watching an intimate moment between two people in love?

"Fine, then. Let. Go." She rips her hand away.

I'm sorry? Am I missing something here? I silently ask myself. I mean, I know Theo is only reacting this way because he's trying to watch out for her, but fuck . . . this is weird.

I take a moment and sweep my eyes around the surrounding area. The thick brush of trees we're standing in line the outer corners of the field and hug each of the far sides of the ledge.

"Okay, why don't we just head back to the rest of the group?" I offer aloud, desperate for a solution out of this rapidly growing, awkward situation. My head is pounding, and sadly it's not from the beer.

"Fine," Brielle says, staring unnervingly back at my best friend. She turns back toward the field and starts walking again. Theo is close behind her.

I watch the two of them walk off in front of me. Theo's mouth is moving as he and Brielle carry on talking, but I'm too far away to make out a single word.

Sighing, I raise my hand up to pinch the bridge of my nose, as my eyes trail beyond them to Becks. Fuck it. Right now, there's only one thing I need to be focusing on, and that's kissing the girl I've had a crush on for months. I don't care if Theo says she's not into me. I like her. So I'm going for it. Tonight.

With a deep breath, I fix my hoodie and take the final step out of the tree line and into the clearing. As I do, a gust of wind carries up my hood and rustles my hair. Theo pulls out his phone and checks it. I see the screen come alive in his hands, and then his expression darkens.

"What's up?" I ask.

The only time I ever see him look like this is when something's up with his dad—the asshole drunk who likes to play the role of a father in public, but in private, he's the lowest form of a man—a devil in disguise. He really believes that none of us know he hits Theo. We're not blind. We've seen the marks he leaves behind.

"Um, nothing . . ." Theo finally answers me, shoving his phone deep inside his pocket. "There's just this thing I forgot I have to do for my dad tonight."

"Thing? What thing?" Brielle spins around when she realizes we're no longer following her.

"It's . . . er . . . actually, I can't say." He rubs at the back of his neck. "But I should probably head out. My father's pissed I haven't already left."

I know I'm going to regret asking, because I know the shady shit his father is into, but I have to know. "Where's this "thing" you have to pick up?"

"Crossroads."

"Crossroads—shit! That's . . . fuck! Well, nice knowing ya, man!"

"Oh shut up, Mason. Theo can't go there alone!"

Brielle's eyebrows knit along the center while she flashes me a look that terrifies me as much as the idea of going to a place like Crossroads.

My sister is known for being the wild one in our group. You tell her she can't do something, or that she shouldn't, and she makes it her mission to prove you wrong. And drunk Brielle is worse. All I need is for her to start an all-out brawl, which Theo and I will have to save her from.

"Okay, fine. How about I go with Theo and you stay here?" I offer.

Theo nods in agreement with me.

"Sorry, boys. I'm going. Becks too!"

"Where are we going?" A familiar voice asks. The voice that tempts my dreams and that's stolen my heart.

I pinch my eyes shut before I turn to the side and find Becks standing just off to the right. Her golden eyes are glossy as she stares up at me.

"Nowhere . . ."

Brielle swats my arm, then says, "Crossroads, bitch.

"Oh hell yes! When do we leave? I know this sick bar that we could—"

Bar?

What bar?

Becks knows about bars?

"No! No way! It's not happening!"

I turn to Theo, hoping he'll back me up, when I see he's shaking his head. Our conversation earlier today about my needing to "play it cool" idly drifts through the back of my mind.

Right. Shit.

"Look, Brielle, it's not a good idea," Theo says. He pushes a hand through his hair again, like he's nervous about whatever he's going to say next. "This place is not the best crowd, and if something happens it's not going to be good. It would just be easier if you stay here. I can't afford to be distracted while I handle this, and I don't have time to babysit you."

Oh shit. *Here we go.*

I take a giant step back.

"Babysit!" Brielle yells. "Are you joking me?"

Becks walks backward to join me at my side. Neither of us want to be within spitting distance of Brielle when she's pissed.

Brielle pushes up on her toes and locks her eyes with Theo's. "For your information, I don't need a babysitter! In case you haven't noticed, I'm not a kid anymore!"

"Aren't you though? You're like what . . . fifteen?"

I choke back a laugh when I see the anger twist along my sister's face. I haven't seen her this pissed since Dad told her that Santa wasn't really a fat, jolly man who came down our chimney to deliver her presents—that he was really just Mom in a fuzzy, red robe.

I snap back to the moment at hand when Becks's elbow slams into my side, urging me to intervene. "Oh, ugh . . . okay, you two." I take a wary step in their direction. "Maybe we should all just take a moment and—"

"Shut up, Mason!" Brielle yells before she turns back to Theo and jams a finger into his chest.

Well, I tried.

Brielle wastes no time and continues, "I'm sixteen you asshole! But I'm not surprised you haven't noticed because you've been too busy shoving your tongue down Jessica's throat every chance you get!"

Wait? What?

What does Theo kissing Jessica have to do with any of this?

"God, it was the one time, Brielle! Get over it! Besides, she kissed me! When are you going to let that go?"

Theo rolls his eyes and I worry that she's pushing him too far. I shuffle my feet a step or two, when Theo does something that catches me off guard—he gently laces his fingers around Brielle's wrist.

"You know what? It doesn't even matter how old you are. You've got Luca, remember? What about him, Brielle? *And* you just broke things off with Chad . . . you can't pin this all on me."

As the voice of reason, Becks takes the chance to jump in and say, "I have an idea. How about we all go, but everyone who's not Theo stays in the car? That way we're still there if he needs us, but we're not in any danger. Then . . . afterwards . . . we can all hang out?"

I feel like my head is about to explode as I try to figure out what the hell Brielle and Theo are really arguing about, when I see something flash in between them, like they're only just realizing that they have an audience.

Theo drops her wrist.

Brielle rolls her eyes.

"Great. Now that that's settled, Brielle, why don't you go tell Luca we're leaving. Knowing where we're going, it might be better if he comes too," I say after a minute passes.

Theo lets out a chuckle. "Oh no. I don't want that guy coming."

"Oh, he's coming." Brielle smirks, pushing past Theo to join Becks who's already walking back to gather her things.

Theo and I hang back and watch them walk away.

"What the fuck is up with your sister, Mason?"

"Hey, I don't want to hear it. You're the idiot who provoked her."

We meet the girls and Luca by the car, and after an hour of driving, we pull into the parking lot of Redd's Bar. I watch as Theo gets out and heads inside. The look on his face does nothing to ease the knots I feel tightening within my stomach. Brielle has been quiet the whole way over, but now that we're parked, she's suddenly bouncing against the car door.

Becks whispers something in her ear, while excitedly fluffing her hair.

What the fuck?

"Oh no! Brielle, no!" I spin around in my seat when I finally realize what they're planning. "The plan was to wait in the car! I turn to Becks, pleading, "Becks . . . come on. Luca, help me out here!"

"Come on, Mason. Live a little." Becks smiles at me.

Beside her, Brielle opens the door and hops out. Luca follows. They rush toward the bar's front door, but I can't bring myself to move. I tighten my grip on the steering wheel, and silently yell, *Fuck!*

Aside from all the shit I'm going to get from Theo about letting them go inside . . . aside from the fact that something is obviously going on between my sister and my best friend . . . there's something else not right about this situation. I can feel it in the air; a change that has my nerves on edge. It's less about where we are and more about who it is that sent us.

"Let's go, Mason!" I hear Becks call from outside the car. She motions for me to join her, teasing me with those fucking golden eyes.

I squeeze my own shut and try to ignore all the warning bells ringing inside my head.

Fuck it! I open the door and get out.

What's the worst that can happen?

present

chapter one

H oly crap, Bree! This is it!" Becks says, taking a giddy step forward. She hands our ID's to the bouncer, groaning to herself when she spots Luca waiting for us by the door.
"Remind me again, why you let the goody-goody come?" she asks, her short, auburn curls brushing the top of her shoulders as the wind picks up.

"Be nice," I tell her, hoping that for once she'll listen to me. Luca's the only reason I did show up.

Aside from the fact that this place is in the wrong part of town, everything about being here screams trouble. The old Denton cotton mill transformed into Haze, the shiny new nightclub all of campus is talking about.

Forget the gangs I know that patrol every corner, and the mass hysteria that seems to go hand in hand with any college hot spot. They aren't what has me on edge tonight. My father is. He would kill me if he knew I let Becks talk me into ditching my study group. Especially if he finds out where we are.

Cops make the worst parents.

Well, Detectives, in my case. You can never lie to them. So, on the off chance we are caught, Luca's my get out of jail free card. My father loves him. He tolerates Becks.

"You're all set," the bouncer interjects, finally feeling satisfied with our ID's. He hands them back to Becks, then stamps each of our hands in bright blue ink. The word: "UNDERAGE" in bold. "You look like you're out to have some fun tonight. You sure you wouldn't rather stay out here with me, beautiful?" he asks, his voice sounding as if someone took sandpaper to his vocal cords.

He leans into where I'm standing and smiles, my nostrils instantly burning as the small barrier his gum held lifts and the smell of stale smoke quickly overwhelms the space around us. I tuck a strand of my dirty blonde hair back behind my ear and roll my eyes at the bouncer, who's a little too comfortable invading my personal space.

"I . . . um," I start to say, when I feel Luca's arm slip around my lower back. The soft material of my blouse pulls along the center under the weight of his grip.

"She's all good, man, but thanks." He smiles politely, gently guiding Becks and me through the aluminum doors.

I turn in time to see his brow furrow as he examines my outfit. The soft blue of his eyes is paler under the harsh glare of the entry hall lights.

Here we go.

I know that look. He hates it. I knew he would. The ivory blouse and silver sequined skirt, which Becks made me wear, barely reaches the top of my thighs. Hell, even I hate the idea of showing this much skin.

"Just say it," I tell him.

"No. No, it's just. . . y- you look. . . I—" A playful smirk presses his lips as he crosses his arms in front of him. "Look, you're beautiful, Bree. I just think that next time you might remind Becks that she doesn't need to be *so good* at dressing you. I feel like I need to give you my coat."

"God. . . you're such a cliché, Luca. Brielle looks hot! Besides, all the naughty bits are covered!" Becks yells as she reaches back to grab my arm. I wriggle under her grip as she drags me behind her to an empty area nestled between the bar and the restrooms.

Inside the club, everything is alive with the color blue. The solid LED bar top that's off to our right, which pulses between a mix of ice blue and a darker, midnight color. Even the light display playing over the dance floor is blue. I look at Luca, trying to gauge his reaction when I see the mammoth of brick walls, behind him. My eyes follow the wall, all the way to the top, trying to assess its height, when I see two extended levels of the club.

Holy crap.

This place is huge.

"Whoa. Hello, Haze." Becks lets out a laugh. She sweeps her eyes around the room as tightly packed bodies of college students, dance in groups along the floor. She wrinkles her brow down at her beige-colored dress and gently pats her lower region. "Looks like mama's getting a new plaything tonight."

"Oh. Good. God," Luca chokes, his hands shooting up to cover his ears. The tips of his fingers push into his jet-black curls as he shakes his head.

"Oh no, don't you start," I say, feeling more like a referee than their best friend. Luca smiles brightly and pulls me to his side. The spicy smell of his cologne instantly works to calm my nerves.

"That's okay, Bree. He doesn't—oh. . .for fuck's sake! You've got to be kidding me," Becks huffs, whipping around to face us as two figures lock eyes on the three of us and begin walking over. She swats Luca's arm, but misses, hitting him squarely in the chest. "What the hell! You invited them?"

Them?

Luca shrugs, looking equally as confused. "Don't look at me. Why would I invite—"

"Well, hello, handsome!" a girl exclaims, the neckline of her amber-colored dress, rising and falling at a rapid pace. She spins a lock of her red curls between her two fingers and licks her nude painted lips. "Isn't this a surprise!"

"Um. . . Hi! I'm Brielle. . ." I say when neither Becks nor Luca speaks up.

The girl turns to look at me. Her tawny eyes are blazing as she says, "Penny" in a flat tone, then swivels back to Luca with a flip of her hair. She reaches out and places a hand on Luca forearm, the pads of her fingers digging into his skin, as she chirps, "Come. Come sit with us."

"Oh hell no, I'm not—"

"That sound's. . .great, Penny. Thanks," Luca finishes for Becks. He wards off another one of her attempts at hitting him, before he waves for the girl to lead the way.

"I. Hate. You," Becks groans, shoving Luca's arm when Penny's a few feet ahead of us.

He motions for her to start walking. "Well, at least we can agree on that."

We arrive at a lounge area, which is positioned directly next to a bar where a massive U-shaped, white leather couch sits. We round the side, when I notice two other girls and a guy busily tapping away on their phones. Trying not to give anyone a show, I tuck my dress tightly underneath me and sit down.

"So, did you see Wesley when you came in?" Penny yells straightaway. Her eyes lock on Luca as she leans into his side. The viselike grip she has on his arm grows tighter by the minute.

Um . . . am I'm missing something here? Is Luca seeing someone he didn't tell me about?

I shift in my seat, listening to the leather material squeak under the bare section of my thighs.

"Wesley who?" I ask, suddenly desperate for some sort of clarity. I look up and see Penny staring at me with a not so subtle look of surprise. "What? Is he the owner or something?"

"Not quite. Wesley's the manager here, love," the guy sitting on the opposite side of Becks says—the one who was too preoccupied when we first arrived to be bothered to look up from his phone.

Pausing midtext, he lifts his eyes to lock with mine. Leaning forward, he lowers his phone. His English accent is the first thing I notice about him. The second is his hair. It's short and black, much like Luca's, only not as thick. The tips of his ends are perfectly spiked along the front.

He crosses one leg over the other, then stares at his watch. "I thought everyone knew Wesley."

I shake my head when the name doesn't ring a bell.

"So, Luc. I assume this is the lovely, uninformed creature you're always going on about," the guy Penny was walking with when she first saw us says. His short, red hair is combed viciously around his face, the distinctive highlights bringing out the tawny flakes in his eyes. "Damn, you're a lot hotter than I expected."

"Ethan!" Penny frowns at him through thick lashes. Her expression becomes lax as she leans over Luca's lap and whispers, "Just ignore him. I'm pretty sure he was dropped on his head when we were kids."

"Whatever. Don't pretend you haven't noticed, sis."

It's then that I notice the obvious similarities between the two, and I mentally kicked myself for not realizing it before. They're twins. Like Ethan, Penny's hair is red, but tamer in the sense of the style. They both have the same tawny eyes and slender frame. In fact, the only difference I can find between the two is the shape of their noses. Where Penny's is short and bubbled at the end—much like her personality from what I can tell so far—Ethan's is the nose of an aristocrat, with a wide bridge that falls to a slightly curved tip.

Ah, crap.

It all makes sense now.

These are the annoying, rich twins from Becks and Luca's history class—the ones Becks loathes more than guys who wear deep V-neck shirts, and people who bite their string cheese.

"Trust me, if Wesley was the owner, you wouldn't want to meet him, sweets." Ethan smiles, coolly. His bloodshot eyes are full of contempt as he picks at something on his cuticle. "That guy's a rich, unpredictable asshole who hates everyone *but* Wes." He leans back against the seat. His arms move to cross behind his head. "Well, Wes and pretty girls like you. But I wouldn't mess with him. He'd ruin you."

I turn my attention to the dance floor and purposefully ignore him. *Seems like there's plenty of rich assholes around here tonight.* I arch my brow, hating the fact that he called me sweets.

"I don't know," the girl sitting next to Ethan says. With her extended eyeliner and bright blue eyes, slender frame and slow movements, she reminds me of a cat.

Her black, shoulder-length hair is styled perfectly straight, sweeping over her collarbone every time she moves.

"I don't care what he is. I'd sure as hell let him be mean to me for a few nights—if you know what I mean. The guy's fucking hot!"

"Please." Penny laughs. She turns to her brother, and the two of them lock eyes, seeming to share the same thought.

"Being easy, isn't exactly an attractive trait, Hallie. Why would he ever waste his time on a night with you?"

Ethan pulls the girl onto his lap, laughing as he does. He clamps his hand down on her waist and nuzzles into her ear. "True. You've got my attention though," he says.

Now that's a disgusting thought.

"Gross!" I suppress a gag, feeling mildly offended for this girl.

When I sense Ethan's eyes settle on me, I look up in time to watch him snatch his glass from the top of the table, toss the remaining of his drink back, as he mumbles something inaudible.

Whoops!

Did I just say that out loud?

On that note . . . "I think I'm going to walk around," I say. Sitting here is doing nothing to help ease my already rising nerves. In fact, it's only making it worse.

Luca moves to follow, but I stop him. Not that I believe for a second that Penny has any intention of letting him go.

"I'm fine." I smile, silently wishing—not for the first time tonight—that I hadn't let Becks talk me into coming. Economics is more bearable than these two.

chapter two

THEO

T he last few weeks have been a fucking nightmare. The ice machine died. Twice. Half of the VIP furniture I order to replace the ones ruined by last week's bar fight was delivered to the wrong address. And for some reason, our waitresses seem to think that I could actually give a fuck about their personal lives.

Why the hell do I care that Cameron's boyfriend is a cheating, bastard? Or that Macie's friend came down with the flu? As long as the guests are happy and I'm free to come and go as I please, that's all I care about. I opened Haze to have a quiet place where I can handle my own shit. My real job. Privately.

In my environment where I control what happens. I didn't open it to spend my time worrying over other people's problems. I deal with enough problems as it is–mainly my father's. Problems like (fuck) this girl!

I inhale a sharp breath as one of my dad's current "problems" teeth drag along my neck. The action rips me from my thoughts. "Oh, sorry," her voice catches as she leans forward to push her chest in my face.

I roll my eyes and try to focus.

Damn, I almost forgot she was there.

"You're good," I lie, trying not to sound like a complete asshole, since I plan on fucking this girl tonight.

She pushes me back against the seat and straddles me. Her mouth slowly works its way up to mine. I can tell that she's really into this by the way that she's practically panting on top of me, but I can't think about that. I shift against the seat and adjust myself. The uncomfortable way she's practically choking my dick underneath her makes it hard for me to get into the mood.

"God, I want you so bad," she whispers, her hands sliding down to palm me through my jeans.

What the fuck did she just say?

I pull back and look at her. Her blonde hair and blue eyes, vaguely reminding me of someone I knew a long time ago, before I fucked up and ruined it all.

"Do you normally talk this much?" I ask. More so for the fact that, if she did, I would definitely need to invest in a good pair of earplugs down the road. That, or make sure to keep the music turned up loud enough to drown out the sound of her nasally ass voice. Nothing's more unattractive than a chick who doesn't know when to shut the hell up.

She obviously didn't see this for what it is—a transaction. It's the type of business arrangement that only guys like our fathers make in order to cover up shady deals they don't want hashed out in the public eye. Well, the first half of our meeting had been about that. This . . . this is purely a distraction. A way for me to pass the time, since Wes is forcing me to stay to establish my "presence" within Haze as its owner.

Why? I don't fucking know.

Everyone out there already knows who I am and who my father is. Shit, half of them are on his payroll. The not so secret, consigliere to the notorious crime boss of Dallas, Giovanni Russo. Guns. Drugs. Women. My father dabbles in it all. He's been on the FBI watchlist for as long as I can remember. On top of that, he's also the reigning leader on the ballot for shittiest father ever. I swear he only brought me into the business to keep me from turning him in—which I would have. Happily.

I squint my eyes when I see the curtain, shutting out the rest of the partygoers from our private space, shift, and Wes pops his head through it.

"Sorry to interrupt, but we have a situation out here."

Of course, we do.

How could we not when most of the guests consist of blue-collar criminals and their white-collared bosses? Throw in the alcohol we're shoveling out, and I'm surprised that it took this long for something to happen.

"Hurry back," Katrina moans and rotates off my lap.

I tuck my dick up along the waist of my jeans and step out of the lounge.

"It's Devon," Wes says the moment the curtain closes behind me. Pointing toward the dance floor, I follow his finger and see the crowd gathering around Devon and a short blonde.

I hum amused. Yup, they're definitely readying themselves for a fight, which, with Devon, there's always a pretty good chance of that. That bitch loves the adrenaline high, almost as much as I do.

"Okay. And?" I raise my brow, waiting to hear how this is my problem. Even without a gag for Katrina, anything is better than having to mess with the shitshow that is Devon O'Brien. "Isn't this why you hired those jugheads, you call "bouncers" for?"

"Really, man? We both know, you're the only one who Devon will listen to when she's like this," Wes says, motioning for me to hurry. "Please."

Damn it.

He's lucky we're friends.

If it were anyone else asking, I'd tell them promptly where they could shove it.

"Fuck. Fine." I shake my head, tossing him a look over my shoulder as I yell, "You owe me though!"

I'm halfway through the crowd, when I can hear the gentle tone of blonde girl's voice. It's soothing and sweet, and in no way a match for someone hoping to hold their own against Devon. But the closer I get, I know there's more to it than that. The voice is oddly familiar in a way that I can't put my finger on but am immediately drawn to.

I feel my hands curl into fists against my sides as I step into the circle.

"Is there a problem here?" I interject, and at the sight of me, all eyes drop.

Devon shoots me a glare from the far side of the circle, and even from where I'm standing, I can see that her eyes are wide and bloodshot. Great. She is drinking again.

The last time she found herself drowning at the end of a bottle she nearly killed herself, and me. But, hey, that's an issue for a different day. I need to focus on getting blondie over here away from Devon before I have the fucking police at my back door.

Switching my focus to the short blonde standing in front of Devon, I take a few steps forward until I see her shoulders start to turn. The second I catch those green eyes I feel like I know better than my own, I freeze midstep.

What the. . .? Brielle?

I don't believe it.

I allow my curiosity to get the better of me, as I step back and rake my eyes down her slender, petite frame. Damn. I should have come back sooner.

Unlike most people who know my reputation and fear me for it, Brielle doesn't cower when I look at her. Rather, I watch as she openly does the same. I see her eyes hover on the tattoos that cover most of my arms and try not to laugh when I see how taken aback she seems to be by my appearance.

Wait a minute.

What the hell is Brielle even doing on this side of town?

Scanning the crowd, I look for an answer, but every eye stays pinned to the floor. I'm not sure what pisses me off more. The fact that, whoever the fuck she's with is either too much of a coward to step up, or that she's somehow found her way into this mess in the first place. I shake my head. She always did like to keep us on our toes. Her brother and me, I mean—mostly me. But who the fuck would be dumb enough to let her sneak off in a place like this?

Once more, I skate my eyes down the length of her as she fidgets, nervously, and pulls at the hem of her skirt. Damn it. Why the hell did it have to be her?

chapter three

BRIELLE

I bounce between bodies like a pinball as I fight my way to the bar. Elbows jab into my sides, shoulders ram into my head. Just another one of the perks of being five foot two. I can almost see the top of the bartender's head, when I feel a heel catch under my foot, sending me tumbling into the person in front of me.

"Hey, watch it, bitch!" a girl snarls, shoving me off with her arm. The smell of the whiskey on her breath hits me in waves. "The fuck is your problem?"

Bitch? Really?

I take a step back. Ever since we arrived, I feel like I've crossed over some invisible line and found myself in the middle of a Quentin Tarantino movie. I've heard more curse words than I do in a normal week—and I live with Becks—so, that's saying something.

"I'm so sorry," I say, watching her sway. The girl's dark brown eyes are almost predator-like as she scowls down at me from hooded lids. "I tripped and—"

"You're sorry?"

The guy she's with tries to pull her back while yelling all the ways that I'm not worth the energy.

Thanks?

But with a growl, his efforts are futile because she shoves his hands away, yelling, "You gotta be . . ." her words trail off into a garbled mess I can't decipher.

I bite my lip. Crap.

This girl looks like she's the type of person who loves getting into fights. She has, what my father calls, "the look." Blown-out eyes. Matted hair. The beaded, sweat-soaked forehead, and worn nails. She's either high, or currently coming down from one. And by the smell of her breath, anything could set her off.

It's then that a voice breaks through the crowd—deep, rich, and strangely . . . familiar.

"Is there a problem here?" the voice asks, and at the sound of it, all eyes drop to the floor.

If I were smart, I'd fall in suit with everyone else around me, but instead I do the opposite. The lure of suspicion wins out over my better judgement as I turn and come face to face with its owner. The second our eyes meet, I have to lock my knees so that I don't faint.

"Do I need to repeat the question?" he asks, his tone clipped and annoyed.

I feel my jaw drop as I take in a deep breath in an attempt to steady myself.

No.

It can't be.

"Theo? Y- You're back?" I stumble my words as I attempt to answer him. Knots form in my stomach and twist in a way that make me feel sick.

What the hell is he doing here?

Staring up at him clinically, it's easy to see why he's so handsome, with his dark green eyes and brown, slightly tousled hair. The exact type of guy I often try to avoid. He's too attractive for anything good to ever come out of dating a guy like him. The sort of guy who has more girls vying for his attention than he knows what to do with.

With his chiseled face and muscular frame—apparent even under his black T-shirt and jeans. For whatever reason, whatever *it* is, I'm immediately rendered defenseless. The only thing I hate more than feeling this way is the look on his face as if I had somehow disappointed him with my answer.

"It's good to see you, Brielle," he says. The corners of his lips pulling back into that devilish grin I've always loved. The memory of the last time I saw it is something I'm not ready to relive just yet.

I close my eyes, hearing the crowd around us take a collective breath and hold it as he steps in my direction. *Should I be afraid like they all seem to be?* The thought is there and gone before I have the chance to really think about it. I open my eyes.

"Why didn't you . . . you didn't reach out?"

It could have been the lights, or my imagination, but the second I finish, I swear its shock that crosses his face. Although as quickly as it appears, it's gone, leaving me to wonder if I'd imagined the whole thing.

"Didn't know I needed to," he says. His eyes linger for a moment longer before shifting to a figure standing a few feet beside me. "Devon, do I need to repeat myself?"

Devon?

I turn to the girl with the raven hair.

"Wait. You're asking me? This little tramp bumps into me, and you have the audacity to ask *me* if there is an issue? *Me,* Theo?"

Theo looks unfazed as he mutters a quick, "Yes."

Devon's body stills then in a terrifying way. The array of emotions that flash across her face are hard to keep up with. But, eventually, she collects herself. "I . . . apologize." Her tone is rigid. Each word laced with venom.

"Thank you. And like I said, I'm—"

"Great. Now that that's settled, leave," Theo interjects, his voice claiming the space and stopping me from finishing what I was about to say. "I'll cover the cab fare, but you can't stay here. I told you, I won't put up with you when you're like this," he finishes, his words dripping authority as he stares Devon down.

Rather than acknowledging his demands with a response, Devon simply turns and disappears into the crowd. Each step in the opposite direction sends a wave of shock, which penetrates the crowd and causes it to quickly disperse.

What the hell is that all about?

I've never known Theo to be so rude?

He made his point; he didn't have to keep embarrassing her in front of everyone.

"Brielle," Theo calls my name, the noticeable shift in his tone makes my head feel dizzy. "Hello?"

He edges closer when I don't answer him and moves until he's standing directly in front of me. I inhale a deep breath, cursing my own body as I feel my skin prickle at the nearness of him. He smells exactly as I remember—of mint and newly upholstered leather.

He scratches his stubble, and I swear he's covering a grin when he says, "Stunned silent. Now that's a side of Brielle I never thought I'd se—"

"You didn't have to do that. It wasn't even her fault, *and* she apologized," I say the words aloud before I realize I've said anything at all. "If anyone should be forced to leave, it's me."

"What's that? You want to know how I've been? Yeah, no, I've been great! Thanks for asking," Theo says. The cocky grin he's wearing, almost completely gone as he moves to step around me.

"What?" I hear the rise in my own voice, feeling as annoyed as he seems to be, but I can't stop. I follow him. "That's not what I asked, Theo!"

"Well, that's the only answer you're going to get. You have no clue what you're talking about." He whips around to face me, his tone is as cold as ice.

He takes a step closer. His shoulders are even with my eyes. I can't help but feel like he's testing me in some way. Pushing me to see where my boundaries lie after all this time. *Is he trying to dominate me?* The question is there and gone before I have the chance to fully acknowledge it.

"Look, I don't know who you're here with. But, for your own good, it's probably best that you find them and leave. This isn't a playground for kids, and I don't have time to babysit."

Hearing his words, I blush and numbly take a step back. His eyes bore into me with an intensity I'm unable to place. Curiosity? Amusement? Desire? My mind freezes then, tasting how ridiculous I sound. *Desire?* I shake my head at the thought. I must have forgotten who I was talking to. This is Theo after all. The guy who's always been too busy being everyone else's number one man, to ever stop and see what he has in front of him. Add in this new bad-boy persona he's adopted, and it's like I don't even recognize who he is anymore.

"I'm sorry. Who are you?" I manage to say.

The muscles along his chest flex as he inhales a deep breath. He's struggling with himself, and whatever it's about, it's winning. "Someone you should stay away from." He shifts his eyes. "You're not the only one whose changed, Brielle. But you're definitely too good to be hanging around here."

Glancing around, people have started to pick up on our history and are nosily circling us. Their questioning stares, and lingering curiosity, practically solidify every concern that tells me I should turn around and run. Fast. That this rude guy is not the same polo wearing, video game playing boy I knew growing up.

"Theo," I plead with him. But for what, I don't know.

I watch as he shakes his head. His hazel eyes peel off toward something in the distance, and I drop the hand I hadn't realized I was holding out to him.

"I can't," he says. The internal battle he seems to be waging drives him further away from me. His expression turns cold and distant. "You should go."

"Bree! There you are!" Luca's yells.

The wave of relief I feel, washes over me as I turn and find those soft blue eyes. "We were just looking for you. Becks is having a moment and—" Luca freezes midstep. His eyes shift up to the apparent stranger standing next to me, and if even possible, the air thickens to a more uncomfortable state. His gaze sweeps between Theo and me, and with a look of disgust, he mutters, "What the hell are you doing here?"

"Wait. You're here with Luca?" Theo half laughs. His smile only mildly amused. The laugh itself is deep and would be attractive were he not using it to taunt Luca. He turns to face him. "Damn, and I thought my night couldn't get any worse."

Wait?

Did he say worse?

Luca narrows his eyes at Theo as he reaches out to pull me to his side. Theo tenses at the action, but thankfully he doesn't react.

"Thought you left town? If you cared at all, you'd do us all a favor and leave again."

"Luca!"

"Wow. Is that a threat, Garrett?" Theo says. His voice tight as each word is used to challenge Luca in a way that

makes me increasingly uneasy. I see his hands curl into fists as
he lifts his chest and takes a step in Luca's direction, the rich
green of his hazel eyes darkening.

"You know exactly what it is, Wescott."

"Whoa. Okay. Enough." I push my way in between
them. "Why don't you both just take a step back?"

I can feel the danger of the situation growing as I try to
understand where it's coming from in the first place. When
Theo left, we were all fine. What changed? I look down and
notice Theo's hands, and the slight bruising scattered along his
knuckles. What the hell? *Someone you should stay away from,*
his warning echoes inside my mind. But as much as it probably
should, it doesn't scare me. Theo may have changed, but I don't
think for a second that he would ever hurt me.

I watch him smile as if he read my thoughts. But the
smile is tight and doesn't reach his eyes. He looks to Luca, then
back to me. "Fucking course," he says as a form of recognition
slides across his face. "You two now, huh? Mason always said
it would happen." He takes in an exaggerated breath. His eyes
are still dark, but his expression is beginning to lighten.

Wait. What?

Hearing Mason's name, Luca places a hand along my
lower back, and I fight the urge to remove it. It's been a while
since anyone's been brave enough to openly mentioned my
brother in front of me. Not because I didn't want them to, but
because of what happened the night he died, and everything
that's happened since.

"How dare you," Luca snaps. His words are rushed.

I wrinkle my brow up at him in hopes of ending
whatever argument they're choosing to hash out in the middle
of the club, but he ignores me or simply doesn't see.

"I see someone grew up and decided to finally grow some balls," Theo says without an ounce of humor. "I've already kicked your ass once, Garrett. Don't make me do it again in front of her."

"Okay, enough!" I yell when I catch them start to move again. I raise my hands and press a palm against each of their chests.

"It's not me you should be worried about," Luca says, while taking a step back. "It's him you have to watch yourself around. You haven't changed at all, have you Theo?"

I can tell by the rapid rise and fall of Theo's chest that his temper won't be so easily satiated. I turn to face him and look at my hand, noting how his chest is rock hard against my palm. I try not to let my mind run away with me as I think about what his chest might look like without his shirt on.

Is it covered in tattoos, too?

A couple of seconds pass before I recognize that Theo's breathing has slowed, and he's watching me. I lift my head and our eyes meet, and immediately he reacts to it; the color of his eyes lighten to a pale green. He raises his hand as if to cover mine, and it's then, in that moment—that lasts no longer than a second—that I can finally see the tiny resemblance of the old Theo. The sweet one, who would stay up late just to make sure that I made it home okay, and the one who was always so playful and fun. But in the blink of an eye, it vanishes. The hard-pressed, bad-tempered version of him seizes control.

I drop my hand.

"I . . . I need to find Becks."

chapter four

We arrive back at the massive couch and find Becks and Penny blissfully distracted. "This is Mark, Liam, and Graham," Becks exclaims, pointing to each guy separately as she says their name.

I watch them squirm uncomfortably in their chairs as I sit down next to Luca. The one wearing our schools University of North Texas fraternity jacket kinks his brow in my direction.

"Yes, they were nice enough to keep us company." Penny's nose crinkles over the rim of her drink. "You know, since Luca had to go looking for you, and my brother decided to take his turn on the campus bicycle."

I cut my eyes to the dance floor, when I notice Ethan and Hallie are in fact missing. Then turn back and flash the guys a meek smile, choosing to ignore Penny's blatant attempt at getting a rise out of me, when a petite waitress turns her attention toward our group. Her arms precariously holding a tray of drinks.

"Hey, y'all!" she greets us. Her heavy twang and wrist tattoo that reads "Made in Texas" makes me smile. She splits the tray between the two cube tables, cautiously making sure to set each drink as close to the center as possible. "I hope you're thirsty. Mr. Wescott asked me to send these over to you guys."

"Wesc—wait. Wescott?" Becks shifts her weight and slides to the edge of her seat.

Without question, I take a drink from the table in front of me. The pink-and-orange one that smells tropical, a nice reprieve from all the blue, and raise it to my lips. The fruity concoction tastes delicious on my tongue as I gulp down almost half the glass. I don't even try to hide the massive stamp on my hand that's meant to indicate that I'm not twenty-one. Twenty is close enough—at least, it is tonight.

"Um, thanks," Becks mutters to the girl, narrowing her eyes as she shoots me a look of concern. I can tell that she wants to ask me what the hell she must have missed, but, thankfully, she lets it go. For now, which is good since I'm not even sure what I think myself at the moment—only that, my stress levels have officially peaked.

The waitress nods her head, then walks off when I hear Becks gasp. Her hand darts under the table to take hold of mine as she leans into my side. I turn my eyes in the direction that she's staring in and find a tall guy, with a muscular frame and broad shoulders standing next to our table. His tangled mess of blond hair hangs down, covering most of his face as he works to smooth it back.

"And you'll tell your father how much we appreciate him stopping by," he tells the couple he's with. We can't see their faces, but by the way this guy is talking to them, they have to be important.

Beck's jaw practically drops to the floor the longer she watches him, and it takes all I have not to burst out laughing. I think she's found her new plaything. When I hear the name Russo, I lean in further trying to get look, when I notice the other guy he's standing beside. Theo. And he's not alone.

Adorned with a tall, gorgeous woman tucked under his arm, I try not to let it bother me but it does.

What the hell is wrong with me?

As if just noticing him, Becks twists to the side. The knots in my stomach twist to an uncomfortable state.

"Can you believe that asshole?" Luca groans, then adjusts himself so that his arm now drapes behind me.

"Hold on. So you do know Wesley?" Penny chuckles from her seat. The three guys she'd been entertaining suddenly appear to look awkward without her constant attention. When we don't answer her, she motions with the hand that's carefully holding her drink back at the guy with the blond hair.

"No, but if he's anything like the guy standing next to him, I'm good," Luca says automatically.

I lick my lips and taste remnants of my cocktail. I take another sip, purposefully ignoring the guilty feeling that's building in the pit of my stomach. It's clear I need to talk to Luca about what happened between Theo and him, but seeing the way he's reacting, I'm not sure if tonight is the right time to do it.

"Wait, hold on! Theo? How the hell do you know him?" Penny asks as I watch her eyes grow to the size of large grapes, while she shoves her drink at one of the guys. It spills on his lap but she could care less.

"Of course we know him." Becks rolls her eyes in the typical Becks sort of way. She reaches for her own drink, pinched between her legs, and takes a small sip. As if feeding off Penny's curiosity, she continues, "The man basically lived with Brielle for a whole year after his mother died. He's like the big brother we never wanted. Or at least he was. . . before Mason. . ."

I cut my eyes to the floor, when I feel everyone looking at me.

"What? Before what?" Penny nudges Becks to continue.

I inhale in a quick breath and tuck my hands tightly in my lap. The sequin material of Becks' skirt digs into my skin. "She was going to say before my brother died. Five years ago. His name was Mason."

Looking up at Penny I ready myself for whatever she's about to say. She doesn't exactly strike me as the sympathetic type.

"Oh. My. God. This is fucking awesome!" Penny laughs. She looks over her shoulder and eyes Theo, who's momentarily watching us. "Oh Ethan is going to be so pissed when he hears what he missed!"

"When he hears what? That we know him?" Luca chimes in beside me. His tone sounding as if he was readying himself to come to my defense.

"Well, yes! But mostly that she does," Penny says, then glances back at Theo again. "*And* . . . from the looks of it, that it definitely seems like someone's down for some major reminiscing," she says. A smug smile slowly spreads across her mouth. Her tawny eyes slide back to look at me. "He hasn't taken his eyes off of you. Apparently, you are his type."

"You have no idea what you're talking about!" Becks is quick to come to my defense.

"God, chill out, would ya? All I'm saying is that—"

"No, seriously—" Luca jolts upward—"just drop it. Brielle would never go for him."

Penny's smug smile fades as she takes her drink back. It's clear that she doesn't agree. But she's thankfully taken the hint. Flexing his arm, Luca pulls me into his chest.

"I think I'm going to need another drink," he whispers into my hair.

I wrinkle my nose and shoot him a warning glance. Unlike Becks and me, who only managed to get drinks because

Theo had them sent over, Luca is twenty-one. "I thought you weren't drinking tonight?" I tease him. He doesn't answer me, but rather sits there, silently appraising my every move. I feel my cheeks begin to heat in an uncomfortable way. "What?"

"Nothing. Just thinking." His tone is so natural and light, that I almost believe him. But knowing Luca, I know it's so much more than that. I turn forward and shuffle my feet while I think of what to say. I can feel Becks glaring at me.

This is it. This is your chance, I silently tell myself. It's the chance to tell him the truth about how I really feel. But the only word my mouth can form is "Oh."

All right. "I'll be back. I'm going to run and grab a beer. I'm not much of a cocktail kind of guy." Luca stands up from the couch. He works his way around the far side, leaning back at the last second to shout, "You want anything?"

I shake my head and he disappears. I know I'm being a coward, but I keep my eyes glued to the floor. I don't dare look at Becks for fear of what she might say. I know whatever lecture she's got in store for me, she'll be right. What I'm doing with Luca is selfish and unfair but I'm scared. If I tell him the truth about how I feel, he may leave, and I don't know if I'm ready to take that chance. I don't know if I'm ready to lose another person I care about.

We stay for two more rounds of drinks, until I've sufficiently had my fill of Penny's *I'm better than you* attitude. On the way out, I keep my eyes laser-locked to the floor just to avoid any possibility of seeing Theo again. Throughout the night I managed to see enough . . . of him *and* the girl he has superglued to his arm to last a lifetime.

The next morning, I find myself lying in bed, just staring up at the ceiling. Thanks to all the sugar in those cocktails I drank, I tossed and turned for hours after Luca dropped us off.

Memories haunting my mind as I think about Theo and this new, darker side of him that I'm not sure I really like. *This isn't a playground for kids.* Theo's obnoxious voice plays in my head. The fact that he still views me as a "kid" pisses me off more than I'd like to admit.

An hour later, my stomach growls alerting me that it's time to get up. I roll from my bed and throw my dirty blonde hair up into its usual messy bun. I can feel the knots pull in my neck as I wrap the bun twice with the rubber band, too tired to care. I pass a mirror, but I don't bother looking. I know I'll hate what I see.

"Morning," I say in between a yawn, when I turn the corner into our kitchen and find Becks, seated and helping herself to a bowl of cereal.

"Ah, sleeping beauty finally wakes!" She laughs and sets down the book she'd been reading.

My eyes shift to the clock on the stove, widening when I notice it's already close to one o'clock in the afternoon!

"So, is it just me, or are you kind of freaking out too?"

"Freaking out?" I lean against the counter. My mind is still sifting through random thoughts from last night. "About what?"

"Oh I don't know." She smiles, spooning milk into her mouth as fast as she can. "You don't think it's strange that after all this time, Theo just randomly shows up. *And* on the one night you actually agree to come out with me."

Tilting her bowl, Becks lets the milk pool against the opposite side before she makes quick work of finishing off the tiny pieces of cereal. When she finishes, she wipes her mouth.

"Wait. You don't think he's going to want to hang out again, do you?"

"Yeah, no. That's not going to happen!" I nervously bite at my bottom lip. I think Theo was just as surprised to see us as we were to see him. In fact, I don't think he has any interest in hanging out with us, ever. At least, I didn't until she just mentioned it.

"Hey, so, whatever happened with Wes?" I try to move the conversation along, remembering how—at the last minute—Penny called him over to the table to introduce us. But when Luca and I left, to stop by the bathrooms, Becks had stayed behind to talk to him.

"Oh yeah!" She shoots forward in her seat and pushes the book further up the table, as she leans her elbows along either side of her bowl. "I can't believe I forgot."

"So? What happened?"

"What happened is I found out that man is perfection! He's sweet and handsome. And he asked me to come back tonight to hang out with him. Well . . . he asked both of us to."

"Both of us?" I say, and she nods her head. "No. Becks, I can't."

"Oh please. I need you."

I arch my brow as I watch Becks silently plead. She crosses her hands in front of her chest. "Please! Please! Pleeeeease! I'll love you forever and ever."

"No can do. I really need to study. If I fail this exam, my father will lose it. It's worth half of my grade."

"Oh, come on. You never fail, and your father can learn to loosen the reins a little." Becks rocks side to side excessively. The wooden chair creaks under her every time she leans to one side.

Because I know she won't relent, I give in and say, "Fine. But we're not staying out long."

"Yay!" She jumps up from her seat and wraps her thin arms around me. "I told him we'd be there around ten, so you'll still have plenty of time to study before we go."

"Oh you did, did you?"

"Yup. And before you try to worm your way out of it, just know, I'm picking out your outfit tonight."

"What? No. No!"

"Yes! You desperately need to find a man, Bree. You've been single for too long. And nothing in that closet of yours is going to help."

A man?

When the hell did this turn into operation get Brielle a boyfriend?

"I don't need a man, Becks. I'm fine."

"No, you're really not."

I arch a brow at her across the room like *excuse me?*

"All I'm saying is that Mr. Darcy may be steamy when it comes to those classic literary novels of yours, but it's not your legs he's burying himself into. . . it's Elizabeth's."

I turn around and busy myself cleaning the few items we have in our sink, trying to erase the image her words provoked. When I finish, I go to the refrigerator and pour myself a glass of juice.

"Look! At the very least, maybe meeting a guy might would help you relieve some of the stress you put yourself through. You know, by letting someone else do all the work for once."

I lean back letting her words sink in before bursting out loud in a fit of laughter. "Did you seriously just insinuate that I—"

"Flick your bean to *Pride and Prejudice*. . . yes."

"Oh my God, Becks!"

I close my eyes. The blood under my cheeks ignites as I feel my jaw drop. Great. Now I'll never look at Jane Austen the same way ever again.

"I don't do that!" I tell her.

I could never. Have never. Nor do I plan to start now.

"Okay! Okay!" Her face twists with an uneasy look. "Geez, and y'all say I'm the unusual one."

chapter five

THEO

O verall, I think it was a pretty great turnout last night." Wes
follows me into my office. I throw down my keys and the
stack of papers he so graciously shoved at me when I first
walked in. *Fuck, he's annoying today.* I just arrived, and ever
since then, it's been a never-ending strand of opinions from him.

I drop my eyes down to my desk. His trail of thoughts
finally comes to an end as he collapses into one of the chairs in
front of it and says, "She's coming here tonight so I guess we'll
see."

"Who is?"

"Who? The new girl I was just telling you about! Man,
you never listen." He fumbles with a pen on my desk. "Becks . .
. something, I think. She's pretty hot. Great rack."

At the sound of the name, old memories I've worked so
hard to bury flood my mind, and an image of another girl—a
short, blond in white—resurfaces. The thin-ass top she wore and
barely-there skirt showed her womanly features in a way that
affected me more than I'd like to admit. It was like no time had
passed; everything I felt for her before was back.

I cut my eyes to Wes and watch the confusion build
behind his eyes. Jesus, what does he want . . . approval?

"Well, good luck with that." I feign interest at the idea of
Becks and him "talking." If only so he'll hurry the hell up and
leave.

But I can't hide my smile.

Becks doesn't talk. *She eats guys alive.* I know from experience, watching her and Mason together. That girl had him so wrapped; he couldn't see that she was just leading him on.

To distract myself, I begin sifting mindlessly through the stack of mail currently weighing down my desk. I expect him to leave, but instead, he shoots out of his seat.

"Wait. You know her?" The excitement in his voice annoys me. Damn it. So much for hurrying this conversation along. Now I'm going to have to give him something, or he'll just keep pestering me.

I sigh and take a seat. "She is . . . was, one of the girls who ran around in my group," I eventually relent. "A freshman, my senior year. Her best friend was my best friend's younger sister."

I pause when another memory resurfaces. The quick flash of Mason's image passes over my mind, and of a young Brielle beside him.

"Oh shit." Wes smiles and nods his head. Seeming to be content enough for now to move on. "Well, I'm just going to see how it goes. I really wanted to talk to her friend, but she had some asshole with her who was being a serious cock block."

I laugh, picking at the frayed edges of a notebook.

"Luca." I shake my head. The irony not lost on me that for the first time, ever, I'm grateful for Luca's, annoyingly accurate, obsession with Brielle. Then I remember the way he slid his hand around her waist, and I'm over it. I take a deep breath and try to relax my hand—the one currently choking a section of Target ads.

"What?"

"Not what, who. The asshole," I tell him. "His name is Luca."

"Huh. Well, either way, I told Becks to bring her tonight. She's a ten, man. I'd fu—"

"Don't . . . finish that sentence," I threaten him. The thought of him in bed with her makes my blood boil. That annoying desire to punch something pricks at my nerves, like an itch between the shoulder blades you just can't scratch. I take a deep breath. "Brielle is off-limits," I repeat the words her brother said to me more times than I can remember.

"Oh, I see." Wes grins. He grabs the paperweight off my desk, tosses it back and forth a few times, then stops. "You like her."

The fuck?

"No. I definitely do not," I say, my answer quick, too quick. And unfortunately, for me, Wes isn't as dumb as he looks. He instantly picks up on it.

"What the hell happened to Katrina, man? I saw you giving her 'the look' just last night," he chokes. The rise of his voice has my pulse racing, and I shoot him a warning glance. The fuck is this? Therapy hour? "Damn. Okay. Point made. She's yours," he yields. "Have them both."

"Brielle is far from mine, and Katrina and I. . ." Fuck. Why the hell are we even talking about this? "Don't you have inventory to do?" I ask, wadding up a section of ads to toss at him. "I mean, what the hell am I paying you for?"

"Because the girls need something to look at when they come to this club of yours?" He laughs, smoothing his hands down the front of his shirt. "And because you're shit with people."

I shake my head, my daily limit of stupidity getting dangerously high.

Wes stands with his back is to me, as he slowly creeps to the door. He turns around at the last second to add, "You sure you don't like her, man? Because I could get behind a threesome with—"

"Do you want me to kick your ass? Get the fuck out of my office, Wes!" I yell. He's clearly joking, trying to provoke me. That asshole. He always likes to piss me off. Little does he know that I've kicked other guys' asses just for thinking as much. Even being a best friend has its limits. Something I learned a long time ago.

I sit back down and pick up the stack of new hire documents he left on my desk. They're all the same. Nice hair. Big boobs. I toss them down. Instead, I close my eyes and let my mind's eye finds its way back to her—to Brielle—of her standing there, staring back at me, while everyone else had turned away. She was so pissed that I'd sent Devon home, but what she didn't know was that I did it for her own good.

I exhale a deep breath.

Fucking Wes! Why did I let him talk me into opening a club here on campus anyway? It's too close to home. To her and to our past. I knew I was bound to run into her, but I definitely didn't expect for her to show up so soon, especially not with *him*. Watching Luca lavish her with his hands took everything I had in me not to reach over and strangle him.

He's always wanted her, and now that he has her, I have what I need to move on. Closure. Reassurance that she's okay and that she hasn't been miserable since I left. *Not that it would affect me either way if she was*, I quickly remind myself.

Brielle Sutton was always too good to ever be with a guy like me. If I wasn't good enough for her then, I sure as hell am not good enough for her now. Not after everything I've done.

In that moment, I stand and grab my keys. There's no way I can fucking work now. I'm too riled up. If I don't leave,

I'm only going to continue to think about it until, eventually, I'll tear this club apart. I pull out my phone and quickly dial Katrina, telling her to hurry and get dressed. Like it or not, I needed to feel something. Anything. I just need a release.

chapter six

BRIELLE

I change my mind. I'm not going," I say, shaking my head repeatedly. The reflection of the random blonde girl, staring back at me is one of false familiarity.

"Oh, you're going," Becks calls from the closet, her copper eyes burning as she hurries to continue her search for something. "And you're wearing that dress. So deal with it."

I work my hands down the front of the dress. The olive color gives the illusion that I'm tanner than I actually am. *Okay.* Yeah, no. I can do this! It's not that short, I suppose. I spin to the side and squeeze my eyes shut. God, who am I kidding?

"Becks, there's literally no back to this!"

In a fit of anger, Becks tosses the lone heel of the pair she wants to wear, and then stomps over to me. "I swear, if I left my other heel at Derrick's, I'm going to be pissed." Her eyes assess my dress again. "Nope. It's perfect. Now, if you'll excuse me. . . I have to go call Derrick and pray his girlfriend hasn't found my other shoe. And that, if she has, she hasn't killed him with it yet. They're my favorite pair."

Okay . . .

I feel my eyes grow wide. The laundry list of issues that one sentence held is not something I want to tackle, when I still have the entire night ahead of me. I'm picking my battles tonight. Closing my eyes, I force myself to walk out of her room. No matter how long I stare, the reflection isn't going to change. I know I'll only talk myself out of going if I do.

I'm halfway to the kitchen, when I spot Luca sprawled out on the couch.

"Hey!" I smile, tucking my dress under me as I plop down beside him. "You just get here?"

"Yeah, Becks let me in while you were in the shower." His blinks at the television screen as if he's fighting to stay awake. "I didn't know you two were going. . ." his words trail off as he finally turns and looks at me. His dart back and forth in an insane way.

"Okay, it's not *that* bad."

"Brielle, what the—you can't be serious about wearing that!" he sputters. His sleepiness has completely subsided.

"Excuse me?"

The dress is short; I'll give him that. But short, to me, is anything above mid-thigh. And the back is . . . well, the back is nonexistent. But, it's not like I'm not hanging out everywhere. Like Becks says, *'all the naughty bits are covered.'* I mean, I let her talk me into a lot of things, but I'm not a complete pushover.

Seeing my reaction, Luca backpedals. "I don't mean it to be rude." His words are broken in the way they always get when he's nervous about something. "I just mean that people may get the wrong impression about you, seeing you in that, and since I have that thing with my mom, I can't be there to—"

"Okay, I'm ready!" Becks interjects as she exits her room. I smile and turn to her, seeing she's wearing a gorgeous, navy sequined dress. "I know." She smiles brightly. "I look amazing."

"Wesley is going to love it," I say and stand, making my way over to the door. I grab my keys and my phone from the tiny table in the entry hall and shove them into my clutch. "Look, I'm going to have my phone if anything happens, or if

we need saving, okay?" I turn toward Luca, trying not to leave
on a sour note.

"What the hell are you talking about?" Becks laughs,
reaching around me to grab her phone before she snatches my
keys and tosses them at Luca. "You can't drink and drive.
Luca's our ride. Why do you think he's here?"

Wait. What?

I turn to Luca. "Is that okay with you?" I ask because it
seems like once again, Becks forgot not everyone lives to serve
her.

"Yup! Yes!" Luca smiles and rushes toward the door.

I shoot a look at Becks, but she just waves me off.

"Oh, stop," she groans. "You and I both know he would
have found a way to do it anyway."

When we arrive at the club Wesley is waiting for us
outside. He smiles and waves us over. I can tell by his
expression that he's surprised to see Luca in the driver's seat,
but he doesn't say anything.

"Come on. Let's head inside." He waves us behind him
as we walk around the line and straight back.

"Damn! How cool was that?" Becks laughs, clearly
loving the way everyone in line had stopped and stared at us as
we walked by.

"Pretty crazy," I say, not sure if I'd consider being
glared at by a hundred or so people, who've been waiting in line
for over an hour, "cool."

Wesley ushers us over to the bar that's shaped like a
square, motioning for us to take a seat.

"I feel terrible about this, but one of my bartenders
turned out to be a flake and quit this morning. So I'm stuck
covering her shifts until I can hire someone new." He reaches

for a pair of shot glasses and begins to pour something brown into each of them. "But I also didn't want to cancel."

"She quit, huh?" Becks smiles, leaning over the bar top to grab one of the shots and tosses it back. "I bartended a bit last year. Depending on how tonight goes, I might just let you talk me into helping you with some of those shifts."

Wesley's jaw drops as Becks sets the glass down and motions for him to hand her the other. Turning my head I try to pretend that I'm not completely a third wheel, when my eyes are drawn to the dance floor. From this far away, I can see the blanket of smoke that floats in a thin layer across the room. It looks like something out of an old horror film that appears just before the monster does.

"Brielle? Hello?" Becks waves a hand in my face. "You alive in there? Wesley asked you a question."

"Oh shoot. I'm sorry, Wesley," I offer and turn around to find both of them staring. "What was your question?"

"That's okay! I. . . ugh . . . I asked if you wanted a drink." He smiles. "And please, call me Wes. Only my mother calls me by my full name, and I hate it."

I smile and nod my head. "Okay, Wes. I'd love a drink."

"You got it!"

The night trails on, and like I promised in the car, I keep to myself. *Like a fly on the wall,* I repeat Becks' words in my head. But, not two seconds after Wes hands us our second drink, a huge party comes in and swarms the bar. Most of them are frat guys, so poor Wes is having to make drink after drink as they down their shots like water.

Becks grabs my hand and leans over the bar to yell, "We're going to go dance!"

"Come again?" I try to resist as she pulls me behind her.

The group of guys, keeping Wes busy, whistle behind us as we walk away. Becks just flips them the finger and keeps moving.

We dance for what feels like hours, until we make the decision to head back to the bar for another drink after the heat has set in and we're both covered in a light sweat.

"Damn. I like a woman who knows how to move." A guy sitting in the stool beside me licks his lips. I pretend not to hear him. Instead, I stare down at the end of the bar where Wes is and silently beg for him to hurry back. "I mean, I could watch you all night. You . . . those legs. . . that—"

"Gross, guy. Neither of us are interested in anything you've got going on. So save yourself the time and take it somewhere else." Becks leans around me to snap. Her copper eyes are alive under the blue back glow of the bar.

"Well, I wasn't talking to you. Was I?" the guy raises his voice. His hand reaches out to touch the bare skin along my back while he leans into my side. The feel of his fingers moving over my skin makes me shudder in disgust. His beer breath, nauseatingly potent, as he mumbles, "I was talking to sweet tits."

Sweet tits?

"Ew, get the fuck off her!" Becks shouts, eliciting Wes to look up from where he's standing, down at the other side of the bar. I see his face screw up in anger, and he immediately drops a glass.

I shove the guy when I feel his hand skim the lower half of my dress. His other hand fumbles with his drink, causing it to spill on my arm.

"Hey! What the fuck do you think you're doing?" Wes barks as he rounds the bar to step in between me and the guy.

"I just wanted to talk to the pretty blonde," the guy growls, probably more annoyed that I spilt his drink than the fact that he is being confronted for being a creep.

"Well, now you can talk to the bouncer as he walks your ass out of here!" Wes yells. As if on cue, two guys walk up and escort the guy away from the bar and out the front door. Wes turns around and places his hands on my shoulders. "Are you okay?"

"Yes, thank you," I say and take the towel he hands me.

"Fucking creep!" Becks grabs the other towel from the bar top and starts wiping the drink off her dress. I wrinkle my brow up at her, curious as to what she's really more pissed about: The drunk guy hitting on me or her potentially ruined dress?

Wes hurries around the bar and hands us two more towels. "We're about to announce last call. Why don't you two head back to the office? You can clean up and then we can hang out after we close?" He hurries with fixing a drink while he waits for our answer.

Becks looks up at me, her hand still mindlessly wiping the bottom of her dress. I can tell that she wants to stay but doesn't want to be the one to say it—probably worried about what Wes will think if she does. So before I can talk myself out of it, I say, "Sure." Because what's the worst that can happen? Someone else spilling their drink on me?

chapter seven

I sit back on the leather chaise and run my hands up my arm. The soft material is cool against my exposed skin.

"Somehow, I don't think you should be sitting there," I say as Becks twirls the chair around behind the desk and rolls her eyes at me.

"Oh please. It's just us." She leans forward. Her fingers trail a stack of files that lie in disarray across the desk's top.

Shaking my head, I pull out my phone and see that it's close to two in the morning. So much for not staying out long. I roll my eyes. I'm move to put it away, when I see the text notification from Luca and open the message app.

Hope ur having fun. Txt me when u need me.

My fingers trail the screen as I quickly type out a response.

Sounds good. Thanks.

I start to wonder if he had already fallen asleep, when the phone goes off, and the screen comes alive in my hand.

Welcome. See u soon.

"Looks like they're hiring more waitresses," Becks says as I look up and find she's holding one of the files. Her eyes filter down the page as she reads. "There's no way those boobs are real."

"Becks—"

Down the hall, a door slams shut, startling us. I can see Becks panic as she throws the file down and races over to where I'm seated. Her hands fluff her hair, while she prepares herself to see Wes again. I set my phone down on the couch and stifle a laugh, when I hear the door pop open. But when I raise my eyes, I feel my heart constrict. It's not Wes.

Not even close!

Stumbling into the office is the tall blonde from last night. The one with the perfect legs, and great hair that seems too perfect to be real. She throws herself against the closest wall, and a body comes with her. That's when I see him. Theo. He pulls her from the wall and shuts the door.

"Oh, God," the girl moans, her hands working to lift the back of his shirt as he walks her further into the room.

"Stop. Talking," he growls into her neck. His hands reach down to lift her legs, expertly wrapping them around his waist. The spiral of black-inked tattoos dance under the soft glow of streetlights that bathe the office in a warm light.

Oh my God.

I cover my face with my hands, my cheeks burning as I try to think of a way out of this. My own personal form of hell. Sadly, the only way out of here is through the door and that's obviously not going to work.

No. No. No. This isn't happening, I silently think to myself as I pull my hands back, only to see Theo press himself into the curve of her body. His hands are quick as he grabs her bottom and carries her with him.

Becks reaches for my hand and covers her mouth. She is definitely enjoying this way more than she should be.

"Tell me I'm pretty," the girl moans, and I silently die inside.

Feeling nauseous all of a sudden, I close my eyes while focusing on trying to steady my breaths. This is so uncomfortable. What the hell is Theo doing here anyway?

I shrink back into the chaise and cover my face again. With every moan I feel my heart sink, and I'm instantly angry at myself for feeling anything at all. So, Theo has a girlfriend. So what? Why should I care?

"Yes. Take. It. Off." Becks claps, as I look over to see Theo's shirt being tossed to the ground.

"What the fuck?" Theo turns around to face us. The abrupt way he drops the girl on the desk, sends papers flying off the back. He eyes Becks before turning to me, and I watch the color drain from his face. "Where the hell did you two come from?" His voice is so loud that it echoes. "Get out!"

"Oh come on! As if you mind giving anyone a show." Becks simply smiles at him. Her ability to downplay even the most embarrassing situations, a talent I've witnessed more than a handful of time. "Now, be honest with me. Have you been working out?"

"Um . . . is everything all right in here, ladies? I heard some shouting, and I—" Wes calls out from the hall, leaning into the room. His eyes shift between Theo and the girl, the two of us and then Theo's shirt; a sly smile spreads across his lips. "Oh shit."

Theo's eyes meet mine again, and within a second I'm on my feet. No one has to ask me twice to leave.

"Wait. We're leaving? Now?" Becks whines still sitting comfortably in her seat.

"Wes, get her the hell out of here!" I hear Theo yell from outside in the hall. I hug the corner as Becks slowly gets up and strides across the room.

"Fine. Rain check then." She laughs.

Grabbing the handle, Wes starts to shut the door, when I hear Theo curse under his breath. At the last second, I look up, and catch his eye through the crack in the door. He looks more pissed than I would have expected him to be, which only hurts more because it must mean that he really likes this girl. Then, the door shuts, and he's gone.

"Drinks?" Wes struggles to keep a straight face.

"Yup!"

"Definitely!" I walk back to the bar.

Four shots and two drinks later, and I forget why I was so mad.

Theo who?

"Um, Strawberry Shortcake?" Becks laughs as she slams her glass down on the bar and slides it back to Wes. This little game he start two shots back, where he mixes something and we have to guess what it tastes like, is harder than it seems.

"What? Not even close," he says, disbelief clearly etched across his face. He shifts his focus and waits for me to guess.

I lift the glass and finish the drink. The sweet concoction goes down easily, a gentle burn replacing it. I'm well beyond my usual two drink max. I set down my glass and shrug.

"Maybe . . . I don't know . . . Jolly Rancher?" I'm slurring, but I'm past the point of caring. I don't know why but watching Theo and that girl earlier affected me. It stirred up old feelings, and is messing with my head. But since Becks is refusing to let me text Luca so that we can leave, what the hell else is there to do?

"Close." Wes smiles, grabbing my glass. "It's Pink Gummy Bear number three."

"Number three?" I ask loudly. "You made that up! Gummy Bears don't have numbers." I can't stop myself from laughing. "There's just the red one, the green one, the pink, and—"

"Look, don't take it out on the name just because you two are the absolute worst at guessing games." He smiles.

Becks cackles on her stool and almost falls off.

"Okay. Okay." Wes laughs with us, pouring something brown into each of our glasses, which he's been shaking for the past minute. He wipes his hands, then slides them back. "Last one."

Raising my glass I swirl the brown liquid around before smelling it. Mmm. It's sweet and reminds me of chocolate. I take a sip. "Oh wow," I moan. It's absolutely delicious. I open my eyes and cover my mouth, embarrassed when I see Wes is watching me. But I can't help myself. It tastes too good. I take another sip and try to fight through the dizzy haze that is my mind until I realize that the flavor is familiar. I lick my lips.

"So, you like it then?" Wes grins from behind the bar, his eyebrow shooting up.

I nod my head and then finish the shot.

"It's Snickers!" Becks yells from her seat, waving her empty glass in Wes's face. "That was an easy one."

"No! Wrong again." He leans back and captures her glass with his hand. "You're up, Brielle. Don't let me down."

I roll my glass between my fingers and bite my lip. "I don't know." I hand mine back to him. "Maybe . . . Reese's Peanut Butter Cup?"

"Yes! Finally!" He reaches out to high-five me.

"Thank you. Thank—"

"What the hell is going on in here?" A voice appears behind us. The harsh tone catches me off guard and I whip around, nearly falling out of my seat.

"Are you drunk?" Theo's eyes fixate on me from across the room. The gentle concern I hear in his voice makes me smile, until I remember how he looked pinning that girl to the wall. Before I know it, he's at my side. With one hand, he grips my lower back and, with the other, he holds my arm. He curses under his breath, then mutters, "Jesus, Brielle."

"I'm fine," I say, even though I know it's a lie. I can feel the liquor burning its way through my veins.

Theo's hand on my back gives rise to goose bumps that spread along my skin. He looks down at my dress, then back up at me. The tiny muscles in his jaw pop under his stubble. "What the fuck, Wes? How many drinks has she had?" He glowers at his Wes as if he plans on killing him.

"Chill out. She said she's fine." Wes rocks his head from side to side as he rounds the bar and takes a seat next to Becks, who's twirling a strand of her hair between her fingers.

"Um, hello. Still here." I glance between the two guys. The hard glare pressed along Theo's face softens the moment our eyes meet.

"What the hell are you doing?"

I crinkle my nose at the question, when I find that the response I really want to give is too heavy of a conversation for how drunk I am. So, instead, I wrap my other arm around his neck, and let him lift me back into my seat. I can smell the mint on his breath as it hits my cheek.

"You smell good."

"And you smell like a pillow case on Halloween." Theo laughs and pulls back to look at me. I feel something in my chest pinch when I remember how much I love his laugh.

"Well then, you must be happy. I know how much you like candy."

"I love candy."

A figure moves in the distance, and it's the girl from before. I watch her examine Theo and I together; an angry expression pulls along her mouth.

"Sorry to break up . . . whatever this is. But do you plan on coming back to your office sometime today, Theo? Or am I just going to have to finish off what you started on my own?"

I lean around Theo's shoulder and find that, thankfully, she does still look normal enough. Definitely not like someone who just recently had sex in the back of a club. Or at least, I assume. I wouldn't know, personally.

Wait.

Did she just say . . ."Your office?" I loudly interrupt. The heaviness of the alcohol is stripping away my manners. "What does she mean *your* office?"

Theo laughs once, seeming amused by me. "This is my club."

"What? But you just got here?"

"Actually, I've been back for a couple months now," he says. The corners of his mouth draw back into a handsome smile as he leans into the back of my stool. It's then I feel the warmth of his breath behind my ear before he whispers, "Not that I care, but does Luca know where you are?" His tone is so calm, but I can't tell if he's being serious or if he's mocking me.

What does Luca knowing have to do with anything?

"Hello? Theo are you coming or not?" the girl whines. Her long legs cross at the ankles as she picks at her nails and leans against the wall. "Better yet, let's just head back to your place."

His place? I grimace at the idea.

I watch Theo's face fall when she finishes, and at the same time, I shift away toward the opposite side of the stool.

"Katrina, go back to the office and wait for me there," he tells her. His words are cold and low.

Sighing dramatically, the girl turns and heads back down the hall.

"Well, she's lovely. You always did know how to pick them." I try not to laugh, turning around to face the others. I rest my head on my hand and lean over the bar top—not sure why the idea of them going back to his place bothers me so much.

I try no to notice that he hasn't moved.

"Brielle—"

Suddenly the entry door slams shut, and the sound of muffled voices and multiple pairs of feet shuffle toward us. I twist around in my stool, when the ceiling lights click on, and I'm temporarily blinded. The harsh glow of the florescent lights bleaches the room and makes me feel like I'm back at a police station.

I blink, and when my eyes settle it's like looking at the place with new eyes. Much like the outside of the club, the original walls of the old mill are visible; the perfect blend of red brick and solid concrete that span the length of the interior and give off the feeling of warmth. Along the sides, large wooden beams reach up into the ceiling and give meaning to the placement of cocktail tables and lounging areas, which surround them.

I'm not sure what I expected it to look like, but I'm surprised to see that Theo has made the effort to build the club's renovations around the building's original architecture—almost as if he cared about trying to preserve its history.

"Whoa," Becks says, "this place is huge."

"Yeah, Theo did a great job with it. It was a steal, really."

"It's—"

Beautiful, I silently finish her sentence.

"Hey, look, new girl," Ethan says when I see the wild mess of red hair round the corner.

Oh, great. It's that guy.

His tawny eyes slide across the room. "I heard I missed out on some interesting revelations last night. My sister just couldn't stop talking about you."

"Really? Shoot. And here I was preferring that neither of you thought about me at all."

"Damn. I like her," the guy standing beside Ethan says, and I instantly recognize him as one of the cellular zombies from last night. The sound of his English accent and those jet-black spikes aren't something I would forget. I tilt my head and watch him walk over to the bar and take a seat. "Nice to see you again, love."

Like he used to years ago, when random guys would flirt with me, Theo squares his shoulders and moves to stand between us. He's easily a foot taller than the guy, as he stares down at him with a murderous glare. "I'm sorry, who the fuck are you?"

"Oh that's Blake," Ethan says as if that will mean anything to Theo. "And sorry about the impromptu walk-in. We saw Wes's truck and wanted to see if he might be down for having a little after-party. Hope it's cool. We bribed the bouncer, and he let us in."

Theo turns to Wes, who throws his hands up. "Don't look at me. I had no idea about this."

"Oh come on, Theo." Penny moves across the room. She circles Theo, like a hawk circling its prey, and works her way until she's standing directly in front of him. She flips her long, red hair over her shoulder and runs a hand along Theo's chest. "Don't you want to play?"

My eyes grow wide, and my jaw falls slack as I turn around and cut Becks a glance. The tiny ounce of relief I feel is reassured when I find that, much like me, Becks looks equally taken back. I hold my breath, waiting for Theo to answer.

No. No. Say no!

"Fine. But only if porcupine over here keeps to his own fucking lane."

"His lane?" Penny's brow arches at Theo's statement. Her eyes slide between Theo and me. "Right. Just to be clear, whose lane is she in, again?" She points to me.

Theo takes a step and turns toward me. "Can I talk you for a moment?"

I nod my head.

I allow him to help me down as he leads me to the full-length window wall, on the far side of the building, that overlooks the giant field out back. He releases my arm. "I don't care who you call, but you need to leave. Now."

Hold the phone. . .

"Why do I have to leave?"

"Because I—fuck! I don't have to explain myself to you, Brielle. Just fucking leave!"

I look back over my shoulder and see Becks laughing at something Blake said. Then Katrina steps out of the office hall. The sight of her prompts a memory to flash across my mind— of Theo and her, barging through the door. Their lips locked as he pressed her against the wall.

"Is it Katrina? Are you worried I might say something and ruin whatever you've got going on with her?"

When he doesn't answer, I roll my eyes. "Theo, I'm not leaving."

"Yes, you are."

"No, I'm not. Mostly because I haven't even texted Luca yet. So he's at least fifteen minutes out. But also, because I don't want to."

Theo sets his jaw, then turns to look out the window. "Of course he's waiting for you. He's always been such the good, little pet."

I stifle my temper and walk over next to him. My heels wobble the whole way until I'm able to steady myself on the glass panel.

"Okay, maybe I could have done without that last shot." I hedge, fixing my dress as Theo shifts his stance to face me.

His eyes trail down with my hands as I run them down my dress, smoothing out the creases. The weight of his stare ignites the skin along my cheeks.

Focus Brielle! I hear my conscious yelling at me. *You're mad at him, remember?*

Right.

"Look, I get it. Something happened between you and Luca, but he's my best friend. So whatever it is, I don't care. Just stop talking about him like that."

"Best friend? What a load."

"Excuse me?"

"You heard me." Theo laughs. The rude tone in his voice, makes me want to reach over and smack him. "I think we both know that's not all he is. But, hey, I honestly don't care what he is. He's nothing to me."

I glance back at the group and find Katrina watching us. Her long, blonde hair is draped over her shoulders. I look up at Theo and see those brilliant green eyes of his. Is that what he expects from the people he hangs around with? For everyone to blindly follow his commands? Like Devon did when he told her to leave?

I drop my eyes to the floor, feeling my anger swell in my chest. Just who exactly does he think he is now? I'm not some child; I refuse to be bossed around!

"Luca aside, I'm sorry if my being here is uncomfortable for you. But deal with it! You don't get to tell me what to do, Theo." I watch his eyes grow wide and hear his breath catch in his throat, but I can't stop, "If either of us should be the one to leave, it's you. But I appreciate your concern."

I turn to leave, but Theo reaches out and grasps my wrist. "Will you just listen to me? Damn it. I'm telling you to leave because I know the type of after-party Ethan is referring to, and they turn ugly. Fast. Trust me, you're not going to want to be any part of it."

I rip my hand back from his grip. "I'm staying Theo, deal with it. Besides, it's your club. Why don't you make them leave if you really don't want them here? I can't leave Becks."

"Because their parents are—" He tightens his hand into a fist. "Forget it! You wouldn't understand!"

"I might if you tried to explain it."

"Just—forget it. We'll both stay. It's not like I wouldn't rather be doing anything else with my night. Now I have to stay to watch out for your ungrateful ass."

Ungrateful?

"How am I ungrateful? I didn't ask you to stay, Theo. I told you to leave!"

"Fine. You want me gone? I'm gone."

I squint my eyes at the back of his head as he starts toward Katrina.

"Hey, Theo!" I yell when he's about halfway to her. He pauses, twisting his head to the side to look back at me. "Make sure to tell her she's pretty."

A smug smile spreads along his lips. "Have a nice night, Brielle." His jaw flits under the skin, as he continues, "I know I will."

chapter eight

S omehow I just knew that somewhere Luca was waiting for Brielle, and sure enough, I was right. That guy is obsessed. He's probably been sitting in his car, watching his phone for hours—like the "good" guy that he is—just waiting for her to call. Fuck. I hate him. I hate that I let my temper run away with me too.

Out of all the people in my life, Brielle is the last person I ever want to hurt. So much so that after I left Katrina's house at two forty I've been driving around for the past hour, just trying to cool my head. For someone whose life revolves around chaos and fixing other people's problems, I've learned to demand control. Control of the room, and the people in it. But like a drug, control is addictive. Just ask my father. I need it, crave it, and when I don't get it, I get pissed.

And with Brielle, she just loves to test me. She always has. I made the mistake of slipping up with her, once, because of certain feelings—feelings I allowed to cloud my judgement. It's because of that mistake that I almost lost Mason *and* her that night.

It isn't until Wes calls me and asks if he can offer Becks the open bartending position that I finally feel like I can breathe again—not because of Becks but because he told me they were still at the club, which means there's still a chance that I can see Brielle. If I hurry. . .

I know I need to apologize for being an ass, but damn it if I wouldn't rather just avoid the whole thing. I kill the engine, and head inside Haze, spotting blond waves the second I walk through the door—only, they aren't from my girl, but Wes.

Fuck. Did I just say, my girl?

Brielle. It's not Brielle.

I set my keys down on the bar top. "Ugh, how's everything going?" I shift my eyes around the room and swallow the urge to call out her name. Instead, I focus on the obvious, which is . . . this place is a fucking mess. I check my watch. Eh, we're still five hours out before the morning cleaning crew arrives. One problem at a time.

"I swear, it'll be clean before Barb gets here." Wes shoots me a glassy look when he reads my expression. His smile is bright, but I'm not convinced. I lean over the bar and find a passed-out Becks lying on his lap. "And before you ask, I have no clue where Brielle is."

I shake my head and shrug as if I don't understand what he's insinuating. "I didn't ask where she was." But inside, I'm ready to tear his fucking limbs off. What the hell does he mean he has no clue where she is? The place isn't that big.

I crane my neck, when I hear her laugh echo from the office hall. When I turn back around, Wes is downing the last of a bottle of Jack Daniels. "And women say romance is dead." I point down at Becks. "Take her home."

"But what about . . ." Losing his train of thought, he lets his words trail off, while rubbing the back of his neck.

"Brielle? Yeah, let me worry about Brielle," I tell him, and for some reason, I can't hide my smile. The idea of Brielle being trapped inside my truck, forced to talk to me as I drive her home, makes something weird kick up in my chest. I twist around and notice Ethan and Penny are missing, too, as well as that asshole with the pitchfork for a head. "Where's everyone else?"

"Blake took off with Brielle, and the twins left for a party over in Aubrey," Wes says, slowly peeling himself out from under Becks. The hard rap of her head as it hits the ground when he forgets to hold it up, makes me cringe internally. "Whoops."

He shoots me an arrogant smirk that makes me want to reach over and punch him. But I won't. I've got other things on my mind, like who the hell this Blake guy is, and why he seems so interested in talking to Brielle.

"Just get her home. Safely. Call a cab if you have to; just don't drive."

I wait until he nods before I head to the office. I reach the hall, when my phone goes off. Jesus, it's Katrina. I decline the call and see the string of notifications that have been accumulating since I left. But I'm purposefully ignoring them because: a) Who the fuck does that, especially, when you know, and they know, that they're being rejected? b) I know that if I do answer, she's going to want to know why I left as early as I did, and I can't juggle that ball of crazy while I'm trying to talk to Brielle.

When I reach the office, I find the door is shut. That's when I hear it—the sound of Brielle's innocent laughter, which dredges up memories I've long since tried to forget. Like. . .how much I actually love the sound of her laugh. I swallow my nerves and open the door, praying for Blakes sake that I don't find the two of them enacting a similar scene that Brielle found me in, earlier this evening.

But, thankfully, she's alone.

I step into the room when she turns and sees me.

"Theo?" She's sitting on the floor with her legs drawn up to her chest. The half-empty glass in her hand looks mostly watered down. She peers up and over the top of a book, seeming surprised to see me. But whether that's a bad or good thing, I'm not sure. "What are you doing here?"

I don't answer her as my mind dawdles on the mossy hue of her eyes. Her hair is now pulled into a bun that shows off her slim jaw and neckline. I let my eyes drift over her body until I notice that she's set the book down and is watching me.

Damn it.

I force a cough and point down at the book.

"What's so funny?"

She hesitates, probably having caught on to me, before she picks up the book and opens it. The page she'd ended on is dog-eared, in a true Brielle sort of way.

"Oh, it's just this book I found in your lost and found."

"We have a lost and found?"

She tilts her head, her full lips pulling back into a smile. She taps the floor beside her. "Come read with me. I just got to a good part. It's a love scene." Her words are light, but I can tell that there's more to it than that.

"A love scene, huh?" I half laugh, half choke.

The idea of her reading an erotic novel almost amuses me as much as it terrifies me. Before I know it, I find myself wondering what she would think if she could read my thoughts right now. My girl and a million different—all filthy— scenarios. Each one of which ending with her panting and moaning my name until she's begging for me to fuck her, which, I would, happily. There's only one difference . . . she'd be too spent to laugh.

I take a deep breath and run a hand through my hair. Shit, I'm struggling here. Maybe this isn't such a good idea.

"Let me guess," she says, her head falling back to rest on
the leather chaise behind her. "Per usual, you hear love scene
and immediately think of sex. Am I right?" When I don't
answer, she closes the book and stands up. Her eyes hold mine
as she walks the short distance to where I'm standing and taps
the book to my chest. "No wonder Katrina is in such good
shape. She has to be, with that dirty mind of yours."

My smile drops instantly, and I narrow my gaze. The
sound of Katrina's name on Brielle's lips is foreign in a
nauseating way. I have to admit, I thought she'd still be too
pissed to even want to talk. Most girls would be.

I see her waiting for me to respond, so I say, "Says the
girl who's reading kinky, sex stories over here." I shake my
head, trying to recover. But I can tell she's noticed. I watch the
corner of her lips curl into that seductive grin of hers—the one I
love so much. Shit. Did I just say love?

What the fuck is wrong with me?

Brielle bites her lip and I can't seem to look away. Jesus.
Why does she keep doing that?

"Did Becks say something to you about me?"

What?

"No," I say. What the hell is that supposed to mean?
And because I'm a nosey asshole, I ask, "Why? Is there
something I should know?" I let out a breath, watching her as
she sits down and sets the book by her side. The flimsy bit of
paper rubs the outside of her thigh, and for a split second, I'm
jealous of that book touching her when I can't.

"Forget it. I thought you were . . . it's nothing."

Right. I'm sure it is.

I feel the muscles in my jaw tick as she picks the book
back up. She licks her lips, then presses them together. With all
the talk of sex, I feel my curiosity pique. Suddenly, I can't help

but wonder what it is that she, herself, imagines when she lies down at night and touches herself. Does she think of the men in her books? Does she picture Luca?

At that thought, I tighten my fists, forcing myself to take a breath. The idea of her even thinking about finding pleasure with him makes my skin itch. The kind of anger that can only be solved with a fight, a hot shower, and a good fuck.

"Why aren't you out there with the others? And where, um—I close my eyes—"where is that Blake guy?" My right hand moves to my face, as I pinch the bridge of my nose, trying desperately to think of something other than her and whatever is going on in that book.

"Well, I got hungry. And he. . ."

I take in a deep breath and try to steady myself. The better part of my inner mind begins scolding me, giving me all the reasons why I should turn around and leave. I should just call one of my guys and have them take her home, but for some reason, I can't get my damn legs to move from this spot.

"Theo? Did you hear me?"

Nope.

"Sorry, yes," I say, then cross the room and slide down in the seat beside her.

Sitting this close makes our shoulders brush against one another's, and like she used to—back before any of the bad shit happened—she leans into my side. Her head nestles atop my shoulder, while she tilts the book up so that I can read along with her.

"Hey, I should really be getting you home—"

"Shh, this is the good part."

I roll my eyes at the sheer control this girl has over me, and I eventually relent. For a minute, I allow myself to forget that any time has passed, and I pull her closer to me. When she doesn't resist, I press my lips into her hair and breathe in the smell of her coconut shampoo. Everything about her is so familiar. But it's also excitingly new.

"Hey, are you okay?" I hear her voice. The subtle concern behind her words makes me freeze, and in a matter of seconds, she shifts to face me. Shit. What just happened?

"Come on, Romeo. I think you need some air. You look a little pale." She smiles, reaching out with the back of her wrist and presses it to my forehead. "I swear, you're such a guy. Any talk of intimacy, and you start to sweat—"

I reach for her wrist and take hold of it. Whatever else she was about to say quickly fades away. For the next few seconds, she sits, quietly appraising my every move. With her free hand, she reaches out and touches a spot along my chest.

"Your heart's racing." Her words are soft and breathy. But I feel the exact opposite. I feel like it's stopped.

"Brielle, I—"

I force myself to stop talking when I hear the sound of someone beating on the door. If it's Wes, I swear I'm going to kill him. Then I'll thank him for stopping me from doing something stupid. I've never been more grateful for his nosey ass tendencies than I am in this moment. Besides the fact that Brielle's drunk, I have to struggle trying to keep my head straight, especially when it comes to her. Too much time alone with her clouds my judgement.

Halfway to the door it opens to reveal Blake. He peers around my shoulder and takes a giant step into the room. When his eyes find Brielle, she smiles and waves. But before he can take another step, I block his path. "The fuck are you doing in here?"

"Theo," I hear Brielle's gentle warning. I turn around and watch her close the book and set it on my desk.

I take in her appearance and wonder why the hell she's so calm, all of a sudden. Is it me? Was I projecting my feelings for this girl on the situation? Or is she just better at covering it up?

I watch her walk to the door, her hand pulling it open the rest of the way, as Blake stares openly at her body. His eyes rake up and down the length of her while she makes her way down the hall. I curl my fists.

"You ready to get out of here, love? I kept it warm for you."

Kept it. . . warm?

"What the hell did you just say to her?" I grab the guy. My hand fists at the collar of his tattered shirt, and I shove him into the wall.

"Theo, stop!" Brielle yells. Her hand gently works to peel away my fingers until the last of the material is sprung from my grip. She steps between us. "Just calm down. What the hell is going on with you?"

With me? Was she planning on going home with this asshole?

"Her soup, man. I was talking about her soup. She said she was hungry, so I left and went to get her something other than peanuts and leftover bar food."

I grit my teeth, trying to push back the building desire to punch him square in the jaw, but instead I take a step back. Leaning over Brielle, I point my finger at his chest. "That better damn well be the only thing you meant."

"Seriously? Now you're threatening him?" Brielle's disapproving tone hits me, and I look down to see her face screwed up in anger.

Jesus. I laugh.

She's right. What the hell am I doing?

I press the palms of my hands against my eyes and head into my office. Brielle calls out to me, but I slam the door shut. I need space. I don't know why that guy staring at her bothers me so damn much. But it does. This is why I didn't tell her that I was back. Whenever I'm around her, I lose the ability to think clearly. A classic example of a damned if you do, damned if you don't situation.

I waste the next ten minutes mindlessly shifting papers around the desk. I push a hand through my hair, take in a deep breath, and walk out to the bar. The second I do, I see them. My eyes are pinned to the way he subtly leans into her while he talks. She smiles, but I can't tell if it's forced or sincere.

Breathe, I tell myself as I feel my hands ball into fists. I look at Brielle and—not for the first time—I notice the girl of my past is now a woman. The curves of her breasts and the thickness of her ass makes my dick jump with excitement.

The fuck am I doing?

Brielle is an adult. If she wants to go home with this asshole, then by all means . . . I have no right to stop her. But when I catch his hand brush a spot along her knee, pausing for a second too long. My reservations elude me.

"Are you fucking dense?" I practically rip Brielle off her stool and pull her to me. Really I just need to get her out of the way so I can kick this guy's ass.

"Theo!" Brielle tries to worm her way free from my grip. "What's your problem? We were just eating."

"Yeah, well, I guess that's better than the alternative."

"The alternative?"

"You." I turn my attention to Blake. I point my finger at him, feeling Brielle's tiny hands pull at my wrist, as if she could hold me back if I wanted to hit him. "What the fuck are you doing?"

I watch him struggle for an answer until he raises his sandwich. "Eating."

Jesus. This guy must have a death wish. I half laugh at his answer and fight the urge not to punch the panini out of his hand. I know I'm blowing this out of proportion, but it's like I can't stop. I'm too far gone; I'm seeing red. "Get the fuck out of my club."

I grab my keys off the bar and begin making my way towards the back door. I hear tiny footsteps trailing after me, but I'm not in the mood to stop.

"Theo, wait."

With that, my feet halt. Damn it. Even my feet are against me. I turn around, finding no other option, and frown when I notice her shaking.

"What the hell was that?"

"What else should I have done? Fucking let him finish his sandwich?" I roll my eyes. *I'd much sooner shove it down his throat.* I cut my eyes to the ground, to the boxes lining the wall. I exhale a breath and kick the closest one. "Do you like him or something?" I feel myself spiraling now. The small smile she offered him and the way she allowed his touch replaying in my mind, like a sick joke.

"Stop." Her tone is soft, but I can hear the anger she's suppressing. When I look up, I see something flash behind her eyes, like an old memory resurfacing.

"Stop what?"

"Stop talking to me like this."

Her voice is low. I watch her take in a deep breath and release it.

"This isn't like you. What happened to the old Theo who was kind and sweet, and—"

"I don't know what to tell you. Maybe you just didn't know me as well as you thought you did."

"I don't believe that."

I roll my eyes. "That's the thing, Brielle. I don't care what you think. Or what anyone thinks for that matter. If you haven't noticed, a lot has changed since you knew me."

Damn it. I shouldn't have said that.

Brielle looks down the hall toward the bar, the same time the front entry door clicks shut signaling Blakes departure.

"Right. Silly me." She twists to the side. "I'm . . . um . . . I'm gonna go."

I call her name, when she starts to walk away, but she ignores it. I quickly jog around her and block her path. I touch her shoulder, but she shoves it off.

"Don't, Theo. I just want to go home." She tilts her head up to look at me. But I find little relief in the fact that she doesn't move to try and go around. "I can't do this right now. I can't go there with you. Think what you want, but we were honestly just eating."

"Come on, Brielle," I say. My eyes trail the length of her, as if her body needed an explanation for how easily she affects men. "There's nothing innocent in the way you make guys feel."

Immediately, the soft tone vanishes in front of me. Her cheeks quickly turn red as she narrows her eyes in frustration. "Can you stop it already? Leave the act behind. I already have Luca trying to take Mason's place. I don't need you doing it too!"

Luca? Mason? What the hell just happened. Am I missing something? What did I say that would make her say that?

"Wait. Hold on a second. Brielle . . ." I reach my arm out to grab hold of her, while she tries to push around me. Neither of us are taking note of the lone box that I kicked earlier, which is now sitting in the middle of the floor, until she stumbles, and we fall face first to the ground.

Instinctively, my first thought is to catch her. But in the mess of things, it doesn't work out that way. "Shit, are you all right?" I ask, my voice etched in panic. I had inevitably fallen for her—or on top of her—but I'm thankful to find my arms absorbed most of my weight.

I feel her hands pressing against my chest. She's lying motionless, staring up at me with those damn green eyes. Her blonde waves have fallen, framing her face; the smell of her coconut shampoo quickly overloads my senses again.

"I, um. . ."

For a second, I let my mind drift as I shift my weight onto one arm. With my free hand, I brush a strand of her hair, which is resting over her lips, off to the side. The soft, pink fullness of them ignite a sense of need deep within me—an all-consuming desire to have my way with her. . .to push the limits of what she knows is possible.

I tell myself to get up, but I am no longer in control. Rather, I'm being driven by another part of me—a part that I'm not embarrassed to admit is beginning to inch its way down the leg of my pants.

"I'm sorry," she says. Her words are breathy and weak. "I wasn't paying attention."

Right.

Without another thought, I roll over and stand up. My mind is a jumbled mess as I reach down and lift her to her feet. As usual, she is light, fitting perfectly in my arms.

"No, it's not your fault." I take a step back, suddenly in need of some distance between us. I push a hand through my hair and force myself to look at the ground. "Um . . I can give you a ride. If you want. That way you don't have to bother Luca."

I can see her hesitation. She doesn't trust me. But being who she is, she also doesn't want to say no. "Sure. A ride would be great."

chapter nine

T he next week goes by quickly, and to celebrate the start of the weekend, Luca and I grab lunch on the square after our history class. We would have invited Becks, but after two shifts together and countless hours spent "texting," she and Wes have officially decided to declare themselves an item. Like any other new couple, they're practically joined at the hip. And I couldn't be more happy for her.

"Melle's Mushroom?" Luca's asks. His voice, muffled through the phone.

"Sounds good to me. Meet you in ten?"

"It's a date!"

I arrive a few minutes early, so I hurry inside to grab us a table. Luckily, it's still early enough that there aren't too many people around just yet. Even with it being a Friday, pizza and burgers before noon isn't every college student's ideal choice. But it is ours. When Luca arrives, the waitress comes over, and we place our order. Not too much later, our food arrives, and we both scarf down half a pizza and share a side of fries.

"I was thinking about heading up to the Drafthouse and catching a movie tonight," Luca says as the two of us waste the last few minutes walking around the square. "Want to come?"

"Sure!" I smile up at him. "I haven't been to a movie theater in forever."

"Really? Cool. Pick you up around six?"

"Works for me."

Later that night, as we arrive at the gas station, Luca hops out to work the pump. The flashing neon lights flicker every so often behind his head, as he leans down to look at me through the driver's side window.

"Want to go grab us some candy?"

"Is that even a question?" I accept his wallet from his outstretched hand. I smile and open my door. "Any requests?"

"You know what I like."

I turn around and walk inside, happy I decided to come. Luca's been in such a playful mood all day. I love when he's like this. Playful Luca is always way more fun than brooding Luca. I spot the candy section and almost skip to it. The cashier up front waves to me as I turn the aisle. Eying the Snickers bars, I reach for one.

"Snickers, huh? By that little noise you made the other night, after the Reese's shot, I wouldn't have guessed that." The familiar voice whispers over my shoulder. I turn around and jump back, thankful when Wes is able to steady me before I take the whole display down. "Oh shit. My bad. Are you okay?"

I nod. "Yes, thank you." Dusting myself off as if I had actually fallen, I say, "I, um. We. . . we're headed to the movies." I smile, holding up Luca's wallet. "Luca and I, I mean. Where's Becks?"

"Oh, she caught a last-minute shift tonight." He takes a step back. "I'm here with the boys. Were all about to head over to K.O. and watch Theo's big fight." He reaches around my shoulder and grabs a Snickers for himself. "You should come if you want. Luca, too."

"K.O.?"

"You know, Knock Out?" he says, but the name doesn't register. "The bar just outside city limits . . . the one with the boxing ring . . . and the fights . . . and, seriously? You've never heard of it?"

I shake my head.

"Hey, man. You ready to—"

I look up to see Ethan turning into the aisle. His eyes make a broad sweep around us, until he settles his focus on me. "Ah, fuck. What the hell is new girl doing here? Are you, like, stalking us or something?"

I narrow my eyes at him.

"Shut the hell up, Ethan. Brielle's cool." Wes turns around and slaps the Snickers bar to his chest. "Just for that, you can pay for being a dick." His tone flat. Then he turns back around to face me. "So, what do you think? Want to come?"

"Brielle, everything okay? The cars filled up. You ready yet?" I hear Luca walking up behind me. He's probably been wondering what the hell was taking so long to buy a Snickers, a KitKat, and two bottles of water.

"Oh yeah. Sorry. I ran into Wes and we started talking." I press my lips together. I can hear my mind screaming at me to walk away and go to the movies. But I'd be lying if I didn't say the idea of going to Knock Out didn't sound interesting. Well, not the idea of watching Theo fight, but if I go, maybe he'll change his mind. "He just invited us to go to Knock Out with them. They're going to watch—"

"You want to go to K.O.? No! Hell no!"

"Whoa, man." I watch Wes's eyebrows pull in. "There's nothing wrong with K.O., Theo and I go there all the time."

"Oh well, that makes me feel better, because Theo being there must mean it's safe."

I catch the anger spark behind Wes's eyes, and before anything happens, I slide between them. Just in case.

"Luca didn't mean that," I hedge, trying to prevent a fight from happening before we even arrive at the place. "Right, Luca?"

"Wrong. I've been there . . . it's not the best crowd."

"Luca, please."

"No, Brielle, please. I enjoy watching me dig their own graves."

I turn to Wes and touch his shoulder. His sea-blue eyes fall to my hand, then move up my arm and settle along my face.

"Why don't I just text you if we end up going?" I smile sweetly.

"Ya, I think that might be best." His lips crease as he runs his tongue along the front of his teeth. "I'll put your names down at the front."

"Thank you!"

Luca and I walk back to the car after purchasing what I'd originally gone in for. He holds my door for me as I get in, and I can see he's busy trying to piece together his defense. He shuts the door when I'm in and walks around to his side.

"Brielle, I know what you're thinking. The whole fighting, bad boy stuff, as cliché as it is, is attractive to women. But, I just—"

"You think bad boys fighting is hot, Luca?" I tease him.

"Ha. Ha. I said to women, and I only know this because you and Becks made me watch that vampire TV series about ten-billion times last summer. I just don't think it's a good idea."

I suck my bottom lip in between my teeth and bite it. I fully understand why he's saying this. I mean, hell, I think it's insane for something like this to even exist. But it does, and yet, I still want to go.

"Look, what if we only went just long enough so I can see the place—if only so I can say I've been there once. We don't even have to sit with Theo if you don't want to. Wes said he was fighting anyway."

"Of course, he is." Luca rolls his eyes. "Brielle, have you seen the guy? He's built like an NFL linebacker and covered in tattoos. I know you probably think he's still the old Theo, but that guy is long gone. And this new version is trouble."

"Yeah, maybe you're right."

"I mean, what would your father say if he found out you went to a bar that has a secret boxing league? Because I already know what he'd do to me. He'd kill me and lock you up for temporary insanity."

Crap. I hadn't even thought about my father, or what he'd do to Luca if he found out he was the one who drove me there. I look up when I hear Wes's voice snap at Ethan across the parking lot. His blond mess of hair is draped in front of his face, like it usually is, as he tosses Ethan a Gatorade across the tailgate. A minute later, they pull out and speed off while we're still parked.

I close my eyes, fully aware that there's a good chance I'm going to regret this, and say, "Luca, I want to go."

"Seriously? After everything I just said, you still want to go?"

"Yes."

Luca runs a hand over his hair, then pulls out of the parking lot. "Fine, but we're not staying long."

We drive the rest of the way in silence as I look out the window. Fifteen minutes ago we passed a building and I haven't seen one since. At the next light, Luca takes a right turn. And another mile down, we come up to a big field where a hundred or so cars and trucks are parked, surrounding a lone building. The building itself is massive and is easily fifty-thousand square feet, or more. It looks like a venue one might rent out for an event more than a bar.

"This is it?" I ask, leaning under the rearview mirror as we turn in and round the front, looking for a place to park.

"Yup. This is the place."

In bright, bold letters, the words: "KNOCK OUT," are lit up in red over the entrance. Luca finds a place to park up close, when we see Wes and Ethan cross over the parking lot and meet up with Theo. I cut my eyes back to Luca and notice the worried look on his face.

"Everything is going to be okay, Luca."

"Yeah, you say that now."

I laugh then hop out of the car. I wait at the trunk for Luca, when a group of guys leaving are passing by. Seeing them, Luca grabs my arm and rips me back to him.

His sour expression is confusing at first, until he leans in to whisper in my ear, "See what I mean?"

At first, I'm not sure what he means. A group of guys leaving a bar, is a pretty normal sight. But when I take a closer look, I see the guys are covered in blood—lots of blood—up their arms, around their hairline, and across their face.

"What the hell?" I inhale in a quick breath. My fingers dig into Luca's arm.

Oh yeah.

This place definitely isn't legal.

"You sure you still want to go?" Luca almost seems excited for a moment.

I turn back to the bar and catch another group, shuffling out the door. Two of them pull out their cigarette packs, while the other two hang back and lean against the concrete wall. I barely get a glimpse inside enough to see the corner of the ring before the doors slam shut.

If Becks were here, she'd tell me to suck it up and move my ass—and that I need to stop being so scared of what my father thinks and just live in the moment. I rub my hands together and pull at the frayed end of my shorts.

"Yes, now come on."

I link Luca's arm with mine, and we start to walk up to the bar's entrance. I barely make it a step before I catch Theo's eyes spot me from across the lot, and instantly I feel the weight of his stare, which is full of the slow, burning anger that I saw the other night at the club. I avert my eyes, feeling my cheeks heat up.

I hate that he had to see me like that. I found out from Becks, the next morning, that I'd passed out in his car and that that he had to carry me inside and put me to bed. Put me to bed! Like a child!

"Um, I'm sorry, but what the fuck is she doing here?" Theo yells out loud. The twenty or so guests walking around out front all stop and turn to stare.

Yup, I'm already regretting it.

chapter ten

W hat the hell are you doing here?" Theo repeats, his eyes shifting from the bar to me, then back to the bar. He pushes past Wes, barreling through four guys, and meets me at the door. His expression contorts from shock to confusion, to full on anger, as he grabs my arm and drags me over to the side of the building.

"Do you realize where you are? You don't belong here." His eyes dart between Luca and me. "What were you thinking, bringing her here? Take her home! Now!"

I shake my head and push past him. But the second I take a step, his hand reaches out and grasps my arm, twirling me around to face him. "Stop grabbing me!" I yell and pull my arm away.

"Then stop walking away from me and I will."

He exhales a breath and pauses. His eyes flit behind me and out into the parking lot. Being this close to him, I can smell the spice of Katrina's vanilla perfume on his shirt, and I hate the fact that it's there. "You're not going inside." He shakes his head. A smug smile spreads along his lips.

Ugh! "I'm not some high schooler anymore, Theo. I'm an adult. I don't need you, or anyone, to protect me. I can go wherever the hell I please."

Cinching his hands around my hips, Theo pushes me against the cement wall of the building. I feel his fingers dig into my skin as he leans over me. His eyes rest on my mouth. I can tell by the look in them that he's deliberating what to do next.

"Do you even know what goes on in there? The type of people that hang out at places like this?" he says in a low voice.

I swallow the lump that's forming in my throat and feel my pulse begin to race. "You mean people like you? Aren't you here to fight, Theo?"

"I warned you to stay away from me." His hands slip from my waist. The smug expression he was wearing begins to fade as he twists his head to the side and glares at Wes.

"Yeah, well, you've said a lot of things before."

"Clearly I haven't said enough."

I turn around to walk away, and the first thing I see is Katrina glaring at me. Her sunflower-yellow romper and all-white heels make her look like the perfect summer Barbie doll. I bite my lip. God, does this girl ever have a bad hair day?

Forcing myself to smile, I drop my eyes to the simple T-shirt and shorts I'm wearing, for what I thought was going to be a casual night at the movies. Katrina walks up to Theo's side and grabs his arm. Her perfectly manicured nails press into his skin as she stands there—her blue eyes like daggers.

As if reading my mind, Theo wraps his hand around Katrina's waist, and pulls her against his side. I try to look away, but my eyes focus on the action. As if to solidify the action's intended meaning, he tosses a smile in my direction.

"Look, you seem like a nice girl, so I'm going to try to break it down for you." Katrina wrinkles her brow, her bottom lip pulling to one side. "Go home. Obviously, Theo doesn't feel like babysitting tonight, and honestly, you're a little annoying."

Annoying? What the—

"Katrina," Theo groans a low warning. He drops his arm as if to further show his displeasure with her, when she rolls her eyes. The act itself is so overly dramatic that for a second, I wonder if she were to hold it any longer, would her eyes actually stick to the back of her head.

I shift my stance and cut my eyes over to Luca. I can see the warning signs etched on his face, and I shudder thinking what might happen if my father were to find out where I am again—a thought that irritates me more than anything, because it's like living on a leash. Before Mason, I never used to care what anyone thought, but now it's all I seem to be able to do.

Looking up at Katrina's smug face, my competitive side—the side of me that's more like the old Brielle than the one I hide behind today—wants to prove that smug face wrong. Why shouldn't I go? I'm not a child anymore. I can protect myself. And what better way to prove it than by showing them. Here. Tonight.

"Brielle, maybe we should leave." Luca reaches out to touch my shoulder. "We can still catch the late night showing if we hurry."

Theo's face falls instantly. "Yes. You'd better hurry, Brielle. I know how much you love the previews," he says dryly, his voice so full of sarcasm I can't help but laugh. The tattoos in black ink that stretch over the length of his arm flex under the spotlight.

"Nice try, but I'm still coming inside." I smile as sweetly as I can manage. When no one says anything, I skirt around the three of them and head toward the door. "Come on, Luca. Live a lit—"

I make it a step, trying to ignore the eerie sense of déjà vu, before fingers reach out and grasp my arm.

"Hey, get the fuck off of her!"

"Easy, lover boy."

I turn around and shoot Theo a look.

"I said stop grabbing me!"

Theo looks down at his hand, hesitating for another minute, then releases me.

"I'm asking nicely. Please. Leave."

Katrina lets out a long breath. "For fuck's sake, just let the girl come in. I'm so bored of this. It's not like she's going to last very long, anyway."

I bite my tongue to keep my rude comments to myself, as Theo motions for Katrina to come closer. She does as he asks, and when she's finally at his side, he leans into her ear and whispers something that elicits her to walk off and head into the bar.

What the. . .?

So, it's safe for Katrina to go in alone, but not me?

I cross my arms, pointing after her.

"What's wrong now?" Theo half laughs. His smile is soft, but the anger behind his eyes is still burning.

"Seriously? You even have to ask?" I shrug my shoulders as I look up at the distorted image of someone I once knew. "Who the hell are you? I thought you just said the place isn't safe, yet you let her go inside. Alone."

"Katrina can handle herself."

"You're such a hypocrite." The words tumble from my lips before I can manage to stop myself. "I don't know how Katrina puts up with you, because I would never want to be with someone like—"

Theo glares aggressively at me. But there's more to it than that. With one hand, he grasps my wrist, and with the other, he grabs my elbow. He pulls me to him, my arm sliding along his side, until there's barely any space left between us. I can feel the rise of his chest with every breath he takes.

"Damn it, Brielle! Why are you so insistent on fighting me? I'm just trying to keep you safe so that nothing happens like it did in the. . ." his voice trails off.

"In the past? Is that what you were going to say?"

I feel Theo's heart beat against my wrist and close my eyes. The steady rhythm is soothing even during all the craziness that's ensued. I open my eyes, suddenly aware at how everyone around us is staring. The closeness that Theo seems to want feels more intimate by the second.

"You don't own me, Theo. You don't get to just show up in my life after five years and start bossing me around. It doesn't work like that."

"Fine," he says, stepping back. His hands release me, while I wrap my arms around my waist and hold them there. "Whatever. Just don't come crying to me when you don't like what you see."

Theo hurries to the door, yelling, "Hurry up, then, if you're coming!"

Luca reaches out and pulls me to his side as we walk to catch up with Theo. "What the hell was that?" he whispers in my ear. But, honestly, his guess is as good as mine.

A short, bald guy, standing just past the entrance, stammers when he sees Theo, who reaches in his pocket and pulls out an invitation of sorts. It's a small, yellow card, about the size of an index card, which seems to have had its fair share of use.

"They're with me," he says without hesitation, and we're immediately waved through.

Inside, the room is flooded with bodies so tightly packed that no matter which way you move, you're bound to bump into someone. The air is thick inside, a medley of blood, sweat, and dirt. For a bar, this one is definitely unique. Aside from a few tables and booths, most of the space is taken up by a series of stadium-styled seats, which extend up the length of two walls. And sitting dead center in the room is a boxing ring.

We meet up with the others shortly afterward, and together, we go to the table that Wes has waiting for us, close to the ring. I take a seat next to Luca and shift the basket of half-cracked peanut shells further down on the table.

"What can I get you to drink, handsome?" I look up and find a waitress in a corset and short, shorts batting her eyes at Luca.

He smiles back at her, placing his left arm around the back of my chair. "We'll have two draft Dos Equis pints," he says, moving his right hand to touch my knee as he leans toward me.

I look up and nod in agreement.

A smile plays along Luca's lips. I don't know who the act is more for—the waitress or Theo. But I'm not going to embarrass him by shrugging him off. For all I know, he just wants to shut the girl down politely.

"Got it." The waitress smiles and turns to walk away.

"Oh wait." I cut my eyes over to the rest of the table. "You forgot to get their order."

"Oh, I know what they want."

I press my lips into a line. Right. Of course she does. I forget they're probably here all the time. I look over to Luca and smile sweetly, suddenly grateful that he's not the kind of guy who has waitresses know his bar orders wherever he goes. I relax back against my chair and take a breath. So far, this place isn't that bad.

It's then I shift my eyes to Theo and Katrina. The aggressive look he's wearing momentarily catches me off guard.

"What?"

"Nothing," Theo says. The corners of his lips curl back into a look that reveals some resemblance of disgust. "Just thinking about how cute you two look together."

I lean forward and adjust myself.

Well, this was going to be a long night, I think to myself, just as my eyes catch sight of the large display hanging over the bar. Its detailed list of names is followed by a series of numbers scaled from one to ten. The four letters marking the top left column are "T. H. E. O."

What the hell?

"What's that?" I ask just as our drinks arrive. I smile at the waitress and take a sip of my beer.

"Seriously?" Katrina turns her attention to me. "Do you know nothing? That's the leaderboard, duh! And my baby is undefeated."

Did she really just call him "baby?"

"Theo, my man!" A voice breaks through the dull roar, and I turn toward its owner.

"Mack." Theo smiles back. The two-clasp hands almost immediately. He points to the ring. "Is there going to be a fight tonight, or . . .?"

The slender man with the stark widow's peak breaks out into a slow chuckle. "Yeah, Tucker and Liam are about to hop in; they've been talking trash all night so it should be a good one." He continues to laugh. "But, hey man, how do you feel about taking on a newcomer tonight? The guy's been throwing around so much shit. Honestly I was happy when I saw you walk in."

I look over at Theo in time to see him cut his eyes at me.

He raises his hand and pushes it through his tousled brown mess of hair, before turning back to the guy and answering him, "Ah, maybe later, man. I've got some old friends out with me tonight. We're just here to catch up."

Mack hums like *ah*.

"Wait, what?" Katrina snaps.

I feel myself relax and let out a breath I hadn't realized I was holding. I'm happy to hear Theo reject the offer. I definitely don't want to sit around and watch him fight.

"It's all good, man," The guy smiles, giving him a small pat on the back. "I'll just tell him to fuck off."

Theo laughs, turning back toward the table after Mack walks off and back to the bar. But for some reason, I can't shake the uneasy feeling I get and decide to keep my eyes on Mack. I watch him round the side of the bar, when I see that the "guy" he'd been referring to is none other than the drunk from the bar.

The creep Wes had thrown out last weekend.

Oh, crap.

Mack's lips move as he tells him that it's not going to happen tonight, and apparently it's not taken well. He mouths the words "fuck you," before walking away. Eliciting the creep to turn around and glare in our direction. The moment his eyes meet mine, I look away.

Theo narrows his eyes as if reading my thoughts. "What's wrong?"

"Well—" I feel Luca's hand reach for mine before I cut my eyes back to the bar. "Oh dear God," I say when I see he's abandoned his drink and is walking toward us. "Funny story. . ."

Feeling impatient, Theo turns around in time to watch as the guy steps up to the table. His silvery hair is matted down to his head. His brown-black eyes are dilated and on edge. I keep mine fixated on Theo, hoping that he'll send the guy away before he has the chance to recognize me. Although, in all honesty, by the smell of him, it's probably fair to say that he's too drunk to remember much of anything.

"Hey, man," he slurs. His eyes lock on Theo.

Theo sighs and adjusts himself in his seat. His shoulders tense. He looks down at his hand, casually resting atop the table, seeming bored already. "Sorry, do I know you?"

The guy half laughs at Theo's question before taking a step closer. His hand slams down on the table with brute force. "I hear you're the person to beat around here, yet Mack tells me you declined to fight tonight," he states, his breath pushing across the table and burning my nostrils. How the hell is he still standing? He smells like he drank the whole bar.

The room falls silent as two guys step inside the ring. Both of them have their heads craned as they watch for Theo's reaction. The tension is palpable.

Theo glares at him. "I guess I missed the fucking question."

Oh, no.

As much as he deserves to have his ass kicked, I doubt it would be much of a fair fight. He's easily two feet shorter than Theo, and probably a good forty pounds lighter.

"Ha! Yeah, so what's up? The legend not all he's hyped up to be? Or are you just not wanting to dirty up your face around these pretty ladies?"

I watch the muscles in Theo's jaw clench.

"Do it, baby. Fight'em. Kick his drunk ass."

"Yeah, fight me, baby." The guy mocks Katrina.

What the?

I shoot her a look, wondering what the hell it is she's doing? Who pushes their boyfriend to fight someone?

"Theo . . ." I barely whisper his name. The part of me that still cares for him, begging him not to do it.

"Look, you're obviously drunk," Theo begins, sitting up straight. I watch the muscles along his arm flex as he reaches for his drink. "So, I'm going to give you the chance to walk away before I change my mind."

"I doubt that; I really do." The guy leans into Theo's face. Their noses are so close that they're practically touching.

I feel the drag of Theo's chair while he throws it back and stands up. "Do you have a death wish, asshole?" He shoves the guy back. The guy stumbles to the table next to us and falls against another guy's drink.

The situation suddenly feels dangerous, and before I know it, I'm on my feet and standing in front of Theo.

"Please," I say, desperate for him to listen to me as I reach out and take hold of his hand.

I start to relax when I hear his breathing slow as he laces his fingers with mine. And when I hear the guy get back to his feet, I turn and look over my shoulder before taking a tiny step to the side. I don't want to risk him accidentally trying to get to Theo, then missing, and hitting me instead. Theo would kill him. That I was sure of.

"Oh, you're fucking getting in that ring, and I'm kicking your—"

"No. I'm not." Theo shuts him down, then raises his hand to the bouncer and waves him over our way. "But your ass is leaving this bar."

"The hell I am." The guy spits out at Theo as two gorillas of bouncers come barreling through the crowd and grab at his sides.

"Yes. You are."

I turn to shoot Luca a look that says, "What the hell did we get ourselves into?" But then I hear the guy yell, "You!"

Twisting around instinctively I immediately regret it. "It is you. The dancer!" he yells.

"Don't you fucking talk to her!"

"Theo, don't!"

The guy just laughs. "I knew I'd see you again, Sweet Tits."

Crap. The guy just doesn't know when to shut up.

"That's it. I'm gonna—"

"No, please. Just ignore him, Theo. He's not worth it." I take the chance to remind him.

He pulls me with him, his body turning to follow the guy as the bouncers lead him through the room.

"Who the hell was that, Brielle?" Theo asks. His eyes dart down to my face for a split second before he snaps them back up again.

"Nobody." I work to keep Theo from trailing after the guy. I cut a quick glance to Wes, who, thankfully, hasn't ratted me out yet, and bite my lip.

"I'll see you real soon, Sugar Lips," the guy calls from the entrance. I close my eyes briefly, not sure how much longer I can keep this up. "I'll make sure to give that mouth and ass of yours something better to do next time I see you."

I shut my eyes and keep the pressure on Theo's chest. "No. No. No. No," I beg him, but I'm losing against his strength. "Theo. Stop. Look at me." Next to the bar I see two doors leading to a patio and begin pulling him toward them.

"Get away from me, Brielle."

"Not going to happen. Come on. Time for a break, Mister."

I'm surprised when Theo lets me move him, but I don't waste time trying to understand why. I look over my shoulder at

Luca and flash him an apologetic smile. "We'll be right back," I promise as I catch Katrina groaning.

Luca just nods. He clearly doesn't want to put up a fight with Theo, who's already so on edge. Not that I blame him.

"Hurry back, Bree. I'll order some food," he calls from behind us, as we disappear out the back door. The silent hum of the change in atmosphere makes my ears ring.

chapter eleven

W e step outside, and I can feel Brielle watching me as I break away and move to a spot near the wall. I can't believe I let her talk me down from fighting that fucking asshole; I never back away from a fight. I lean my back against the cool surface of the concrete and inhale a deep breath.

I'll make sure to give that mouth and ass of yours something better to do next time I see you, that fucker's voice echoes inside my mind, and I slam my fist into the wall.

"I should have kicked his ass," I say and run my hand through the top of my hair.

"No, you shouldn't have. The guy has issues, and I don't see how the two of you fighting, solves any of them."

No, but it would make me feel better.

I toss my eyes down at her and raise my brow. Her full lips pull back into a small smile as I shake my head. Damn it. How the hell can someone so irritating be so damn cute that I have to fight the urge not to smile with her?

"You make me crazy," I tell her before I have the chance to stop myself.

"I could say the same about you."

She comes over to lean against the wall beside me. A strong feeling of déjà vu takes hold of me, and I smile, letting myself succumb to it. I turn to my side and pull her to face me. The two of us probably look like a strange sight together—her innocent appearance and my known reputation. But I couldn't give a fuck. I reach up and tuck a strand of her hair behind her ear. My hand lingers just a second longer before I drop it to my side.

"I need to know," I say, knowing she'll understand what I mean.

I watch her roll her eyes and bite her lip. *Fuck, if she doesn't cut that shit out . . . so help me*. She shakes her head before pushing off the wall and moves just off to the side. My mind is suddenly grateful for the extra space the wall gives us. I need to relax. No. I need to go beat that guy's ass.

"He's just a guy that hit on me at Haze, then spilled his beer all over me and—"

"Wait. That's who Wes threw out?" I growl, pushing off the wall.

"No, wait! Theo, don't!" I feel her hand on my arm and I immediately halt. Jesus. How does she have so much control over me? I look down at her hand, then to those amazing green eyes of hers, pleading for me to listen. She drops her hand. "He isn't worth it, okay? Please, don't make me watch you fight."

Damn it. If this girl wasn't my fucking weakness, I'd tell her to fuck off and go and find that guy. Instead, I lift my hand to her face and brush my thumb over her bottom lip. My mind instantly goes back to the last time we were alone together, and the feel of her body under mine.

"What would you do if I kissed you?" I say the words aloud watch the curiosity build behind her eyes.

Her smile wavers as she contemplates something. But, too soon, she lifts her chin from my grasp and turns her head back in the door's direction. I almost want to laugh, but can't, when an image of her and Luca rears its ugly head in the back of my mind—of her relaxing back into his arm, and him with his fucking hands on her.

"What? Don't want Luca to see us together like this?"

"That's not fair."

"How so?"

"How so? Theo, your girlfriend is literally sitting inside, waiting for you to come back."

It's my turn not to look in the direction of the door, as I let out a small laugh. "Katrina is not my girlfriend," I say in a matter-of-fact tone. "She's just the daughter of some asshole my dad is currently schmoozing. I don't date."

"Does she know that?" I can hear the disapproval clear in her voice.

I move towards her then, watching as she matches me, step per step, in the opposite direction. Soon I have her right where I want her—cornered against the wall. Her breath catches every so often while she waits to see what I'll do next. I press my hands to her sides and lean into her. The feel of her body so close, loosens my reserve to push her away.

"You'd better be careful, Brielle. Or I might think you're jealous."

"There's that cockiness I haven't missed. Go ahead. Think what you want."

"So you are jealous." I pull back and find her green eyes lingering on my mouth.

Her full lips purse, and it takes all I have not to close the space between us and claim that innocent mouth of hers. The only thing stopping me is my selfish desire to hear her say it, because, if nothing else, it tells me that I haven't been the only one losing my damn mind.

"Say it. Tell me you're jealous of Katrina, and I won't go after that asshole."

Her lips part further, as a vision of them wrapped around my cock flashes across my mind, like a bad joke. Fuck, I want this girl. What the hell is wrong with me? I look down to the cut of her shirt and smile while eyeing the modest amount of skin that swells over the top of it. I lick my lips and raise my hand to run my finger along the curve of her breasts, unable to help myself.

She presses her lips together and closes her eyes.

"Say it, Brielle," I groan, impatiently.

She lets out a soft moan, and I lean down to kiss the corner of her mouth, greedily wanting to steal it for myself. I can feel my cock straining against my jeans, and impulsively, I push it against her hip. She inhales a sharp, quick breath and holds it.

Jesus. I need to stop, or I'm going to scare her away.

What the hell is she doing to me?

"Okay. I- I'm, jea- jealous . . ." She relents, and I tilt her chin up and kiss the side of her neck—not sure if I was rewarding *her* for finally giving me what I wanted, or if it wasn't because I needed it more than her.

I hear her gasp and feel her nails dig into the back of my arm as she leans back against the wall and slowly gives in to the moment. She allows my touch. In fact, I think she wants it just as badly as I do. And like the asshole I am, I have no intention of stopping—no matter who she's dating. Or "friends" with—so she says. Whatever the fuck that means. She was mine first.

"Wait. No. Stop. We can't do this again. I need to get back to . . ."

I drop my hand and take a step back. Damn it, if she doesn't know how to ruin a mood. Even when Luca isn't here, the fucker's still a damn cockblock. I move to a table closest to us and take a seat, then sweep my eyes over at the audience we seem to have amassed. Does no one have anything better to do?

Brielle comes around and sits in front of me. Her petite frame and perfect curves make it impossible for me to want to look beyond her and at the onlookers, who, on any other day, I'd tell to fuck off.

"It's not what you think. I told you, Luca and I—"

"Yeah. No. I get it."

I run my hand across my chin, cursing myself for allowing the moment to even happen. I keep forgetting that this is one of the reasons why I left in the first place. I've always wanted this girl too damn much.

"Not like it meant anything anyway. Just a little fun."

She looks at me, and I can see the hurt cross her face before she says, "Fun. Right."

Twenty minutes later, when Liam becomes conscious again, he asks for a rematch, and the thought of another fight is Brielle's final straw. I'm not surprised at all, Brielle has always hated seeing people in pain. But it's weird seeing her get so upset for someone she's never met before. I mean, I have to admit, it was far from a fair fight. Tucker annihilated Liam in under a minute. But the guy knew what he was getting himself into.

After they leave, I replay the moments that led to her leaving, up to the part when I had to sit there and watch as she leaned into Luca's side and asked him to save her from this place. Shit. Kalie, the waitress, couldn't bring the drinks fast enough at that point.

It's around midnight, when we head for the truck, and a figure steps into view. Behind him, I can see the outline of four others shifting nervously.

Jesus.

Right on time.

I knew this asshole would be waiting for me. Guys like him never learn. I tilt my wrist up so that I can look at my watch, then shrug out of my jacket, handing it to Katrina to hold. Eh, I got time.

"You ready for our fight?" he says, and I can tell from his voice that he's sobered up since our last encounter. "There's no one to hide behind, now that your bitch is gone."

I turn my head to the side and crack my neck. My hands are already itching to be released as I curl them along my sides. This is what I've been waiting for—the adrenaline high only fighting can give. I was robbed of it earlier tonight out of fear of what Brielle would think, but now that she's gone, there's nothing stopping me. If for no other reason, fighting helps me feel something when I otherwise can't.

An image pricks at the back of my mind but I bury it. *Real men don't let others define them,* I let my father's words fill the space instead. I gave up letting myself believe I could ever have what I truly wanted long ago.

I widen my stance and point to his friend on the right. "Just remind him tomorrow, he asked for this."

Half an hour later, and two fights in, I open my eyes and hold my breath. The musky smell of the locker room, singeing my nostrils. After that fucker dropped—not two minutes into the fight—I had the sudden urge to let off some steam. Mack couldn't have been more excited to see me walk back in.

Ah! I inhale in a deep breath through my nose, then release it. I'm pretty sure this last one bruised a rib. Fucking asshole.

"Ew. Yeah, he kicked you good," Katrina's annoying ass voice is in my ear.

"I'll be fine." I grab my side, and using my legs, I pull myself up off the bench. "Thanks for the concern."

I pull my T-shirt over my head—with no help from this girl—and hear my phone buzz. I pull it from my pocket. Who the fuck. . . oh. . . it's *him.* My dad. Of course he'd text me now. I don't know who else I expected it to be. It's not like Brielle's going to want to talk to me much after tonight. After we had gone back inside, she shut me out. Other than the few side glances and short responses, she pretty much kept to herself. Even my best attempts at getting a rise out of her had failed.

I may have taken things I bit far. I just couldn't resist. She's always been like a drug to me. The more I'm around her, the more I crave her. It's unhealthy.

I look down to find three separate messages from my dad.

Did you talk to Katrina yet?

Get her to go, Theo!

No excuses.

Fucking prick. I toss my phone back on the bench and cut my eyes over to Katrina for a second as I pull the legs of my jeans up. Jesus. I grab my side; this bruised rib is going to be a problem for a while.

"You ready to go?" I ask Katrina and quickly shrug on my leather jacket.

"Yup."

She jumps off the bench, pulling her bag over her shoulder. Her long, blonde hair trails behind her as she walks to the door. She pauses only long enough for me to open it for her. When I do, she tosses her hair and carries on.

You're welcome.

I used to think having manners mattered with girls. But with Katrina, she expects it so much that I almost hate to do it just so that I can piss her off. I let the door swing shut behind me as I step out amid the hundreds of people packed around the ring as another pair begins their fight.

I shoot Mack a nod when we reach the door. That asshole owes me still for tonight's win, but I'll get it later. Shit. I should make him pay extra for his friend fighting dirty. But I won't. It made for an interesting twist. He's lucky I only knocked him out. I could have done a lot worse.

We exit the bar, and I see my truck. I pull my keys out of my pocket and start it remotely so that by the time we're inside, it'll have cooled off for Katrina. Not that she'll notice as she's barely looked up from her phone for more than a second.

Why the fuck am I being so nice to this girl again?

Oh, yeah. My dad.

His problems are my problems. At least, that's what he likes to say. When he first mentioned the idea to me of Katrina and I getting together, and his need for me to keep her happy, I was okay with it. Anything is better than getting your hands dirty for a dirty cause. But even I have my limits.

Add in everything with Brielle—the little blonde angel who's not so little anymore—and now a month and a half seems like more work than it's worth. It's my fault though. I shouldn't have allowed myself to get too close to Brielle. But damn me to hell if I didn't enjoy the way her body felt against mine. I mean, it can never happen again, but I enjoyed it.

Katrina hops up onto the passenger seat. Her eyes are still glued to her phone. I shut the door, and silently yell, "you're fucking welcome," as I walk around the hood. Jesus. I'm still on edge. If I didn't have a bruised rib, I'd go back in, but it's already half past one, and I need to get Katrina home.

I pull into her parent's driveway half an hour later and kill the engine. I sit for few minutes listening to Katrina's nails

typing away as the engine crackles in the background. I look up
at the dash and see the clock reads two o'clock on the dot.

　　　Closing my eyes, I rest my head back on the seat. I
wonder if Brielle is home right now. Or if Luca is staying over
at her place tonight. I inhale a deep breath and squeeze the
steering wheel. The leather tightens under my grip. I'd like to
think that Brielle might still be a virgin—that she might have
waited, but seeing how protective Luca is, I doubt that it's all in
the name of friendship.

　　　I look over at Katrina, but she isn't paying attention.
Fuck, this girl is annoying. She's still on her damn phone! "Put
that shit away, or I'll toss it out the window," I growl.

　　　Her slender fingers peel back from her phone. "Okay.
What's bugging you?"

　　　"You are. You and that phone."

　　　"Oh yeah?" She turns toward me then and pushes her
phone into her bag. Her lips part as she leans into me. Her hand
moves down to press against the zipper on my jeans. "Want me
to make it up to you?"

　　　I brush her off.

　　　"No thanks. Not tonight."

　　　All I can think about is a pair of damn green eyes, and
the look on Brielle's face when I made the comment about
kissing her. *Yeah, well, you've said a lot of things before,* she
had said. She isn't wrong. Before Mason died, I said a lot to
her. Promised a lot. But after what happened with . . . things got
ugly fast.

　　　Katrina's expression twists into a look of disdain.
"What? What did you just say?"

　　　"I said I'm good."

　　　"What the fuck is your problem today, Theo?" She yells
at the top of her lungs. "You're acting crazy."

"Nothing's wrong," I lie. An image of Brielle pricks at the back of my mind, but I will it away. *Luca. She's with Luca.* I feel the need to remind myself.

She grips the door handle but pauses before opening it. "Don't you like me?"

No!

"Yes."

At the sound of that, she climbs over the console and sits on my lap. I'd roll my eyes and tell her to get off, but really, what choice do I have? Apparently, I still have to worm her into coming to the ball with me, and I can't very well do that if she's pissed. This is the job.

"Then fuck me, Theo!" she yells—her eyes wild and needy. "Or I'll just have to find someone else who can."

I wrinkle my nose up at her. Is this girl for real right now? She actually just told me to fuck her or she's going to find someone else? I'd rather risk a night with Devon.

I watch her hands trail the line of my zipper until she works it down and takes hold of me in her hand. I hesitate for a moment, not sure what I expect to feel, as she strokes the length of me. I look up at her.

"You like that, baby?" she asks, while leaning forward to place sloppy kisses on my neck. I close my eyes. Jesus. I'm hating this. More so because it's Katrina. But also because this girl has no idea what I like. She's all over the place, and it doesn't help that my mind is too. "Theo?"

I don't answer because I know I won't be able to lie right now. Instead, I grab the seat lever and pull it. The seat immediately reclines, as I wrap my arm around her waist and flip her under me. I know I'm going to have to take charge if I stand any chance of getting through this. "Stop. Talking."

I lower my head and allow her to kiss me as I listen to her moan my name. My pants hit the floor, and I feel her hands on me again. "Yes, kiss me," she groans against my lips.

"I told you to stop talking." I shake my head. This girl seriously isn't helping me get in the mood.

Make sure to tell her she's pretty. Brielle's words flash in my mind, and I pinch my eyes shut. The image of her standing there, smug-faced and disgusted with me, ignites something under my skin. I shake my head to clear the memory but it's no use.

"What the hell's wrong with you?" Katrina barks.

Her hands grip me harder. I wince and pull back to the side. What the hell is she pouting for? It's my dick she's choking!

"Nothing," I say, feeling the anger seep out of my words, as my manhood is brought into question. The simple fact that Brielle is able to mess with my head, even when she's not here, pisses me off even more than Katrina's judgmental glares.

"Then what's taking so long? Do you need me to—"

"Just give me a second."

Jesus, she's fucking annoying. I try to focus as I let my mind drift off to a distant memory. The need to salvage my time with Katrina wins out over my pride. I sigh and give in to the memories that I store behind a wall. I grab Katrina's hips but imagine that they're *hers*.

"Oh, there you are." Katrina squirms. Her hand, folds over me as she works my length from top to bottom. I take in a breath and reach for one of the condoms I keep in my console for emergency type situations, such as this one. I grab it and slip it on. If I'm going to get through this, then I have to focus.

I lean back while she undresses and then spread her legs with my knee. "Let's make this quick," I say, and she nods her head.

With one last glance at her house, I thrust into her—my mind a jumble mix of blurred lines as I desperately try to hold on to the memory. But with every moan Katrina makes, she threatens to kill the moment.

Fuck. I groan into her neck and pick up the pace.

Each minute that ticks by, passes like an eternity. And when I finally finish, it feels like a small victory. I check the dash. Two thirty-one. Jesus. Thirty minutes have never felt so long.

I give her a minute to recover before I open the door and wave her ass out.

"God, you're such a dick." She stumbles, adjusting her bra straps. I toss her bag to her and fall into my seat. "You're lucky I love it."

Yeah. Lucky.

chapter twelve

I stand awkwardly, shifting back and forth within the same small section of tile at Café Maria's, and cut my eyes over to Becks. Wearing an all-black, zip-up hoodie, and short black shorts, her fingers dance across her phone's massive screen.

Apparently, hanging out at a local café was Becks's idea of flying under the radar. She found out this morning that Derrick's girlfriend *did* find that heel. And yes, she's pissed about it.

"Um, I have a Grande Peppermint Mochaccino for a . . . Brielle?" the barista calls.

"That's me," I say aloud as I quickly step up and reach for my cup. "Thank you!"

I walk back over to Becks, who's still in line waiting, before I leave to snag us a table against the back window. It's been two weeks since our night at Knock Out, and honestly, I've needed the time away to clear my head. With everything coming up this weekend, I can't afford to let myself get caught up in the "what if's" our little moment outside might have meant. Why Theo asked to kiss me. And why I wanted him to.

I take a seat and toss my bag in the extra chair for Luca. He wasn't sure if he was going to make it out of his exam in time to meet us. But I'd rather have it just in case. I lift my cup. The heat radiating off of it is scalding as I press my lips to the plastic lid and blow slowly. I definitely am not trying to burn off all of my taste buds within the first sip.

The smell of peppermint rises from the cup and kisses my nose. Mm. . . I smile, remembering how much Mason used to love this drink. *It's like Christmas*, he would say. God, I miss my brother. I can't believe it's been five years now.

I pull out my phone and tap the screen. Great. I'm now an hour late at picking my mom up from the house. She's going to kill me. Today was supposed to be our annual shopping trip for the memorial—Wednesdays are when they put out all the fresh buffet platters.

I open my messages and quickly type an apology before hitting send. Well, there goes my Friday night plans. Looks like I now have a date with my mom. And Kroger's.

Sighing, I crumple back against the wooden frame of my chair. I hope this weekend passes fast. Every year, for the past four years, the Suttons have hosted a party the first weekend in October to commemorate the loss of my brother. It's usually super sad and ends with my parents drunk and passed out on the couch. But two years ago, Becks, Luca, and I started our own tradition.

After all the formal stuff ends, we all sneak away to the D.O., our old High School party spot, and light a bonfire. We still drink—don't get me wrong—but it's more of a celebration than a memorial. I think Mason would have preferred it that way; he was never a fan of sappy stuff.

Lifting my eyes, I smile as Becks whirls into her seat. "Okay, so the party starts at six, right?" she asks.

"Nope, seven, but you can get there at six and help me decorate—"

"Ah! It's cute how after these years, you still think I would ever help decorate; seven it is." She smiles. "Then it's off to the D.O. directly after, right?"

"Yup. Luca, said he's going to grab the alcohol so we should be all set."

"Good."

I can see something else brewing behind her eyes as I lift my cup and take another sip.

"What?"

"Oh nothing."

"Becks . . ."

"Okay, well, it's more of a question actually." I blow into my lid again, then take a sip, listening to her babble. "Are you inviting Theo Saturday?"

"Theo?" I almost spit my drink at her. The sound of his name invokes a vision of him pinning me against the wall at Knock Out as his finger slowly trailed across my chest. I feel a strange, throbbing sensation when I remember how much I had liked it and cross my legs, squeezing them tightly.

"No, why would I?"

"Well, he was Mason's best friend. . . and now that he's back home—"

"Yeah, but I don't think that's such a great idea," I interject, letting my mind wander.

The idea of the two of us being back there, together, after all this time, is almost too painful to think about and of itself. I set my cup down and run my finger in circles around the rim. No, I can't invite him. The last time Theo was there, it was the night Mason died. Having him come would open too many wounds. For me, for us, and for my family. . . right?

"Plus, what about Luca?" I ask.

"What about me?"

The two of us turn around and find Luca hovering behind us, a steaming cup of coffee in hand. I cut my eyes to

Becks as I remove my bag from his chair. When did he get here?

"Nothing, nosey." She's quick to recover and rolls her eyes for added effect. I watch her tap her screen, the tiny clock illuminating over a picture of her and Wes. "Oh, shit. I'd better run. I've got to get to work before Kallen has a heart attack."

"Kallen?" Luca asks, taking a sip from his coffee. I crinkle my nose at the sight. How the hell does he drink that—black with no sugar and no cream?

"Yeah. He's the new trainer at the gym I work at during the week. He's an ass if you ask me." Becks sighs, standing and reaching for her bag. "I swear, I keep praying that Wes will let me take on more shifts at Haze because the tips there are more than I make at this hourly shithole."

"Bye, Becks," I call after her.

"Bye, bitch!"

Becks twirls around at the last second to yell, "Don't forget my Claws, Luca!" as she pushes the door open and strolls out.

"She knows it's like fifty-five degrees out there, right? We had that cold front come in."

"Yup."

"Huh. Well, I'm just amazed anyone willingly employs that girl." He laughs. It's a hearty laugh and I smile at the sound of it. "Wesley must have it bad."

"Appears so."

When Saturday comes, it's pushing six o'clock, when I finally finish arranging my mother's collection of Mason photos, proudly in the foyer. He would have hated being on display like this. I finger the ends of my hair and smile at my favorite one. The one with the two of us, laughing at the pool the summer before he died. I press my finger to his face. Everything was so much simpler back then.

Forcing myself to cough, I clear my throat and fight back the tears threatening to ruin my mother's perfection. She, like Becks, always likes to go the extra mile when it comes to appearances. For my mother, it's more about her gain in community status than simply doing it to get attention. Being the only real estate broker in our tiny town has made her this way. It's a taxing job . . . or so she says.

So when my mom insists on helping me get ready, I don't argue. It's easier than hearing her speech about what would happen to our family name if I didn't. Her brokerage is what's keeping me from having to have a job like Becks. I don't need a Kallen bossing me around. I already have enough people trying to control me.

"Done." I smile as I walk into the dining room, awaiting my next set of orders. I pull out a chair to sit, when the doorbell echoes throughout the house. I double-check the clock. "Who the heck could that be? It's not even half past six."

I can see the worry written clearly along my mother's face. She hates it when things don't go as planned. "Well, go answer it. Whoever it is can help, I guess."

I walk down the long hall and open the door. My mouth falls open when I find Theo, standing, in a white T-shirt and black jeans, holding a dozen red roses on the other side. The knees of his jeans are torn. His biceps are pulling at the sleeves of his shirt. He smiles down at me. That nagging throb between my thighs is suddenly back and in full force as I take in the sight of him.

I shake my head, all too aware of how I must look.

"W-What are you doing here?" I stumble, trying to get my words out. My eyes wrap the length of his perfectly chiseled body once more.

"Brielle, honey. Who is it?" I hear my mother's voice coming up behind me. I push the door open the rest of the way, and she wraps her arms around Theo.

What the. . .?

"Okay, does someone want to fill me in?" I arch my brow at his smug face and roll my eyes. "What are you doing here?"

"Brielle don't be rude. I invited him."

"These are for you," Theo says, the corners of his lips pulling back into that devilish grin as he hands my mother the roses. The moment his arm extends, I see my mother's smile draw tight.

"Oh, Theo. Were you going to change here?" My mother's voice is strained.

He laughs half amused. "Is something wrong with my clothes?"

"Other than them being covered in holes?" I shake my head.

I can see my mother starting to panic. Her eyes shift back and forth rapidly between Theo, his clothes, and his tattoos. I know that if I don't do something fast, she'll have a meltdown. Losing Mason wasn't the only thing she lost five years ago. She lost her patience too.

I take a step toward her and reach out to touch her shoulder; I hate seeing her worry like this. "Um, hey, Mom. Why don't you let me handle this? I can take Theo upstairs, and I'm sure Dad will have something that he can borrow."

I watch her shoulders sag as she relaxes, letting out a breath. "Good thinking, dear." She waves her hand for Theo to hurry inside. "Well then, chop, chop. People will be here soon, you two!"

I cut my eyes to Theo and find he's grinning from ear to ear. I shake my head and playfully swat his arm. *Of course he's excited about this*, I silently say to myself, then turn and walk up the stairs. "What are you smiling at?"

"Nothing," he says as he follows behind me. "I just forgot how cute your obsessive need to problem solve is."

Cute?

Theo thinks I'm . . . cute?

Ugh! No wonder he left when he did. No one ever chooses the "cute girl." Ten minutes later, and we're nowhere closer than when we started.

"If this one doesn't work, then I give up." I half laugh, shifting atop the bed.

So far, I've hated all of the options on him; my father's collection isn't the greatest. Something about palm trees, frilly peacock feathers, and weird teardrop dotted things, just don't scream Theo.

"That's okay. I like a girl who knows how to take her time," he calls from the closet. The rich sound of his laugh creeps out from beneath the door.

"Well, if they weren't all just *so cute* on you, we'd be done by now."

Theo peeks his head out from behind the door. "I knew that bothered you," he quickly replies, then steps out. His hand motions to the tie hanging around his neck. "I think I need a little help."

He comes around the side, and I take in the sight of him. *Holy hell,* I think to myself as he moves to stand in front of the floor-length mirror. The solid-charcoal dress shirt against his all-black jeans and the black tie he has draped around his neck looks amazing on him. I swallow hard, the air rapidly getting hotter in the room by the second.

"See something you like, Brielle?" He smirks. He's so cocky that it's unreal—as if he needs me to tell him how handsome he is.

"I, ugh, I was just. . ." I say and scoot off the bed. Crap. The way this boy affects me, I'll never understand it. "Sorry." I try to smile, my cheeks betraying me as they burn under the weight of his stare.

I pad over to where he's standing and reach for his tie but he stops me. His hand takes hold of my wrist. I notice his eyes are darker than usual.

"Don't apologize. I like seeing when I affect you." The words roll off his tongue in a way that sends goosebumps racing down my spine.

I shiver inwardly before pulling my hand back. It's then that I catch the slightest bit of imperfection as I look up at him. The deep cuts and splashes of bruising—almost fully healed— that play along the features of his face. I immediately think back to that night at K.O., when something flashes in his eyes. I push away from him.

"You said you would leave him alone, Theo!" I head for the door, but he's quick on his feet.

"I did, but he was waiting for me out in the parking lot."

I shake my head, looking up at him. "You expect me to believe that?" I snap as I try to push around him. But it's no use.

"Let me go, Theo."

"No."

I move to shove him, but he's faster than me. Before I know what's happened, he spins us around so that my back is to the wall while he presses his body up against mine. *Why do I always let him do this to me?* I wonder as I look up and find our faces are only an inch apart. His lips are too close for me to be able to think straight. I want to push him off or yell but I can't. I'd be lying if I said a part of me didn't want to let it happen—to let him kiss me. . . and more.

I shift uncomfortably and tilt my head back to rest against the door. I feel my cheeks start to heat and, annoyingly, he notices. His eyes roam down my body and hovers over a certain spot. I swallow hard, a knot forming in the pit of my stomach.

"Theo, I. . ." I begin to say, but stop myself.

I drop my eyes to a spot on the carpet, but he lifts my chin, gently forcing me to look up at him.

"What do you want, Brielle?" he asks, his expression soft. "I need you to say it."

I can feel my heartbeat pounding in my ears as I release a breath I hadn't known I was holding. I let my eyes drift down to his mouth and I bite my lip.

"I want—"

"Brielle? Theo?" I stop talking the moment I hear my mother's heels padding down the hallway. Her voice calls out as she searches for us. I cut my eyes to the door, then to Theo and then at our appearance. "Guests are arriving. Ya'll about ready?"

Oh, this was going to be hard to explain. . .

Two hours later, the memorial is almost over, and I'm starving. I grab a plate from the buffet table and begin making my way through the line.

"Hungry, are we?" I jump when Luca's voice rushes up behind me, startling me. I turn to my side and shoot him a look. "Sorry." He raises his hands in defense before he reaches out and takes my plate from me. "What's got you so jumpy?"

"Nothing worth repeating." I pick up a pretzel stick. My eyes sweep out towards the family room in search of Theo but he isn't there. I take a deep breath and try to relax. "Everything's fine," I offer Luca, not sure if I was saying it more to reassure him or me.

We reach the end of the buffet line. My plate is full. Holding out his arm for me to take, Luca escorts me over to an empty spot at the table, where the two of us sit and pick at the bounty.

Thankfully, now that all the speeches are done, people are starting to clear out. So, I don't need to stop and talk every few minutes. These people's annoying need for me to relive Mason's final moments, just before everything went to hell in a handbasket, is an annual tradition of theirs, which I wish would stop. Don't they know that's not how I want to remember my brother?

"So." Luca smiles, seemingly happy all of a sudden. "I have everything loaded in the car, so we're all set to leave as soon as you're ready."

Oh crap. I drop the rolled-up slice of turkey I'm holding and brush my hands along my thighs. Just when I think I'm in the clear. "So, um," I begin, but chicken out. Reaching for my water cup, I quickly gulp down a few, rather large, mouthfuls.

"What's wrong?"

I close my eyes and take a deep breath, then set down my cup. *Please, don't make a scene,* I silently beg him in my mind. How do I tell Luca that after my mom caught us in her room that she may have . . . she definitely did . . . invite Theo to join us?

"Theo's coming. Tonight, I mean."

The expression that quickly overtakes his face is exactly what I had been dreading since the moment Theo had agreed to come. "Please don't kill me."

"What? Why, Brielle? Why would you invite that asshole?"

"Luca, please. . . just listen to me."

"Asshole?" Becks interjects.

The short, purple dress she's wearing sways as she comes around the back of my chair and sits down on my lap. Her purple painted fingernails, skim over the selection of deli meats until she finds a slice of ham and pops it in her mouth.

"Luca, no one wants to hear about the kinky-ass shit you're into, okay?" She grins playfully, then reaches for my drink.

Luca slaps his hand over his face. "Dear God. We're talking about Theo, Becks. Theo!"

"Oh." She brushes her hands before reaching for a Ritz cracker. "What about him? Did he tell you that I invited him?" she asks. The calm tone of her voice sounds as if she doesn't think anything about it. "Wes, too."

"Wait, what?" I say and push her up off of my lap. "You invited him too? I thought I told you I didn't want him to come?"

"I'm so confused," Luca says to no one in particular.

"Well, you did, but I thought you just meant as to like . . . here. To the boring stuff."

Is she serious right now?

"Becks. . . you know that's not what I—"

"Okay, freeze, Brielle. What's going on?" Luca turns to me then. His eyes are searching the far depths of my own as if the question is about more than the simple invite.

"What's going on is, after a comment my mother made a about it when she found us together upstairs. One thing led to another and now he's coming. Although, apparently Becks invited him too. But, look, it's not a big deal. He probably won't even come."

"Oh, he's coming." Becks half laughs. "Luca, over here, forgot my Claws. So, he and Wes are going to grab them on their way over."

"Your mother found you two together?" Luca repeats my words to himself. "Upstairs?"

"Really, Sherlock, of course that's what you would take from all of that." Becks snaps at Luca, launching her half-eaten cracker into his lap. "Not that you forgot my Claws?"

Closing my eyes, I stand up from my seat. "I better go tell my parents that we're headed out." I force myself to smile as

I turn and start toward the kitchen where my parents always hang out. My mind trips over what the hell I'm going to do, now that I know Theo is actually going to come.

chapter thirteen

THEO

W hy the hell did you invite so many people, again?" I yell at Wes. My head pounds as I sweep my eyes over the endless sea of random people I've never met, dancing mindlessly around the fire pit. Leave it to Wes to turn a quiet night out into a massive party.

I cut my eyes back to Brielle. The rich green of her own eyes are cast down as she sits next to Luca on a spare log. The two of them are laughing hysterically.

What the hell's so funny?

Luca raises his hand to brush something off Brielle's leg, his fingers lingering along the curve of her knee. Even from here, I can see the blush that spreads across her cheeks. Damn it, I hate that asshole. I watch them for a moment longer; my hands curl along my sides with every second that he doesn't remove his hand.

I take in a deep breath.

"Chill, man." Wes smiles as if reading my thoughts. The cool tone of his voice makes me want to punch him in the throat.

I turn to face Wes, ready to ask him who the fuck he thinks he is, telling me to chill, when I find Becks grinding against him. I take a step back and force myself to look away. Jesus. I'm never going to be able to unsee this.

"Becks said it was all good," he continues. His tone is placid and too matter of fact for my liking. "Besides, with just the two girls, it would have been a sausage fest."

"Right." I sigh and pinch the bridge of my nose.

I cut my eyes back at Brielle, but it's a wasted of effort. She isn't paying attention. Damn it. I knew that our little moment would cost me some ground with her. She's with Luca, and yet again, I found myself pinning her to a wall—something I really need to stop doing because, regardless of her relationship, in no way will Brielle ever fit into my world.

Shit. If she knew what I did, she'd probably never speak to me again.

And her dad would have me arrested.

"Oh shit." Wes slaps my arm. The grin on his face immediately darkens. "There's your distraction, man."

I turn and look over my shoulder as I watch Katrina's slender frame break the tree line. Fuck, how the hell did she find me? The last thing I need tonight is her whiny ass hanging all over me.

It must have been Wes, I think to myself. My legs move before I've even finished talking. Of course he did. He invited everyone. I lean down and grab a beer. "I hope you brought enough beer."

"Hey, handsome," Katrina coos as she strolls up to where I'm standing.

I shoot Wes a lethal glare, but the coward retreats back to Becks before I could do anything further. Asshole. Lifting my beer, I take a swig and feel the semi-cool liquid glide down the back of my throat.

"What the hell are you doing here, Katrina?" I ask plainly.

"Well, to see you of course." She smiles, her right hand reaching up to snatch my beer from my hand.

Her eyes scan the crowd around us as she tilts her head back and chugs a few sips. She hands it back with a force, and at the moment, I don't know who's more disgusted—me, because she's practically stalking me, or her after tasting room temperature beer.

Katrina purses her lips and gasps when her eyes fall to a certain blonde. "I see the brat's here," Katrina groans. "Remind me again why you entertain these peons?"

"Katrina—" I raise my voice in warning for her to tread carefully.

"I know, I know," she interjects, waving her hand in front of her as she does. "She's your ex-besties, little sis," she groans again. "I just don't see why that matters."

I close my eyes and try to remain calm. Fuck my father for making me put up with her. He's such a prick.

"Theo!" I turn, hearing Wes's voice trail across the pit. "Get your ass over here."

Without question, I excuse myself and work my way towards Wes. Maybe Katrina might leave if I ignore her long enough. Along with Becks, I find Wes is seated within a large circle of random people—Brielle and Luca included.

"What's going on?"

"Sit your ass down, Wescott," Wes slurs, leaning back. He wraps his arm around Becks's waist and pulls her onto his lap, pointing to her empty spot on the log. "We're going to play a game."

"Oh, I love a good drinking game." Katrina works her way around the opposite side of the circle and takes a seat. "Which one? I could go for some Truth or Dare. . . or a little Seven Minutes in Heaven, perhaps?"

She winks at me but I turn away. Why am I not surprised those are the type of games she wants to play?

"Ah. . . no." Wes squints, half laughing. "We're playing, Never Have I Ever."

"Oh."

"Yeah. Okay. Does everyone have a drink?" Wes yells around the circle. "Good. . . now, who wants to start?"

"I will!" Becks yips, all too eager as she squirms atop Wes's lap.

I press my lips together and try not to say anything when her legs part, and I see she isn't wearing any underwear. I shake my head. How the hell are her and Brielle friends? They're nothing alike. Wes definitely has his hands full with her.

"Hmm, Never Have I Ever . . ."

"Maybe we should start with someone else," Luca groans. "We could be here all night."

Oh shit.

I silently laugh, but others aren't as concerned about being heard. I watch as Brielle turns and swats Luca's arm. Her eyes are piercing as she glares at him. It was definitely a fucked-up thing to say. *Never have I ever been so impressed,* I silently think and shake my head. Luca looks up and catches me watching, but I just offer him a sly smile.

That's right, asshole. Keep it up.

I need all the help I can get.

"Ha. Ha," Becks says. Her cheeks are slightly red, but otherwise she seems unaffected. "Never have I ever been a dick."

I roll my eyes and take a swig of my beer. *Here we go.* Becks may not have been talking about me, but there's no denying I am a dick more often than not.

The game ticks on, eventually taking on a whole new level as more and more people take their turn. By this point, Brielle's taken all of one sip, and even then, I'm not sure how much I believe it.

I drop my head and laugh as I begin to form a mental list of all the firsts, I'd love to help her explore—if she really is as innocent as she portrays to be. But I doubt it. Not with Luca always lurking about.

"Hmm, never have I ever . . . been in love," a random girl admits.

The circle erupts with laughter, but I can't find the humor. It's then I catch Luca tilting up his beer and downing a good portion as he locks eyes with my girl.

I suck in a breath.

Now that's hilarious.

"Your turn," I hear Wes say, his attention directed at me. "Theo? Did you hear me?"

"Yeah, I heard you," I groan and push a hand through my hair. What the hell am I going to say? "Ugh. . . never have I ever. . ." I start, my eyes searching for something I could use when I quickly spot Brielle sitting across from me. Her blonde waves fall over her shoulder and hang there, while Luca leans into her side to whisper something in her ear.

Jesus, that guy just doesn't give up.

I lose myself for a second, when those full lips of hers pull into that perfect fucking smile. But it's a moment that barely lasts longer than a second, before I remember who it's really for.

"Never have I ever kissed Brielle." The words fall out of my mouth before I have a chance to really think about what I said at all—or what I'd do if anyone were to move to take a drink.

I watch from my peripherals as Brielle whips her head towards me, her mouth slack and her eyes wide.

Oh yeah.

She's pissed.

She's going to kill me for this, but the look on Luca's face is worth it—his bugged-out eyes, and clenched jaw. But it's also not enough.

"Oh, wait." I grin, lifting my drink and taking a nice, long gulp. I watch Luca press his lips together as he squeezes the beer bottle in his hands. I can tell that my little white lie is slowly killing him on the inside. And I love it.

"Excuse me?" Katrina snaps from her seat. Her eyes wild.

"Theo," Brielle snaps, and I try not to think too long about why the idea of us kissing would be this upsetting to her. If she wants to get technical, it's not that much of a lie. We did kiss. Well, I kissed her—her neck. The corner of her mouth.

But then Luca raises his cup and takes a sip. The action causes Brielle to avert her eyes.

"Oh. My. God." Becks bursts out laughing, wriggling within Wes's grip. "I fucking *love* this game."

"Really, Becks," Brielle exclaims.

"Right, well, I guess it's my turn." Luca turns to Wes then, sporting a stupid-ass smirk.

Wes nods as I clench my hands. I'm dying to hear what this goody-goody has to say.

"Hmm. What to say. Oh, I know . . . how about, never have I ever killed my best friend . . ."

chapter fourteen

BRIELLE

I close my eyes and suck in a deep breath. No. . .no. . . no. This is not happening. Surely, I'm just drunk. I can feel my inner mind reeling as I choke on how thick the air has become.

"Oh shit," Becks is the first to break the silence.

I open my eyes and jump up when I hear Theo's voice drawing near. "You just don't learn, do you?"

"Theo, wait," I beg him, but he's moving too fast. "Theo!"

I turn in time to watch Luca stand from his seat just before Theo lands a punch straight across his jaw. The sound is deafening, and it echoes across the field.

A few of the girls around us start to squeal, and with it, the circle splits. If I were smart, I'd follow suit and leave the two of them to finally hash out whatever issues they're hiding, but my legs refuse to move.

"Wes! Get in there!" Becks calls from beside me, as a flash of blonde pushes by. "Do something!"

I blink in time to watch as Luca hits the ground—his face a bloody mess from the long gash that now lines the top of his cheek. It's not until I'm standing in front of Theo that I realize I've moved at all.

"What the hell, Theo?" I yell at him.

I can hear my voice catch but I ignore it. I use my hands to shove him back as Wes continues to try and pull Theo away from the group. Theo's eyes snap down to meet mine head-on.

They're wide with shock. Then, his lips part as if he were about to say something, but he stops himself.

Luca takes in a shallow breath, and immediately I bend down to sit by his side. "Oh thank God." My shoulders sag in relief when I see he seems to be okay.

"You've got to be fucking joking." Theo chuckles before adding, "Fuck this! I'm out of here."

I turn my head to the side and watch as he brushes Wes off his arm. He tosses his beer into the fire pit, then starts walking toward the tree line.

"Becks, help me." I wrap my arm around Luca's waist and help him sit up. Leaning against the log, Luca tilts his head back, his cut bleeding heavily.

"It looks worse than it is," he whispers softly, a small smile playing along his lips. "Face wounds are always the worst."

I shake my head and slap his arm.

Hard.

"Ouch! What the hell was that for?"

"For being an idiot!" I yell, rocking back on my heels to stand up. "This is just as much your fault as it is his." I turn to Becks. "Make sure he doesn't bleed to death; I'll be back in a minute."

"Brielle, wait!"

I follow the path I saw Theo take, ignoring Luca's blatant attempts to have me stay, and step into the thick brush of the tree line. Crap. My inner mind instantly recognizes where I am. I close my eyes and take a breath. Of course he'd come here. This was their spot. I can't count the amount of times I found Theo and my brother out here—rarely alone if I remember correctly, which was never a fun part for me.

I take another step, noticing how overgrown it's become. I haven't been up here since that night, five years ago. It's strange how it feels like that was just yesterday—like if I keep walking, I'll eventually run into Mason and his famous brotherly glare he liked to use, when he felt I was intruding on "guy time."

I hear a branch snap, and my mind snaps with it.

"Not now, Brielle," The irritation in Theo's words is clear, as they trail from somewhere up ahead. "Why don't you do us both a favor and save whatever speech you've come to give for your boyfriend."

I shake my head and bite my lip. Boyfriend? Seriously? "Luca is not my—ugh . . . you know what? You're impossible. Haven't you learned better by now, than to tell me what to do?" I laugh and take a couple of steps further.

I don't know why he's so insistent upon the fact that Luca and I are dating. We're just friends. I also don't know why I can't admit that. Maybe I like the thought of Theo being jealous, because, at least then I know he still cares?

I blink hard, letting my eyes adjust as the moonlight comes in sprays through the treetops behind us, and I finally see how close he's standing to the edge of the cliff.

"Theo, please . . . just talk to me." I hear my voice stumble before I realize that it's my own. The sound of his name on my lips is weighted with an emotion I can't place.

Twisting within his stance, I watch as he turns towards me, his eyes shaded as he walks over to where I'm standing. "What do you want, Brielle?"

"To talk? I guess," I say, shrugging my shoulders, confused as to why I keep making an effort, when he clearly doesn't seem to care.

He's so hot and cold with me, it's hard to read him. One minute he's rude and pushing me away, and the next, he's pushing me up against a wall, kissing my neck and sparking feelings and sensations I've never felt before.

Theo is Theo, I remind myself. **Handsome. Annoying. And complicated.**

"I- I don't know. Never mind." I roll my eyes and turn to walk away. "This was obviously a mistake."

"No. Wait. Don't go." He sighs. His fingers folding around my wrist as he grasps it and pulls me back to face him. "Please. I'm sorry, okay?"

"Don't do that," I snap and pull away from him.

"Do what?"

"Don't feed me some stupid apology because you think that I'll forget what just happened."

He crinkles his brow and shakes his head, a wry smile playing along his lips. "That's not what I'm doing."

I purse my lips together and take a few steps back. Behind us, the music picks back up as the party carries on without us. Everyone else may be able to forget, but I can't.

As if reading my thoughts, Theo drops his eyes to the ground, his expression growing serious. He kicks a rock.

"What the hell just happened?" I ask when I can see he's retreating back into his thoughts. "Talk to me."

"And tell you what, Brielle?" he finally says. His tone is more aggressive than I expected. "The guy was being an asshole so I hit him. End of discussion. I mean, fuck. What do you want from me?"

I tilt my head up at him and tap my foot. "So you don't think you started it with the whole "never have I ever kissed Brielle" thing?" I glare at him. "What was that?"

As I watch the tension build behind his eyes, I can see he's struggling within himself. The moonlight behind me shifts and illuminates the features of his face, making the hazel color of his eyes appear as if it's been washed out.

"I don't know why I said that," he says, but I can tell he's lying. What is he hiding? "Why were you avoiding me?"

Avoiding him?

I wasn't avoiding him.

"Don't be insane. I wasn't avoiding you . . . I was . . . just hanging out with Luca."

"That's a load of bull."

"Excuse me?"

"You heard me. I wonder what Mr. Perfect would think if he knew that you were practically panting for me to do something to you back in your parents' bedroom."

I suck in my bottom lip and bite it. Hard.

"I wasn't panting! You're the one who keeps shoving me into walls and kissing my neck. You're sweet one second, then a jerk the next. What the hell do you want from me, because I can't keep up?"

"I don't want anything from you."

I take a step back and set my eyes on him. Not for the first time, I struggle to recognize the old Theo under this mask, which he seems to put on when he feels attacked. I get it. A lot has changed since Mason's death. Even I have had to bury certain parts about myself in order to move forward—to be the better daughter for my parents. But I never thought he'd drift so far. Be so cruel. Especially with me.

"Fine. Then why don't I do us both a favor and leave."

"Do whatever you want," he challenges then, raising his voice. His expression is cold and emotionless. "Run back to Luca. It's what you're good at."

I feel my eyes growing wide with shock as I let his words sink in. A knot forms in the base of my throat and I swallow it. "I don't need this." I turn around, but before I can take a step, he wraps his arms around my waist and pulls me to him without permission or apology. "Let go, Theo, or I'll scream."

"You should scream," he says, and I know he means it. "I'm no good for you. You should be with Luca. Mason was right."

I close my eyes and relax my body against his chest, tilting my head back to look up at him. I can feel his heart beating as his eyes zero in on my mouth.

"If you didn't want me, then what the hell have you been doing?"

"You think that I don't want you?" I feel his grip loosen as the words fall from his lips.

I crinkle my nose and take advantage of the moment to spin around inside his arms. My hands rise to steady myself against the hard muscles of his chest.

"What else am I supposed to think? You said it yourself back at Knock Out: "It meant nothing anyways." That it was all just a little fun."

Theo drops his head back for a second, like he's debating how to answer my question, when, instead of pushing me away again, he wraps his hands around my wrists. He leans forward, his forehead resting against my own as he meets my gaze. He tightens his grip, then guides my hands down his torso . . . then lower, until they fill with the length of him.

"Never doubt that I want you, Brielle. Believe me, I do."

I release a breath I hadn't known I was holding and lick my lips. The muscles along my stomach clench as I feel a pressure build between my thighs. I squeeze them together trying to stifle the sensation, but it does little to help.

God, how does he always do this to me?

"I-I want you too." I hear the words slip from my lips.

His hands release their hold on me, which I know is his way of offering me control over what happens next. I can feel the warmth of his breath caressing my cheek. My heart is pounding a mile a minute.

A handsome smile tugs at the corners of his mouth, as his eyes slowly travel down the front of me. I feel my cheeks heat up, when the crisp night air picks up, and a breeze carries through the trees. It briefly helps to soothe the heat rising in me. *I don't want anything from you*, his words flash like a warning across my mind.

I take a wary step back.

"Maybe we should—"

But before I can finish, I feel his hand push into my hair, while his lips crash against mine.

As he kisses me, his tongue sweeps across my bottom lip. I moan into his mouth, but he swallows it with his whispered words. "Kiss me, Brielle." His tone is pleading—so, I do.

His arm encircles my waist. He walks us backward, and I jump when I feel the massive stone wall brush the back of my legs. Its hard, cold exterior is a nice relief from the heat he provokes. I move my hand to his chest, but he grabs it and presses it next to my head. With his free hand, he bends down and pulls my right leg up to his waist. His hips rock into me with a measurable force.

"Fuck, Brielle," he groans into my neck, his breath, warm against my skin. My nipples pucker under the weight of his words.

He pulls back to watch as he runs his hands along my side—each touch meticulous and deliberate. When he stops, I can't resist. I pull his mouth to mine. I don't know what I'm supposed to do, but I know that I want to touch him. With that thought, I break the kiss, but he shifts his assault. His lips quickly move to trail kisses along my chin and neck, grazing a spot just under my ear.

In the distance, there is a shuffling of noises, which I can't register. Assuming he's heard it, too, I think he's about to pull away, when he dips his head and rakes his teeth across my collarbone.

"Oh shit." Wes's tone is mocking as he stumbles into the small opening.

Theo releases me, but I'm thankful when he doesn't drop his arms just yet. Instead, he leans toward the side Wes is on to cover me from his wandering eyes. My whole body suddenly feels weak and drained.

"Get the hell out of here, Wes!" Theo yells.

"Yeah. Ugh, yup. I'll just . . . I'll tell Becks you'll be out in a minute."

I watch Theo's chest rise and fall rapidly and wonder if he notices how our moment has affected me too. When we're alone again, he leans down and presses his forehead to mine. He closes his eyes. "Why couldn't we do that five years ago?" His question is full of emotion.

Not trusting myself to speak, I raise my hand to run my thumb along his bottom lip and take a breath. I can see a fire in his eyes before he takes in a deep breath and steps away from me. The muscles along his chest flex as he pushes off the stone wall.

I take a moment to collect myself and shift my eyes to the arms of his sleeves, noticing how they're pulled tightly against his biceps. *He really is muscular,* I tell myself as I think back to Luca's comment and when he said that Theo was trouble.

I'll admit, the simple black T-shirts and ripped jeans are a lot different than what I was used to seeing him in—which was mostly Polos and a lot of Calvin Klein. I won't lie, this new edgy look is growing on me. It's hot and oddly suits him.

At the sound of faint wisps of music, filling the silence surrounding us, Theo's expression suddenly grows distant and serious as he looks out at the tree line.

"We should go," he says after a minute, sighing. His back is now facing me, as he turns to look out over the side of the cliff. "This was . . . um, fun. Thank you."

Thank you?

Nodding, I bite my lip—not knowing what the hell is happening or why he suddenly seems so far away. "Wait . . . um." I nearly choke at how awkward this has become. " Did I . . . did I do something wrong?"

"What?" He turns around. "Why would you think that?"

I wrinkle my brow up at him and tilt my head. *Umm, maybe because we just kissed for the first time, ever—just two seconds ago—and you're already running away,* I want to say but I don't. Instead, I shrug off his question and move to go around him.

"Brielle, wait. What just happened?" he calls behind me as I work my way back down the tree line.

"Nothing, Theo," I snap, pausing when I reach the brush. I look back at him, then to the bonfire. Luca's slumped frame, catches my attention as Becks hands him another beer.

With the next step I take, I'll be in the clearing.

"Look, you didn't do anything wrong," he says, his chest brushing the back of my arm as he moves to stand behind me.

"I just don't want you to think that the kiss has changed anything. I really did mean what I said before. You deserve better than me."

I turn to my side, hoping that I'll see some trace of hesitation, but there isn't any to be found. What the hell is he talking about? I deserve better than him? Why is he pushing me away, again?

I force myself to look away; this constant whiplash of emotions he provokes is tiring.

"Right." I half laugh when I think about everything that's happened. God, compared to what he's used to, he probably thinks I'm pathetic.

"Brielle, talk to me."

"I think I should probably go and check on Luca." I keep my back to him, then step into the clearing. "Have a good night, Theo."

chapter fifteen

O uch!" Luca winces as I replace the makeshift ice pack, which I made out of two beers wrapped in a towel, with a cold one. "He really got me good. Is it still bleeding?"

I roll my eyes, knowing all too well that he's enjoying this a little more than he should be. Luca has always been a poor patient. Whether it be a paper cut or the flu, he's notorious for milking his injuries. Flipping my hair to the side, I peel back the corner of the pack in order to get a good look at it. It stopped bleeding thirty minutes ago.

"I think you'll live." I smile softly. The baby-blue of his eyes darken as I lean back and sit on the ground in front of him. "You know, this could have all been avoided, right?"

"Yeah, well, he started it." A playful smirk presses his lips, and I feel myself smiling along with him. "There's just something about the guy that bothers me; we'll never see eye to eye. He's already trying to worm his way back into the group."

I drop my eyes to the ground, my fingers playing with the damp towel from his old ice pack. *Well, tonight couldn't have turned out any worse*. I half laugh at the thought. Then again, Mason would have loved it. The drama. The fight. This is the type of stuff my brother lived for.

He'd never admit it—that would imply that he cared more than what a typical guy is supposed to—but I knew him better than that. Blame the high-altitude or the beer, but

The D.O. always has a way of making people go crazy. I scrunch my face and shake my head.

"Did I miss something? When did you and Theo start hating each other?" I look up at him. "I feel like you've had it out for Theo ever since—"

"It's more than that. Things with Theo are . . . complicated," he answers automatically, dropping the hand he was using to hold the ice pack and sits up. "Let's not talk about it, please."

"Well, it can't be too complicated if you threw it out there in front of everyone," I feel the need to add. "Luca, Theo didn't even tell us that he was home. I doubt he's going to want to rejoin the group."

"So, his showing up everywhere is, what? A coincidence?"

"Yes. Maybe?" I shrug. "I don't know."

"Exactly."

I sit back, letting his words sink in before bursting out loud in a fit of laughter. "Luca, where is this coming from? Are you. . .? I don't know, jealous?" I genuinely ask.

"Jealous? Of Theo? Hell no! But his money, good looks, and overall easiness to life, which he seems to think he deserves? Yes!"

I squint my eyes. So he *is* jealous. "Look, Theo is Theo." I reach out and touch his arm. "Him being back isn't going to change anything, especially not between the three of us. You and Becks are like family to me."

"But what if I don't want to be just. . ." Luca's eyebrows knit into a line. "I just don't want to see you get hurt."

What?

How could that happen?

"Why would Theo hurt me?" I ask, my breath hinged.

"Because anyone with eyes could see the way he acted around you back then. Hell. Even the fight that got Mason killed only got started because that guy at the bar made the mistake of hitting on *you*. He's just bad news, Brielle."

"Wow." I half laugh when nothing else comes to mind.

I choose to overlook the fact that he basically accused Theo of being the reason my brother is dead, which he couldn't be more wrong about.

"I- I'm sorry. That came out a little harsh."

When I don't answer, Luca shakes his head. His right hand moves to the back of my arm, as he pulls me to my knees. I glance around at the crowd around us and find several people watching us, including Theo, Becks, and Wes.

I watch Theo roll his eyes before leaning into Katrina to whisper something in her ear. I wonder if it's an apology for his actions during the game—and everything that happened since.

Katrina lets out a soft moan and pulls him closer and kisses his cheek. I guess that's a no. *Who's running now?* I silently scold Theo, remembering how earlier he accused me of doing the same thing with Luca. God, he's such a player. Why did I ever think things would be different with me?

"Brielle?" I feel Luca's breath, hot on my cheek, as his fingers slip under my chin, and he draws my face gently around so that our eyes meet.

I suck in my bottom lip and hold my breath when I realize how close we are.

What is he doing?

No, don't do this. Not now!

Friends Luca—we're just friends.

"Brielle? Did you hear me?"

I lift my chin out of his grasp and lean back. "S-Sorry," I whisper quietly. "What did you say?"

"Nothing," he offers after a minute. His eyes sweep over to Theo and Katrina before he leans back and replaces the ice pack over the top of his cheek.

Before I have a chance to think about it, I reach out and take his hand. I half expected him to pull away, but instead he folds his fingers around mine. His thumb rubs the soft skin along my wrist. I wish he can my mind and see just how much he means to me, but what if he can't accept it? I feel like I've let his feelings for me hang between us—unanswered—for so long that no matter what I say, it'll never be enough.

"Luca, I—"

I chicken out.

"I mean, you . . . you've got to stop blaming Theo for Mason's death," I say. The outer edges of my eyes, beginning to well up with tears when I think back to that terrible night. "I don't blame him, and neither should you."

His grip on my wrist tightens slightly, but his words are soft. "Hey, don't cry." He sighs, releasing me, then tosses the ice pack down to his side. His right hand moves to brush the top of my cheek as a lone tear slips from my eye. "

"Okay, what the hell are you two doing?"

Luca drops his hand, sucking a breath in between clenched teeth, as we both turn to look up at our friend. A very drunk Becks is swaying beside us. Her eyes are glossy, and her hair is a mess. I push my eyes past her and see Wes is watching us. His grin is stretched from ear to ear as he dances alone to the music.

"Come on guys. This is a party for God's sake," she's shouting as she falls to the ground beside me and pulls me into a hug. Her slender arms wrap around my neck while she pushes her nose to my ear and whispers, "Did you finally tell him that you just want to be friends?" But she's drunk so she ends up yelling it instead.

Oh my God.

That's just. . . that's perfect.

"O-Okay, Becks . . . m- maybe we should find you some water."

"No water. Just beer." She hiccups, pulling back from my arms and taking my face between her hands. "Oh. My. God. Can you believe how fucking hot Wes is?"

"Here we go. Okay," Luca stands, brushing the back of his jeans. "On that note . . . I'll go grab that water for you." He motions to Becks. "Brielle, you want anything while I'm up?"

"No, thank you."

He nods, then turns to walk away.

"Ugh, I thought he'd never leave," Becks grumbles loudly, leaning back against the log. "You're welcome for saving you by the way. P.S. . . . it was Wes's idea."

She turns around and throws Wes a small wave. Then blows him a kiss, which he stumbles to grab before shoving it deep into his pocket.

"Becks, I didn't need saving," I groan, when my eyes flint behind Wes's broad shoulders, and I see Katrina is now sitting on Theo's lap. A low burn heats my cheeks as I bite back some very heated words. On top of everything else tonight— guilt—is not something I wanted to add to my life. I can't believe I let Theo kiss me.

"Luca and I were just talking about Mason."

"Mason? Why were you talking about him?"

I squeeze my eyes shut and try not to let my emotions get the best of me. *She's drunk,* I remind myself. She doesn't know what she's talking about.

"Nothing," I finally say, then force myself to ask how she and Wes are getting along—if only because I know talking about him makes her happy.

"We're doing great!" She smiles, clapping wildly. "Come dance with us. We both know Luca will still be crying over this tomorrow; the guy is a man-child."

"Be nice." I laugh trying to sound normal, but I see the array of emotions cross Becks's face—she worried for me. It's the same look she gave me the day we found out when Theo first left—worry that I won't be able to move on. I shake my head and smile when I can see the wheels in her head start to turn. "Thanks, but . . . I shouldn't."

"What? Why?"

"It's . . . complicated." I shrug. Never have I ever used a word so much in a single night. I can't help laughing silently to myself.

Becks holds her finger up to me and works at swallowing something. Oh God, if she pukes on me, I'm definitely going home. "Please tell me it isn't because of the slut, Katia," she finally answers after managing to calm the alcohol-ridden bile currently working its way up the back of her throat. "God, she's a clingy one."

I bite back a laugh. "You mean, Katrina." I smile, but Becks just waves me off.

"Whatever. All I know is that the girl whines more than Luca, and that's saying something." Becks shakes her head. "And I'm not the only one she's been annoying; Theo's been pissed at her all night."

I whip my head to the side, surprised by her answer, only to find Katrina sloppily kissing the side of Theo's neck. *Yeah, he really looks upset.* I roll my eyes. Becks must be drunker than I thought.

"I can see that." I crinkle my nose. "Anyway, I should really get back to Lu—"

"Luca needs to stop playing to your weakness." She leans forward and takes a hold of my hands. "He'll be fine for a few minutes. Trust me."

She squeezes my hands and pulls me up with her. I twist around, hoping I'll find Luca, but he's across the pit talking to that Penny girl I met the first night at the club. Her long, red hair is pulled up into a messy bun, and she's leaning into his side.

"Come on." Becks starts dancing in front of me. "You know you want to."

I fight my smile and watch Becks as she breaks out her weird robot moves. "Fine," I relent after she pulls out the mime tricks. "But only until Luca gets back."

"Oh please, like he wouldn't get a rise out of watching you dance," she squeals, pulling me with her toward the pit. "I'm talking a full six inch rise. Well, it's Luca . . . so maybe four."

"Becks." I playfully swat her arm.

"What? I was talking about his mood." She laughs along with me, her arms pushing me out as we dance to the beat of the music. "But I'm sure that would rise too." She winks at me.

I shake my head. "That's so wrong."

"But so true."

By the time the third song kicks on, I can feel myself relaxing as I give into the music. It doesn't take long before Wes decides to join us, and I find myself dancing more on my own than with Becks. I don't mind; I've become used to Becks leaving me in order to chase after a guy. Or two.

"Here," I hear a voice behind me and I spin around.

"Blake? What are you doing here?" It's Ethan's friend, the one Theo almost punched a panini out of his hand the other night at Haze.

He extends his right hand as he offers me the drink. "I thought you might be thirsty after the way you've been dancing." He smiles and bites at his lip nervously.

I look down at the drink and see that it's unopened, then glance back up at him. "Thank you." I smile before reaching out and taking the drink. The cool feel of the bottle against my palm is a welcome relief, as I twist off the cap and take a sip. "How did you know I love the black cherry flavor?" I tease while eyeing the label of my Mikes Hard Lemonade.

"Don't all gorgeous girls like you crave something sweet?"

I half laugh at his attempt to compliment me. My body sways to the beat as I watch him squirm in front of me. Maybe it's this new relaxed mood I'm in, but I like seeing him like this—on edge and nervous. Even though I can't see anything ever happening between us, right about now I can use the distraction of a nice, cute guy.

"That was cute." I smile back at him.

"I can be cute sometimes." He smiles, sucking his bottom lip and bites it again. "Why do I feel like I'm going to get into trouble talking to you?"

I feel my cheeks burn from his question as I tilt my head to the side and see Becks watching us. She motions me on with her hands as Wes gives me a giant thumbs up. The two glide by, connected at the hip, and I roll my eyes, thoroughly embarrassed, when I see Blake notice.

"Um, sorry about that." I reach out and rest my hand on his arm, laughing as I work to recover. "They're a little enthusiastic."

Blake's eyes shift between me and my hand; a handsome smile tugs his lips. "Hey, I'm perfectly fine with that."

I avert my attention and shift nervously. My mind spins with all the reasons why I shouldn't be talking to him; Theo being the first and foremost. I close my eyes and push him from my thoughts. How I still let him creep back in even now, while I'm talking to Blake, baffles and confuses me all at the same time.

I lift my eyes and immediately find the dark green of Theo's staring back at me. I look away.

"Do you, ugh. . . want to . . . dance?" I ask after a minute and reach out for him to take my hand.

Blake takes no time to think about it and twists me around. "I'd like to take you out on a date," he whispers into my ear when he pulls me into his arms. "But I'll start with a dance."

chapter sixteen

I can feel my blood boiling as I stare out in front of me and watch the asshole from the other night dance with Brielle. His grubby, little hands press into the soft curves of her waist as he holds her to him like she's already his. *Too bad she's already taken,* I silently say, not sure who I'm saying this more to. . . him or me.

I clench my fists against my sides and work to control my temper. Where the hell is Luca anyway, and why the fuck isn't he kicking this guy's ass? When I told her she deserved better than me, I didn't say it for her to ring the damn dinner bell and toss herself to the wolves. I mean—

"Fuck." I jump as Katrina's boney ass digs into my leg again. That's it. I wipe my neck of her slobber, then push her up off my lap.

I inhale a deep breath and try to relax. Between Katrina's failed attempts to get me in the mood and Brielle dangling this fucker in front of my face, I'm on overload. Besides, Brielle isn't even watching anymore, so what's the point? So much for getting the distraction I need. I grip the neck of my beer bottle and look down to the ground. No, what I need is Brielle.

Jesus. What the hell is wrong with me? I push a hand through my hair and lean back. It's annoying how much I want her. No matter what I do, I can't get that girl out of my head. The way her lips taste; the feel of her skin under my hands. Just the sound of her voice is like a contact high for me. I instantly perk up and feel alive.

It doesn't help she's fucking sexy, and she doesn't even know it. Just the thought of kissing her makes my cock hard.

Damn it.

Why the hell did I push her away again?

"Umm, hello?" Katrina groans as she stands in front of me, arms crossed, tapping her foot, like the spoiled brat that she is.

I roll my eyes. God, this chick is annoying. I swear she's her own cockblock. My father can't seal this deal fast enough so that I can be done with her pouty ass.

"What the hell was that?" she adds as if hearing my thoughts.

I shoot her a warning glance. "Not tonight, Katrina. I'm not in the mood."

"You're never in the mood anymore."

Not for you.

I roll my eyes again and lean around her, when I catch Brielle walking off with porcupine guy. His arm is wrapped around her waist as he leads her to a spot over by the tree line.

What the fuck is he doing now?

Sitting up, I try to get a closer look. He pulls out his phone and sets it in her hand. Her emerald-green eyes come alive against the screen's bright glare, as those grubby fucking fingers of his push into her hair. She smiles innocently and quickly begins tapping her fingers across his screen.

Fuck this shit.

Enough is enough.

"Theo?" I hear Katrina's voice fade into the background while I stand and hurry toward them. This guy is in for a rude fucking awakening if he thinks he's going to get with my girl. In an attempt to save time, I cut through the crowd of people dancing, when I find Wes and Becks nestled in the middle of it all. Shit. I knew I should have gone around.

"Whoa, whoa. Whoa." Wes reaches his arm out to block me. I shift my eyes between the two of them and groan when I find they're both wasted. "Brielle's fine, man. Leave the poor girl alone to have a little fun."

The fuck?

I whip my head to the side. My chest rises and falls rapidly, as I feel the impending need to get to her weighing heavily on my shoulders.

"Step aside, Wes. I won't ask again."

Wes shifts his stance and squints his eyes. He looks as if he's trying to read my thoughts but is failing at it. "Yeah, okay, man." He sighs. I watch his expression drop instantly. Lifting his hands, he takes a step back.

"You have something you want to say?" I growl, twisting to the side to look up at my friend. His casual demeanor dials my anger up a notch.

"Nothing, man." He shakes his head. "I'm just waiting for you to admit that you have actual feelings for this girl."

Feelings?

Nodding, I roll my eyes when I don't know what else to say. I hesitate a moment longer before I push around him and make a break toward Brielle. My legs are working to take two steps at a time as I search the tree line for where I last saw her. But she isn't there.

The fuck?

I can feel my heart thumping loudly.

Where the hell is she?

"Looking for someone?" I hear the familiar voice rip through my inner thoughts.

"Fuck off, Luca."

"Yeah, see, I can't do that," He laughs, stepping in between me and my line of sight. "I think it's about time we had a little chat."

I arch my brow while looking down at him and then I roll my shoulders back. *Relax,* I tell myself. Brielle would never speak to me again if I let Luca goad me into another fight—not that I would consider that one-punch knock out from earlier a fight. Or the one from five years ago after he confronted me at Mason's funeral, even if I let that one last a little longer.

I scoff, reliving that embarrassing moment for Luca and shake my head. God, this guy's a pussy.

"A little chat?" I press my lips into a hard line; I don't have time for this. "Is there a reason you're wasting my time?"

"I want you to leave Brielle alone," he growls, shrugging his shoulders as he does.

I stare openly at him for a couple of seconds; I just knew I must have misunderstood him. Luca isn't dumb enough to actually threaten me.

"What the fuck did you just say?" I ask, hearing the rise in my voice and watch as the coward winces.

Yeah, that's more like it.

"You heard me."

I laugh, half amused and take a step toward him. "Look, as much as it humors me to listen to you, you don't want to go down this route." A wicked smile pulls at the corners of my mouth. "It will be the last thing that you do."

"Unless you want me to tell Brielle about what really happened the night Mason died. You won't touch me."

I can feel my pulse quickening as I narrow my eyes at him. My feet press firmly into the ground as I prepare myself;

the skin along my knuckles are itching for release. "It's pretty hard to say anything if your mouth is wired shut."

Luca's eyes grow wide with shock; I almost laugh.

"So, what?" he says, shoving his hands into the deep pockets of his jeans. "You get Mason killed, decide to leave for five years and then come back and expect to still have any sort of claim over her?"

The fuck? I look around.

Is he really wanting to do this now?

Here?

"I did not kill Mason! He was my best friend!" I yell, my mind reeling. As much as it pains me to admit, I had to hand it to him. For being such a little bitch earlier, he was actually managing to hold his own pretty well.

"Fine. But then, if you cared about his friendship, you should honor what he wanted all along and leave Brielle alone."

"I won't do that," I say in a matter of fact, surprising even myself. Because I mean it. "I can't."

"You think she will love someone who killed her brother?"

Love?

The word flashes in and out of my mind before I have the chance to really process it.

I can feel what little nails I have digging into my palms as I inhale through my nose and out through clenched teeth. The image of Mason lying shot, bleeding out, pricks at the back of my mind—the bright, neon lights of Redd's Bar, pulsing in the distance.

I close my eyes and will away the memory.

For years, I've struggled with the guilt, trying anything to forget. I've buried myself in women, alcohol, and my father's work, but nothing seems to help. Nothing can take away the pain I feel, losing my friend, my home, and Brielle all in one night. I fucking hated myself—still do in some ways—because no matter what I do, it doesn't change the fact that he's gone.

If only I had seen the signs sooner, reacted faster, maybe I could have prevented the whole thing. I'd gladly die a hundred times if it meant Brielle could have her brother back.

I rub my hand along my jaw, then take a step in Luca's direction. "I'm going to tell you this one last time, and for your sake, you'd better make sure your ears are fucking clear. I. Did. Not. Kill. Mason."

"Well, not directly."

I shake my head. The hell is his problem today? If I didn't know any better, I'd think Luca wanted me to hit him . . . but I do know better. This dumb fuck is just in love—not that I blame him. Brielle can make any man willing to do some crazy shit for her.

I feel my pocket buzzing, and I reach in and take out my phone. I'm thankful for the pause until the bright light of the screen roars to life in my hand and my father's name appears. Jesus. Does everyone want a piece of me tonight?

I stick up my hand to silence Luca when I hear him groaning in front of me, then I reject the call. It's not like I didn't know what he wanted anyway; he's only called four other times this week for the same exact reason. He's making sure that I've asked Katrina to The All Hallows Eve Ball, where he plans to seal the deal with her father.

The short answer is no.

I haven't.

For some reason, every time I work myself up to asking, my thoughts are clouded with images of Brielle and I choke. That, and the fact that spending four hours trapped with her in a room, makes me want to rip out all my hair.

I look back at Luca. "Listen, I'm not going to fight you. All I want is to find Brielle," I say, pausing before I choose to add, "You two aren't really together, are you?"

He shifts uncomfortably and crosses his arms. Fuck. That's what I thought. At least, is now. No one, in their right mind, dating Brielle, would ever be okay with another guy making a move on her.

"Why would you ask me that?"

"Because unlike you, I've never been good at sharing."

"Well, maybe it's because, unlike you, I trust her," he offers, but even he doesn't believe it. Luca rolls his eyes in a way that would shame Katrina out of her title. "What is it with you? Why can't you just let her go? There are plenty of other women out there you could fuck with. Brielle deserves more."

I feel my muscles flex at his choice of words when, out of the corner of my eye, I catch Brielle walking toward us. I sweep my eyes around her but see no sign of the hedgehog., but he's gone. Shit. Now, who am I going to take all this pent-up anger out on?

I relax my hands and feel the tension in my shoulders ease up the closer she gets.

"Please tell me you two aren't fighting again?" Brielle's soft voice carries through the air.

"No." Both of us answer her at the same time.

"Well, good."

"Can we talk?" I ask and reach out to touch her hand.

She steps back before I can touch her and crosses her arms. "Sure." She nods her head, turning to Luca as she does. I can tell from the look on his face, he's got a fucking opinion about it, but thankfully, for him, he keeps it to himself. "Will you start packing up?" She smiles at him. "It's getting pretty late."

Late?

I tilt my wrist and look at my watch.

It's barely ten thirty?

"Brielle," I begin the second Luca's far enough away.

She raises her hand to cut me off. I pause, seeing the struggle behind her eyes and silently curse myself for causing it.

"Just, stop. This doesn't have to be this difficult. We obviously are better at being friends. We should just—"

"Fuck, no," I say in a matter-of-fact tone. "I have plenty of friends; I don't need another."

I watch her brow lift. Her eyes are wide with shock.

What?

What did I say?

"Well, sorry to burst your bubble, but I am not Katrina!" she shouts, shaking her head as she does. She throws her arms down to her sides and takes another step back. "I thought you knew me better than that, but I guess I was wrong."

When I see her turn to go, I reach out and grasp her arm. But she jerks away from me.

"Stop grabbing me, Theo. I won't tell you again."

I watch her about to leave again, but I step in her way. My fingers close around the back of her arms as I keep her close. "What the hell just happened here?" I ask, my eyes searching hers, trying to find an answer. How did me trying to tell her that I want us to be more turn into a fight over Katrina?

"I would never think that."

"Then what is this? What are we doing?"

I inhale a deep breath and hold it. Fuck. I can't seem to catch a break tonight.

"Shouldn't you be telling me, Brielle? Aren't you with Luca?"

I watch an array of emotions flash across her face as she works to come up with something to say back. What the fuck is it with her? Why did she allow me to believe that they're together? Does she secretly have feelings for the guy?

A minute trails by with no response, and suddenly I'm over the whole thing. "You know what?" I take a step back. "It is late. Just tell Wes I'll see him tomorrow. Have a nice night, Brielle."

She calls out behind me, asking for me to wait. But this time she isn't in control. After a ten-minute hike down the hill, I arrive at my truck and hop in. Damn it. I slam my hand against the steering wheel. And before I realize what I'm doing, I pull out on the road. I don't even waste the time debating; I just drive and eventually pull into the parking lot of K.O. My body is aching for a different kind of release.

I open the door and head in. Oh good, Kalie is here tonight. I smile, seeing my favorite waitress hurrying toward me.

"Hey, baby! The usual?" she coos. The black tank she's wearing seems to only be holding on by a prayer, and those tight-ass shorts of hers accentuate her in all the right places.

"You got it, and do me a favor, please, and tell Mack that I'm here."

"So, it's that kind of night, huh?" she asks and lays down a napkin to let the other girls know I've been helped.

"You don't have to say it like that. I do have a title to uphold, you know."

I watch Kalie shake her head before she hurries off to place my order. I turn to the side and offer Mack a wave after I see she passes along my message. I feel myself relax as I look up and watch the sorry sacks of shit currently working off their stress.

"You're up next." Kalie smiles, setting down my beer. "Mack said he has a surprise for you," she adds, and I turn back to Mack. "I'll be back in a minute with your wings!"

Mack tilts his head toward the end of the bar, and I follow it with my eyes. "Fuck." I say aloud to myself when I see who he's referring to. Even though it's dark, I'd recognize those fuckers from a mile away. They're the four figures who stood by and watched as I beat the shit out of their friend and broke his nose.

I roll my eyes and turn around in my seat. Lifting my beer, I take a big swig of it and sit back. Unfortunately, for them, I wasn't even half as mad as I am tonight.

This . . . this is going to be a fun night.

chapter seventeen

My tiny two-bedroom apartment is a sight for sore eyes, as I hurry up the steps and work to unlock the front door. Thankfully, Luca doesn't ask to stay when we pull up the driveway. After everything that's happened, I think he knows I desperately just need some time alone.

I unlock the door and wave goodbye, then walk inside and allow myself a minute to cry, before I wipe the tears away and force myself to pull it together. I will not be one of those girls—the ones who cry over Theo Wescott. I've seen it happen too many times, and I always swore to myself that I would never be *that girl*.

No, instead, I'll bury myself in *Pride and Prejudice* and a pint of mint chocolate chip ice cream. It's what I always do. . . when Chad, my ex, cheated on me. . . when Mason died. . . when Theo left. I chose to give up pursuing English as my major so that I could get "a real career," as my mom had advised. But at least I can still wallow the way I like—she hasn't taken that yet.

I make it halfway through the book, when I hear a weird scratching noise coming from the front door. I roll off the couch, crouching behind it, to investigate, when Becks comes falling through the door, with Wes.

"Shh. . .! Brielle is sleeping!" she yells. "Follow me."
Well, at least someone had a good night.

I roll my eyes and shake my head, waiting until they're tucked away in her room before I return to my spot on the couch. I definitely didn't want to take the chance of them seeing me. Talk about an awkward situation.

Drifting off somewhere in the middle. I wake up the next morning to Wes poking at my cheek, and I realize that I must have passed out on the couch. I blink my eyes open and choke back a scream when I see his all-too-cheerful grin staring back at me.

"Morning, B." He laughs, obviously amused at seeing my reaction.

B.? I think to myself, wondering what that's all about.

"Damn! You're even more gorgeous without makeup. Theo's a lucky guy."

I sit up and push the stray hairs back from my face.

"Thanks, but Theo and I aren't together." I offer a weak smile before I lean over to the table to grab my water from last night. I hear his feet shuffling around the corner, before I feel the couch slouch down beside me.

"What do you mean?"

Setting down my cup, I turn toward him.

Oh. My. God.

"Wes!" I shout when I find him sporting nothing but a pair of black boxers. His chest is glistening as if he's just come from a morning run, and the length of him strains against the opening of his boxers while he sits there, watching me. "Put that thing away!"

My hand moves to cover my eyes.

This is not happening.

I did not just see Wes sporting a massive boner.

"Whoops. Sorry." He laughs, shrugging, as he reaches behind me for the pillow I slept on. "Morning wood."

I look away when my cheeks heat. "Um, anyway—" I drop my hand—"I mean, there's no Theo and me. We're just friends."

Wes crinkles his nose. His hand moves to rest atop the pillow. *Mental note to self: Wash the pillow.*

"Does he know that?"

"Yes," I groan, leaning back against the cushion, and toss my hands up. "Although apparently, he already has too many. So maybe not. I don't really know anymore. He's confusing."

I look over when Wes bursts out laughing. "What's so funny?"

"Nothing, I just. . . you just. . ." he stumbles. "Theo is the most straightforward guy I know," he finally says. His hand musses up his blond hair even more as he stretches back along the arm of the couch. His leg accidentally bumps our coffee table. "He's more blunt than my nana . . . maybe you're not hearing him correctly?"

I tilt my head back and look up at the ceiling.

What the hell is going on around here?

Am I really talking about Theo with his best friend? While he's practically naked, sitting next to me on my living room couch?

I slap my hand over my face.

Ugh, this has to be a dream.

"Look, all I'm saying is, maybe you two should sit down and talk." He smiles at me. "Who knows, you may even be surprised at what he has to say."

I squint my eyes at him. My mind questions why he's grinning, but before I can ask what he's hiding, Becks barrels out of her room.

"Hey, what happened to 'just grabbing some water'?" She arches her brow at him as she lunges over the back of the couch and falls between us.

I pinch my eyes closed when I find Becks is equally as naked as he is. "God, will you two please go put some clothes on?" I laugh, because, really, this is more of the two of them than I ever want to see.

"Tempting—" Wes smacks his lips—"But I think I'd rather let Becks take some more off, first."

"Only if I get to do it with my teeth," she says.

Though my eyes are still closed, I know Becks is smiling. The cushions shift beneath me, which leads me to assume they stood up. I listen to the shuffle of their footsteps until they're far enough away and then I drop my hand from my eyes.

"So, uh, yeah. . . I have a few errands to run. I'll see y'all later," I call out to them just before Becks's bedroom door slams shut. There's no way I'm going to stay here with all the sex going on. God knows what I might witness next.

I shake my head and push up off the couch.

I need to listen, I hear Wes's voice inside my head.

What does that even mean?

Of course, I listened to Theo; he was pretty clear about how he felt the whole night—pushing me away after our moment together, then flaunting Katrina in front of my face the next. Then he even had the nerve to tell me he didn't want to be my friend. I mean, maybe I am clueless, but I just don't see how else I could interpret any of those things.

I hurry to my room and quickly change, before grabbing my keys and running out the door. I feel my phone go off in my lap and I flip it over. It's Luca inviting me out to lunch at the mall. I shoot him a quick response, telling him I'd love to, then put the car into gear. Maybe a day out, shopping and hanging out with Luca, is exactly what I need.

"Hey, Bree," Luca calls out to me from the back booth, as I smile and work my way around the hostess stand.

"Hey!" I smile at him, but it fades quickly after I arrive at the table and see his face. "Oh, my God, Luca." I reach out and cup his chin. "Your face looks terrible today. How are you feeling?"

He tosses his hand in front of him and nudges me to take a seat. "It's really not that bad." He laughs, but I can tell it's an act. "I'm glad you could make it. I was worried you might be mad at me."

I tilt my head and flash him a look. "I'm not mad." I pick up my menu. My mouth is already watering as I look at the daily specials. "I mean, you and Theo definitely took things way too far last night but I'm not mad. Just—"

"Good God, please don't say disappointed."

I drop my menu and choke back a laugh. "I was going to say hungry." I feel my lips betraying me as a small smile escapes them. "I'm just really hungry."

"Oh, well, good." He smiles and sits back. "I was worried you might say disappointed." He pushes his menu back and forth with his finger along the tabletop.

"Well I'm not.."

"Good."

"Good." I offer him a playful wink; my sour mood from earlier quickly evaporates.

"So want to hear about the newest upgrade I did to my car?" he ask, launching himself forward in his seat.

"Luca, don't take this the wrong way," My tone is light as I lean my arms against the table. "But unless your car has magically been upgraded into a food truck . . . let's not talk about it until after we eat. My brain needs fuel before I can even begin to think about processing your car talk."

He lets out a hearty laugh, then picks up his water. "Deal."

We barely finish our meal, when Luca launches into the conversation about his cat back exhaust system—or whatever the heck he called it. After lunch we decide to finally go see that movie we had planned to a couple weeks ago.

Once the movie is over, Luca offers to escort me to my car. "I had fun today!" I smile up at Luca, pulling him into a hug; the soft material of his jacket brushes against the side of my face. "Thank you for walking me to my car. I needed this."

Luca reaches his arm up to take my hand, uncoiling it from around his arm and spins me playfully. "Anytime. I love our day dates."

Day dates?

Love?

I offer another weak smile before turning toward my driver's-side door. There's that word, again: love. He's used it all day. I bite my lip and try not to unintentionally read more into things. A part of me really wishes that I could feel something for Luca. By every definition, he is the perfect guy— he's loyal, dependable, doesn't lie or fight.

He's the complete opposite of everything Theo represents, and I know he's who Mason wanted me to be with, but no matter how many times I try, there's always something holding me back. I even went as far as letting him kiss me a few months ago, but there was nothing behind it. It's nothing like the way I feel when Theo's kissed me. We're just better as friends than anything more. Why is it so hard for me to say the words, 'We're friends, Luca. Nothing more."

Is it guilt?

Hope?

Luca stops me from leaving just as my fingers brush the cool metal of the door handle. So close. I let go and turn around. *Please don't make me do this.*

Staring up at him, the sky is dark now as the harsh security lights of the parking lot cast shadows across his face. I can see something building behind those baby-blue eyes of his, but no matter how much I try, his expression is unreadable. My lips part to ask him what he's thinking, when out of the blue, my phone starts vibrating hastily in my pocket.

I stumble back and quickly fish it out, watching Luca side-eye me. "Uh, sorry." I crinkle my nose up at him. "It's probably Becks wondering where I am."

"No. You're fine."

I tap the screen, and sure enough, Becks's name appears. I unlock my phone. "Oh crap," I say aloud.

"What's wrong?"

I use my finger to scroll down the notification log; a crippling feeling washes over me when I see Becks's name is listed almost a dozen times. In each of the messages, she tells me to hurry and go to Haze. I bite my lip.

"Becks needs me at Haze." I know that's probably the last thing Luca wants to hear.

"What? Why the hell would she ask you to go there?"

I squint my eyes when I hear the aggressive tone to his words. I press my lips into a thin line and open the door.

"I don't know, but whatever her reason is, it must be important. Becks never blows me up like this. I'm sorry, but I have to go."

"Brielle, hold on. You . . . you're way too worried to drive. Let me take you. Besides, if Becks is in trouble, maybe I can help."

A small smile breaks my lips.

"What?"

"Nothing. I just never thought I'd see the day where you would offer to help Becks, willingly?" I nudge him playfully with my elbow.

He leans over me, his face unreadable, and I hold my breath. "I care more than you think."

chapter eighteen

W e pull into the back of Haze, like Becks requested, and I hop out while Luca parks my car. I'm surprised when I find the back door is cracked, and no one is around or waiting for me. I sweep my eyes around the half-empty lot, slowly edging my way inside.

"Hello," I call out as I step into the dark hall. I can see the lights from the dance floor flashing far off in the distance; the sounds of drunken stupor are barely audible.

Oh, yeah.

This isn't creepy.

Not at all.

If my father were here, he'd scold me for hours about going inside without backup. Moments like this are what scary movies are derived upon. I can just see it now—the opening scene where the blonde girl dies because she was too worried for her friend, to wait on the guy parking the car.

I take a couple of steps toward the lights, when Becks appears out of nowhere from Theo's office. Her knee-high, black boots, and silver-sequined dress, flashier than a 1970's disco ball. I blink through the darkness and try to focus on her face. Even in this light, I can tell by her expression that she's on edge. Her lips are pursed, and her eyes are wide. She's as pale as a ghost.

"There you are!" she's yells, the high-pitched tone of her voice pierces the back of my eardrums. "What the hell took you so long?"

"Sorry. I was with Luca? Why? What's wrong?

She reaches out and takes my hand, dragging me behind her and into the office. The massive swarm of bodies parading around the room shroud the area in a thick heat.

What the hell is this?

"Becks, what's going on in—"

I feel an arm snake around my waist as a sweat-soaked ape of a man pulls me into the crook of his arm. "Sorry, gorgeous, but the owner isn't up for guests tonight."

Guests?

I wrinkle my nose in disgust. His musky cologne is almost as potent as his body odor.

"Back the hell off, Eddie. Trust me. We need her." Becks whips her ponytail around and scolds the guy. He flashes her a blurred expression.

"Okay, Becks, it's time to start talking."

"Everyone out!"

I look around, when I hear Wes scream from somewhere further inside the room. Becks pulls me to a wall as it slowly empties. The chaos of people clamoring to get out reminds me of a hoard of zombies from one of Luca's favorite movies.

When the room is clear, I'm surprised to find Theo slouched back in his chair, with a bottle of whiskey in hand. His eyes are glossy, and his hair is a disheveled mess—more than it usually is. I shake my head, feeling my nerves swell up inside my chest when I see that familiar, distant look cross over his face. He's clearly wasted.

I let out a long breath and look down in front of him. That would explain the slew of iced waters covering his desk like a bad display of paperweights.

"What's going on?" I ask as Becks and I watch Wes scroll mindlessly through Theo's phone. His eyes shift over the screen in a nervous manner.

"We need you to talk some sense into Theo."

Talk some sense into Theo?

"What? Theo doesn't listen to me."

"Sure, he does." Becks turns around and sucks in her bottom lip. "But even if he doesn't, we . . . Wes and I . . . we need you."

"What? Why?"

"Well, don't freak out," she begins, her hands folding over one another continuously.

Okay, now I'm scared. Becks is seriously freaking out. I haven't seen her this wound up in a long time.

"Theo's been sta—."

"The fuck is she doing here?"

The two of us turn when we hear Theo shout. The rest of the stragglers hurry out of the room. The sound of the door slamming shut is deafening. Wes and Becks immediately avert their eyes, which is never a good sign. As long as I've known Becks, she has never been scared of anyone or anything.

I watch as Theo tries to stand, but he stumbles and falls back in his seat. Wow, he must really be drunk. I silently prepare myself. I've only ever seen drunk Theo a handful of times before, and it's never pretty. I can't imagine this new version of him being any nicer.

"I asked a question!" His eyes dart between Wes and Becks. When neither of them answers, he twists his chair to face me. "You need to leave. Now!" he barks. His words echo off the glass window, and it rattles within the frame. If I didn't know Theo would never hurt me, I might have cringed.

What am I doing here again?

I turn to Becks. "Yeah, I'm gonna go . . ."

"Yeah, you should!" Theo continues to yell as he works himself into a half-standing, half-leaning position, and rounds the side of his desk. "Unless there's something else you want to lie to me about?"

"Lie to you?" I press my lips into a hard line. "What the hell are you . . ." But I stop when I see it. The deep red stain that covers the entire side of his plain, white T-shirt. I point to it and say, "You're bleeding."

"Yeah, that's usually what happens when you get stabbed." Theo chuckles. I fail to see the humor in it, and before I know what I'm doing, I run to him.

"What the hell is wrong with you? How are you so calm?" I yell.

I'm trying to push up the side of his shirt so that I can get a closer look, but it's molded to his skin. I pull my hands away, tears welling up inside my eyes, when I find they're soaked in his blood.

"What the hell is going on? Why hasn't anyone called for an ambulance or something?"

"Brielle . . ."

I feel myself start to spiral. "W-wait a second. Let me think! Becks, I need something to apply pressure with."

"Brielle . . ."

"Wes, stop scrolling and dial 9-1-1!"

"Brielle!"

"No!" I whip my head back around and blink away the tears. All I can think is that it's happening. Again. My mind is racing with images of Mason and the gunshot wound that tore through him and left a gaping wound that would forever scar my family.

"No! I can't lose anyone else."

"Whoa. No, hey," Theo whispers and reaches down to fold his fingers around my one wrist as the other pushes into my hair. His demeanor has completely shifted as he leans into me. "Shh. No, don't cry, baby. I'm fine. It's only a little blood."

Only a little blood? I yell at him inside my head.

I can feel the slight sway in his stance as he holds on to me, and suddenly I worry he might pass out.

"Theo, this is not a little blood. What the hell happened? And why are you so drunk?"

Wes looks to Theo for approval and Theo nods. "It was that asshole from the bar. Apparently, he didn't take too kindly to Theo breaking his nose a few weeks back. So, he's had his friends patrolling Knock Out for payback, and when dummy over here decided to show up last night, they jumped him. Well, at least, they tried to." Wes frowns, his expression heavy. "I found him like this when I came to get the club ready for opening."

"Okay. Did you call the police?" I ask. "I can call my dad. I'm sure he would—"

"No, Brielle, you can't." Wes shakes his head, looking back down at the phone. "Trust me, they got what they deserved."

"Jesus. Can everyone just calm down? I'll be fine. It's just a scratch," Theo says. His hands move to wrap his side as if to try to alleviate some of the strain.

Some scratch. . .

As if reading my thoughts, Theo sighs, and slowly makes his way to the leather chaise. "Look, it happens. I just didn't see the asshole had a knife until he was already on me."

"I can't handle this. I'm calling the police."

"Brielle, just, come here," Theo whines, motioning for me to come to him. "Wes is working on calling my private doctor. So, you don't have to worry. It's nothing that hasn't happened before."

Come again?

"I am?" Wes asks, seeming relieved.

Is that why they wanted me here?

To convince Theo to see his doctor?

I squint my eyes up at him and tilt my head. The usual rich green of his own is washed out. I feel like I should do something, but I'm still stuck on the "this has happened before."

"Just hurry up and dial before he changes his mind," Becks mumbles under her breath. Her voice rips me from Theo's gaze. She lets out a small laugh and turns to me. "I'm just glad you're here now. Being the voice of reason is not my strong suit, especially with a patient with as thick of a head as Theo's." She quickly fixes her hair, tossing it back into a small bun. "Plus, I am not good with blood."

"It's ringing," Wes calls out to the room before walking past me. I hear the phone rings once before an older sounding man answers it. "Yes, hello. I'm calling for Theo Wescott," Wes begins, his voice surprisingly steady for someone who just found their best friend stabbed. "He's, uh, sick . . .? Oh . . . yup, that's it. Stabbed, yes. Where? Right side."

I turn toward Becks and am happy to see that she is equally as shocked as I am about this whole thing. "I, uh, I'm going to step out for a minute," I whisper to no one in particular, and quickly turn toward the door.

I walk a step before I feel myself begin to crumble and decide to lean against the wall. *Focus, Brielle,* I tell myself. My mind is running through a mental checklist of things I can do to keep myself busy.

He's not going to die. "It's just a scratch," Theo's obnoxious words tumble through my mind, and I cling to them.

Those waters looked old; I'll just go grab another. I have to keep myself busy, or I'm going to lose it.

He's not going to die, I remind myself again.

I run to the server's station and grab a couple of glasses of water. I sure hope he has enough coasters for all of these. I would hate to leave water stains all over his desk.

I turn around and freeze midstep. My hands rock forward as one of the glasses threatens to spill and I swallow hard, trying to force down the knot that's formed in my throat, when I'm met by two sets of blue eyes.

A slight pang of guilt resonates in my stomach as I watch a pissed-off Katrina, and a confused Luca giving me a wide-eyed stare. "Oh, hey." I look down and see that I'm still covered in Theo's blood. "Thirsty?"

chapter nineteen

G ross. I'm good." Katrina shrugs, crossing her arms in
front of her as she stares openly in disgust. Her bright red
heels, stamp beneath her as she rocks back on the heel.

I nod, turning back toward the server's station and set
down the three glasses.

A simple no would have sufficed.

I barely manage to get them on the counter before Luca
rushes up to me. "What the hell, Brielle! Is this your blood?" he
asks, his breath beating against my neck. He moves his hands,
tugging on the lower edges of my own shirt, but I gently stop
him.

"No. It's, um. . ." I nervously twist out of his grip. My
eyes shift up to Katrina as I step in front of her. "It's not my
blood. It's Theo's," I give her the answer as if she had been the
one with the question.

They may not be boyfriend and girlfriend, but they
obviously have something between them, especially since Theo
likes to throw her in my face any chance he gets. I can only
imagine how I would be feeling if I were in her shoes, seeing
me like this when I first heard the news.

Katrina shifts anxiously and wrinkles her brow in a
furious manner. For a minute, she seems like a completely
different person—levelheaded and calm.

"Wait a minute. Theo's hurt?"

Oh, so she does care about someone other than herself.
My mind tosses the joke around before I remember the
circumstances. An image of Theo sitting slack in his chair
flashes across the back of my mind.

"Yeah, come on. I'll take you to him," I say, then reach
around for the glasses before I take off down the hall.

"Ugh. . . be there in a sec." Katrina calls after me.

The short walk back to the office passes in silence.

"Here. Drink these," I say and thrust one of the glasses
at Theo. "It'll help you sober up."

"There is only one thing that could make me feel better,
babe." He smiles, flashing me a dimpled smile. "And it's not
water."

I roll my eyes and set them down beside him anyway.
"Yeah, well, it's the only thing you're getting from me so you
might want to drink up."

"Damn!" Wes bursts out laughing. "Ah, man. I never
thought I'd see the day, Theo Wescott can't land a girl."

"Shut the fuck up, Wes." Theo smirks, but it lacks the
usual passion behind it.

Katrina enters shortly after, and sprints to Theo's side.
Her hands move to encircle his neck as she plops down on his
lap. The force of the action makes Theo lurch forward in
response.

Yeah, that's not going to help with his pain! I silently
scream at her. I stand awkwardly at his side, like an intruder, as
I watch Katrina fawn all over him.

"I'm fine." Theo pats her back. He lifts his eyes from her
shoulder and immediately finds me.

Our eyes fix for a few seconds as Katrina hugs his neck.
Eventually, the moment passes when she pulls back. Hers snap

down to the red stains covering his side. Theo presses a towel just under his rib and holds it there.

"Shit, baby, you bled all over my dress."

Katrina covers her mouth and looks away. Her blue eyes latch on to a spot on the ceiling, as she moves to the far wall. Her blonde, pencil-perfect hair is wound in a tight braid.

I cringe inwardly when I hear her call Theo baby, remembering that he had just used the same word on me.

Stop thinking about it!

Focus on something else.

I roll my eyes and walk over to where Wes and Becks are standing; I notice Luca is keeping to himself by the door.

"Um, so what did the doctor say?" I manage, surprised that I was able to sound a lot calmer than I felt. On the inside, I'm in full panic mode.

"He's on his way," Becks is the first to answer me.

I turn away from the group and look out the glass panel that lines the one side of the door. I can see the solid build of Eddie's right arm and leg, and I focus on it. My mind is a million miles away.

Theo slowly paces back to his desk, and Katrina sits along the now empty chaise, sighs, and sucks in a rather large breath.

"This is insane. We should be taking you to the hospital!" I yell to no one in particular.

I turn around when I hear Luca laugh and stare at him incredulously. He presses his lips into a hard line, as if he's biting back what he really wants to say. Instead, he says, "Theo can't go to the hospital. Don't you get it, Brielle? He'd be implicating himself."

Implicating himself?

What does Luca think Theo did to them?

Murder them?

I turn back to Theo, who's swirling his chair around from side to side. No . . . Theo wouldn't . . . wait. Did he?

"What do you mean?"

"What do you think, Brielle?"

"Luca, that's enough!" Wes steps in between us. His broad shoulders roll back as he squares them with Luca's.

"Whatever. She asked."

Half an hour later, the doctor finally arrives and is escorted back into the office. As he crosses the room, the large space slowly feels smaller by the second. He casts a solemn expression when he sees Theo.

Well, he definitely doesn't like to sugarcoat things.

I cut my eyes to Becks after we both notice how young he is. By the sound of his voice over the phone, I was expecting a short, elderly man with a briefcase and salty hair. This guy was far from that. I take a step toward Theo when I see him wince as the doctor removes his shirt. The wet material drops to the floor, revealing two large, jagged wounds.

"Oh my God," I gasp when I see the two wounds start bleeding heavily. The minimal protection his shirt provided was now stripped away.

Without a thought, I cross the room and gently grasp Theo's good arm. I can feel the tears pricking at the back of my eyes, but I will them away. "Doctor, is he, um . . . is he going to be okay?" I know he'll be the one to give me an honest answer.

"Call me William." His words drip confidence.

The doctor—William—is very handsome, with his chiseled features, dark brown eyes, and charcoal-colored hair. He squats down and leans close to Theo's side. The expression on his face is disinterested and unnervingly calm. I guess that's a good sign. . .?

"It's not too serious. Just a scratch compared to others I've seen. But he'll need sutures." William breaks from his examination to glare up at me, and I swallow hard, feeling my cheeks flush. I thought doctors were only this attractive on television shows and in movies. "The better question is are you okay? You look pale."

I nod, when I hear Theo scoff beside me.

He pulls his hand from mine and drapes it over the back of the chair. "Hate to say I told you so, but . . ." his voice trails off as he groans. The muscle beneath the wound that's closest to his rib cage flexes. "Just stitch it up like last time. And hurry."

I look to William, waiting for him to tell Theo that he's insane. But he simply nods and begins pulling equipment from the medium-sized leather bag he brought with him.

"Whatever you say. I guess this means you aren't going to want the local either?"

"Eh, I'm numb enough. What do you think the alcohol was for?"

"I'm not going to answer that." William twists around, holding a scissor-like instrument in his hand; the tip of one is clamped down on a giant, hook-shaped needle.

"Wait. Hold on. What's happening here?" I nearly choke at the idea.

"Oh, would you calm down." Katrina snarls her upper lip, crossing her legs in front of her on the chaise. "The guy fights all the time. You heard the doctor—it's nothing."

"Nothing?" I glare at her.

What is she?

Blind?

"You might be a bitch, Katrina, but you're not ignorant."

"Ooookay," Wes chooses this moment to interject. "Maybe we should all take five."

"Whatever," Katrina sneers, rising from her seat and makes her way to the door. "I'm going to the ladies' room. I'll be back in a minute."

Soon after, everyone leaves the room but me, and as William works to suture the wounds, I can't help but notice how calm Theo is. He's perfectly still the entire time. And other than a few sharp breaths, it's like he doesn't even notice the one-inch needle threading through his skin.

"Almost done." William pulls back, and he peels open the last suture pack.

I can't resist the urge to comfort Theo, and before I know what I'm doing, I reach out and touch his arm. My thumb soothes the pain, which I know he has to feel, as I brush it back and forth over the soft skin of his torso. I see a bit of scripture tattooed vertically up the length of his left side, and I run my fingers along it. It's in another language, but as I say the words in my mind, they sounds beautiful.

"Oh good. You're almost done." Wes returns to the room and sighs, letting out a small laugh. He grabs his phone out of his front pocket and brings the screen to life. "Hector, yes. Bring the car around in twenty. Thanks."

He turns back to the door when Katrina appears. She looks like a woman on a mission, as she glides into the room and settles back down on the chaise.

"Katrina, are you coming?" Wes asks, then cuts his eyes to me. He shrugs, adding, "Someone needs to play nurse tonight, and I don't fit the outfit."

I bite back the ache that his words bring when he automatically assumes it should be Katrina.

Katrina is the obvious pick, my inner mind reminds me. It's not an actual nurse Theo needs, but a distraction. I can read between the lines.

William ties off the last suture and laughs under his breath as if hearing my thoughts and shakes his head.

"You got something to say, William, say it." Theo groans, pulling his shirt back on.

"Oh, nothing."

"I could beat it out of you." Theo rolls his eyes in annoyance. "Or do you not think me capable?"

"No, I believe you." William's tone is serious and weighted as he and Theo lock eyes.

I can feel my pulse begin to race. My mind is reeling, when I look up and find Theo's face is as pale as a ghost. I squeeze his hand gently, and I'm happy when he returns the gesture.

"It's just that, and no offense—he turns then, throwing Katrina a pitying look—"your friend's asking the wrong girl for the job."

Wes furrows his brow as a sense of understanding washes over him.

"But that's just my opinion."

I look down to Theo's hand and release it. The sudden heaviness I feel as everyone's eyes turn on me, makes my head spin.

"What do you say, B?" Wes jerks the bottle of pills from William's hand and turns toward me. "You up for the task?"

I turn back to Theo.

"It's your choice." He smiles sheepishly and stands up from the chair. I cut my eyes over to where Katrina's sitting, but she seems to have disappeared.

"Uh, I guess," I finally say and bite at my bottom lip. "I'll just need to stop by my place and grab a few—"

"Don't worry about that, beautiful." Wes smiles. His devilish grin causes an uneasy feeling to form in the pit of my stomach. "I'm sure there are plenty of clothes left there for you to choose from."

I pinch the bridge of my nose. Right. I bet there is.

"That is, unless you two choose to do a whole different kind of healing." Wes winks, nudging my arm. "One that involves very little clothing at all."

chapter twenty

T heo's truck pulls into the back lot the moment we walk outside.

"You know I expect a full recap of everything that happens, right?" Becks laughs, wrapping her arms around my side, pulling me into a hug.

"Is Wes staying over again tonight?" I fix the strap of her sequin dress. The image of her staying alone in our apartment is somehow unsettling—not that I'm worried that Becks, of all people, couldn't defend herself. It just seems lonely.

She pouts her bottom lip, pulling me closer. "No, but I'll be okay. Just make sure you don't do anything I wouldn't do, all right?"

Luca walks up behind us. "Really, Becks?"

I turn toward him and suck in a deep breath.

"What? You do know who she's going home with?" Becks half laughs. "I know that's what I would do if I were her."

"Becks," I warn, shaking my head, silently begging for her to stop. I know she's teasing, but I can see the tension building in Luca's shoulders. He isn't going to see it like that, and I don't need a full-fledged meltdown on top of everything else.

"Well, thankfully, Brielle isn't you," he snaps all of a sudden. "She doesn't fuck everything that breathes."

What the hell? My brain freezes. I can feel the shift around us as every eye turns to gawk at us.

"And she sure as hell isn't going to start with Theo!"

I see Wes move to head toward us, but Theo pulls him back. "Leave it," he says.

"What? You wouldn't be pissed at that?"

"He's not mad at Becks."

I feel something in my chest constrict when I hear Theo's response. I almost think drunk Theo is somehow more levelheaded than normal Theo at the moment. But then I remember that now is not the time to be thinking about him.

"Okay. Whoa—" I tilt my head at Luca—are you okay? Where the hell did that come from?"

When he doesn't answer, I cut my eyes at Becks and give her a look, signaling for her to give us a minute. I wait until she's over by the truck before I choose to press him further.

"Luca, what the hell was that? Becks is only tea—"

"Yeah, everything is always such a joke to her." He tosses his eyes and runs a hand over his face. "You know, I am just so sick of all of this." He pauses, taking a step back. "This is all just an act to get you alone, Brielle. He wants you. I told you this would happen."

I take in a breath and reach out to touch his arm. "Okay, Luca, you need to calm down. You're not making any sense. You can't honestly think Theo would let himself to get stabbed just to be alone with me?"

"No, Brielle, this is such bullshit."

"What is?"

"Everything. The stuff with Theo . . . us . . . tonight."

"Fine. So then, let's talk. Luca, you're my best—"

"Don't. Just stop."

"Luca we've been friends forever." I swallow the lump in my throat. I can't wait anymore—he deserves to know how I feel. He needs to hear the truth. "But I can't force myself to feel something that isn't there."

Luca tosses his head back and laughs hard.

"You've never even given us a chance, Brielle." He shakes his head. His hand reaches out to grasps my elbows as he pulls me closer. "I mean, we share an amazing kiss and then he shows up, and now you're rushing off to be with this asshole. I don't understand."

From the corner of my eye, I can see Theo watching me. His expression is tense as his eyes zero in on Luca's hold on me. His steely gaze threatens to murder Luca on the spot. I know that if I don't find a way to resolve this fast, something bad is going to happen.

"It's not like that," I finally answer Luca, but even I know it's a lie.

For some reason, whatever it is, Theo and I share something that I can't explain. Even though we may never be together, it doesn't change the fact that a part of me will always love him. But I can't break Luca's heart by telling him that. Selfishly, I still need him in my life. . . just not in the way he wants to be.

Wait.

Did I just say *love*?

"Theo and I, we . . . we have a history; I can't explain it. He makes me—" I begin to say, but Luca cuts me off, waving his hands in defeat.

"What you two are is dangerous." He shakes his head, his right foot scuffing back along the pavement as he steps away from me. "I don't care how long it takes, or what I have to do, but I will prove it to you."

He's staring off somewhere in the distance, when I catch a figure moving to my left. Katrina. The sight of her hits me like a ton of bricks, as I realize I hadn't thought about how my leaving with Theo—or how any of this—might make her feel.

"Just go, Brielle." Luca's voice snaps me back to the moment at hand. "It's obvious you want to. You didn't even try to put up a fight."

"Luca, I . . . I don't know what to say."

He doesn't answer, merely shrugs his shoulders, and walks away. I stare after him for a minute before I turn around and head toward the truck. I'm standing next to Becks, when I see Katrina and Theo arguing on the other side.

"What the hell is in the air tonight that's making everyone go crazy?"

"Beats me." Becks laughs, tilting her head to the side. "But it's awkward as fuck."

I smile at her and open the back door to the truck. I offer her a small wave before I climb in and shut the door behind me. Inside the cabin, I can hear every word Katrina and Theo are saying. I cross my right leg over the other and try to tune them out, but it isn't working.

"I don't know, Theo, but my daddy isn't going to be happy when he hears about this," Katrina snaps.

Her daddy?

What the hell is she?

Five?

I roll my eyes and suck in a deep breath. Would it be rude if I asked the driver to turn up the radio?

No. No. I better not.

"Your daddy isn't my concern," Theo says in a mocking tone, and I feel my eyes widen in disbelief. "I told you from the beginning that this was all just for fun."

"You're such an asshole, Theo. Why are you acting like this?"

"Acting like what?"

"I don't know; you've just changed. Ever since she's shown up, you've started acting like a—"

"Like a what, Katrina?" Theo takes a step toward her. His tone is shaky and on edge. I cut my eyes to the side and notice he's leaning heavily on the door. "Go ahead, tell me. What am I acting like?"

"Like a jealous dick."

I feel my lips part when I see she looks just as defeated as she sounds.

"You're insane." Theo shakes his head at her, pushing off the door, and turns toward the parking lot. "I don't—"

"Yeah, I know. The great Theo Wescott doesn't date." She rolls her eyes. "So then, why is she going home with you and not me?"

"What the hell are you talking about? I didn't pick."

"You fucking told her it was up to her!" Katrina yells, obviously having reached her limit for the night. "You can lie to yourself, but you've got a shitty poker face."

Katrina rocks back on her heel and gathers herself. Her eyes, cutting toward the passenger side door until she catches me watching. Crap. I look away, feeling my cheeks flush as I try to ignore the sound of my heart beating throughout the cabin. That's what I get for being nosey.

"Look, I'm sorry," Theo answers her, drawing her attention away from me. "But I'd better go."

She narrows her eyes then, her expression darkening as she turns, and saunters away from him. Her right hand rises behind her as she flips him off, and disappears into the night.

Well, at least she kept her class.

I smile and shake my head.

As we're making our way to Theo's home, I'm surprised by how long we've been in the car, when the driver suddenly turns off onto a long cobblestone driveway and heads further east. I look around, trying to see any signs of a house, but there's only darkness.

Where the heck are we going?

After another minute, we arrive at an entrance and I see the name "Wescott" engraved in the stone walls, which line both sides of the large wrought iron fence. I cut my eyes up to the driver's seat and watch him punch in the code.

Does Theo really need this much security?

The gate opens a second later, and we continue down the driveway. From what little light the moon gives off, I can see big, beautiful trees planted in rows, which canopy together and darken the road. I wonder how it looks during the day, but I can only imagine it's like something right out of a fairy tale. When we finally reach the end, there's a break. The grounds beyond it open up and out to reveal a massive castle of a home that sits up on a hill.

I feel my mouth drop as I stare out my window in awe. The house is gorgeous. The outside is lined with tall, marbled pillars that wrap along the entire exterior. The front door is an impressive double-doored entrance set within a stone wall; each side is carved out of thick, mahogany. Along the sides, windows and sliding doors are positioned every few feet from one another.

"This is where you live?" The words slip from my lips as we pull to a stop in the circular driveway.

"This is the place," Theo says, joining me in admiring the grandeur that is his home. Both of our necks crane up in an attempt to see beyond what the windows allow. "You ready?"

"Yes, please." I smile eagerly up at him from the back seat. He does his best to return it with one of his own, seeming to like my reaction, but it doesn't reach his eyes. I wonder if he's in pain.

Theo takes my hand and pulls me along. I smile seeing the small bump of his enthusiasm and that he seems to be walking more steadily as we make our way up the brick steps to the front door. My mind spins as I step through the doors and find that the inside is designed like something out of a movie.

The foyer is just as I imagined—massive and lined with stark white walls and a crystal chandelier, which hangs perfectly in the center of the room. I glance around and see three main sections that break off. And directly in front of us, a massive staircase frames either side of the entry to the living room. Both rows of stairs leads up to connect on the next floor and so on, and so on, for two floors higher. My mind struggles to find a word that sufficiently describes just how exquisite it all is.

Before I can ask for a tour of the rest of the house, Theo grabs my hand, and we climb the first row of stairs to the second floor. The base where both sets of stairs meet pushes out into another grand foyer, where another set of double doors sits beyond it, with two rooms on either side that face one another.

"This is my room." He smiles, pushing the doors open for me to walk inside. At the sight of his massive four-poster bed, he begins moving at an elevated speed before he collapses on it.

"I'm happy to see you moving around so easily." I squint my eyes in his direction, taking a step further into the room. "Why am I here, again?"

"Excuse me, ma'am. Sorry to intrude. But if you don't need me, Boss I'll happily lock up and be on my way." Hector says from the doorway.

"Yes, you're good, Hector. Thank you."

Nodding his head, Hector turns and hurries out of the room. The way he practically runs away tells me that he obviously doesn't care to be in the lair of the beast any longer than he has to be. Laughing at the thought of this, I look back at Theo and then walk up to the side of his bed, bending over to lean beside him.

"So, do you need me to get you anything before I wander off and find myself a room?"

"Find a room?" Theo turns his head toward me, the corners of his lips pulling back into a devilish grin. "I thought this was a sleepover?"

I roll my eyes and playfully swat his good arm. "Oh really, well, something tells me this is exactly why your doctor didn't want Katrina coming home with you tonight." I smile at him but it's forced. My shoulder leans into his side, and I have to fight the urge to keep it there. "You have to rest."

"I am resting. Come on. What if I promise to behave myself?" His eyes trail down my back.

"Theo, no. We can't—"

"What?" he groans, rolling over to face me. "You're here to take care of me, aren't you?"

I freeze at the statement and turn away from him. The idea of sleeping in the same house as him is hard enough. But to be in the same bed . . .

"I can't." I turn back, smiling and bite my lower lip.

"Can't or won't? Because if you keep biting that damn lip, I won't be able to let you go."

I blink my eyes shut and turn away from him. The memory of what happened yesterday, at the D.O., hits me in waves. I used to think that I was impervious to his charms. But after yesterday, I can see why he would think that I could so easily be persuaded into something more—a thought that embarrasses me almost as much as it excites me. I always thought Theo would be my first.

I scoot to the far side of the bed when I feel a deep throb pulse between my thighs and a heat creeping up, as it ignites under my cheeks.

God, what the hell is my problem?

From everything I know about him—from everything I've heard—I should be running away. Not lying in his bed. Alone. I glance to the side and catch his eyes watching my mouth. A playful spark burns behind his eyes.

"Theo, I hope you don't think I'm going to sleep with you just because you're injured," I say, licking my lips. The subtle way he's leaning closer isn't reassuring at all.

"What? I would never think that."

"Good because I won't." I feel the need to repeat myself.

"Okay. . . what's going on with you? I never said you would."

"No but Wes—"

"Jesus. You're such a girl." He rolls his eyes and then pushes up on his elbows until he's directly in front of me. "Look, not that you even bother to ever let me defend myself, but much to your disbelief, I know you're nothing like Katrina. You're pure and innocent, and good. It's one of the reasons why I loved being around you so damn much back when we were friends. Well, that and . . . your incredible sense of getting into trouble. Never a dull moment with you."

"No, of course," I say.

My mind instantly clings to his choice of words—as in "friends" being past tense. I pinch a section of my cheek between my teeth and roll off the bed.

"Thanks for clarifying that."

chapter twenty-one

BRIELLE

W ait. Hold on. What just happened?" Theo asks, annoyed, motioning for me to come back to the bed. I drop my eyes to the carpet and move across the room. The thin material of my dress kicks up as I walk over the grates of the air conditioning vent; I forgot that old homes like this don't have central air.

"Nothing, you just . . . just forget it."

"Okay then," he says, pulling himself up off the bed. I lift my eyes and notice he's moving slower than he was a second ago. But I let it go. "Come on. I'll show you to your room."

My eyes follow his broad shoulders out into the hall as he runs a hand through his thick head of hair. We make an immediate left turn and come up to the next room. Inside, the walls are a soft blush color with splashes of floral designs throughout. The bedding is an ivory hue.

The room is easily two times the size of mine and Becks's entire house. It contains a long walk-in closet, bookshelves, and private bath, which is fully equipped with a massive walk-in waterfall shower (with *five* different showerheads) and a double sink. I cut my eyes to the corner when I catch the massive clawfoot tub.

"What the—" I suck my bottom lip into my mouth, trapping the curse word I was about to say.

Oh, I'm definitely going to take full advantage of that tonight. I let a smile slip. My mind already calculating the perfect bubble bath cocktail, as my eyes peruse the bubble bar. The hundred or so variety of smell combinations makes my eyes grow wide.

"I knew you were going to like that." Theo laughs, walking over to the tub to run his hand along its smooth surface. "You know, the guy who I bought this house from—"

"You mean this castle." I feel my lip tug to the side as I flash a playful grin at him and cross my arms.

He shakes his head, a handsome grin playing along his lips, as he rubs at the stubble that thinly sprays his jaw. "I knew I should have just taken you to my flat."

Excuse me?

"You have a flat?"

"Yes. In Dallas." Theo shrugs as if it's not that big of a deal. He stands and leads me back into the main bedroom. "Anyway, his wife loved the garden out back; it's apparently, why they bought the property in the first place. But, unfortunately, shortly after they moved in, they found out she was terminal. Leukemia is what I heard. So, when she became too ill to venture outside her room, he had this room built for her. The entire floor used to be one solid room if you can believe that."

I can.

"When I first toured the property, I came in here, and when I saw the tub it made me think about all the times you used to get so pissed when Mason would lock you out of the bathroom when you wanted to take a bath. It's one of the reasons I decided to buy it."

Theo thinks about me?

His gaze slices to mine and it strips me bare.

Trying to bring the conversation back around, I say, "I love that. The story, I mean. It's . . . romantic. The floral designs. He brought the garden to her." I swoon at the thought of someone loving me that much one day. "Wait, so why are there three rooms then? Why not just two?"

"Oh, well, the other was for her nurse."

"Oh, right. That makes sense. Is it as big as this room?"

"Oh yeah. It's the same size. Rumor has it that the husband and the nurse were having an affair, so naturally, it only made sense to just keep everything equal."

Of course—naturally!

What was I thinking?

I roll my eyes, while I silently wonder how one might decorate a mistress's room, when a thought hits me. "Well, thanks for not putting me in there." I giggle and pull at the bottom of my dress. The soft lace kisses the top of my thighs.

"Oh no. I'd never do that to you." He laughs along with me, as his hand moves to support his side before leaning into the doorframe.

I can feel my heart begin to flutter when I realize that Theo chose to put me in the wife's room rather than the mistress's. My mind secretly wonders if maybe he really didn't believe I was just another Katrina and that maybe he thought I could be something more.

"I turned it into my game room."

Well, I spoke too soon.

Closing my eyes, I shake my head.

"Right," I whisper, faintly. Guys and their video games, I swear. The memory of Mason and him, seated on the floor of his room, "raiding" loudly all throughout the night quickly flashes across the back of my mind. I miss those days.

"Hey, are you okay?" I look up as I hear him suck in a quick breath. I reach my hands out to help him move over to the bed, but before I can even manage to touch him, he pulls away. "Sorry. I was only trying to help," I say. But I should have known he wouldn't want the help. It's tough trying to care for someone who thinks their invincible.

"I'm fine. I just need to go lie down for a bit." He tries to keep his voice even, but I can see the pain masked behind his eyes. I press my lips together, and take a step back, nodding my head in submission.

Out of the corner of his eye, he looks up and watches me for a moment. "Don't worry. I won't die on you." He smiles. His shoulder leans in to nudge me before he walks out of the room and into the hall. "You should, ugh, you should call Luca." He clears his throat. "I'm surprised he even allowed you to come in the first place."

Here we go.

I narrow my eyes at his back when he continues to walk away from me. "I don't need permission to go anywhere, Theo. You and Luca seem to forget that I'm not that little girl you once knew! You're not my brother! You don't get the privilege of weighing in on my decisions."

At that, he stops and turns around. His deep green eyes are blazing but then he lets them slowly travel up and down my body, in an almost aggressive way.

"I'm not playing big brother with you, Brielle! I never have!" he yells. I rock back a step, my fingers playing with the hem of my dress while I look up at him. "But since you're still playing games, maybe someone should."

I take a breath and hold it, then release as I say, "Playing games? Excuse me?" I shake my head, stepping toward him.

My heart is beating a mile as I feel myself getting angrier by the second. "What the hell does that mean?"

Theo breaks away from me and turns his attention toward the stairs. His eyes stare off into the distance, as he if he's debating what he wants to say next. He draws in a deep breath, then lets it out.

"I know you're not with Luca, Brielle."

I hold my breath for a moment before saying. "I never said I was."

"No. But you sure as hell didn't correct me." He drops his head, sighing loudly.

I shift nervously, my heart beating so loudly that I'm practically drowning within the sound. "Theo, you haven't been here! You left—for five years—but Luca. . . he was here. I didn't correct you because I didn't think it mattered. I'm sorry if you thought there was something more going on, or if you felt like I owed you—"

"Enough!" Theo yells. He spins back around and heads in the direction of his room. He reaches the door and opens it, pausing only for a moment to say, "There's food in the kitchen if you get hungry. Make yourself at home. Goodnight."

He lifts his head, as if he were going to look at me, before he changes his mind. In the last second he walks inside his room and shuts the door.

For the next hour, I sit on my bed, hoping that Theo would come back and talk to me, but when he doesn't I finally give up.

Screw it.

I move into the bathroom and step up to the sink.

Out of the corner of my eye, I notice the clawfoot tub; a sly smile spreads across my lips. After the day I've had, this is exactly what I need—a nice, long bubble bath. I skip over to the tub and turn on the faucet, then plug the drain with the stopper.

I'm not playing big brother, his words are still on constant repeat in the back of my mind. I try to unravel the hidden meaning behind them, but I'm confused.

The truth is, I don't blame Theo for being mad at me; I would be mad at me, too. God, why didn't I just tell him the truth? Is it because, if I'm single, it would make things easier for the two of us to slip up and fall back, thereby, ruining *us* all over again? Or is it because I'm really that scared of losing Luca?

I ease my way into the tub. Crap! The water's hot. But the heat against my skin instantly works to calm my nerves, as the scent of apple medley swirls around in the steam that perforates the massive haze of bubbles. I smile and slink down further.

"Enjoying yourself?"

"Theo!" I hurdle forward when I hear Theo's voice fill the room. My eyes fly open, and my lips part the second I am able to focus.

Leaning against the sliding door, Theo is bare from the waist up. My muscles instantly clench. His brown hair is even more disheveled—if that's at all possible. I lick my lips as I hungrily rake my eyes down the front of him; a pair of black pajama bottoms hang from his hips, which highlight a very deep V. I swallow the knot in my throat that's threatening to choke me. How it's possible that he's even more muscular and handsome than I had first imagined.

He watches me with a steely gaze, his expression unreadable as he pushes off the door and steps further into the room. Without thinking, I wrap my arms around my chest. The mountain of bubbles, which currently cover my naked body, are not nearly enough to shield the hunger burning in his eyes.

"You're. . . ugh. . . you're out of bed," I struggle to get the words out. "Why?"

He settles himself in the chair that's tucked precariously under the vanity, and I'm thankful that he's at least keeping his distance—for now. I guess five years really did change him. My eyes slowly drink in the sight of him.

Stop drooling! I yell at myself and snap my mouth shut.

"I couldn't sleep. Figured we should talk," he says simply, pushing a hand through his hair. "I was. . . ugh. . . looking for you when I heard the water running."

"Oh." My voice catches, as I lower my eyes down to check the level of the bubbles. I nervously wriggle my toes. "Well, you found me." I try to smile in an attempt to lighten the mood.

A low burn eases its way up my thighs, while I feel my pulse beating in my ears; the delicate throb pulses at my core, beating hastily in tune with it.

"So, I have." He arches his brow at me. An amused lilt plays within the tone of his voice. "You know, that tub was made to hold two?"

Like a thief, he captures my gaze and pins me with it. His expression is predatory as he licks his lips, pulling the bottom one and biting it.

Oh, this could be bad.

"Sorry. . ." I stumble and rush to sit up, forgetting for a split second that I'm completely naked, before I quickly slink back into the tub. As the bubbles begin to melt away, more of my skin is revealed. "What. . . ugh . . . I'm sorry. What did you want to talk about?"

He shrugs away the question. My stomach tightens as I watch him stand. As if on cue, I cross my legs and pull them up to my chest.

"It can wait," he says.

He moves slowly. His hazel eyes are holding me trapped as he steps up to the foot of the tub and leans down to rests his arms on either side of my head. The hard-packed muscles of his chest press atop the remaining bubbles. My mountain of protection is now more like a small hill.

I inhale a quick breath the instant I feel his lips brush the side of my neck. A thousand, tiny electrical currents come alive while I lean into his touch and wait for something to happen.

"Do you even know the things you do to me?" he whispers against my skin. I squeeze my legs tighter and fight to ignore the less than subtle ache that's throbbing between my thighs, but it's no use. He knows what I'm doing. "I can help you with that." His tone is serious as his eyes flint down to the bubbles. The intensity behind them is one I've only seen a handful of times.

"Theo, I . . . I've never—"

"Brielle," he whispers. His teeth nipping at a spot just below my ear. "Let me show you how good I can make you feel."

Reaching his hand into the tub, Theo slips it under the water. His fingers skim the top of my knee, then smooth their way down my thigh. I gasp when a feeling rushes down my body to the spot between my thighs, the pressure building as a soft moan escapes my lips.

I feel his lips brush the corner of my mouth, and I turn into the kiss. In anticipation, my back arches off the cool ceramic of the tub. His fingers slowly start to move around in quick circles against the spot where I'm most sensitive. I close my eyes and let the feeling wash over me. It's something I've never felt before.

The building pressure knots somewhere deep within my stomach. I raise my hand, wanting to run my fingers along the ridges of his washboard abs when I graze a thin slip of tape.

Parting my lips, I attempt to stop his assault. My conscious temporarily caught up in the whirlwind of emotions, as I debate whether or not this would be on the list of restricted activities while he recovers from his wounds.

I tilt my head back on the tub, trying to steady my breathing as I look up and watch his eyes darken.

"I can handle it, baby," he says and presses a soft kiss against my lips. Once again, his ability to read my mind amazes me. "Do you trust me?" He smiles, his eyes holding my full attention.

I nod, which I can tell pleases him. He brings his hand up to my chest, and gently teases the area between my breasts. But he doesn't stay there long, as his hand disappears again under the water. He applies some pressure as he works his fingers in small circles. The rush of pleasure instantly builds once more. Without warning, he slips a finger inside of me. The initial shock startles me and causes me to moan.

"Fuck. You're so tight."

I feel my cheeks burn as I wonder if I've done something wrong, when his lips claim mine. His tongue dips down and sweeps over my bottom lip. I inhale a sharp breath, and in response, he nibbles it.

"I love your lips."

"Really?" I moan into his mouth until he crashes his lips against mine.

With his other hand, he skims my collarbone before he dips down and cups my breast. His fingers expertly tease my nipples while he pinches them. My senses are on overload, as I feel the muscles in my stomach clench.

"Theo," I call out to him. His finger moves in and out in a steady rhythm.

I part my lips, ready to beg for mercy, but he stops me. His lips are against my own as his tongue pushes into my mouth. The pressure builds further, and I rock my hips into his hand, desperate for relief. I feel the warmth of his breath drag along my collarbone as he brushes his lips over my tender skin and then nips at it.

"Tell me you want this, Brielle."

"What?" I then moan when I feel his lips move up my neck.

"Tell me. I want to hear you say you want this. That you want me."

"I want you." I inhale a quick breath and hold it as I feel a tightening deep within my stomach. As if reading my thoughts, Theo's fingers pick up the pace, and I feel like I'm hovering at the edge of a cliff. "Theo. . ."

"That's it, baby. Come for me."

Those words are all it takes for me to lose myself. My legs start to shake as my vision goes white, and I press my eyes shut. My back arches off the cool surface of the tub. The sweet ascent of pleasure surges deep from my core.

A small smile escapes my lips, and I open my eyes to find Theo watching me. He smiles in return and then presses his lips once more against my mouth before removing his hand.

"Enjoy that?" he teases, raising his fingers to his lips and sucking them. "Fuck, I want to taste you."

I giggle, not knowing what to say, but suddenly find myself wanting to return the favor. I cut my eyes to a certain area on his pajama pants and feel a wave of energy take over when I see the large bulge staring back at me. But there's something else that catches my eye too.

It's then I notice the swatch of blood that's spreading along the corners of his bandages. William's voice, dawdling on about being careful not to pop a stitch rings in my ears.

"Theo, you're bleeding," I manage, my words still too breathy for my liking.

"It's fine, baby."

"But your doctor said. . ." My voice trails off as I sit up and take a closer look. My left hand gently holds his side as my right works to make sure he didn't tear anything. Slowly, I pull back the corners of his bandages but find the sutures are fully intact. "We need to change your bandages." I frown, looking up at him. The intensity of the moment we just shared together is deflated.

Theo sighs but doesn't argue. Rather, he stands and walks out into the bedroom. The muscles in his back tense as he moves to sit down on the bed. I turn to the sink and silently curse myself for leaving my towel so far away.

Crap.

I turn back to find Theo has his back to me. Hesitating a moment longer, I pull the plug and stand up slowly, waiting to see what he will do. After a few seconds, I hop out, and wrap a towel around myself. Then, I walk across the room to my purse and take out the small emergency kit the doctor gave me before we left.

When I have it, I pad over to where Theo is sitting on the bed and close the distance between us. The look in his eyes is incredulous as I work to change his bandage.

"You know, I could really get used to seeing you like this." A wry smile pulls at the corner of his mouth.

"Oh really? Like what?" I smile back, clipping the end of another line of tape.

I'm thankful that I actually made a point to pay attention when the doctor explained how to do this—unlike Theo, who chased his antibiotics down with a straight shot of tequila.

"Wet and touching me."

chapter twenty-two

THEO

I squeeze my eyes shut and force myself to look away. Damn it. This continuous torture of having her so close, and so wet, is fucking with my head. Did I really get away with touching her? I squint down and sneak a peek. Her blonde hair is wrapped in a fluffy bun, and her delicate fingers are skimming my burning skin.

Jesus, the things I want to do to her. I feel my cock straining against my sweats, but all I want to do is dive between my girl's thighs and taste her. Fuck, I want that so damn bad. I've never minded the act of going down on a girl before, but I've never craved the possibility as much as I do with Brielle. And when I'm done, I want her to feel me—all of me—over and over again, until she's begging for release.

Having noticed my tunnel vision, Brielle bats her eyes and looks up at me. Oh no. I know that face. I wet my lips. "Brielle, I'm fine." I choose to focus on those swollen lips of hers, imagining just how good they would feel wrapped around my cock. The chance to finally claim that feisty mouth is doing nothing to help stave off my need for more.

I inhale a deep breath and lean back. I need to cool off. If I move too fast, I could scare Brielle away. Not that I could keep her—no matter how much I want to. The truth of the matter is, she's safer away from me. Without me. Another reason why I'm pissed that Wes asked Becks to call her in the first place.

And another reason why I didn't object to Katrina coming instead. Brielle is too good to be buried under all my shit.

In one swift movement, she decides to rip the final bandage off the rest of the way. The adhesive lining grips on to my skin, mercilessly. I watch the edge of the wound pull, causing the very bottom suture to stretch and tear. Before I can even blink, a thin line of blood trails down and drips along the white sheets.

"Oh my God," Brielle gasps as she reaches for a dry washcloth and presses it to the wound. "I am so sorry. I thought it would help if I went faster. I—"

"Brielle, it's fine." I reach out to reassure her. This constant need of hers, to worry over me, still catches me off guard. "It's just a little blood."

I pull her close to me; the smell of her coconut shampoo encircles us. The feel of her hands on me are somehow turning my insides out. I smile and press my lips to her forehead. Damn it, if this girl isn't my fucking weakness.

"Should we call the doctor? Do you think he'll have to replace the stitch?" "Oh. My. God. He's going to regret sending me to come instead of Katrina, isn't he?"

I press two fingers under her chin and tilt her head up. "I'm fine. It takes a lot more than a popped suture to hurt me." I'm not lying when I tell her this. Even if it were a big deal, I'd rather bleed out than call William back.

I saw it on Brielle's face when William first arrived. She was impressed by him—and *of* him. It didn't help that he couldn't keep his fucking eyes to himself either. It took all I had not to throw his ass out. But if I did, I'd still be bleeding, sitting in my chair at the office and surrounded by a shit ton of people I care nothing about. At least William had the sense to suggest

Brielle should be the one to come home with me. If he hadn't, I would have gladly accepted more drugs.

I lock eyes with Brielle, and she parts her lips. The better part of my mind scolds me in all the reasons that I should leave before allowing this to go any farther than it already has. But, greedily, I am unable to resist the urge to be closer to her, and I press my lips against hers.

In a matter of seconds, I have her straddling me. Her legs are squeezing against the outside of my thighs as she rocks her hips against my cock.

"Fuck, Brielle," I groan and reach around to cup her ass. "If I knew how much you liked playing doctor, I would have suggested it a long time ago."

Running her fingers through my hair, she gently tugs a fistful, forcing my head back. She shifts her weight and rocks up on her knees. Those full fucking lips are teasing their way up my neck, until I can't wait any longer. I pull her down to me and groan against her lips.

I press my hands against her back and try to mold her body against my own. Fuck, I want this girl. Bad.

"Can I . . . um. . ." Fuck, this is awkward. "Can I take off your towel?" I ask, fully prepared to get a stern "hell no" and a slap to the face.

If she were any other chick, I'd rip the damn thing off, fuck her, then move on with my life. But this isn't just a random ass girl; it's Brielle. I'd rather face rejection, than ever push her into doing something she isn't ready for.

I can see the hesitation building behind her eyes, but she surprises me, yet again, when she leans back and nods.

Holy fuck! I almost jump. How the hell did I manage to get so lucky? I stumble in disbelief, but before she has the chance to change her mind, I reach for the knotted towel, covering her swollen breasts, and tug it free. My cock grows a full inch as my eyes greedily devour the length of her perfect fucking body.

I half choke, my mind temporarily seizing, when, for the life of me, I can't understand why Brielle would be interested in me at all. I feel like I've been given a gift that I didn't deserve. The girl of my dreams is finally within reach.

"Can I do something to you?" she asks. The gentle tone of her voice makes me want to do even more dirty things to her, as I lean forward and brush my lips against hers.

"Can I ask you a question first?" I hear myself say, not realizing until after I've said it, that I said anything at all.

Jesus. Don't do it, Theo, my conscience pleads. That son of a bitch I often tune out, for whatever reason, is deciding to ruin this moment for me.

"Of course." She smiles and sits back on her thighs.

Oh, fuck. . . fuck. . . fuck. . . fuck, I silently repeat, trying not to think about how close I am to being able to roll her over and taste her.

I lick my lips.

"Um, w-why did you come here?"

"What? What do you mean?" she asks, crinkling her nose in that cute way she always does when someone asks her a question that surprises her.

She tilts her head to the side and crosses her arms to cover her chest. Shit. I can already see it—that invisible wall building back up behind her eyes. *Nice going, conscious. All you had to do was shut the hell up. But no.* Damn it. Why do I feel this undeniable urge to protect this girl, even from myself?

"I know, you know what I'm talking about, Brielle," I reluctantly answer. My tone treads the harsh line of open honesty and makes me sound like a complete dick. It's not as easy as I thought it would be. "After everything that happened with Mason, why don't you hate me too?"

She immediately drops her hands to her side and rocks off my lap. I watch her fold the towel around her petite frame, then sit back down on the far edge of the bed. The distance between us hurts more than any knife wound could.

"Stop." Her voice weak.

I can't help wondering if she's about to cry.

"Stop what?"

"Why?"

I take in a deep breath. "Why what, Brielle? Talk to me."

"Why are you trying to ruin this? You always do this." I can hear the constant break in her voice, and I know that if I keep pushing, she's going to fall apart. "I thought you wanted this . . . I thought you wanted me."

"The fuck? Of course I do! I've wanted to be with you since the first time we met— that day I saw you floating on that damn flamingo inner tube in the pool. This isn't easy for me. I mean, fuck. I lo—" I pause, choosing not to finish that train of thought. Instead, I take the safe route. I decide to tell her the truth. A different truth. "It's just, I don't deserve you. I wasn't good for you then, and I sure as hell am not good for you now."

Brielle laughs, but I know better than to think she's finding any humor in what I say. No, she's pissed. Worse. She's fuming. "You're unbelievable." She turns to leave, but her feet barely have the chance to brush the floor before I reach out with my bad arm and grasp her waist.

"Answer the question, Brielle. We can't avoid this forever." I roll my eyes, feeling her try—and fail—to break away from me. The pain from holding on to her courses through my side, but I bite it back because I need to know.

"What do you want me to say, Theo? That I've felt guilty every day for what happened that night? That I wish you hadn't pushed me out of the way?" she shoots back defensively, but I expected that.

Brielle is too selfless of a person to not assume that this, in some way, is all her fault—that she was the reason Mason's killer chose to fire that gun—when in reality, that couldn't be further from the truth. She presses her hands firmly against my chest and holds them there. The intensity of her emerald eyes burn until I relinquish my hold on her.

"I want you to admit that this . . . will never work." I motion between the two of us. My heart thrums loudly in my ears as I hold my breath and wait for her to say something.

"I know." She sighs. The tears she's been holding back now slip down the sides of her cheeks, one after the other. "It's all just too confusing. I loved you, Theo. *Really* loved you. But then Mason was killed by that crazy, drug dealer at the bar, and everything changed so fast." She bites her lip. "You just left. And I was hurt for a lot of reasons but never because I blamed you. You didn't pull the trigger. I was there. You tried to stop it."

"No, but Luca is right." I finally let out the breath I've been holding for what now seems like an eternity, not willing to accept her answer. With a gentle hand, I wipe away her tears. My thumb lingers a second longer, brushing over the top of her bottom lip. "It was because of me and because of my feelings for you that blinded me from the danger of the situation."

I stare back at her as seconds quickly turn into minutes, and I wonder if it shouldn't be me who breaks the silence first. On second thought, no. I better not. I know that if I do there's a very good chance I might slip up and ask another question, which has been eating away at me ever since the first night I saw her: Does she have feelings for Luca?

This is the same question that nearly knocked me over, again, tonight, and the night of the bonfire—a hit worse than an unexpected kick to the gut during any match I've faced at K.O.

"I don't love him," she offers as if having read my mind. I stare openly at her, trying to understand why she so willingly brought it up. "I know you, Theo." She does it again. She reads my fucking mind. "I saw you watching us in the parking lot. I know you heard him."

"Oh," I say as Luca's words echo in the back of mind. "So then . . . you finally kissed him because you, what? Really care about him as a friend?"

Brielle reaches out and playfully swats at my chest. "He kissed *me,* you jerk!" She smiles, but it fades almost as quickly as it appears. "It was earlier this summer. I told him I didn't want to force any feelings, when there are none, but Luca's told me before that he thinks it's just because I'm scared."

"Scared? What would you be scared of?" I feel a slight twinge of excitement as I wait for her to respond.

"Because I've never opened up with a guy like that. At least, not since . . . you." She hesitates, looking down at my chest before lifting her hands to cover her face. "And because I'm still relatively new to a lot of things."

Jesus.

"You're a virgin?"

I watch her tilt her head to the side. The corner of her mouth slowly pull into a sly grin. "Would that be a problem if I am?" she says in a matter-of-fact tone.

Does it make me an ass if I say it would be easier if she wasn't? Because, at least if she weren't, I wouldn't feel like I was completely corrupting her. In a perfect world, I'd like to think I would be someone deserving of her. But I'm not.

"Theo?" she calls my name, leaning forward to gently push me to lie back on the bed. Her fingers softly graze the tender skin around my wounds.

"I don't know whether it's a good sign that the bleeding has stopped or if I should start to worry." She looks at me with concern.

I press my lips together to keep from grinning like a fucking idiot when I say, "Maybe it's just been diverted elsewhere for now."

"Theo Wescott, you've got enough going on to be thinking of *that* anytime soon."

I shake my head. "Eh. . . I heal fast."

Brielle drops her head and stares at her hands. Her eyes glint up at me every so often as I watch her debate on how to respond. It's a damned sight to see. Brielle has always been beautiful, but somehow over these past five years, she's graduated to so much more than that. Beautiful almost seems too simple. I shut my eyes and pause, trying not to slap myself across the face.

Fuck.

What the hell is wrong with me?

I sound like fucking Wes when he smokes too much pot—a master of contemplating even the most minute of details. I roll my eyes. At least my high school English teacher would be impressed.

I look up when I feel Brielle's fingers stop moving, and to my surprise, she's watching me. The dark green of her eyes hold my full attention as she moves to straddle my waist. Her hips slowly lower down until her body is flush with mine. Her bare sex teases my cock when I think about the fact that the only thing keeping me from filling her is the thin layer my fucking sweatpants provide.

Jesus. This girl may be innocent around everyone else, but with me she definitely likes to play with fire—something I'll gladly endure.

"Brielle, wait." I hold my breath.

My fists are clenching as I try to fight the effect she has over me. I'm losing. It's not that I don't want her because I do . . . want her. I just don't know what would happen if I lost her again.

"I need you to know," I tell her, trying to make sure I choose my words carefully, "I want to do the right thing here and take it slow. But I'm weak and, selfishly, I can't resist you." I pause and release another long breath. "So I'm leaving it up to you to tell me what to do. I could never live with myself if I hurt you."

I can feel my heartbeat pounding against my chest as I rise up on my elbows just so I can be closer to her. I let my eyes drift up to her mouth, as she sucks in her bottom lip and bites it. Her emerald eyes are daring me under thick lashes to make a move.

Damn it.

Is she teasing me?

That's not helping either, baby.

"Can I ask you a question now?" She smiles sweetly, and I nod my head. "Can I touch you?" she whispers. Her hands hover over the waistband of my sweatpants.

I can barely nod yes, while I try to wrap the idea around my mind that this is actually happening. "Y-Yes, please," I practically beg her, then roll my eyes, annoyed, when I hear how needy I sound. I clear my throat. "I mean . . . do you, um . . . do you want me to show you how?"

She answers me with a kiss as her body leans down, closing the gap between us. I push up further on my elbows, wanting more. My tongue teases the far corners of her mouth as I pull her to lie beside me.

Her hands travel down my pecs with a featherlike touch while she uses the pads of her fingers to skim the skin. I inhale a sharp breath when she curiously treads the ridges of old wounds and circles them. Damn it. *Please, don't ask.* The thought of trudging up all my buried secrets in one night is daunting.

"What happened here?"

Fuck. I half laugh. I can't seem to catch a break.

"Which one?" I ask honestly, focusing on her, waiting for the fear to build behind her eyes. For most girls—the ones like Katrina—my history is usually a turn-on. But because of who Brielle is, I wouldn't blame her if she ran away.

"Are these all from him?" she asks, her words soft, gentle, and knowing.

I cut my eyes away when it all starts to hit too close to home. I buried this shit for a reason. I want to tell her but I can't. "Some, yeah." I keep my head turned, not wanting to witness the horrified look she has to be wearing, when I'm jolted. The feel of her lips lightly pressing against my skin, catches me off guard.

I watch her with a muted sense of shock. Why the hell isn't she running?

"Brielle, are you sure about this?" I feel the need to ask again, if only just so I could hear it. Her fingers are now trailing the lines of my tattoos.

"I don't need you to protect me, Theo," she offers after a moment. "I want you. I always have. I still. . ."

Still what? I feel my heart stop.

Then finally, she says, "I still care about you, Theo."

I lean back slightly at her response while reaching a hand out to brush a long strand of her hair that has gone awry. "Trust me," I whisper. I'm more serious than I have ever been. "A girl like you needs protection."

"From who? You? Your dad?"

"Yes, Brielle, my father is fucking insane."

She pulls back and bites her lip. "Should I be scared of you, Theo? Honestly?" I hear the hidden meaning ringing behind her words.

I want to tell her no and that I'd rather die than let anything hurt her, but people who live in my father's world rarely have their happy ending. Why should I be any different? The truth is, I am the one who wrecks other people's happiness—the one my father sends in when he needs to make a point.

There it is. . . the issue that started it all. The one, we'll never agree upon, and the one, undeniable truth that will never allow us to be together. If I can't promise her safety on top of everything else, I don't deserve her.

"Yes," I say, my breath ragged and uneven. I draw in a deep breath in an attempt to steady the sudden rise of my pulse before I continue, "You should be very scared."

chapter twenty-three

I hear the light click on before I realize I'm no longer alone. "Brielle?" Theo squirms hazily as he blinks his eyes over to where I'm sitting at the kitchen bar. His hair is mussed up and his voice scratchy. *God, he's handsome.* "What are you doing awake?"

My cheeks burn when my eyes adjust, and I see that he's wearing nothing but a pair of black boxers. The hard muscles of his chest and biceps flex as he rubs a hand across his face. The labyrinth of black-inked tattoos, which cover a wide range of his upper torso, draw my attention. *You should be very scared,* his warning echoes in the back of my mind.

I press my hands against my thighs and sit up. The long, black T-shirt he gave me to sleep in is loose and hangs just above my knees, the soft, cotton twisting under me as I cross my legs under the stool.

"I. . . ugh. . . I couldn't sleep." The insomnia is probably my mind's way of trying to make sense of everything that's happened today.

I pinch a handful of my T-shirt's neckline and raise it up to my nose, breathing in the smell of his cologne. I've missed it. It's the only thing about him that hasn't changed. The strong tones of mint and newly upholstered leather. It fills me with a sense of comfort and familiarity from memories we share that feel like a lifetime ago.

"Brielle, it's three in the morning."

I toss my eyes to the side of the room. "Wow! Handsome, rude, and he tells the time too." I roll my lips over the top of each other before adding, "Lucky me."

Theo strolls to the fridge, pulling it open. His hand instinctively reaches for the milk. He shuts the fridge door and heads to a cabinet directly to the right. "Funny. Would you like anything?"

"No, thank you." I smile, raising my mug. The warm ceramic is calming my nerves. I watch him pour half a glass before capping the milk and returning it to the fridge. "Why are you up?" I ask and sip some more of my tea, thankful that he had enough sense to stock the good kind of chamomile—my favorite, Twining's.

Should I be scared? I allow myself a second to think about it all over again. But like before, I arrive at the same conclusion. It just doesn't make any sense. I know Theo; I know he would never hurt me. When I'm with him, it's like being able to breathe after drowning for so long. Even with this new side— darker and ruder—he makes me feel wanted.

He closes the fridge, ripping me from my inner thoughts, then walks around the island to join me. "I. . . ugh—" He laughs and rubs his hand against the back of his neck. "I actually couldn't sleep either. I hate where we left things."

I sigh, flipping my hair to the side. I wasn't expecting him to actually answer me.

He sets the glass down, his index finger skimming the rim. "I haven't told anyone this, not even Wes, but I came back to Elm Brook a few years ago. It was my Sophomore year at Texas Tech—I screwed up, and let my father talk me into doing something to someone who . . . who didn't deserve it. After that, I just needed to see you, even if it was only for a second, but you weren't home."

"Theo, what are you—"

He raises his hand to halt my words. "The point is that I left, and your life turned out the better for it. So it's easy for me to think that everything would be a whole hell of a lot easier if I could just walk away. But I . . . I don't think I can." He pushes a hand through his hair before he edges the glass further up the counter, twisting his stool toward me as he does. "I would never do anything to hurt you, but I can't sit here and look you in the eye and tell you that nothing will ever happen. My world is— the thought of anyone hurting you—"

"You mean because of your dad?"

"No. I mean me." He pauses. His expression is neutral. "My father is a lawless prick. But you don't know the things I've done since I left. Terrible things."

I freeze when memories of a bruised and beaten Theo, stumbling into my family's house after another fight with his dad, floods my mind. I cringe, remembering how old some of those scars were. My heart is breaking for a young, Theo who was forced to live with someone so cruel.

"Theo." My face fills with concern before I set down my mug. My hands still warm as I reach out and brush my fingers over the three small scars lining the right side of his collarbone. He shivers under my touch. "I remember these now. You got them just after that baseball game with Denton High."

I inhale a slow, deep breath, feeling the tears beginning to well up behind my eyes. I was the first one to find him— drunk and asleep, curled up outside on our trampoline. He'd been beaten and was bleeding. The image of him lying there stirs emotions I haven't felt in a very long time. "I can understand if you're concerned about your father, but I know you'd never hurt me."

Recognition flashes across Theo's face and he stills. "I can handle my dad. What I can't handle is the idea of something happening to you."

"I'm stronger than you think."

I pinch my eyes shut and start to pull my hand away. But in one, quick motion, he grabs ahold of it and laces his fingers over my wrist. My heart sinks. "W-What are you doing?" I ask when I notice he's staring at me. He licks his lips.

"Nothing, just . . . come here."

I hear the hitch in my breath, when I feel his fingers pressing into my skin as he moves his hands up the sides of my legs. The hem of the shirt I'm wearing slides up my thighs while he raises it. His hands reach down to cup my bottom.

In a matter of seconds, he lifts me onto his lap. His hands slowly move up to my waist as his thumbs rub small circles along my bare stomach. "I love your body," he whispers against my neck. His words are shaky, as I feel a part of him slowly begin to harden beneath me.

I flush and look away. How is it that Theo and I manage to go from arguing one minute to my straddling him the next?

"You do?" I mumble and lean into his kiss.

I close my eyes and give in to the feeling, when he pushes a hand into my hair and pulls my mouth back down to his. His lips close over mine, claiming me as he teases a series of playful kisses with his tongue until we're both left panting and wanting more.

I rock my hips against him and moan.

"Hold on to me, baby," he mumbles. His hands move under my butt as we slide off his stool and he stands. I wrap my arms around his neck and lean into him before he heads towards the staircase.

"Wait, Theo, what about your—"

"Kiss me." he groans, taking two steps at a time as he ascends the stairs.

We come up to his room, and I can feel his hesitation as his hands slowly release me. My body slides down the front of him. I feel his erection press into my stomach and my heart stumbles. "Are you sure about this?" He breaks away from kissing me. His voice is ragged, and a hunger burns behind his eyes.

"No. I mean, yes." A smile plays along my lips. "I mean, I want you. But I . . . maybe we should—"

I giggle when all of a sudden, Theo opens the door, scooping me into his arms and carrying me into the room.

"Welcome back." He chuckles as we fall onto his bed. My legs wrapping around his waist as I pull him to me. He presses against me, and I feel the muscles in my stomach clench.

He knots his fingers in the base of my shirt and moans. The feeling of his boxers' soft fabric rubbing against my body is heavenly, causing me to arch my back.

"Lift your arms, baby. I want to see you."

I nod and sit up, raising my arms above my head. Without any hesitation, Theo grips the bottom of the shirt and removes it. "Fuck, Brielle." He inhales a sharp breath, sucking his bottom lip as his eyes hungrily wander over my body while I lie sprawled out in nothing but a thong. "You're going to be the death of me."

I blush, feeling my cheeks heat to an uncomfortable degree. My heart is racing as I stare up at him. I love the way

Theo sees me. It somehow makes knowing that he's been with other women a little easier to swallow.

"Wh- what happens next?"

With his knee, Theo edges my legs apart. His hands travel up my waist. "Well, at the moment, I'd like to keep kissing you." He flashes a wide grin.

"And after?"

I gasp when I feel his teeth graze over my collarbone. "And after that, I think we should *both* try to get some sleep."

Wait. What?

"So, you . . . I mean, we. . . we're not going to—"

Theo brings his mouth to mine and kisses me. He waits for permission before he deepens the kiss, his fingers smoothing their way up to cup my breast. "I have five years to make up for. But all of that can wait until you're ready."

chapter twenty-four

BRIELLE

I wake up to the sun in my face and Theo's arms draped across my waist. Squinting in the direction of the light, I find that the curtains have been drawn back, revealing a beautiful floor-to-ceiling window overlooking the pond and gardens. *A view to buy a house for,* I remember Theo's story from last night. The thought slightly taints this moment as I think about how hard it must have been for the previous owner's wife.

I know from experience how hard it is to be cheated on. I can't even imagine how hard it would have been to watch the affair going on and not be able to do anything about it. She deserved better.

Theo squirms when I sit up and scoot off the bed, but he doesn't wake up. My toes brush the carpet, and I'm thankful that the bedrooms are the only places that don't have hardwood floors—something I found out last night before I ended up in the kitchen.

I move to the window to get a closer look, sucking in a sharp breath as I sweep my eyes over the landscape. The gorgeous trees and rolling hills beyond the gardens make for an incredible sight. But it doesn't take long before a large farmhouse-styled table catches my eye; the far end of it is set up for two. Delicate looking ivory plates with navy chargers, hand-rolled linen napkins, and silver-lined cups adorn the table. It's extravagant, sure, but beautifully arranged.

I roll my eyes at the lifestyle Theo lives, which I never knew about. I cut my eyes over to him in bed, and as always, I notice his tousled hair. I mean, I know his family is from old money. But still. This is . . . unexpected. No wonder Katrina is so obsessed with him. This looks like the type of luxury she's used to having and raised to expect.

I notice the huge selection of breakfast choices neatly arranged along the center of the table and my stomach growls. My mind is already planning what I'm going to devour first, when Theo's phone buzzes to life on the nightstand. I quickly pad over to it and silence it. After everything he went through yesterday, he deserves to sleep in a little longer.

I sit down on the bed, my fingers clutching his phone, when I think about all the things in Theo's life that I don't understand. All those other scars he bears—most of them, in some way, because of his father. It's no wonder he's so guarded.

I turn my head to the side and stare down at his knuckles; the light spray of bruising and the harsh, jagged lines where his skin tore looks irritated. "I need answers," I whisper, waiting for a response that will never come. I curl my hand around the other. "I still love you."

Theo straightens out, and I fear he's heard me, but his soft snores set my mind at ease. *Oh shoot!* I mentally say, when the sheet is tugged down and I can see his bandage is bloody. It's not enough to be alarming, but I hate seeing it at all. This is all my fault. He's hurt right now because of me. I cringe, thinking back to everything that he's done, which I should have known better than to let him—like carrying me when I have two perfectly good feet. But that's the problem with us. When we're together, we forget ourselves.

I cut my eyes to the bedroom door and decide I should grab the medical kit. Standing up, I walk toward the door. My fingers brush the cool metal of the doorknob, when I hear rustling on the bed. Theo wakes up, groaning, and slowly slides up to sit back against the headboard. "Are you running out on me?" He laughs, shaking his head.

"No." I smile, seeing that playful grin stretching along his lips. My body is already moving toward him, before I even realize I've turned around. "I was just going to grab my clothes. I figured your T-shirt probably isn't the most appropriate attire for breakfast with his majesty," I tease. My fingers pulling at the bottom of my shirt.

Theo tilts his head and rolls his eyes. "I think I'm missing something here." He shakes his head again. "But if you're saying that you want to be my queen . . ."

"I'm also going to grab the medical kit. You're bleeding." My index finger points to the bandages along his side, red-soaked and loose. "You shouldn't have carried me last night; you probably tore something."

"But I gained so much more." He laughs. He reaches out to me. "Come here," He pauses, leaning forward to grab me by my hips and pull me to him. My legs encircle his torso as I settle on top of his lap. "Proper breakfast attire, huh? I can help you with that because, in my opinion, you're definitely wearing far too much."

I let my head fall back as Theo begins kissing my neck. His lips trail my jaw as his hand pushes into my hair and grabs a handful.

"Mm," I moan, feeling the length of him rubbing me. "My mistake."

What was I worried about?

Smoothing his one hand up my back, he loops the other around my waist, forcing my body to rock against him. I lean down, needing his lips on mine. Our hips move together until we're both panting.

So, this is the perks of morning wood?

My stomach clenches at the thought of last night. My need for this man surprises me as I reach down and press my hand against him. My fingers are already skimming the waistband of his boxers, when he reluctantly grips my hand and stops me.

"As much as I want *this* to continue," he whispers, "and fuck, do I want this. Eliza, my. . . er. . . well, I don't really know what she is—my housekeeper? I guess? She's like family, and if we don't go down soon, she will come up here."

Theo has a housekeeper?

I purse my lips as I wrap my arms around his neck. The tips of my fingers dig into his shoulders.

"Brielle," he breathes against my lips, while I tease him, pressing my center against his erection. He's trying but failing to put up a fight.

I look down at him and whine.

Did I just seriously whine?

Hooking my fingers in the neckline of my shirt, I pull it over my head and toss it to the floor. Theo's eyes grow wide, and he licks his lips. That spark behind his eyes is now blazing.

"Fuck it." I feel his arms lace around my waist as he twists me around. I hit the mattress, my hair billowing around me. Theo chuckles, smoothing my hair back before his lips part. I can feel his heartbeat pounding against my chest. "Do you trust me?"

I nod, fully aware of how out of character I'm behaving, when he uses his knee to spread my legs apart. I weave my fingers through the top of his hair as he licks and sucks my skin until he settles himself between my legs. He pauses seeing my little, black thong, but it doesn't stop him for long. My back arches the instant I feel his tongue loop around the thong's base, then he takes it in his mouth and pulls it down and out of the way.

"Theo!" A voice shouts from outside the bedroom.

Who the? "Oh crap," I whisper, hearing footsteps stop just outside the door. He really wasn't joking about her coming up here to get us.

"Don't make me come in there!" The voice calls again.

"That's Eliza." Theo rolls his eyes. "Yeah, we're coming!"

I bite my lip and squeeze my legs shut. Oh God. . . did she hear us? Did she hear me? Theo rocks off the bed to grab his shirt for me to put on. "You'd better get dressed. She really will come in."

I barely have time to slip the shirt over my head before the door handle sounds and a short Latino woman, with chocolate-brown eyes and blackish-silver hair, barges in the room.

"Jesus, Eliza. A little privacy please!" Theo barks, but the woman pays him no mind.

"Oh hush, and put some pants on." She waves her hand at him before adding, "And for the love of God, tuck that thing. The breakfast table is no place for that." Shaking her head, her eyes fall to me after he disappears into the closet.

I cross my arms in front of me, hugging myself. Thankfully, whatever sexual build-up I was feeling died the minute she pushed through those doors. I raise my hand when she continues to stare openly at me. "Hello." I smile weakly. My stomach ties up into knots. I feel sick. "I'm sorry . . . if you,

you know. . . if you heard—"

"Oh honey, it's nothing I haven't heard before." Eliza shakes her head.

Um, okay? Thank you?

Walking further into the room, she starts making the bed—even with me still in it! "Although, you are the first one to ever make it to breakfast—sleepovers aren't usually *his* thing."

Stepping off the bed as she rounds my side, I watch as she flips the comforter into place and smooths it down. Is this what a walk of shame feels like? We didn't even do anything. . .

"You'd better find your clothes, dear." Eliza smiles before heading toward the door. "We've got company."

Company? There are other people here?

Eliza opens the door and steps out into the hall as Theo pushes his way past her and into the room.

"Hold up, did you say company?" he asks, moving to stand in front of me when he can see how uncomfortable I am. His upper lip is pulled back into a scowl. "Who the fuck would show up at this time? Is it—"

I watch as Eliza rocks back on her heels, closing her eyes as she inhales a quick breath. I can read her anxiety from here. Whoever's here is bad news.

"It's your dad, Theo." Eliza drops her head, her finger moving to scratch, her brow. "And he's not alone."

Ah crap. Mr. Wescott. Here? Now? I look down at Theo's T-shirt and cross my legs.

"Yeah, so you two had better pick up the pace." She shakes her finger at Theo and me. "Whatever he's got going on, he's out to kill. Oh, and I hope you like waffles, dear. Chef Travis made enough to feed a small army."

chapter twenty-five

W hat the fuck is this asshole doing in my house? I watch his hands press softly against Brielle's lower back. His eyes hold mine as he leans down to whisper something in her ear. Jesus, he's such a prick. He's lucky I don't beat his ass just for showing up at my house in the first place. Now he's trying to put on an act and touch my girl. I don't think so.

"Did you need something?" I ask, reaching out to take Brielle's hand and guiding her to stand behind me. I set my jaw when I watch my father's eyes linger.

"Oh, yes, Son." He smiles, tossing his eyes, suddenly bored with this game of cat and mouse. That sadistic fucking grin he's choosing to wear wraps from ear to ear. "I'll let you escort the lovely Brielle to the table and then I'll meet you in the study. It was nice to see you, my dear. You've grown up to become such a beautiful woman. Your brother, Mason, would have been proud."

Damn it. He just couldn't help himself, throwing Mason into the pot to let that hang over her head while I'm away. First Luca, and now my father. This girl's going to make a run for it; I just know it. I would. There's a limit to the amount of doubt one person can take, and lately, we've had a lot thrown at us.

Minutes later, I push through my office doors and prepare myself for a fight.

"Ah! So nice of you to join me, Son." I hear the asshole's voice the second the doors slam shut behind me. "I like what you've done with the—"

"The fuck is this? I made it clear when I moved back that you're not welcome here!" I yell, silently cursing that Brielle wouldn't let me leave until I agreed for her to change my bandage. Who knows what he's helped himself to while I've been gone?

He raises his hand to silence me, and out of habit, I shut my mouth. It's a bad habit and one that I am working to get over. *You don't scare me anymore,* my mind fumes.

I pause and take a breath as memories flood my mind. Images of him looming over me with his belt. . . a boot. . . my mother's antique hand-sculpted vase. Hell. Anything he could grab—at least, before he gave up and started using his bare hands. He would look at me and see his own personal demons—whatever it was that week. Such a pathetic, poor excuse for a father. A child abuser.

After everything he did—to me and my mother—he's as good as garbage in my eyes. But I'm not an idiot. The man's a monster. A monster with an army. Thankfully, with knowledge, comes experience, and if you spend enough time in hell, you learn a thing or two about how the devil operates.

I touch the three tiny scars and remember the night Brielle found me. She didn't ask questions or pry. She just sat down next to me and started telling me about some stupid guy named Damon from one of her shows. The guy sounded like a complete dick, and I didn't see the point of her story, but I didn't have the heart to tell her that vampires were the last thing on my mind. So, I let her carry on. Plus I liked the sound of her voice. It was comfort enough.

"Excuse me?" My father exclaims, ripping me from my inner ramblings. His voice is hinged as he slowly sets down his phone.

The pain meds I took while getting dressed are starting to take effect. I didn't want to tell Brielle but she was right. I shouldn't have picked her up last night. I just couldn't help it. There's just something about that girl that triggers me. She's like my own personal drug. The longer I'm around her, the worse it gets. But fuck it if she wasn't worth the pain.

Like always, it seems my father has made himself at home, rummaging through my things, sitting at my desk. He gives me a quick once-over, his eyes growing ever so slightly before he spins around in the chair to face the window. The gardens, the pond, and my girl are in full view.

"I am ashamed of you, boy. Mason Sutton's sister? I thought I taught you better than this," he growls. The veins in the side of his neck threaten to pop. "But here you are, acting like a child and risking my legacy—all for a stroll down memory lane."

I turn my head and look out the window at Brielle. Even from here, I can tell she's stressed, pushing her food around her plate, when she would normally be going back for more. "Brielle has nothing to do with this." I raise my voice, my tone surprising even me.

My father cuts his eyes in my direction and adjusts himself in the seat. Normally, I don't like to risk triggering him, but I feel the undeniable urge to protect her.

He rolls his eyes.

I knew all that earlier shit with Brielle was just for show. My father hates her and her family. It's because of them that people really started to shine a light on what was happening in our small town. Rumors landed into the ears of those willing to listen. Too bad my father is a master at playing the innocent one.

"Oh, but she does," he continues. Tossing down the wadded piece of paper he's holding, he stands to face me. My poor chair reflexively spins around until it settles in its natural state. "That little bitch is obviously toying with your mind, making you weak. You should be helping me seal the deal with Mr. Overshire, yet here you are chasing pussy and having breakfast."

I take a step toward him and try to talk at a slower pace. I want to make sure he hears me clearly. "I suggest you tread carefully, Father."

For a split second, I watch that iron-clad exterior of his weaken. The man behind the façade is finally realizing that I'm no longer a child he can easily manipulate.

He steps around the chair and pushes it out of the way. "Oh." He chuckles. "Don't tell me you've fallen for her?" His voice is eerily calm as he leans across the desk and grabs the paperweight. My eyes are laser-focused on the solid, aluminum piece as he tosses is back and forth between his hands.

Fuck. I grit my teeth and dig my feet into the floor, preparing myself for what's to come.

"That would be hard, considering you know I don't date," I say, knowing that my father is baiting me. If I'd said yes, it would be another reason he'd use to back up his choice to have her handled. I refuse to allow him to hurt her.

It's then my father rears back and launches the paperweight. Luckily for me, his aim is true, and he skims my arm. Nothing truly visible. Nothing permanent. I know him well enough now to recognize his methods of proving a point—the point being that he's bigger, stronger, and smarter than I am, and that he's the one in control. But that's no longer the case anymore. And he not only knows it, he's threatened by it.

The first initial impact feels more like a paper cut as it slices at my exposed skin. I can feel the warmth of my blood while thin lines streak down my arm and drip from my hand. But I don't move. I don't even breathe. Like most predators, if he smells fear, he'll attack, and I refuse to take that chance with Brielle just outside. I may be able to handle my father, but it's the ones I can't see that pose the most threat. My father never goes anywhere alone.

I watch him openly with disgust as he clenches his jaw, smooths his hair back, and collects himself. Sick bastard. He's the only person I know who gets off on inflicting pain.

"Look, the choice is simple. If you want to keep that perfect, little piece whole, then end it. Now." He straightens his tie. "Us Wescotts aren't bred for relationships." He walks up to me and places a hand on my shoulder, his thumb driving into my fresh cut as he leans over to whisper in my ear. "You can play hero all you want, boy, but I know you." He smiles grimly. "You're just like me."

No, you're wrong, I want to say. But I know that would be a lie. Deep down, I can feel it. It starts out as an itch—a need to take control. Every time I throw a punch, win a match, or pick a fight. I feel the adrenaline rush—that high. It's addicting. I may not be as bad as him, but it's imprinted in my DNA.

But does that make me the same as my father?

The idea that there could be a chance pisses me off more than anything. He withdraws his thumb and moves to stand on my other side. "This lifestyle. . . it isn't for the weak, and that girl of yours is going to get you killed. She's a fucking weed. A weakness."

He shoves me forward at the same time that his leg comes up to knee me in the gut. I fall to my knees. He waits for me to stand up before he walks to the door. As I do, my sides are screaming in pain. I watch him open the door. His free hand brushes down the sleek material of his suit and then he grabs his jacket from the stand.

"Call Katrina. I don't care what you have to promise, but you will bring her to the ball."

"And if I don't?" I manage to steady myself long enough to add, "If I'm done?"

"Well, I would hate to see any other harm come to the Sutton family." His tone is placid. His face, emotionless. "I'll see you next week, Son. If you haven't asked her by then, well, I think you're smart enough to know what will happen."

Moments later, I'm looking out the window, watching my father drive off. His men are in tow. Fucking Katrina. She must have whined to her "daddy." Of course he came here. He would never let anything threaten his business or his money.

I push a hand through my hair and pinch the back of my neck. Something tells me that Brielle wouldn't be up for the kind of relief I'm used to seeking out after a run-in with my father. And I don't want to push her when she's not ready. But damn it. What the hell am I going to do now?

As much as I don't want to admit it, I'm falling for Brielle. That is, if I ever even stopped at all, and I know she feels the same. She hasn't told me yet, but I can see it in the way she looks at me. It's the same way I imagine I look at her. I can't turn my back on her, again. I would lose her forever. But can I really jeopardize her life because of my own selfishness?

"There you are."

I feel my tension fade at the sound of her voice. Brielle's gentle tone and those innocent fucking eyes draw me into her, as I turn and watch her walk through the back doors.

I pull her into my arms and kiss her forehead the second she's close enough. My mind is spinning as I try to decide what to do.

"Your father seemed to be in a good mood today." She pulls her chin up to rest it on my sternum. Her emerald eyes looking up at me. "He seemed changed, in a way. Maybe he's trying to make an effort?"

I mentally roll my eyes. If only she knew. My father is the fucking devil.

I lean down and brush my lips against hers, needing the distraction, which she happily delivers. "Can we not talk about my father?" I whisper against her lips. My inhibitions are already fading the longer I'm next to her. I hear her answer in the form of a moan, as she pushes up on her tiptoes to wrap her slender arms around my neck. Her lips part, and I dip my tongue into her mouth, deepening the kiss.

The tiny voice that is my inner mind scolds me in all the ways I should stop. I can't acknowledge that asshole just yet. I've been down this path before, and I know what my father's capable of. The threat is real. But the decision looming over my head to walk away or go to war with my father for the chance to be with her is one I refuse to accept just yet.

chapter twenty-six

BRIELLE

H ey, slow down. You're hurt remember?" I laugh weakly, lifting up on my toes to plant another soft kiss against his lips. I close my eyes and lean into him. "Are you ready for breakfast now?"

Theo runs his hands down my arms and squeezes them. "I was actually thinking about skipping breakfast." He lowers his head. His mouth folds over mine as he sucks in my bottom lip, softly biting it. "What I want isn't on the menu."

Out of the corner of my eye, I watch Eliza disappear around the corner. "Shh," I playfully swat his arm. A slow flutter comes to life in my stomach as I see that spark building behind his eyes. "She'll hear you."

"So?" He arches his brow. His lips curl into that handsome smile I've always loved. "All I want is you, babe. What are you doing today?"

He presses me against the half wall between the kitchen and the dining room. His hand comes up to cup my chin as he crashes his lips against mine. He uses his knee to maneuver his way between my legs. This new appetite he's drummed up makes me wonder if there isn't something more driving him— like a fight with his father. . .

I hear him groan when I pull away, but he redirects his efforts. His mouth moves to my neck. "Hey," I moan and lean into his lips. "Is everything all right?"

Theo laughs and pulls back. I'm thankful for the moment to clear my head. In an attempt to steady myself, I press my head against his chest, waiting for him to answer me when my eyes catch the slight red tint of something wet on the back of my hand. What the hell?

"Theo, are you . . . you're bleeding?" I yell when I realize that it's blood.

I can feel my mind spiraling into full panic mode when I push up his sleeve and find a gash stretching along his bicep.

"It's nothing." He shrugs me off gently and moves toward the kitchen sink. He turns on the water, slapping handfuls over the open wound. "Just drop it, Brielle. I mean it."

Excuse me?

I must have heard him wrong.

"Theo, please," I beg him, trying to tread softly as I make my way over to the sink. I reach out to touch his arm.

"Fuck, I said drop it!" He flinches away from me.

I drop my hand. "Fine."

He hits the water off.

I turn around and begin walking toward the stairs. "I'd better go. I forgot it's Monday; I've got class in an hour."

"Brielle, wait!" I hear him call after me.

Like an idiot, I pause, hoping that he'll offer to tell me the truth of what's bothering him if I stay. Instead, I get, "I'm sorry. Just. . . ugh . . . just drive safe, okay?"

I nod my head and walk out of the room. Is this how being with Theo is? A slave to his mood swings? I quickly change and grab the rest of my things before I head downstairs. I see Theo waiting for me by the door.

"I. . . um . . . I called Hector to drive you since you don't have a car here."

I nod my head and step around him. I wish it were him giving me the ride. At least then I might be able to coax whatever the hell is wrong out of him. I grab the door handle before Theo reaches out and stops me.

"I wish I could tell you, and, eventually, I will. I just need to sort it all out first."

I take in a deep breath. "What could be so horrible that you can't tell me now?" I shake my head. My voice is even and steady as I stare straight into his eyes.

He blinks away. "I'll text you."

"You know, the last time you said that to me, I didn't see you for five years." I let out a breath. I press the handle down and open the door. Hector and the car are waiting just outside for me. I step outside. "Whatever it is, it looks to me like you've already made up your mind about it."

"Hey! This isn't easy for me, Brielle."

I keep walking because I know that if I stop, I might break down.

"Do what you want, Theo. But if you're planning on leaving again, at least have the decency to say goodbye this time."

I reach the car as Hector opens the door. I take my seat and buckle myself in, turning at the last second to say, "Just don't expect me to be waiting around the next time you decide to come back."

Two days have gone by, and I still haven't heard a word from Theo. I'd like to say that I'm surprised, but I should have expected it. He's always been this way with the girls he messes around with. I just didn't think he would ever do it to me.

"Hey, girl!" Becks's voice explodes over the speakers of my tiny car. I reach up and turn her down. I should have waited until I was on campus. Becks isn't someone I normally trust to put on speaker, but I'm desperate to talk to her about what's been going on. The last few nights she's stayed at Wes's.

"Hey." I sigh and sag against my steering wheel. My head rolls along its leather lining as I wait for the stoplight to turn green.

"Uh oh. What happened?" She immediately goes on the defense. "Did Theo—"

"No. It's nothing, really. Just—"

"Oh. My. God. Shut up!" I cover my ears and crack the windows. Her voice is not ideal for small spaces. "You didn't, you slut!"

Oh, good Lord. Here we go. I turn to my side and get a vicious scowl from a soccer mom in a minivan. I mouth a "sorry" to her and roll up the windows. Never in my life have I needed a light to turn green more than I do right now.

"Becks, please—"

"No, bitch! Don't you dare rob me of this moment. Spill."

"Spill?"

"Oh, don't play dumb." I can mentally see her waving me off just by the rise in her tone. "I'm so proud that I could scream. My little Bree finally lost her v-card."

Oh God. "Becks."

"He better have made it special too."

"Special?"

"Yes, Brielle! Losing your virginity is a big deal. How was it? Is he big? Tell me he rocked your little virgin socks off."

"Becks, you're on speaker. And I can't tell you that."

"I swear, Brielle, there is such a thing as being too innocent, you know?" I hear her voice drop. "I get that you're shy with this stuff, but you can't call me, drop the big news, and then rob me of the details. I deserve to know."

"We didn't have sex!"

"Oh," she says and groans over the phone. "Well at least, tell me you did something other than waste the night alone, sitting around with him. That man is sex on a stick."

"Well, he might of . . . I mean, there was a moment when he . . ." I'm hesitant to say the words aloud, not because I'm embarrassed but because it makes what I feel for him all the more real. And if there won't be anything between Theo and me, then I can't allow myself to go there again. "It's complicated."

There's a moment of silence. "God, you're so vanilla." Her tone picks up again.

"Thanks." I laugh unable to hide my smile.

Another short pause.

"Oh shit." Her voice drops another level. "Luca is going to be pissed."

Luca? My mind stumbles to hold on to the name. The image of his face the last time we were together instantly comes to mind. He hasn't been to our class the past two days, so I've completely forgotten about the fight we had. I gently tap my head against the steering wheel as the light turns green.

"Luca and I are friends, Becks," I decide to say, my mind working up an excuse to justify what I did. "Plus, what he said was pretty out of line."

"True, but he doesn't see it that way. He loves you."

I roll my eyes and remember how upset he was back in the parking lot. I'd never seen him raise his voice like that. And his going after Becks was a whole new side of him that I didn't like. I know I have to talk to him, and soon, but I'm afraid of what he might say. "Oh God! You're right."

"He'll get over it, Bree. You can't blame yourself for succumbing to a moment of weakness. Theo is fucking hot; it's normal."

    I flip on my blinker after I pass Spring creek Boulevard, and turn onto College Drive. I wait another minute for a car to pass before I pull into the campus parking lot. "It wasn't just a moment of weakness, Becks," I say as I pull into a parking spot. My fingers twist the key as I hurry to collect my books. "I. . . ugh . . . I'm pretty sure I still love him."

chapter twenty-seven

I clutch the phone to my ear and step out of the car, waiting for Becks to say something. Anything. I can't stand the silence anymore. "Becks? Did you hear me?"

"Oh, I heard you. I'm just waiting for you to admit that this is some kind of sick joke."

I take a second and sweep my eyes around the parking lot. "Look, I know what you're going to say."

"That you're being ridiculous, letting your new fuck-buddy mess with your brain?"

I knit my brows at her word choice and crinkle my nose. "Well, okay, I guess I didn't know what you were going to say," I continue, trying not to let her opinion affect me too much. "But it's not like that; I'm serious. It's like I never stopped loving—"

"Bullshit," Becks snaps. Her annoyance and disapproval ring loud and clear. I turn the corner of the corridor after I push my way inside, and hover along the side, mouth slack as I wait for her to continue. "Brielle, we've been here before." She pauses before saying, "Please correct me if I'm wrong. I mean, has he even reached out to you since you left, what, two days ago?"

"No."

Pause.

"For fuck's sake, Brielle," she whines after a minute. "Congratulations! You're his new Katrina."

"No. Theo wouldn't do that." I feel myself spinning out of control with every word she says. Is she right? Did Theo use me?

"Maybe not the old Theo, but what do you really know about him now?" she continues. Her voice is heavy as if she knows something but is choosing not to tell me.

I think back to Monday morning and to how fast everything went to hell after his father arrived. I wish he would have trusted me enough to tell me what was going on. I wish he would stop treating me like the child he feels he has to protect. God, if Becks is right, then I must look so pathetic to him. I didn't even put up a fight.

Every time I let myself believe that we're finally at a good place, or at least on the same page, he does something like this. I should have read the signs.

"Becks, if you're trying to tell me something, then just say it."

The line goes silent to the point where I'm wondering if she's even still on the phone. I glance at the clock and see that I'm about to be late for class. The tiny butterflies stirring in my stomach begin to make me sick, just thinking about it. "Becks?"

"Oh fine. Fine! But if I tell you, then you can't tell anyone."

I pause, letting her words sink in as I try to wrap my head around what the hell she could possibly have to say. I nod before I remember that she isn't here to see it. "Okay, I won't. Just tell me."

"So it's nothing too bad. Well, I mean it is, but—"
"Becks!"

"Sorry." She catches herself. "I just don't know an easy way to say this."

I suck in a deep breath and hold it as the suspense slowly begins chipping away at my heart.

"Wes told me that Theo's caught up in some pretty fucked-up shit. It started around the time he began working for his dad, and apparently, he's been forced to do some pretty dark things."

"What? What does that even mean?"

"Exactly. I don't really know. Wes was pretty high when he told me, but he seemed genuinely spooked. That was all I could get out of him though, before it all turned into purple elephants and all-seeing turtles. I don't know. It got weird. Whatever it is, people fear him for it. They call him The Grim Reaper."

The Grim Reaper? I silently repeat to myself. Whatever the name means, it doesn't just sound bad, it also sounds illegal. Has Theo killed people?

"This is all just a lot to take in at once." I shrug my shoulders, my resolve wearing thin. "I. . . ugh. . . I better let you go. I can't be late for class."

"Yeah, okay. I'll see you tonight, Brielle."

"See you."

I hang up the phone and hurry down the hall. My mind refuses to acknowledge or accept anything until I speak with Theo—whenever that may be. I need answers, but I want to hear them from him. With a name like the Grim Reaper, I can only think the worst. His father is a monster, and I know that Theo carried a lot of guilt after Mason passed. But I can't imagine that he would fall so far as to possibly hurt others. He's still Theo. At least, I don't think he would. . .

My class ends a few minutes early. Now all I want to do is head home and try to wrap my head around the idea of Theo being his father's lap dog. I push the exit door open and quickly

spot my car, my little Chevy Sonic—turbo, I might add. I pick
up my pace. "Home is only a short fifteen minutes away," I tell
myself, feeling my shoulders already starting to relax. But my
brain is on overdrive.

I squint against the fading sun when I see an all-black
motorcycle pull into the spot next to mine. The rider is dressed
in a simple white T-shirt and jeans. I let my eyes skim the
length of him when I notice his tires are blatantly over the line.

Crap. Getting into my car is now going to be extremely
difficult with all of my books. What the hell is this guy doing?
He's just sitting there, watching me. I pause halfway and sweep
my eyes around the empty parking lot. Should I head back
inside? Call Theo? Luca?

Another minute passes with the two of us doing nothing
but eyeing the other from afar. Screw it, I decide and continue
making my way to my car. Maybe I'll swing my door open and
bump his bike. That would teach him to park over the line. Or
maybe I could just ask him to scoot over? My subconscious
rears to life as usual, and I roll my eyes.

I'm maybe a hundred feet away, when the rider swings
his leg over the side of his bike and pulls his helmet off. What
the . . . Theo?

"You have a motorcycle?"

He pushes his hand through his disheveled waves and
sets his helmet down to hang from his handlebar. "What? I told
you I would get one."

"Yeah, but, that was years ago." I want to laugh.
Memories of Mason and him playing Grand Theft Auto and the
two of them arguing about starting a biker gang, like The Sons
of Anarchy, invade my mind. I mentally toss my eyes at the
idea. It sounded as stupid then as it does now. "When did you
buy it?"

"About a year after I left."

He remains silent as his eyes follow the length of my body, before he lifts them to meet mine. His steely gaze penetrates my thoughts.

Oh, no you don't.

I smile when I know what he must be thinking. Wait. Did he come here to say goodbye?

As if reading my mind, he takes a step toward me. His hand reaches out, but I swat it away. "Brielle, just listen—"

"Save it." I close my eyes. I can't believe he's doing this again. "You're leaving, aren't you?"

"What? No." He drops his hand. "I'm not leaving; I just came here to talk."

"Talk?" I tilt my head up at him. My eyes search his features for any trace that he's lying. But there is none. "Okay, then talk. What are we doing here?" I finally ask the question I've been wondering since before everything happened.

Theo's smile drops, but he doesn't miss a beat. Instead, he leans forward to snatch my wrist, pulling me to him as he wraps his arms tightly around my waist. "Come with me," he says. His voice is barely above a whisper. "I want to show you something."

My eyes flint down at the already scabbed wound lining his bicep. I shake my head. "I can't. I'm sorry." I shrug out of his arms. My body moves to the passenger side of my car. My feet take two steps at a time. I open the door, but Theo is right behind me.

"What do you mean you can't, Brielle?"

"I mean," I begin, watching Theo shut my door after I barely manage to throw my books into the seat. His tall, muscular frame pins me to the door so that I can't walk away from him. I turn my head toward the emptying parking lot. "I can't go with you. I have to get home."

"Is this because I wouldn't tell you about my arm?"

"No." I press my lips into a thin line. "Well, sort of. But it's also about some other things."

"What other things?"

"Theo . . ." I reach up to gently push him away. I need the distance so that I can think, but it's like pressing against the stone wall at the Drop-Off. It's no use; he doesn't move.

"What other things, Brielle?"

"Just . . . things, Theo. About you, your past. And your father and the work you do for him. I mean, what happened when you left here? Who are you? Are you a criminal, or something? Where did you go?"

I half expected him to walk away, but he is unnervingly calm. He opens his mouth, then shuts it. His eyes shift back and forth between my own, searching for something. "If I promise to answer you, will you come with me?"

I stare up into those hazel eyes and feel my pulse begin to race. I nod. Crap, I am pathetic. Why can I never say no to him?

Theo takes my hand and leads me over to his bike. My mind is reeling with all the reasons I should object, but I'm choosing to ignore them. The truth is, I secretly love the idea of Theo having a bike. Of course I don't love the risks that come along with it. But in a way, it makes sense. It's wild like him. Rough, complex, and dangerous.

Dangerous?

Where the hell did that come from?

I watch Theo swing his leg around the side of the bike and take a seat. "You coming, babe?"

I offer him a small smile and climb on behind him. He turns the key, and the motor roars to life, causing the entire bike to vibrate beneath me. "Don't get too excited." He laughs, watching my face through the side mirror. "I might just get jealous."

My arms tighten around his waist. "Just go before I change my mind."

chapter twenty-eight

I watch Theo stumble with a set of keys as I hop around beside his bike, trying to keep warm. The cool, matte, black finish glints under the early moon's light.

When did it get so cold?

I shudder, suddenly annoyed with myself for a number of reasons. The first being that I'm usually a lot better prepared than this. I should have known better than to wear a T-shirt and shorts in October, when the nights can get cold.

"Come on, you'll be warm inside," Theo says the second the door clicks open.

I quickly hurry in after he pushes the door open wider for me to go on ahead of him. The area inside is pitch-black.

"Theo," I call out when the door slams shut.

"Shit. Sorry. One second!" He chuckles from a distance. The playful tone to his voice, makes me want to smile until I hear him slam into something hard. "Fuck."

"You okay?" I bite back a laugh, the lights flickering on the moment I round a small hall.

What the hell?

I squint my eyes.

My hand rises to cover the top of my face as I'm blinded by the stark-white walls etched with thinly painted navy-and-red stripes. Rows of baseball bats, hats, and miscellaneous Texas Rangers memorabilia line the outer walls. I drop my hand. From the outside, the place looks abandoned. Bars on the windows and smashed out security lights. Where are we?

"So, this is what you wanted to show me?" I sweep my eyes around the large space, picking apart tiny details I use as clues, while trying to understand why of all places Theo chose to bring me here.

From the corner of my eye, I watch Theo immediately walk behind a counter that's set in the center of the room. His eyes scanning the variety of bat racks hanging up behind a glass case, where a wide assortment of baseball cards sit completely untouched. I skim my finger atop the closest table and find, like everything else here, it's heavily coated in a thick layer of dust.

"How are you at hitting?" he asks.

My head whips around to face him. "What?"

"Hitting? How are you at swinging a, ugh, screw it. Truth?"

I nod, utterly confused why, of all places, he brought me here.

"The truth is, I hate the way things went down last weekend. It was supposed to be a time spent remembering Mason, and instead, I let my jealousy get the best of me."

I watch him grab a pair of helmets and two bats from the racks. His eyes search underneath of the counter. "Ah." He sighs in relief, bending down to grab a bucket full of gold coins. Each one, only slightly bigger than a quarter. He sets it down on the counter. His hazel eyes lock with mine as he leans over the top, and motions for me to go to him.

"So, naturally, your first thought is to bring me here?" I smile, looking up at him. My hands reach out to snatch the purple bat off the counter, as I step away and take a practice swing. "To answer your question: very good. Mason used to practice pitching on my parents and me." I can't hide the smile I have thinking about my brother. "He always did love playing."

Theo walks around the counter and steps in front of me. He reaches out to take the bat, as he sets it back on the counter. The glass panels of the display case are rattling worse than nails on a chalkboard.

"This place meant a lot to him . . . and me. It was our secret hideout when everything else went to shit. But when the owner filed for bankruptcy, I bought it. Eventually, I hope to see it restored. It may not look like much, but until then, it's all mine."

And he chose me to share it with? I swallow hard. My cheeks heat instantly, and I know he notices. "I've never heard about this place before." I clear my throat, trying to collect myself. The idea of crying when I still need so many answers is not an option I can afford.

Theo bites down on his bottom lip. His rich green eyes hold mine, and I watch the tension build before whatever barrier he has, caves, causing his shoulders to sag in defeat. "My father is the one who cut me."

I hold my breath.

"I get it. You need the truth, and I understand that, but before you say anything, I don't want your pity."

Pity? How could he say that to me? I don't pity him. I love him.

I push off the counter. My legs carry me toward the door. "Brielle, please. Just . . . just listen."

Spinning around, I watch him move slowly across the room until he's standing directly in front of me. "I know you know the type of guy my father is. Or, at least, you've suspected." I nod but keep my mouth shut.

"The first time Mason brought me here, it was after that game with Denton High. I struck out and lost the game for us, and he—like I'm sure you did—put two and two together when I showed up at your house, beat to hell. So the next day, he brought me here. He handed me the bat and told me to keep swinging until I hit every ball in a circuit—because he didn't want my father to ever have the reason to do it again."

I narrow my eyes up at him and tilt my head. Theo's hand comes up to rest against my cheek, and my body relaxes into his touch. My head drops to his chest. "Mason loved you like a brother." I whisper.

"I know, which is why after everything that happened, I left. I was scared. I thought I had no one else left to run to when things went bad. I thought getting away would somehow save me from my father, but all it did was make things worse."

"You had me, Theo. I would have—"

"No. I wouldn't have wanted you to." He turns away. I see the muscles along his back flex under his T-shirt, as he sucks in a deep breath. "I could never forgive myself if anything happened to you because of me."

If anything happened to me? I silently repeat his words. My mind is suddenly wishing for a change of subject. "Theo, your father can't hurt me." I take a few steps in his direction.

"He hurt Mason."

I feel my mouth fall slack as I stare openly at Theo's back. My feet are permanently fixed to the floor. Wait. What? Theo's dad hurt . . . Mason? No. No. No. No. I was there; it wasn't his dad. It was the drug dealer.

I watch Theo turn around; his hazel eyes are almost translucent as he lifts his gaze to me.

"You needed to know."

I can feel my legs beginning to shake as I reach out to him to steady myself. My lungs aching for me to take a breath. "Luca . . . Luca said that you were the reason Mason was dead," I hear myself say. My words are breathy and broken. "But I . . . I didn't want to believe it. Were you in on it? How . . . how could you? Why? Why would your father want to hurt my brother? Why would you let this happen? He was your best friend!"

"What? You can't really think that I would ever be a part of something like that?" Theo is suddenly frantic, his tone, hostile. "He died because my father gave strict orders not to let anyone interfere with his business deal, and I fucked up and let the three of you come with me that night. I was supposed to be in and out, but then y'all came in, and when I saw the guy coming on to you . . . I lost it."

I pause, letting myself remember the night—us pulling into that bar. . . Theo asking us to stay in the car. I pinch my eyes shut. It wasn't Theo's fault. It was mine. I was the reason Mason went inside the bar; he was chasing Becks and me. If I hadn't been trying to make Theo jealous, then Mason would have stayed in the car as Theo had asked, and he'd probably still be alive. But I had to flirt with danger, like I always did back then.

"Luca is right. The two of us together are dangerous," I say and I mean it. I just wanted him to finally tell me the truth about his feelings. And he let his feelings cloud his judgement. I drop my head. We both killed Mason.

"I thought that asshole was going to shoot you, Brielle. So I jumped in front of you. Had I known he was going to go for Mason, things would be a lot different right now. Mason was my best friend. I would have died for him."

"I know. I'm sorry. I just . . . I don't understand why your father would order something like that."

"Because he's sick, Brielle. And because he was hoping something like that would happen so he would have leverage on me, in case I ever tried to leave like my mom did."

I sigh, trying to think of a better way to transition into my next question, but there isn't one. My mind is praying that I haven't pushed him too far already tonight. "Why do people call you the Grim Reaper?"

Theo drops his arms and lets his head fall back. "Fuck. Wes and his big mouth."

He grabs the items off the counter and heads for the back door. "Wes is not the problem here," I call after him. My feet move two at a time as I try to keep up.

We get to the glass door, and I can see the batting cages lining the other side, each one littered with leaves and debris. I hesitate, my mind taking a moment to imagine what this place must have looked like back in the day, when Theo turns around. He pushes a hand through his hair, then rubs at the stubble along his jaw. "Isn't this enough, Brielle? I told you about my father. I brought you here. What else do you want from me?"

"Everything. Why is it so hard to let me in?"

"God, I am going to kick Wes's ass for this."

"No. You're not. Wes is your friend."

"A friend with a big mouth and a death wish."

"I can't take this anymore; this is getting us nowhere." I wrap my arms around my stomach when I feel like I might be sick, and I push through the exit.

"Brielle, wait," I hear him call out to me, but I'm already out the door. I need some distance to think. "Stop running away." I feel his fingers grasp my arm as he pulls me around and holds me to him. "Fuck. What is it with you? I'm trying to make an effort here, but it's not enough. What do you want from me?"

I try to break from his grip, but he's not letting go. "The truth!" I yell at him. "I want the truth."

"And I'm trying. It's not that easy."

"Why? What are you hiding from me? Why is it not easy?"

"Because I love you!" His words echo through the quiet night. "There, I fucking said it. I love you, Brielle. And I don't want to lose you, so I'm trying to be honest. But it's not as easy as you might think because knowing the truth puts a target on your back!"

I cut my eyes at him.

"You, you what?" I feel my pulse begin to rise. My heart swells as tears begin to pool at the bottom of my eyes.

"I said, I love you, Brielle. How do you not see that? I always have."

I eye his lips and try not to think about how badly I want to kiss him. Because I can't. At least, not yet.

"It's also because I'm afraid that if you know the truth then that's it. You'll realize how much of a fuck up I am and you'll be gone."

What are you waiting for.

Say something!

"I. . ." I open my mouth, then shut it. I want to tell him, that I love him. That nothing else matters as long as we're able to be together. But I can't. It's not practical—not when I know he's still hiding things from me. "Why do they call you the Grim Reaper, Theo? What is it exactly that you do for your father?"

I can read the hurt behind his eyes, and I hate myself for causing it. Theo drops his hands, releasing me. "Because I am

The Grim Reaper." The words fall from his lips, his tone hollow.

"You hurt people?" My words, shaky as I work to calm the storm of emotions currently stirring inside my mind.

His face turns pale. "Yes . . . and no. It just depends. My father brings them to me—sometimes I go to them—and it's my job to make them talk. One way or another. At least, it was my job until the job became entertaining Katrina."

I can literally hear the blood pounding behind my ears as I watch him open his mouth, then shut it, time and time again.

I feel myself shaking as I look at Theo in a new light. I see his hands, and I see a weapon. I remember his scars and feel like I'm seeing the aftermath of someone else's pain. How did he make them talk? How badly did he hurt them?

I choose to ask the one question I dread the most. "Theo, have you killed people?"

"Brielle . . . do you really—"

"Answer the question, Theo! Have you killed anyone?"

"No. Never. I'm not a murderer, Brielle."

I rake my eyes across his face, his arms, and his knuckles. "How could you hurt people, Theo, especially after growing up with your father?"

"Because after years of learning how to take a beating, I got tired of feeling weak. So I learned to fight, and I got good at it. Do you think I wanted to hurt them? I didn't have a choice, Brielle. I never have."

I tilt my head to the side. My eyes skim the floor as my mind works to process all of this information. Suddenly a face comes to mind. One with blue eyes and long, blonde hair. . .

"Why does your dad need you to entertain Katrina? Is her dad a big deal or something?"

He nods. "My father is hoping to secure a partnership with him to gain access to his clientele. But I think there's more to it than that. I just don't know what just yet."

"And you're supposed to . . . what? What does he need Katrina entertained for?"

"He wants me to bring her somewhere, make it look like I care about her so that her father is a little more willing to work with my dad."

I close my eyes and take a step back. I need time to gather my thoughts.

"Here." I watch as he shrugs out of his coat and drapes it over my shoulders before he reaches for the zipper. I hadn't realized that I was shivering. "Let me."

Theo zips the coat up just below the base of my neck. The tips of his fingers reaching out to brush across the length of my collarbone.

"Theo, what are we doing?" I peel my eyes away from his and close them, trying and failing not to let myself give in to the moment. I came here for answers.

"I don't know," he says, and I open my eyes when he drops his hand. His expression is suddenly distant.

He walks over to one of the metal chairs and takes a seat. His hands cover his face as he leans over to rest his elbows on his knees.

"God, you know, my father owns everything here?" His voice raises a few octaves as I keep to my spot. My feet are permanently etching their way into the cool concrete as I begin to fear the worst. "The store owners, the drug trades, even the freaking police. Everything."

"He doesn't own my father. And he doesn't own you."

"It's not that simple."

"Yes, it is. You said it yourself. You're good at fighting. So good, in fact, that your father had someone you care about killed in order to get to you. You have a choice. You can leave; he can't hurt you anymore."

"See, that's where you're wrong." Theo drops his head, and I can tell that he's struggling His hands fall away from his face as he turns towards me. The look in his eyes one of genuine concern. "He can hurt me because now he knows my weakness—you."

chapter twenty-nine

THEO

F uck. This is so embarrassing. I should have just kept my mouth shut. Damn it, Brielle *Say something! Anything!* I want to scream. I need to know what's going on inside of that head of hers. I mean. Shit. Did she not hear me?

It feels like forever has passed since I admitted to her that she's my weakness, and she hasn't moved a muscle. Even her expression is unreadable as she eyes me from the same spot by the door where I released her. My mind is racing as I wait for her to speak.

Should I say something? Is she waiting for me to make a move? Fuck. I am so out of my element here. I literally just told this girl something I haven't told anyone else, ever, and she chooses now of all times to go speechless on me? She asked for the truth. . .

Sure, I'll admit, it was a fucked-up thing to do. Telling my girl that I love her—for the first time—in the middle of a fight, but it just slipped out. Maybe it's because she doesn't love me back. Or maybe she knows she won't be able to look past what I've done, now that I've let her in. Now that she knows I'm no better than my father.

I close my eyes and suck in a slow breath. Fuck this. I can't handle the silence for another minute. "This was a bad idea. I should probably get you home." I begin to stand. "It's getting late anyway, and Becks—"

"I'm . . . I'm your weakness?" She interrupts me. Her eyes shift back and forth between my own like she's debating something—as if she didn't already know.

God, if only I could read her mind.

"Isn't it obvious?" My words reveal more truth than I would like and are making me vulnerable to her rejection. I'd be lying if I said I wasn't scared shitless right now. This girl has my heart, and she could crush it in a matter of seconds if she wants to.

This shit is the reason why I don't let people in. I can't stand the waiting, the hesitation, of not knowing how they might feel. Brielle purses her lips, her hand running over the top of her hair. I can see that she is struggling to find the words to answer me as I watch her suck in her bottom lip and bite it. The act takes longer than usual, but I'm unable to look away.

I tense and press my hands over the top of my jeans to adjust myself. My cock is pulsing in rhythm with the beat of my heart, as I try to not think about the fact that we're alone—and that she's staring at me with that innocent fucking look that always makes me want to do a million—all dirty—things to her.

Fuck, I want this girl.

Another minute passes before those perfect lips pull into the softest smile. But my mind blanks, and I'm unable to speak. There are too many scenarios playing out in my head. She takes a step, her feet slowly unsticking from the floor as she walks over to where I'm sitting. Her hands gently press against the top of my shoulders until my back is flat against the chair.

I can see the hesitation in her face. Her nerves probably making her doubt herself as she climbs onto my lap. Her knees brushing the outside of my thighs. Those brilliant green eyes look up at me in shock.

"Say it again," she whispers, her arms wrapping the back of my neck.

Say . . . it?

Which part?

"Y- you're my weakness?" I stumble through the words as my eyes fall to her mouth. Our lips, barely an inch apart.

She shakes her head. "No, the other thing."

Damn it. I lick my lips. She's going to make me say it again. She didn't even answer me the first time, and now she's asking for me to say it again? I sweep my eyes across her face and suck in a deep breath. Her cheeks and nose are red from the cold. I reach up to cup her face with my hands, and without having to think about it, she leans into my touch.

"I love you," I repeat, my eyes holding hers. "I always have."

I barely have time to brace myself before she presses her lips to mine. My arm moves to encircle her waist as I press on her back until our bodies are perfectly flat against one another. I can't help it; I want her. I need her. I don't even care about the fact that she still hasn't said it back. I just want the chance to feel close to her again—like I haven't lost her for good.

I sweep my tongue over her bottom lip and nip at it. The act elicits a moan to fall from those perfect fucking lips as she rocks her hips against my cock. Fuck, this is really happening right now. And here, of all places. . . Damn it. What would Mason think?

With the hand that's cupping her face, I slowly tease my way down her back. My fingers skim the soft skin under her ass, where her shorts are barely long enough to cover. Fuck. Does she really wear this out in public? I lean forward and deepen the kiss. My arm is still locked around her waist.

I hold my breath when I feel her hand on my zipper. The palm of her hand gently teases my cock as she runs down the length of it like she's sizing it up. "Can I . . . touch it?" she asks. Her words are breathy, and her lips swollen from kissing.

"P- please," I manage to mumble. *Smooth, Theo. Real smooth.*

She must have liked my answer because she smiles. Her fingers waste no time as she unbuttons my jeans before moving to the zipper and unzipping it. I tilt my hips, keeping her body pressed against mine, and let her shrug my pants down enough so that she can get to my boxers.

Jesus. She wants this as much as I do. I swallow hard at the thought. My eyes are glued to her movements, like I'm experiencing it all again for the very first time. She pushes her hand under the waistband of my boxers and takes hold of me. Her hand glides up and down my cock in a steady rhythm. "Fuck," I moan. She instantly releases me.

"Oh my God. I am so sorry. Did I hurt you?" She's panting. The swollen peaks of her breasts, peek out at me from where my jacket zipper has worked its way down amid everything. I lick my lips.

"Not at all." I reach out and unzip the jacket further. My fingers tease her soft peaks as I lean forward to kiss a certain spot on her collarbone, which I know she loves. "Quite the opposite actually."

Brielle lets out a soft laugh. "Oh, and that's a problem because . . .?" She tilts her head to the side, mocking me.

I part my lips as I stare out at my little blonde angel. At my cock pressed up against her stomach.

Fuck, she's feisty tonight.

"It's not a problem," I say, but my hands are moving to a mind of their own. My fingers grasp her waist as I reluctantly lift her up and off my lap—my mind still all too aware of where we are. "But if you keep that up, I'm going to want to fuck you. And unfortunately, as much as it kills me, I don't think I can."

"Oh," she mumbles. Her fingers reach for the jacket, and she zips it all the way up.

Shit. Again with the growing of a fucking conscience, I choose now. Mason isn't even here, and he's still cockblocking me with his sister. The asshole. Did he really think Luca was a better choice for her over me?

I stand up and fix my jeans, tucking my cock up along my waist. "It has nothing to do with you, babe." I smile softly, trying to reassure her. The shattered look she's wearing, making me want to rethink my answer. "This place just holds a lot of memories. I just, I don't want to—"

"You don't have to explain anything to me," she interrupts. Her expression is tight. I worry that she's completely misunderstood me, but she surprises me by saying, "You're protecting the memories the two of you shared here. It makes sense. I'm so sorry I didn't think of that before."

I feel myself immediately relax. My shoulders sag as the added stress evaporates. How the hell has she stayed single all these years? She places a hand on my chest, and as usual, my breathing instantly slows. My mind goes blank as I try to remember why I chose to leave her all those years ago.

You can play hero all you want, boy, but I know you. You're just like me. . . My father's words echo inside my head. The reason I chose to bring her here sounds alarms in the forefront of my mind.

I close my eyes. Fuck, I screwed everything up. At the beginning of the night, I had every intention of breaking things off with her—to leave, for good this time, but then I saw her.

For every reason I had that was telling me to go, I found an answer I needed to stay.

"So, you ready to lose?" She cocks her eyebrow, turning over her shoulder to walk to the gear, lying forgotten on the floor. She grabs a bat and a helmet. "Because I hope you don't think that I'm going to take it easy on you since you're injured."

Fuck, I love this feisty side of her.

"I wouldn't expect anything less, babe," I say. My mind chooses this moment to remind me of the fact that she still hasn't told me whether or not she loves me back. My smile drops. "Come on, let's see what you got."

chapter thirty

T heo pulls into my driveway, and I hop off the bike after he cuts the engine. It was too late by the time we left to fetch my car tonight, and a lot has happened since then. Ever since he put a stop to our little moment back at the cages, he's been acting distant. His whiplash of emotions makes my head spin again.

One minute, he's telling me he loves me and the next it's . . . "Well, I guess this is goodnight." He doesn't look at me.

Don't do this.

Talk to me!

I can't stand another minute of this awkward silence. I mean, what happened? He's been so in his head the last hour. I don't understand where it's coming from. Is it because I've been looking for a way to tell him, "I love you," back?

"Yeah." I kick a rock. "I guess it is. Goodnight, Theo."

I can see from here that Becks has left the lights on inside for me, when I suddenly realize that I completely forgot to call her to tell her that I would be home late. I briefly wonder what she thinks I've been up to. She hasn't even tried calling, once.

He's still staring off to the side when I lean in and kiss his cheek. "Thank you for sharing a little bit of Mason with me," I say, thinking about how much it means to me that he chose to open up like this. I still can't believe that Theo Wescott loves me. I always hoped but never imagined it would happen.

But Theo loves me. And I love him.

Maybe I should just say it now—

"You're welcome."

Ugh!

"Right. Well, bye." I turn around so that he doesn't have to see the hurt I know is written across my face. How can he say that I am his weakness when he so obviously holds all the cards?

I manage to open my front door before I hear him running up the steps behind me. "Brielle, wait!" he yells. The desperation etched in his voice surprises me more than anything. I turn around and see the frantic look he's wearing. "I. . . ugh. . . I forgot something."

"You did?"

I inhale a sharp breath when he takes a step toward me. His eyes lock on my mouth before his lips crash against mine. The momentum forces me back until I'm pinned against the doorframe. When he pulls away, we're both panting. "Yeah, I did," he whispers in that raspy voice I love.

Holy shi— He kisses me again, leading me to practically forget how to breathe. My brain stumbles to catch up as I hear him whisper against my lips, "Kiss me back, Brielle. I can't leave it like this."

Leave?

Where is he going other than back to his house?

"Then don't. Stay here . . . with me." I say. My hands gripping the back of his arms. My fingers press into his biceps, afraid that if he leaves, that this could be the end.

I drop my bag and jump onto his torso the moment I feel his hands lifting my bottom. My mind relaxes as I let myself give in to his touch.

As if reading my mind, he carries me through the entry hall, kicking the door shut behind him. "Shh!" I giggle, sweeping my eyes across the small space before I decide Becks has to be in her room. "We can't wake up Becks."

He nods and walks over to the couch. His body flexes under my touch as he sets me down, but he's right on top of me—not giving me a second to rest. His teeth rake at the sensitive spot under my ear, sucking and nipping until I'm a heaving mess. My hand tugs at the bottom of his shirt. The soft material twists in my fingers as I work to push it up the hard-packed muscles of his stomach.

Theo releases his hold on me, and with one finger, he hooks the back of his shirt and pulls it up and over his head. "Now yours," he whispers, his breath hot against my lips. His fingers are teasing my sides as he inches the corners of my shirt up. The pads of his thumbs rub small circles across my skin.

I shrug out of his jacket and barely have time to sit up before my shirt hits the floor.

"You're gorgeous." He sucks his lower lip between his teeth. His eyes slowly travel over my chest, and his fingers skim the tops of my breasts that are spilling over my bra. *How embarrassing.* I shut my eyes. I really should invest in a new bra.

"Open your eyes, baby. I want to see you."

"Sorry. I just, I. . ." I mumble, but Theo reads my mind.

"You have nothing to be embarrassed about. Trust me." He licks his lips while his eyes trail down the length of my body once more. "You're fucking perfect."

I nod in response. My cheeks flush at the thought of him seeing me like this. It's all still so new to me—the dirty talk. . . the way his hands feel as they move over my body. It's like he's always trying to memorize every inch. He doesn't even try to hide the way that he looks at me. How does anyone ever get used to this?

Feeling brave, I lift my hand and gently press it against the outside of his boxers, teasing and exploring the length of him. I swallow the lump in my throat when I think about how big he is.

Is he even going to fit?

Theo groans and leans down over the top of me to place a trail of kisses along my neck. "Are you going to do something with that?" he asks, his words as seductive as everything else about this man. "This is your last chance, babe. If you want to stop, you need to tell me now."

I arch my back when I feel his fingers slip under the thin material of my thong and slowly push into me. First the one and then another. I run my finger over the tip of his penis, and feel his body tighten in response. "I want you," I say. The fullness of his fingers makes me squirm.

"Which room is yours?" he asks. His eyes darken while he stares at me. But he doesn't wait for me to answer. He simply lifts me with one arm by my waist as he continues to thrust his fingers deeper inside me. He carries me into the hall. "Pick a room, Brielle—or so help me, I'll fuck you in the hall."

I pant in between breaths; the pressure building. In another moment of bravery, I drop my hand between us and push my fingers under the elastic waist of his boxers and begin palming him with my hand. My mind secretly hopes that I'm doing this right. He crashes his lips against mine while my back slams against our bathroom door.

"Jesus." He moans. His finger slowly starts to pump faster in and out of me, and his rhythm shifts to match my own. This slow, sweet assault makes me whimper.

"It's the . . . it's the one on the right." I feel a rush of air over my bare skin as Theo kicks the door open—my mind, too far gone to care about how loud we're being. Becks will understand. Hell. She's probably cheering me on.

My feet touch the floor for all of a second before my shorts follow.

"We're going to have to have a conversation about those."

I feel his breath on my neck as he sucks and nips at a spot just under my chin.

"What's wrong with my shorts?" I shake my head. But Theo is too distracted to answer as he drops to his knees. His head disappears between my legs, and his stubble pricks the inside of my thighs.

He withdraws his fingers and hooks them in my thong, pulling it down, and tossing it to the floor. "Can I taste you?"

I blink my eyes open, my body on fire, and stare down at him.

Taste me?

Is it going to hurt?

He waits for my approval, and when I nod, he bends down and lifts me onto the bed. His one arm, holds me to his chest as the other sweeps across the comforter. Textbooks and notepads falling to the floor.

I silently curse my inexperience as he kisses me one more time before his lips move down my chest. I feel his teeth graze across one of my breasts as he dips a finger into the cup of my bra. "Do you want me to take it off?" I ask, annoyed with myself for not having already done it myself.

"Oh, I'll get it." He licks his lips. Then he slips his hand behind my back, and in one attempt, he unclasps it.

I revel in the feeling of my breasts falling free until Theo leans down and takes my nipple in his mouth. The sensation takes me by surprise in a way that threatens to undo me. His free hand expertly works the other as I wriggle under him. I feel the pressure building between my thighs.

"Theo," I moan, and that's all it takes for him to pick up his assault.

I feel his stubble move across my skin as he trails kisses down my body. He settles between my thighs, his arms curling around them as he pulls me to him. I tense, waiting to feel something, when I see he's watching me. His tongue them swirls over my center. He mumbles something under his breath, and the muscles of my stomach clench.

I lace my fingers in the back of his hair and gently tug as he expertly moves his tongue in small strokes. He groans and slowly pushes a finger inside of me. Then another. The feeling is one of pure bliss.

It should make me nervous to know that he's watching, especially during such an intimate moment, but it doesn't. In fact, it's the exact opposite. If anything, it pushes me closer toward the edge. Each fleck of his tongue teases my sensitive spot while his fingers pump in and out of me. I shut my eyes, my fingertips pressing into his shoulders.

My legs stiffen telling me that I'm close when Theo reaches up and snakes his arm around my waist, holding me down as the pressure builds.

"Theo . . ." I whine, my chest rising and falling fast as he begins making small, quick strokes with his tongue. He growls when I push back against him. My body is shaking, and my legs are tensing. I tilt my hips toward him as heatwaves wash over me. I'm close. "I'm about to . . ."

"Come for me, baby. Just let go," he mutters against me, sucking at my sensitive spot. The act is enough to push me over the edge. My vision goes blurry as I come completely undone. I struggle to catch my breath as I lie there trying to collect myself.

"God, you're so responsive." Theo smiles. He moves his knee to rest on the outside of my thigh as he crawls up next to me on the bed. "Just watching you is enough to make me come."

I bite my lips and roll to my side. "Theo," I say in between pants. My fingers numbly make quick work of his jeans as I work them down and off his legs. "Stop talking."

"Fuck, you're feisty tonight." He leans down and presses his lips to mine. The kiss is soft and gentle, but I'm not naïve enough to believe that it will stay this way. "Spread your legs, baby," he whispers, biting my lip as payback.

He drops his hand. His fingers are back circling me, and his movements are fast and rough as he climbs on top of me. My mind is so distracted with everything I've got going on that I barely hear the small rip. I look down to see what he's doing and catch him rolling the condom over his impressive length. "I would have done that," I say softly and sit up on my elbows.

Theo pauses and looks down at the condom. "I could take it off and grab another?" he half laughs. The cute way he's trying so hard to please me, makes me giggle.

I pull him toward my body, my hands curling around the back of his biceps as he steadies himself over the top of me. "I can wait until the next time." I kiss the corners of his mouth. That devilish grin I love so much is playing along his lips. I lick my own, tasting something new when I realize I'm tasting myself.

Theo lowers himself; his legs gently press against my thighs, spreading them further as he settles between them. I inhale a sharp breath when I feel his erection graze across my sensitive spot; the tip of it moves down until it's hovering just out of reach.

"I need you to tell me if you want me to stop."

I nod, well aware that I should be more nervous than I am, but I'm not. I trust Theo entirely, and I know that even if we aren't meant to be together—or that if things were to never work out—I would still want this. I would still want him to be the one I share this moment with. I love him; I always have.

"I will," I promise.

"Just try to relax, baby." He slowly begins sliding himself in me.

I inhale a deep breath and knot my fists in the comforter. There's some pain, but I push through it when I catch Theo watching me.

"How's . . . that, baby?" he pants as he slides slowly in and out of me. I look down and am surprised when I see that he's only using a fraction of himself. "What? What is it?" I hear the panic behind his words. "Do you want me to—"

"No," I quickly say, rising up to wrap my hands around the back of his neck. "I was just wondering why you weren't, you know, going all the way in?"

I blush, hating how inexperienced I sound. Why is it so hard to just say what I mean?

"I will, baby. Trust me, but not tonight." He smiles, bending down to place a soft kiss on my mouth. I part my lips, ready to object that I could take it, but he stops me when his tongue glides across my bottom lip, and he deepens the kiss.

My hands move to his back as Theo begins to pick

the pace, his thrusts becoming gradually less painful as I relax and give in to the moment. It doesn't take long before both of us are panting, the pressure slowly building between my thighs.

"Fuck, you feel too good." His expression grows dark. "You're so tight," he whispers against my lips.

God, his dirty talk is so hot. Hearing it, pushes me closer to the edge, my legs tensing as I wrap them around his waist, urging him to go deeper. I want more. I press my fingers against his back when I feel like I am about to come loose. I pinch my eyes shut.

"You . . . you do . . . too," I stumble.

"Come for me, baby," Theo says, and that's all it takes for me to give in to the sweet release. "I- I'm about to come, baby," he whispers. His breath is ragged against my neck, and his release follows mine shortly afterward. I hear him groan, his jaw tensing as I feel the slightest jerks tease my insides. Each one sends a wave of pleasure surging through my core.

We're both panting when Theo pulls out and collapses next to me on the bed. I wince at the loss of him. "Are you. . . are you okay?" Theo asks between breaths, then rolls to his side and pulls me to him. His face nuzzles into the crook of my neck. I shiver, feeling his breath tickle my skin.

"I'm fine," I answer him honestly. My mind thinks back to when I was digging my fingers into the back of his arms, begging for more. "I'm sorry if, you know . . . if it didn't . . . if I wasn't . . . that good."

"Brielle, I don't think you understand." He presses his fingers under my chin, then tilts my head up to meet his eyes. "That was everything I've ever wanted." He smiles down at me as he quickly presses his lips against mine. "You . . . you are everything I've ever wanted. I love you."

Theo pulls the comforter out from under us, removing and disposing of the condom before he joins me back on the bed. Our legs are entwined as he continues to hold me to him. The two of us not wanting to let the other go for fear of what might happen. Is he still planning on leaving? And if so, for how long?

Ever?

"Theo," I speak up after a minute. My body twists around to face him.

"What's wrong?"

"It's just . . . well, you're not leaving, right?"

I watch his face pale. His hand rubs along his chin. "It's what I should do. The only thing I can do, in order to truly keep you safe." He pauses, then and drops his hand. "But I love you too much to ever walk away again."

I can't hide the smile that stretches across my face. My heart is racing as I rest my head on his chest. My fingers skim the outline of one of his tattoos—some kind of bird with sharp feathers, which branch out from its wings like daggers. "Don't leave, Theo. I wouldn't survive it because. . ." My voice trails off as I take a breath and work up the nerve to say what I've wanted to for so long. "Because I love you too."

chapter thirty-one

M y eyes are burning as I wake up to the sound of someone rustling around in my room. *What did Becks lose this time?* I hazily wonder. My mind still drifting in and out of sleep.

"Can I help you with something?" I moan and roll over to one side. My hair falls over my shoulder as I squint sleepily up at this surprisingly new muscular version of Becks. Holy crap?

"Good morning to you too." Theo lets out a soft chuckle, drops his jeans and pads over to the bed. His arms slide under the lower portion of my back as he brings his body down on top of me. His teeth nip at my ear as he groans into my neck. "Sorry for waking you up, babe. I'm not used to having to sneak out."

I sit up, bringing him with me. My arm clasps the comforter to my chest. "You were trying to sneak out?" I say. My words are shakier than I'd like. Was he really going to leave without saying anything? Did he regret last night?

"What? No!" His lips pull into a thin line as he grabs the comforter and slowly tugs at the corner. "I couldn't sleep so I was going to run and grab something to surprise you with. But now that you're up . . . I'm thinking . . . breakfast in bed?"

My back hits the bed seconds before the heat that his words have stirred, as it slowly creeps up the sides of my face. I let out a quick giggle, feeling him settle between my legs. His hand delicately skims the flat surface of my stomach while he moves to tease my breasts. I squirm, feeling how tender they are from last night's attention but it isn't painful. If anything, it feels even better than before.

I wrap my legs around his waist and pull him to me, my hand moving to the swell in his boxers as I use my toes to hook the back of his waistband and slowly begin to slide them down. The sight of his manhood is still as impressive and intimidating as the first time I saw it.

"And what would you like this morning?" I tease him.

I watch him as his tongue dips out of my bottom lip and sweeps over it. I hold my breath, waiting for his answer, when he leans down to press his lips against the soft spot of my neck. I let my mind drift away, my skin coming alive. My hand glides up and down over his erection; the tip of his head grazes a spot between my thighs with every stroke.

He kisses my jaw, my chin, my lips, once, before he pulls back to look at me. His hazel eyes holding mine as he stares down at me. The seconds quickly turn to minutes. I thread my fingers into the back of his hair and pull his lips to me once more.

"Tell me," I whisper the words against his lips, our foreheads pressed together.

His eyes hastily take in my reaction before he admits, "I want you."

I suck in my bottom lip and tilt my head to the side. "You've got me," I say and release my hands to wrap both of them around the back of his neck.

The tip of his erection fully rides the edge of no return, causing all the air from my lungs to get sucked out. I wriggle under him. His eyes are growing wide as if he's only just realized how close we are. But he doesn't move. Instead, he freezes. His eager need to have his way with me is suddenly halted as he stares down at me. His lips part, then close. I roll my hips over him and moan when I feel my own need grow.

God, I want him so bad right now.

What is he waiting for?

"Fuck, Brielle." He drops his head back. The action forces my hands to his shoulders. He leans back to his knees, closes his eyes, and steps off the bed. "You're making it really hard for me to be a gentleman here," he groans. "I didn't realize that I only had the one condom on me."

"Oh." I bite back a laugh. My eyes drop to the center of his back as he bends down and steps into his boxers. "Hey," I whisper. My arms reach out to grasp his hand. I pull him to sit down on the bed, his back to me. I wrap my arms under his. My fingers trace his chest and the three tiny ridges. "How do you feel about scrambled eggs and buttered toast?"

Theo twists around to face me. He frames my face with his hands. "That sounds perfect, babe."

I show Theo where the shower is so he can "cool off," as I sneak away so I can start making our breakfast. I turn the corner and step into the small hallway. My ears pick up on a commotion happening inside the kitchen. The sound of dishes clanking together, and something crackling on the stove.

I take in a deep breath. Is something burning?

"Burning toast, again." I laugh and round the open frame that splits the kitchen from the family room. The image of Becks in her workout clothes and smoke swirling around the room is what I half expected to see. But I was wrong. So wrong.

"Good morning, B!" I jump back in shock when my eyes land on the naked backside of Wes. With spatula in hand, he tries to flip an omelet. I blink up at the ceiling. My mind is too busy trying not to stare that I can't consciously form a response.

"Phew, you're looking extra gorgeous this morning." He laughs and smacks his lips.

Oh my God. I mentally kick myself. My head shakes as if I could erase the image from my mind. This isn't happening.

"I'm sorry. I just. . . I didn't know you stayed over last night." I recover and walk into the kitchen. My mind kicks into auto drive somewhere between the fridge and the stove as I work around Wes. "Where's Becks?"

I can feel Wes's eyes linger, but I'm doing well enough to crack these eggs without making too much of a mess.

"If I were you, I'd focus more on your shit omelet, than the curve of my girl's ass," Theo threatens him as he comes over and slides his hands around my waist, pulling me toward him. From the corner of my eye, I see Wes's attention quickly snap back to his pan, where his now burnt omelet threatens to send the smoke alarms screaming. "What the fuck are you naked for? Is Becks wearing the pants in the relationship now, or are you just trying to get me to beat your ass?"

Oh crap. I set down the egg I was holding. I'm already preparing for Theo to try something.

"Chill, man. I honestly didn't think with how late of a night y'all had last night that either of you would be up before noon."

"Oh my God." I cover my face. Wes and Becks had both heard us.

Wes dumps his omelet and pan in the sink when he realizes there's no saving it. He presses his hands on his hips. His manhood hanging out in the open for everyone to see. I look up and find Theo glaring daggers at his soon to be ex-best friend.

"Wes."

"Yeah, man?"

"Get the fuck out of here before I lose my patience."

"Yup. Yeah, good idea." He brushes his hands against one another.

I turn back to my eggs and continue to crack them as Theo waits for Wes to leave the room. I drop the shell of one in the bowl that I have sitting off to the side, when I feel Theo lace his fingers around my forearm and flip me around to face him. His body presses me against the counter. His lips quickly claim mine.

"Are you trying to make me jealous?" He growls into my mouth. His fingers skim under the hem of my tank. His chest rises and falls rapidly as he deepens the kiss. He swipes the counter clear, and with one arm, he lifts me up and onto it. Tiny pieces of shell scrape under my bottom.

I pull away, trying to catch my breath. But Theo is insatiable. "Wes is your friend, Theo," I whisper between gasps. I push my fingers into his hair and tug so that he has to look at me. My skin is teeming from his assault. "He would never do that."

"Yeah, well, I'd rather not test that theory." He fights against my grip to press his lips to mine. But I am not giving up so easily. "You're mine."

"Yours?" I arch my brow at him, mocking him. "Says who?"

Theo lets out a muffled laugh. His hands move down to my thighs. The tips of his fingers slowly edge their way up and under my bottom as he squeezes and lifts me onto his torso. I cross my ankles and hold on to his shoulders.

"Says me." He slaps my bottom. The tender sting is pleasurable in addition to all of this added tension. "I love this new side of you." He smiles. "And you. I love you."

My back hits the wall, his arms quickly becoming my new favorite place to be. "I love you," I say, smiling sweetly.

Theo presses his lips to mine once again, letting my legs gradually slide down his front. He's wearing too much. My hands twist at the base of his shirt. How long could it possibly take for him to run to the store? I bite my lip.

"What the fuck, Brielle?" Becks exclaims. The sound of her voice catches both of us off guard and I stumble back. "That's my sexy firemen's calendar you're crushing!"

I turn to the side and see Mr. October is a crinkled mess. Whoops. I scrunch my nose and turn back around. Yeah, he's definitely looked better.

"Shit, Becks. Fucking announce yourself," Theo barks. I peek around his bicep and see a fully dressed Wes saunter over to the fridge. "Seriously, Wes?"

"What? I'm thirsty."

"Get the fuck out!"

I playfully swat at his arm, reminding him of our previous conversation. He obviously hasn't budged from his opinion either. I roll my eyes and dart around him. "How about I just go throw on some clothes, and maybe we eat out for breakfast?" I wink at him. Becks is right on my heels as I walk into my bedroom, and she slams the door shut behind us.

"Okay, you'd better start talking now." She's fuming, but I don't have time to talk calendars at the moment. My mind is more concerned about Wes's safety the longer I'm in here. I walk to my closet and open it. "I love you, but really, Brielle? I thought you were smarter than this. What the hell are you thinking?"

Wait?

That's what she's upset about?

"Becks—"

"No. Don't Becks me," she interrupts. Her hand is moving a mile a minute. "Answers. Now. Spill."

I reach for my simple olive-green T-shirt dress and my all-white Converse. In one motion, I strip the tank top and slip the dress over my head. The soft material glides down my body and kisses the top of my thighs. I'm working on putting on my shoes when Becks slaps a hand over her face.

"You going to add a bra under there, or are we going for a less-is-more kind of thing now?" She laughs, tossing me a bra from my top drawer. "I mean, you got the perk to pull it off, but Theo would probably throw a fucking fit."

"Thanks." I snatch the bra from the floor. It's not my favorite but it'll do.

I smile, thinking about how quickly things have changed. In less than a month, I went from this shy, little virgin to the type of girl who leaves bras in the living room—someone who has intense make-out sessions in her kitchen while her roommate and her roommate's boyfriend are in the other room.

I suck in a deep breath as my fingers mindlessly fumble with the lacey, nude bra in my hands. I walk to the bed. "So, yeah. It all just kind of . . . happened? I guess," I stumble through the words. "He showed up after my class last night and asked if he could take me somewhere to talk."

She pats the bed. "Obviously, it went well. I mean, I'm sure the whole street could attest to that. But, I love you? When did that happen? And how?"

I sit back on the bed. "Is it so bad? I do love him."

"No, it's not a bad thing as long as he actually feels the same way. If he's lied to just get in your pants, a knife wound will be the least of his problems. I watch enough crime shows to ensure his body will never be found."

My head falls back. The two of us break out in a fit of laughter. "Well, hopefully, it never comes to that."

"One can only pray." She smiles. Her hands pull me into a hug. "Now, be honest with me because this is serious. Are we talking full-on cucumber sized, or is he batting with one of those tiny sausages people always try to pass off as a proper meat option?"

"Becks—"

"Okay. Okay. Okay." She shakes her head. "At least tell me he's got a kink somewhere. No one can be that fucking perfect."

"A kink?"

Becks rolls her eyes and crinkles her nose. "Yeah, a kink. A swivel in his stick. A left-handed swoop. Does his dick do this?" Her hands begin to fold. The idea of what she's showing me, looking more painful by the second.

Who the hell had Becks been with that their penis looks like that? A better question, how the hell would that even work?

"Well, maybe it was more like this."

"Oh my God. Becks. Stop." I try to stifle a laugh. I look to the door. "I'm sorry about Mr. October, but we should probably get back out there."

"Eh, he wasn't my favorite." She shrugs. "But next time Theo throws you against a wall, tell him to aim for the one by our pantry. Maybe then he'll see how broke we are and take pity on us."

"Becks!"

"Okay, sorry. You're right." She nods as we move to the door. "Maybe he'll take pity on me. You're fine."

"Becks!"

"What?" She rolls her eyes, her expression completely serious. "Not everyone falls in love with their childhood crush, who grows up to be a smoking-hot millionaire, Brielle. I have needs. And bills. Lots of bills."

chapter thirty-two

THEO

I watch Brielle skip around the corner, breasts bouncing over the top of that skimpy ass tank, and I try not to overreact when I catch Wes's eyes trail her for the third time. Fuck this. If she were any other girl, I wouldn't give it a second thought. In fact, I'd welcome others seeing what only I'm able to achieve. But she's different. This is Brielle. My girl. And I'll be damned if I let Wes get away with it.

"I love you, already? Damn. Someone's growing soft." Wes laughs.

That stupid smirk makes me want to punch him in the fucking face. I roll my eyes, take a step toward him, and shove my forearm against his throat. I can tell by his expression that he's completely caught off guard. But what the fuck did he expect me to do? Nothing? He should know me better than that. If he keeps it up, we may not be friends by the end of the night.

"What the fuck, Theo," he stutters against the weight of my arm.

"You're my friend, Wes, so I'm not going to kick your ass this time. But this is your last warning. Keep. Your eyes. To yourself." I push off him and take a step back.

"Shit. Understood," he chokes out the response.

I walk over to the sink, pushing my hand through my hair as I try to calm my rising pulse.

Wes walks to the table and pulls out a chair. His hand massages his neck. "So, love, huh?" His eyes flit to me as he warily sizes me up like he's waiting for the truth.

I look toward the hall half expecting Brielle to have been back by now. But knowing Becks, she's probably is going to be a minute. A handful of seconds go by before I join Wes at the table, reluctantly.

"Is this where you tell me you have feelings for her too?"

"What? No!"

I nod and shut my mouth. Fuck. This got awkward fast. "Good. I'd hate to have to kill you."

Wes laughs dryly, but when I don't join him, I can see the tension build, as he shifts in his seat.

"Oh, you're serious."

I look up when I hear Becks and Brielle shoot out from the hall. Becks is laughing to herself, but I'm not focused on her. My eyes sweep to my girl, and I drink in the sight of her. Her blonde hair is pulled to the side, and she's wearing some short-ass dress, which barely covers the top of her thighs in a way that I know I will be using to my advantage later.

Damn. I bet that dress would look even better on the floor. I hesitate when an image of my girl writhing on her bed immediately comes to mind. I stand up and walk over to her and wrap my arms around her waist.

"What are you doing today?" I ask her, leaning down to press my lips to her forehead. I'm well aware I have a problem, but fuck it if I don't care. I'm addicted.

"I have class," she says with a frown. She lifts up to her tiptoes and plants a kiss on my mouth. Her hands entwine around the back of my neck as she pulls me to her.

God, I love her lips.

"So, skip it!" Wes yells. A giggling Becks is trapped within the crook of his arm. I turn and shoot him a glare, but he just waves me off. "What?"

Is he serious right now?

"That sounds like fun!" Becks bounces on her toes. "We could all go see the new James Bond movie that just came out. Or maybe the new Harley Quinn one?"

No. Fuck no. There is no way I want to spend the entire day with these two.

"Okay!" Brielle smiles, surprising me. "I'm ahead in my classes anyway. I'd love to go!"

Wait. "What? No." I shake my head. My mind is running a million miles a minute as I try to imagine the four of us on a double date. Becks and Brielle in charge of the seats while Wes and I awkwardly make small talk, grabbing the popcorn.

Nope. Fuck no. Not happening.

Wes is my friend, but I almost just kicked his ass in this very kitchen. If anything, I should be headed to Knock Out, but for some reason, the idea of spending the day with Brielle is enough to stave off that itch—that irritating feeling, I get under my skin to punch something, rather someone, repeatedly.

"What? Oh come on. Please?" Brielle pouts. Her bottom lip is pushed out as she stares up at me with those emerald-green eyes I can't resist.

Fuck. How the hell does she do this? "Fine."

"Hell yes!" Wes shouts. He walks behind Becks and rears his hand back to smack her ass. "Let's go, folks." Jesus. This is going to be a long day.

Half an hour later, we pull up to the ticket stand, and as expected, everyone splits once we're inside. But rather than the girls running off to claim our seats—the perfect middle, middle according to Becks's picky nature—Becks and Wes jump at the chance to go, leaving Brielle and I tasked with the job of grabbing the snacks.

"I wish it were just the two of us." I sigh as we wait for the guy to scoop our popcorn.

"Me too. But it'll be fun. I promise."

The guy behind the counter returns with our popcorn. He drops the two bags down on the counter in a huff, and a few pieces fall off the side.

"That will be fifty-six, twenty." He rolls his eyes.

Shit. Now I remember why I don't come to the theatres anymore. The prices are a fucking joke—not like I can't afford it. But still.

I hand the kid my credit card to swipe through the terminal, and he hands it back. "Thanks," I say and start to sign my name, when I catch him eyeing my girl from the corner of his eye.

I turn to see Brielle, who, as usual, is oblivious and doesn't realize she's got an audience as she works to hold the one of the large bags of popcorn, the three candy boxes, and Becks's frozen Coke slush drink. I feel my temper start to flare when I notice the top of her dress is pulled down to reveal a decent amount of cleavage.

My first thought is damn, this girl should come with a warning. My second, "Is that all you need?" I clear my throat, shoving the thin slip of paper back at the kid, narrowing my eyes.

"Oh. . . um. . . no. I mean, yes. Yes, sir."

I arch my brow and grab the rest of the haul. Brielle is already a few steps ahead of me, waiting at the ticket stand. I shoot popcorn boy one last glare before I wonder if I'm wearing a "fuck with Theo" sign today.

I reach the ticket stand and find Brielle, chatting it up with another asshole. What the fuck? I reach in my pocket and pull out the tickets. "I can't take you anywhere," I say honestly. My temper is getting the better of me.

The nerdy asshole in front of me is still chuckling like a fool, when he looks over the top of his glasses and notices me. He immediately shuts up. His eyes drop to his work like they should have been all along.

"What do you mean?" Brielle smiles. Her casual demeanor only pisses me off more.

"I mean, do you ever go anywhere without being hit on?"

I know I've fucked up when I see her blush and her smile drops. The asshole in front of us nibbles at his lip, and I close my eyes and inhale a deep breath.

"Theatre six is down the hall to your left," the scrawny, little ticket puncher says. I reach out and take our stubs from him, when I notice Brielle is already ten feet ahead of me. "You're a lucky, man. Your girlfriend is sexy."

What the hell did this kid just say to me?

"Are you trying to have me kick your ass, kid?"

"N- no, sir. Please don't do that."

I shake my head and offer the kid a tight smile before rushing off to catch up with my girl. In a stroke of pure luck, I manage to beat her to the door. I slide my arm in front of her, blocking her way.

"We're going to miss the movie." She rolls her eyes and reaches for the handle.

"You make that sound like a bad thing," I tease in a poor attempt to make her smile. "Look, I don't care about seeing this movie, babe." I pull my arm from the door and reach out to touch her face. "I am sorry if I embarrassed you. I just don't like seeing other guys flirting with you."

"Theo, he was just being nice," she says, arms crossed as she stares up at me.

I nod, trying not to risk pissing her off further by telling her just how naive she is to the inner workings of the male mind—especially when it comes to assholes like me! My history of bad decisions weighs heavily on my shoulders. Before we came here, Wes and I had smashed through a pretty lengthy list of girls back in Lubbock. We met on campus at Texas Tech—through a bet—and ever since then, it's been a nonstop party. Until now.

"I'm sure that's. . . exactly what t-that was."

Brielle reaches out and takes my arm. Her fingers wrap my bicep as she kisses my cheek. I bend down and turn into her kiss, the tension in my shoulders unraveling as I do. God, I love her.

"Excuse me."

We hear a voice behind us, causing us to turn around and come face-to-face with an old lady and her granddaughter, who has a wide-eyed stare and a gaping mouth. I roll my eyes. What now? Does granny want a piece of my girl too?

"You're blocking the entrance. Honestly, this is a public theater. . . no one here wants to see that."

Seriously? This lady is pissed about a little PDA, yet the Harley Quinn movie she's about to walk into is perfectly acceptable?

"Oh, we're so sorry," Brielle steps up to say, moving to the side to pull the door open for them. "Enjoy the movie."

That's my girl. A fucking angel . . . sent here to tame this modern-day devil. Too bad she's too nice for her own good. My rottenness will surely corrupt her—if it hasn't already, remembering her new feisty side, which seemed to appear overnight.

"Come on." Brielle giggles. "Let's get inside before Becks gets angry and eats Wes."

"I'm sure he wouldn't mind the idea of that."

"What?"

I shake my head and pull the door open for her to walk in. "Nothing."

"It's about damn time!" Becks shouts.

My eyes flint up to the old woman, who's seated behind our row. glaring daggers at the back of Becks's head. I stifle a laugh. This poor lady. She has no idea what she just bought tickets too. A fucking hour-and-forty-nine minutes of explicit language violence, and sexual content. That's a long time for her to spend rolling those judgmental eyes of hers. They may pop right out of her head.

"Becks, can you go down a little further?" Brielle arches her brow, waiting for Wes to finish grabbing their snacks from her hands.

"Not without dinner and a movie first." She laughs. Wes licks his lips as if thinking about Becks going down *somewhere*, while my girl looks at them, unimpressed.

"Right. Well, we'll catch y'all later," Wes calls behind them, seeing Becks stand. They turn in the opposite direction and begin moving down the aisle.

What the hell? I sit back in my chair.

Brielle mindlessly pops a handful of popcorn into her mouth. "Don't worry; they're not leaving." She reaches for her water bottle.

"Then where are they going?"

"To the back."

The back?

What was the point of getting these specific seats? I begin silently asking myself until I see Brielle flash me a look and I suddenly have my answer.

"Oh."

"Yup." She rocks her head toward me on the seat. Her hair pushes up behind her head. "Becks has this weird obsession with DC Comics. For some reason, she says they make her—"

"Whoa, okay. You know what, I'll take your word for it."

This shit is the reason why I don't do double dates. They're fucking weird.

My mind freezes when I feel Brielle's hand move to my knee. The tiny tips of her slim fingers are swirling over my jeans. "You'll be fine." She smiles as if reading my mind. "After the movie, we'll all go to dinner, and then we're free for the rest of the night to do whatever you want."

"Whatever I want?"

I lick my lips at all the possibilities, when the lights dim, and the preview trailers start to roll. We recline back in our seats as she raises the armrest in between us so she can snuggle against my side. The faint smell of her coconut shampoo teases my nostrils each time she wriggles under my arm.

I catch her feet dancing to the beat of the music. The tiny movements make me smile. The sight of it dredges up an old memory, of Brielle and me, sitting in an empty theatre— much like this one—waiting for Mason to come back with the snacks. Like today, her feet danced to the beat of the music as we played Truth or Dare until the lights cut down. I let out a soft chuckle.

No matter how many times I would talk myself up to it, I could never form the words. The tiny dare I always wished I would have had the balls to ask. . . "I dare you to kiss me," I whisper into her ear.

"What?" Brielle smiles as if she were remembering the memory with me. Her eyes light up in a way that tells me she knows exactly what I'm talking about.

"I said, I dare you to—"

But I don't get to finish. She shifts in her seat and leans up to close her lips over mine. I let my tongue slide inside her mouth, and it's met by hers. The kiss is quick and rough, and when we pull away, we're both panting.

Yeah, take that lady! The childish boy inside of me wants to turn around and yell at her.

"Where did that come from?"

"I've always wanted to kiss you in a movie theatre."

"Well, better late than never. I guess."

I brush her hair to the side as she lies back; the movie jumps into action.

Not much time has passed when I spot the old lady from before, practically dragging her granddaughter down the stairs and out the theatre.

Wow, I'm impressed.

She lasted a whole twenty minutes.

I smile and settle back with Brielle. Someone really should have given her a heads-up. I hope she gives that scrawny ticket puncher a piece of her mind.

The rest of the movie passes in the blink of an eye. I can tell by the way Brielle is jumping around in her seat toward the end that she enjoyed it. She even yelled at one point when things got tense.

"Miss us?" Becks cackles as she and Wes come exiting out of the theatre and find us out in the hall.

I scratch my stubble and bite back what I really want to say. Her hair is a mess, and now there's more lipstick on Wes than Becks.

"That movie was epic."

"Totally." Brielle looks up at me. Her small smile, a tell-all.

Yeah, too bad you weren't able to see any of it. I laugh silently and pull Brielle to me.

"Y'all ready to grab dinner?"

"I already gorged myself back in the theatre." Becks smirks, and I try not to gag. "But I could go for some pizza."

"Oh no. Not Joe's," Brielle immediately answers.

"Oh shit. That's right. Luca's softball team meets there, after practice, Wednesday nights."

Softball? Luca? I try not to laugh.

Either way, I'm with Brielle. I'm already having to share my time with these two. I don't want to risk running into him as well. "There's always Olive Garden," I offer. "Or Saltgrass? My treat?"

Becks walks over to me and slaps a hand on my shoulder. It takes everything I have not to swat her arm away. She stinks of sex—and not the good parts. "I've had enough meat in me for one night, Theo. But thanks for the offer. I'd love some pasta though."

Fucking hell, I groan on the inside, suddenly rethinking my proposition. Pizza would have been faster.

"You can never have enough meat!" Wes adds. The two of them are bouncing off one another like an old married couple. "See y'all there in twenty.

chapter thirty-three

THEO

J ack Mehoff, party of four?" The petite brunette behind the hostess stand smiles. Her eyes are fixated on me as she rounds the side and grabs a handful of menus.

Jack Mehoff? I shoot Wes a look, shaking my head. Fucking Wes. I hand the girl the buzzer. Her fingers take their time to brush against mine before she drops it back on the stand. "You can follow me to your table."

Fucking hell. I wrap my arm around Brielle and pull her to my side, hoping that this bitch will chill her approach. There's nothing worse than girls who can't take a hint. Brielle looks up at me before she thanks the girl. "What?" I lean into her hair and kiss the top of her head.

"Nothing."

We follow the hostess to our table. As requested, we're seated at one of the more private rooms—a small alcove, which could easily seat six, but because I prefer privacy, I made the request. The extra foot room isn't too bad, either.

I help Brielle in her chair, earning a rather toothy grin from Wes. "The fuck are you grinning at?" I roll my eyes.

"Nothing, man."

My phone vibrates the second my ass hits the chair.

Who the fuck . . .?

I reach in my pocket and pull it out. Fucking hell. It's my dad.

Have you handled the situation with the Sutton Girl?
There's no time to waste, Son. The ball is in two weeks!
How are things with Katrina?

Fuck. I pinch the top of my nose. What the hell am I supposed to say?

No?

Fuck off?

I choose Brielle.

No. No, no. Those answers would only result in a target on my girl's back, and I won't let that happen. If I have any chance of making it through this shit, I'm going to have to play his game. Only better. Smarter.

I glance down at the screen before quickly typing a response.

Everything is good. See you next week.

I lie to bide myself more time. Everything is far from good.

I run a hand through my hair, feeling the stress piling up. Shit. This is going to end badly; I just know it. I can feel my nerves getting the best of me after I think about how pissed Brielle is going to be when I show up to the ball with Katrina. Since she left Monday morning, I've done nothing but rack my brain for ways around it, but I don't see a solution.

At least, if I take Katrina, I can help seal the Overshire deal. Maybe then, that'll help soften the blow of my leaving and make it a little more bearable. My father can find somebody else to use as his pawn. And if not, then I guess it's war.

"Hey," Brielle says, the palm of her hand pressing along my cheek, "you okay?"

I set my phone down and take her hand in mine. I lift it to my mouth and gently kiss it. "Everything's good." I stick to my same bullshit answer. It's just easier.

I try to smile in hopes that she won't see just how bad things really are, but I can tell that she isn't buying it. "O-Okay." She drops her hand. Her features hardening as she presses her lips into a thin line.

Damn it.

She knows me too well. I just can't win tonight.

Feeling the frustration of everything starting to weigh heavily on my mind. I need a release, and I doubt Brielle would be open to the idea of a detour to K.O. after we ditch the others. I drop my eyes to her lap. Her hands are folded gently over the top of it. Her short-ass dress is pulled up to reveal a good amount of skin. Fuck it. I *did* say I was going to take advantage of that dress.

I lift my eyes and find Becks and Wes are buried behind their menus, arguing over what appetizer they want to order first. I silently groan and roll my eyes. I knew offering to pay would mean this dinner was going to turn into a full five course meal—or two.

I push my eyes past them and find the rest of the restaurant is oblivious to us. Good. My hands grip the base of my chair as I slowly edge closer to Brielle. She's eyeing me from the side, but, apparently, she isn't talking to me. I reach out and take her hand. My fingers fight against hers as she tries to pull away from me. Doesn't she know there's no use in trying to fight this?

She's laughing when she finally gives in. *Don't worry, I'm going to make it up to you.* I mentally prepare her in my mind.

"What are you thinking about ordering?" she asks, finally relenting to my charms, and licks her lips. Her eyes are focused on the menu lying in front of her.

I cough to clear my throat. "The. . . um. . . the Chicken Fettuccini Alfredo is pretty good." I smile. It's good, but it's not what I want. Maybe it would be if we had the restaurant to ourselves, and for dessert, I'd have her—on her knees—deep throating something other than cheesecake.

I drop my hand from hers and let it settle on her lap. My fingers press into the center of her thigh, and I hold it there. She wriggles from the contact, but I know she isn't about to say something in front of the others.

"What would you like, babe?" I meet her shocked expression with a smile. My eyes are glued to those full lips as they part.

"Um. . . I. . . I. . . um." I listen to her struggling to gets the words out. My fingers slowly creep up higher with every word. "I . . . I . . . um. . . t-the fettuccini sounds good." Her breaths are coming faster now as I slip my hand under her thong, my fingers quickly finding her clit as I begin circling it slowly. "O-oh. . . o-or the eggplant p-parmesan." She places her hand on the table. her fingers gripping the corner so tight that the tips start to turn white under the pressure.

I lift my menu to cover my arm and push a finger inside of her. I hook my foot around the leg of her chair and pull her to me. The wooden frame skids over the carpet until she's out of sight.

"Hmm, are you sure though?" I tease her. "You wouldn't rather have something stuffed?" I add another finger. Fuck. She's soaking wet. I suck in my bottom lip and bite it, watching her try—and fail—to act like I'm not knuckle deep in her pussy. . . and that she isn't secretly loving every minute of it.

"I . .. I . . . um." She closes her eyes and lets her head fall back.

Shit. I lean toward her. My lips greedily claim hers before I pull away, and whisper in her ear for her to pick up her menu. I might be okay with what's happening because I needed it almost as much as she seems to want it. But I'm also too selfish to share this side of Brielle with anyone else. "It's okay; no one's watching," I say when I can see the concern building behind those brilliant green eyes.

She lets out a whisper of a moan as she leans back against her chair. Her legs barely opening wider to allow me more room. But my eyes are stuck on the swollen tops of her breast, my mind wishing I had another hand so I could pay them the attention they deserve.

Jesus. She is sexy as hell.

I lick my lips. My cock is straining against the leg of my jeans. The muscles in her pussy clench around my fingers in a way that has my cock growing to uncomfortable lengths. She drops her hand to my lap and pulls me into a kiss. Soft moans fall from her lips, but I close my mouth over hers and swallow them.

"God, could y'all get a fucking room already?" Becks yells across the table. "If you wanted to make out, that's what the movie was for."

Brielle giggles and pulls away. "Shut the hell up, Becks." She smiles. Her playful attitude draws me to her. I love this new, lively side. It's fucking hot.

I stare at her openly for a second, enjoying the view before I slip my fingers from between her legs. But I can't resist the temptation to taste her again. Never have I been so all-consumed by a girl as I am with Brielle. Closing my mouth over my fingers, I happily lick the salty, sweet mixture from them.

I can see the hunger building in her as she watches me. Her lips are parted, and her brow is arched. But then she remembers where we are. Breaking away, she bites her lip and turns back to her menu. I watch as she sets it down just as I hear someone walk up to the table.

"Yeah, well, sorry. But this is a classy place." Becks grins over the top of her menu. "You can't be choking the gopher under the table and still expect great table service."

"Becks, not now." I look up when I hear the break in Brielle's voice. "Luca, hey! What are you doing here?"

Fuck. I slink back in my chair, then I let my menu fall back on the table. Of course this asshole would be here.

"Hey, Bree," he says, smiling at her over Becks's shoulder. His eyes are laser focused. "I saw you sit down, and I wanted to come over and say hi. We were all just about to head out."

He what?

Fuck. Fuck. Fuck.

I lean around him and spot a group of guys sitting not too far off to the corner. All of them are grinning from ear to ear. Damn it. I move my arm to the back of Brielle's chair. I can feel my nerves pricking along my skin as I wonder what exactly he—they—might have seen. Or for how long he chose to watch before deciding to come over.

I can tell by Brielle's expression that she's wondering the same thing herself. Fuck. There goes dessert. I'm going to be getting an earful instead. "Oh, w-what happened to Joe's?"

"Tate got sick last week so we decided to change it up a bit."

"Awe, poor Tate. Well, how are—"

"Hey, are you still coming over for TVD next Saturday?" Becks interjects. She twists in her chair to look up at him, but he is making a point to keep his attention on Brielle.

What the fuck is he playing at . . . other than softball, apparently. I stifle a laugh when I see him in his little uniform. The tight gray bottoms, long white socks, and the baggy navy shirt. The fuck is this shit, high school? I didn't even know Luca knew how to do anything other than stalk Brielle.

Wait. Did she say, coming over?

"Yeah. That is if Brielle still wants me to?" He licks his lips and takes a step further into our private alcove. Four sets of eyes turn on me as we all wait to hear Brielle's answer.

"Of course I do!"

Wait. "What?" I choose to interrupt.

"Theo, man, isn't that the night of your big fight?" Wes decides now, of all times, to pipe up. His expression is tight as he turns to the side and takes in Luca's appearance.

"Big fight?" Brielle purses her lips. The bubbly, playful side of her is completely gone now. "You're fighting again?"

I arch my brow and shrug. "I never stopped."

"Maybe I should just call you later, Bree?" Luca throws his hands up. "I would hate to interrupt your date."

What the fuck does that mean?

The better part of my mind begins to list all the reasons I should shut the fuck up and let Luca play out this moment. But it's too late for that. The stress of everything coming down all at once pushes me over the edge.

"Do you have something you want to say to me, Garrett?" I sit up in my seat.

"To you. . . always. But it wouldn't do much good now, would it?" He chuckles as a sly grin spreads across his face.

Fuck. So he did see us. That's what this is all about. He saw, and he wants me to know it. "If you've got something to say to me, say it." I feel Brielle's fingers curl around my fist. Her other hand settles on my thigh. I immediately take in a deep breath. "But you should leave before your boys have to carry you out."

"Okay—" Brielle waves her hands between us—"Luca, I'll just see you tomorrow in class, and we can discuss it then. Okay?"

I feel my pulse quickening as I watch the fucker nod. That fucking smirk is daring me to jump up and do something about it.

"Enjoy your dinner," he spits out before he turns around and joins his team.

The group of them are laughing as Luca rejoins them. What the fuck are they celebrating? Luca's ability to hide behind my girl? Damn it. That's the second time I've let her talk me out of a fight. I promise it'll be the last.

"What the fuck was all that about?" Becks crinkles her nose, her expression tight as she shakes her head. "I swear that boy needs to get laid."

"Yeah," Brielle answers automatically. The subtle disapproval in her is stirring something inside of me. "I'll, I'll talk to him."

The fuck? I choke. "Yeah, because you and him, alone, talking is really the best solution." I spit before I have the chance to think about what it is I'm saying.

"Excuse me?" Brielle turns to me. "What does that mean?"

"Oookay, so I'm thinking we could start with some calamari and maybe the-"

"Shut the fuck up, Wes." I glare at him.

"Don't talk to him like that!" Brielle snaps. Her body whips around to face me. I know she's fuming, but like I said, it's too late. I'm too far gone. "Can we talk about this later, please? When we're alone maybe?"

Is she serious?

"Talk about what, Brielle? The fact that you have a habit of protecting Luca? Or that he still believes that there is something between the two of you?" I rub my hand along my jaw. My stubble is a little longer than usual.

"Theo, he's just a frie—"

"He's a crutch, and you fucking know it!" I yell. The look on her face is enough to break me. I hate yelling at her. But what the hell else can I do to get across to her? Let her lie to me? Again.

I reach in my pocket for my wallet.

"Where are you going? A-Are you leaving?"

"Yes, Brielle. That's exactly what I'm doing." I throw down a couple hundred-dollar bills. "Enjoy your meals."

I leave the table and immediately regret my decision to walk away from her. I hate seeing her so deflated. So disappointed. But how can she expect me to carry on, pretending to play nice, after that? She knows how I feel about him. Yet she wants to sit there and pretend that I'm the one overreacting?

No, thank you. I pull at my hair. Fuck, Luca. And fuck, my fucking father. If it's not one, it's the other. Nothing is ever easy.

I can feel my hands curl into fists as I remember how fucking cocky Luca looked, standing there with that conniving smirk pressed to his mouth. Of course he wasn't afraid to speak out at me. He knows Brielle would never let me anywhere near him. The fucking coward. His intentions are only fueled by his own jealousy as he strikes just when my hands are tied.

I jump when I feel a pair of hands wrap around my bicep. The gentle way that they're holding on makes me smile. The anger already begins to resolve from my face as I turn to my side.

What the. . .?

"What the fuck do you want?" I take a step back and break her hold on my arm. The short, brunette hostess with chocolate-brown eyes stares up at me.

"I saw you were upset." She smiles seductively. My eyes trail down her body as they come up and find a tongue sliding across her perfectly glossed lips. Don't get me wrong; she is hot and looks like she has a mouth that could swallow a cock whole. But she isn't Brielle. "I wanted to make sure you were all right. No one should be alone when they're hurting."

I shake my head. Fuck, she's good. "Sorry, not interested," I say. My feet carry me over to the bench, and I throw myself down. "I'm with someone." *At least, I think I am.*

The girl walks over and sits beside me. "You don't look like you're with someone. You look lonely."

I arch my brow. Is this girl serious? "Look, you're hot and all. But I've got enough problems to deal with." I turn my head away from her. "I don't need a meaningless fuck to add to it. Besides, as I said, I'm with someone."

I hear her sigh and lean back against the bench. "It looks to me like you're unhappy. Would she really be angry with you for doing something that makes you feel better? Do you love her?"

What the fuck? I must be losing my edge if this girl thinks that she can talk to me like this? So openly. This bitch is nosier than Eliza.

I sit up and lean toward her, watching as she matches me. She licks her lips and her mouth parts. I wait until I know I have her full attention before I speak. I pace my words slowly so that I don't have to repeat myself. "Do yourself a favor and learn to take a hint. Desperation never looks good on anyone."

I watch her mouth drop.

What?

No comeback?

"Theo?" It's then that I catch a familiar voice in the wind. I squeeze my eyes shut. "I knew it."

Fuck.

I blink my eyes back open to see the hostess-bitch smiling at me. I can only imagine what this must look like. Immediately, I stand and take a step away from the bench. My hands push into the pockets of my jeans as I narrow my eyes at the brunette. I can't catch a break.

"It's not what it looks like."

"Oh, so you weren't about to kiss her?" Brielle raises her voice. She's pissed, and understandably so. I don't even know what I would do if it were me who caught her sitting as close to a random guy as I had been with this girl. "God, I can't believe I thought that you could change."

"Wait, Brielle." I rush after her as she starts walking toward the street. "I didn't do anything. I told her I was with someone."

"Yeah, it really looked like it," she snaps and picks up the pace. Damn, for someone with such short legs, she can really move. "God, you know, Luca was right. You're such an asshole. I don't know why I thought this time could be any different."

Wait. What the fuck did she just say? I reach out and grasp her wrist and pull her around to face me. "You don't mean that."

"Get the hell off me, Theo! Just let me go!"

"No!"

Brielle uses her free hand to push against my chest, but just as it's about to hit, I grab it and spin her around inside my arms.

"Let go, Theo."

"Will you just listen to me, please," I'm begging her. Maybe I should stop, take this as a sign, and let it play out. In the long run, it would be easier for the both of us if we ended things here—with her hating me. I could live with that.

"Fine. Talk then," she snaps, settling inside my arms.

I drop my arms and take a step back. My eyes sweep the parking lot where I can see we've earned some attention. From the corner of my eye, I catch three guys funnel out from the bar. They make their way to the bench and shift nervously back and forth, assessing the situation. Fuck, if they come over here, things are going to get ugly quick.

"Look, I know how it looked, but I would never do that to you. I love you."

"Can you just. . . just take me home? Please."

I lift my eyes, waiting to see Becks's and Wes's judgmental glares, but they're not here.

"Wes and Becks?"

"They're going to stay."

I nod, not wanting to risk pissing her off again, and say, "Okay, let's go."

Twenty minutes later, we pull into her driveway. Hopping off the bike the second we stop, she hands her helmet to me and then heads to her door. I screw my eyes shut.

"Brielle, just wait a minute."

"It's fine. I'm . . . fine, Theo. Just go home."

I roll my eyes and shake my head as I follow her, taking on the steps two at a time. The idea that I was chasing her not even twenty-four hours ago—for a very different reason—not lost on me. Only this time, I'm afraid she won't be so easily be persuaded to listen.

I reach her front door and find Brielle fumbling with her keys. Tears line her cheeks in streaks.

"That's not going to happen, babe." I reach out to touch her shoulder. "I couldn't leave even if I wanted to."

"Were you going to kiss her? Honestly." Brielle asks, and I watch as she turns around and slowly shakes her head. The hurt flashing behind her eyes is hard to see. Like a wound, I feel a subtle pang rip through my chest. I drop my eyes to the ground and arch my brow.

Does she really think I'd risk what we have over a random bitch?

"Do you really think I'd do that to you?"

"I don't know what I think." She wipes her cheek. Her eyes fall to my chest. "All I know is that I came outside to check on you because I wanted to find out why you're fighting again. And I saw you practically moving in on the hostess."

"I didn't kiss her!" I yell. "And sorry to burst your bubble, but I'll never be done fighting—whether it's in the ring or outside of it. I can't just walk away clean."

"What does that even mean? Why can't you stop?"

I reach up and tuck a strand of her blonde hair behind her ear before I drop my hand to my side. "What did you think would happen, Brielle? That my father was just going to let me walk away? It doesn't work that way. Forget Knock Out. If I quit doing what I do for my father, make no mistake, he'll come after me."

"But he's your father!"

"Yeah, well, after twenty-four year's worth of abuse, something tells me that doesn't mean anything to him."

She takes a step back and rolls her eyes. "Fine. You want to fight, then fight. But stop throwing Luca in my face. He's just a friend. You need to trust me."

"Like you trust me?"

Damn it. I didn't mean that.

Brielle scoffs and turns back to the door. "Goodnight, Theo."

"Look, I didn't mean that. You just . . . you have to think about it from my point of view." I spin her back around. God, she's infuriating tonight. "How did it feel when you thought I'd kissed that other girl?"

"That's not the same and you know it! There's nothing to worry about. Luca isn't the problem!" she yells. "It's you. . . and how the second things don't go your way, you instantly revert back to your old ways. Or . . . is this just who you are?"

"Are you for real right now? What is it with you and him? You can't really be this blind," I snap at her, finally feeling my anger coming to a head. She literally told me that they kissed early this summer. How the hell is she going to sit here and tell me that I have nothing to worry about? "And by the way, I may be lashing out, but it's not because of the reasons you think. I'm not the one afraid of doing what's necessary here, you are."

"Excuse me?"

"Look, I'm done. I can't do this with you. You need to choose—Luca or me. You can't have us both."

"Are you seriously giving me an ultimatum?"

I run my teeth over my bottom lip and bite it. *Am I?*

"Yes." Because at least if it ends here and now, I'll know where I stand with her.

"No!"

"No?" I shake my head. "What the hell do you mean, no?"

Brielle turns back to the door and opens it. "I mean, no. Theo, I'm not going to choose. Luca is like family to me. I won't just give him up."

"Fuck, Brielle. He doesn't see it that way. He loves you."

"That doesn't mean that I should just write him off!"

I take a step back, feeling the cold tone of her words, like a slap to my face. "Well, if that's how you feel, then I guess I got my answer."

She drops her bag to the floor. Her breath catches every so often as she waits for a second before turning around.

Fuck this. Fuck love. And fuck this feeling. For once, I can't even blame my father for being the reason that I have to leave Brielle. Because for once, she made the decision for me. She chose Luca. He's the one she wants more. The one she needs.

"I can't do this anymore. All I've done is let you in." The heaviness of it all is severe. This is a whole new kind of pain.

"I love you, Brielle. But I refuse to share you."

chapter thirty-four

THEO

I t's been fifteen minutes since my father arrived with Mr. Overshire, and already my patience is wearing thin. His incessant bitching to have the meeting take place at Haze was nearly enough to make me call off the whole thing in the first place. Besides that, I know who's working the bar tonight. Becks. The last thing I need is for her to convince Brielle that she should come out and her see me—with Katrina, no less—and then turn around and do something, trying to get a rise out of me.

I run my hands over my face, then push them through my hair. Damn it, I'm on edge. It's been a week since I gave her the ultimatum, since she chose Luca over me. I feel like I'm going through withdrawal. I clench my hands into fists and squeeze them. Jesus. I need this night to be over. I need to get my ass to Knock Out, or I'm going to blow up at someone.

I cut my eyes over to Katrina who, surprisingly, hasn't spoken a word to me, and find her blue eyes miles away. I feel my fingers dig into the leather chaise of one of the club's more private VIP balconies. My mind is yelling at me to simply let her be but I can't. The last time I saw her, we both said some pretty hurtful things. In my defense, I had just been stabbed, lost a lot of blood, and was drowning in some pretty expensive tequila. But still, she didn't deserve it.

"No. Absolutely not!" I hear my father's voice catch in the forefront of my mind as I slowly make my way over to where Katrina's standing. I practically drag my feet so as to not draw my father's eye. I know how he can be when he gets in one of his moods, and I am definitely not in the right mind space to handle it tonight. In fact, after everything he pulled with Brielle, he's lucky I even showed up to this shit show. The only reason I did is because it would only cause more problems if I hadn't.

"Don't make an enemy out of me, Tom. You know that's a bullshit excuse," my father's voice snaps again.

I roll my eyes. Fucking pathetic, both of them. How the hell these two plan on being partners blows my fucking mind. Neither of them wants to budge on their offer. Honestly, I don't understand why my father is trying so hard in the first place. It's not like he can't find someone else to take his place. Someone more cooperative. At this rate, we'll be here all night.

Well, not me.

I raise my brow. All it took was one call to Mack, and now my evening just became a whole lot more interesting. It'll be a fun warm-up for tomorrow's big fight. I heard the kid I'm up against is actually pretty good. "Trained by Alfred Alonzo," I hear Wes's obnoxious voice troll through my mind. *Whatever that means.* All I know is it'll be fun to go up against someone who can potentially give it back as good as he gets. He's going to lose—don't get me wrong—but I'll make it worth the overhead it costs to get in.

A certain blonde has left me with more than one demon to face. Why the hell I chose to fall in love with someone who is so damn strong-willed surprises even me. Maybe Mason was the only one smart enough to see the truth. Luca is the better choice. The girl may be my weakness, but she tests me in ways I never knew possible—ways that no amount of change could ever make me good enough to deserve her.

I reach Katrina at the same time that her father reaches for his phone. His chubby, little fingers poke at the screen as he feverishly yells at someone on the other line. I swear the man looks like a damn leprechaun, with his bald head and that god-awful wispy, red beard. His short stature is an oddity compared to Katrina, who must get her looks from her mother.

Katrina, having watched me walk up, turns and faces me. Her expression is amused. "Hello, Theo." She sucks in a deep breath between her teeth. Her eyes gingerly look up and down my body as if she dislikes what she sees. I do the same. "What? No, Brielle tonight?"

I narrow my eyes at her poor attempt at trying to get a rise out of me and lean over the railing. "Katrina, always a pleasure," I lazily say, choosing to ignore her question. My hands fold together as I peer down at the dance floor below us. The bodies upon bodies of clubgoers are completely oblivious to the dangers perfectly poised above them.

She slides toward me, and her shoulder brushes mine. "My father tells me that you're my escort to the All Hallows Eve Ball next week. Is that true?"

I feel a muscle in my jaw clench as I grind my teeth shut, trying to keep myself from saying anything before I have the chance to think. "So I've been told," I sigh reluctantly. "You wouldn't happen to know why that is now, would you?"

"I may have an inkling." She giggles, seeming pleased with herself. "Really you should be thanking me." She smiles and tilts her head toward the side. Her blonde hair falls down my arm like a curtain. The annoying prickle it leaves behind causes my nerve endings to jolt, making me feel on edge.

"And why is that?" I dare to ask.

I already know whatever it is she's about to say is only going to further piss me off, but I also know she's only saying it because she's hurt. I may not remember every little detail that transpired that night, but I do remember seeing the hurt behind her eyes. In all honesty, if I had known how she truly felt, I wouldn't have let it go on as long as I did. I'm a fucking dick but I'm not heartless.

"Because if I hadn't talked Daddy into the idea, then just think about it. You could have walked in with that troll on your arm instead."

The fuck? "Easy," I growl at her. "Leave Brielle out of this."

"Or what? Who are you, but a pawn, Theo? Just like me." She giggles to herself. "It's like you said, this is all just for fun. Only now, I've got the advantage." She leans further into my side. Her lips graze my ear as she breathes her words into my mind. "I know who Theo Wescott loves most in this world."

I reach out and grasp her arm when she moves to walk away from me. She wriggles under my touch, but I don't care at this point. Unlike my father, I couldn't give a fuck what the hell her *daddy* thinks.

I know our little struggle has caught the attention of our fathers when I feel eyes on my back. My father beckons us to join them, obviously choosing to keep a closer eye on me, but I hesitate to move. "For your own good, you'd better keep that pretty mouth of yours shut," I whisper before releasing her.

As if it's fallen asleep, Katrina lets her arm fall limply down her side. Her free hand lifts to massage the soft skin where my hand had held her. "I seem to remember a time when you quite enjoyed my pretty mouth."

I roll my eyes. "I enjoyed a lot of pretty mouths, but don't get it twisted. You were merely a means to an end."

I fully expect to see some kind of hurt but she surprises me. She drops her eyes to the tiny handbag she's carrying, a sly smile tugging at the corner of her mouth. If I didn't know any better, I'd say she wants me to admit it to her that it was all a lie—a ploy for my father to get what he wants. But what comes out of her mouth is, "You disgust me."

"Likewise."

I leave her and walk over to my father, sitting down on the empty seat beside him.

"Oh, good." He flashes a smile, then clamps a hand down on my leg. To everyone else, it would seem like a normal thing to do. Something casual. Only I can see it for what it really is, a fake gesture.

My father is a smart man. He knows that when it comes to business, you have to play the game to win. And Mr. Overshire is a big family man, thus, my father's miraculous transformation into father of the year—a title he plays so well.

"Jameson said someone should be up soon with some drinks from the bar."

Fuck me. I squeeze my eyes shut. Well, so much for discretion.

"Are you two excited about the ball next week?"

It's then that Katrina decides to join the conversation, taking a seat next to me. Her long leg crosses over the other as she presses her heel under my calf. "Of course we are!" Her voice rises a couple of octaves. She wraps her arms around my bicep and leans into my side. "It's all this guy can talk about."

My father turns to me.

"Elated." I feign enthusiasm.

I roll my eyes before spotting a blonde bun out of the corner of my eye, bobbing up the stairs, and immediately my heart sinks. An image of emerald-green eyes and pink, full lips flashes across my mind. Without hesitation, I rip my arm from Katrina and stand up. The gesture leads a thin expression to form along my father's face. But much like before, I couldn't give a fuck. I'm preparing myself for the worst, when I catch the blonde take the next step and two dark brown eyes slide into view.

Oh thank God. I breathe a sigh of relief, then turn back to the group and catch my father's steely gaze. Shit. "Sorry. I . . . uh. . . I thought there was a bug," I say, well aware of how completely fucked I might be—especially when I watch my father's eyes trail behind me to the waitress as realization washes over him.

"I see," he murmurs along with something I can't hear.

I feel my fingers curl into fists.

"Hey y'all!"

I step to the side as the server walks up behind me with a tray of drinks. Jessica? Jasmine? Jeanine? Whatever the hell her name is steps up to the table.

"Sorry it took so long. The bartender said she was making them extra special tonight," she says with a heavy twang.

I bet she did. I shake my head, trying not to imagine just what Becks meant by "special."

Damn it. It looks like getting drunk is off the table. I'll just have to suffer my way through this one.

"Can I get y'all anything else before I go?"

Mr. Overshire reaches for a glass and takes a small sip before setting it back down on the table. "This tastes like sewer water. I'll take a beer. Bottled." Mr. Overshire spits out, reaching forward to grab a handful of napkins, which he uses to dab his tongue.

Katrina offers me a sly smile.

Ever the bitch, I see.

I shake my head and offer the poor girl a smile. "Just the beer, I guess. Thanks."

The girl looks defeated as she turns and starts her descent back down the stairs. Little does she know that she's the lucky one. I'd give anything to get away from this shit. "Excuse us, for a second," I hear my father say as he stands up.

I let out a breath, following silently after him.

"Look, if you're going to say something about the drink, it's not what you think. It's—"

"What are you doing?" he whirls around and asks through gritted teeth. "Are you trying to fuck this deal up for me, or are you just this stupid?"

I take a step back. "You want to try that again? It's just a drink."

I turn my head to Mr. Overshire when my father tosses him a slight wave. I see Katrina is no longer sitting in the same spot but is nestled up beside her father. The two of them are whispering to each other like schoolgirls.

"Lower your voice." My father turns out toward the balcony and rests his elbows along the rail. "I thought I told you to handle the Sutton girl?"

Oh.

"I remember you making a lot of threats," I answer truthfully. I press my hands against my face and rub them over my tired eyes. "But you don't have to worry about her. Brielle isn't going to be a problem." I wave my arms out in front of us. "I'm here. You won. I'm taking Katrina to the ball."

I feel the air kick around us as my father whips toward me. His hands fists the material of my sports coat. "You think this is a game?" he spits out. The whites of his eyes seem to have disappeared completely.

I grab his wrists and remove his hands from my coat. The look on his face, while I do so, is not something I'll likely forget. Because for the first time, ever, I'm the one who's in control. Not him. "Don't fucking touch me again," I say and step in his direction. "It wouldn't be wise."

My father brushes his hair back with his hand and cuts a look toward the two equally surprised figures of Katrina and her father. He licks his lips, tossing his head back in a fit of laughter. When their focus shifts, he waits for some time to pass before choosing to continue.

"Listen here, you little shit," he growls. His voice is as coarse as gravel. "The two of us are going to go over there, and you're going to fall in line. Do you understand? Because if you don't, well . . . I'm sure you can draw your own conclusions. You've always had a vast imagination."

He takes a small step to head back to the table, but I block his path. "Maybe I didn't make myself clear." I clench my jaw. "I did what you asked, which means *you're going to* leave Brielle alone. If you threaten her again, then this—" I motion between the two of us, the Overshires and my club—"this is over. You can come at me all you want, but if you go after Brielle, there is nothing that will stop me from ending you. She's off-limits, and you would do well to remember that."

With a puffed chest, my father narrows his eyes up at me. Like me, he's never been the type of man to back down so easily. "Are you threatening me, Son?"

"That's exactly what I'm doing."

Seconds pass as the two of us stand there, staring at each other. He curls his hands into fists, as if readying himself for a fight, but just as I think he's about to deck me, he releases them. A soft smile pulls along his face.

"Fine. Keep her." He nods his head, fixing his sleeves. "As long as she stays the hell away from family affairs. I'm happy."

He raises an arm to pat me on the back, moving around me as he does. What the hell was that about? I shake my head, distrusting how easily my father relented. He's never been one to bend to other people's wants or needs. I see Katrina rise from her spot beside her father and return to the other seat. I roll my eyes and join her. This is the last time. The last job. After this, I'm done.

I feel my phone ring in my pocket but I silence it. If I had to guess, I'm sure Becks has sufficiently filled Brielle in on what's been happening tonight. But hashing out this specific topic in front of my father isn't exactly ideal. Shit. I'd rather not have it in general. My phone buzzes, again, and I reach in to grab it.

"Is that important?" I hear my father groan. My eyes tear away from the screen to find three sets of eyes watching me. "We were just about to start discussing the legacy of our two families with you both, but if you need to . . ."

I shake my head and bury my phone back in my pocket. Wait.

"I'm sorry. Legacy?"

"Yes." Mr. Overshire decides to jump in now.

The pride he's wearing on his face is suddenly annoying the shit out me. What the fuck do I care about their future partnership plans? They don't involve me.

"We've decided, well, your father suggested, and I agreed, that the only sensible conclusion to ensure our families' ties remain untainted is to make the ultimate bond—a stronger bond between you and Katrina. . . in the form of marriage."

"I'm sorry, what?" "Fuck no!" Katrina and I exclaim at the same time.

The two of us turn to each other in shock. At least, we now have one thing we can agree upon—our mutual dislike of our fucking fathers' dumbass idea.

"Yes, we're sorry to spring this on the two of you. And so suddenly," my father joins in.

Like fuck he is! I want to shout. No way. This is not happening. He can eat shit if he thinks I am going to just lie down and do this for him.

"Sadly, this is the only way." My father glares at me. His expression is tight as if he can read my thoughts.

You're going to fall in line. Do you understand? Because if you don't, well . . . I'm sure you can draw your own conclusions. You've always had a vast imagination, I hear his words echo in the back of my mind. But I'm already on my feet.

"Theo, wait. Get back—"

"No, fuck you!" I spit out as I whip around. "You've lost your damn mind."

My father rises from his seat. "Watch your tone, Son," he warns me, but I've had enough. This whole thing has gone on for far too long. "You wouldn't want to say something you can't take back."

I let out a chuckle and cut my eyes between the two of them. Katrina is still sitting dazed on the couch. Who the hell did they think they were?

"You know what? Go. Get the fuck out." I shake my head. "I'm done."

"Excuse me? Gerald. What is the meaning of this?" Mr. Overshire demands. His judgmental glare is giving my father the stress sweats.

My father marches forward and grips my arm. The sheer force of his hold would have brought down the old me within a heartbeat. But the new me is used to it. Hell. I welcome it at times. "Theo!"

"You heard me!" I shove my father back and yell at them. "Get the hell out of my club. I won't ask again."

Grabbing his daughter, Mr. Overshire slowly descends the steps. I watch my father stumble back a ways before he digs his feet into the ground.

"You will regret this," he says once the Overshires are out of earshot, leering at me from where he stands. Like the flip of a switch, he adjusts his suit, fixes his hair, and then reaches for his things.

"I doubt that!" I yell a little louder than I expected to. "I really do. Find someone else to handle your problems, because I'm done."

He seems to ignore me as he walks toward the stairs. "I'll be seeing you real soon, Son."

I watch him stride down the steps and make his way out through the back. My eyes catch the sight of Becks, shaking her damn head up at me as I lean over the railing, trying to clear my head. Damn it. My ears are ringing. Images from tonight's events replaying through my mind.

What the hell have I done?

chapter thirty-five

My head is spinning as I walk up to the bar. The blue hue of the backlight pulses in tune with the bass—the strobelike effect not helping to ease my nerves. I pinch my eyes shut and try to relax. Jesus, I can't believe I just kicked my father out of my club. If I wasn't so worried about what his end game might be, I'd probably feel relieved. But all I've done now is add more shit on top of everything else.

I look down the bar. Where the hell is Wes? After what my father said, I need to make sure Brielle's safe. I'll hire a security detail and force her to stay at my house. We may not be together right now—or ever again—but I'd do anything to protect her, even if that means calling in old favors and cashing them in. My father may be a powerful man, but I've also got connection—allies made through the many "meetings" my father has sent me to—the ones where I left more than empty pockets in my wake. Broken bones, and broken homes. Sadly, my father likes his lessons to be as demented as he is. But any enemy of my father's is a friend of mine.

I see Becks, in her short white dress, slink around the corner with a glass she's cleaning. Her expression darkens the second she sees me. Fuck. What the hell am I paying Wes for when he's never around? Rolling her eyes, she slams the glass down and starts to make her way toward me. The heels of her knee-high boots overpower the bass as she walks with an

intensity I haven't seen before. Oh, she definitely put
something "special" in those drinks. She's pissed.

"What the hell do you want?" she spits out. The tip of
her tongue brushes over the top of her teeth while she rakes her
eyes over me as if I were the most disgusting thing she's ever
seen. "Enjoy your drinks?"

"I'm just looking for Wes." I shake my head, not
wanting to get into the details or agitate her further. "Do you
know where he is?"

Becks crosses her arms, creasing her expression. "Hmm
. . . I'm sorry. He's out right now. Can I take a message, or
would that be a conflict of interest?"

I push off the counter and cut my eyes back toward the
office. "A conflict of interest?"

"Yeah. You know, because Brielle is my best friend?"
What does Brielle have to do with Wes?

"What the hell are you talking about?" I hesitate,
knowing full well what I'm about to receive. Becks is a fierce
and loyal friend, which means I am most definitely about to
have my ass handed to me.

"For fuck's sake, Theo. Are you messing with me?" She
all but jumps over the bar, trying to get at me. Her arms are
flailing around like they've got a mind of their own.

"Look, I don't know what you think you saw, but—"

"Oh, that's it!" Becks yells. Her heels stomp madly as
she moves to come around the side. "Where the hell is
Katrina?"

"Katrina?"

"Yes! I need to know so after I kick your ass, she's
next."

"Okay, Becks, calm down. I don't know where she is
and I don't care." I shake my head at how insane she sounds.

"I'm telling you the truth. Nothing happened." I let out a slow breath. "Well, I mean, something did happen . . ." Fuck, bad choice of words. "But it's nothing like what you think."

I see Becks rearing back as if to hit me, when she steps up and shoves my shoulder. "You're an asshole, you know that? You led her on back then, and you're leading her on now. Be honest with me. The only reason you were ever even interested in Brielle in the first place is because Mason told you she was off limits. You just want what you can't have."

I can feel my anger starting to rise with every word she lets slip. She thinks I only wanted Brielle because Mason told me to stay away? Where the hell did this come from? Her? Mason? Brielle? Is this what Brielle secretly thinks about my feelings for her? I'm so confused. Worse. I'm pissed. I'm fucking livid. What the hell does Becks even know about love, anyway? And who the hell is she to assume that I never cared for Brielle? She has no idea how I feel. I hardly know how to describe it.

"I'm sorry." I take a step back. "What?"

"You're an asshole but you're not deaf," she snaps.

"Okay, you're a good friend, Becks. And I'm glad Brielle has you watching out for her. But you're wrong. I didn't act on my feelings back then out of respect for Mason, but I loved her then . . . just as I do now." I look up at the VIP section and point at the empty seats. "Which is why I just had to do something I never wanted to do. And why I need to find Wes, *now*." I pause, catching the gold flakes in her eyes. They seem to spark like embers under the flashing lights.

"What does Wes have to do with whatever the hell you just did?" She uncrosses her arms.

I stare down at her and can see that she's not going to help me until I give her something more. I groan to myself, letting out a deep breath and rolling my eyes. What the hell is it with Becks and Wes, feeling like they're warranted with knowing the most private details of my life. Fuck. They really are the perfect match.

I drop my head and stare at the bar top. "Fuck. Fine." I turn toward her and push a shaky hand over the top of my hair. My fingers completely sink into the top of it, reminding me that I'm due for a haircut. I've been a little preoccupied lately. "My father is threatening Brielle because I won't marry Katrina for a business deal."

Becks launches into a succession of rapid blinks before throwing her head back in a fit of laughter. "You're fucked up, Wescott."

"I'm not lying."

"Sure." She backs away when a man in a white dress shirt across the bar, grabs a bottle and starts pouring himself a hearty shot. She heads in his direction but not before adding, "I don't care what the fuck your father wants. Just leave Brielle out of it, okay?"

I follow her. "I can't do that."

I walk up to the man in the white dress shirt and grab a fistful of it. Becks reaches for the bottle just as I slam his face against the bar top. "I don't like thieves. Pay your tab, and get the fuck out of my club," I spit out at the man. After I release him, he tosses a few bills on the counter after I release him, and then stumbles toward the exit.

"Becks, listen to me." I chase her around the bar as she tries to ignore me. "I wouldn't lie about this. I wouldn't lie about Brielle being in trouble." That gets her attention.

"What the hell are you talking about?" She whips around to face me. The guy who's in front of her is waving dollars at her in an attempt to get her attention, which annoys me. I narrow my eyes at the jackass, and Becks pulls the money from his hand.

"Three lemon drops, love. And hurry," he slurs. His eyes linger on her chest. He reaches into his wallet and pulls out another bill, sliding it slowly and facedown on the counter. "There might even be something extra in it for you if you play your cards right."

I feel my pulse pick up, my skin prickling as I press my lips together. What the fuck? I walk over to Becks and step in between her and the man. My instinct to beat the shit out of this asshole wins out over my better judgment. She looks up at me confused when I lean toward the man. Slamming my fist down on the counter, I rip the bill from his hand and pass it to Becks. "Get the fuck away from my bar before I kick your ass," I speak slowly so that he can hear me.

"The fuck? What about my shots?"

"How about some advice instead?" I jerk his hand from the counter when he doesn't move away. "Keep your eyes to yourself. If you want a peep show, the closest strip club is a couple of miles down the road." I turn my head towards Becks, who is watching with a sense of amusement I haven't seen before. "The money stays with the girl; now get lost."

I wait until the guy stumbles away, before I turn around and find Becks smiling. "You didn't have to do that, you know? I can take care of myself."

"Yes, I did. He was out of line." I roll my shoulders, raising my wrist and check the time. "Look, I need to leave and check on Brielle." Sighing, I lift my arm and place my hand on her shoulder. "Are you going to be okay without Wes?" She nods but doesn't say anything. "Okay, well, I guess I'll see you around. Tell Wes to call me when he gets back."

I turn around and start to walk towards the exit, when I feel Becks's hand on my arm. Her fingers clasp around my wrist. "Theo, wait," she whispers. I turn around and stare down at her. "Is your dad really going to do something to Brielle if you don't marry Katrina?"

Searching her eyes for any sign of humor I come up empty. There is none. She actually believes me. "Yes." I suck my bottom lip between my teeth and bite it. "There's more to the story, but I owe it to Brielle to tell her first." I drop my eyes. "I won't lose her like I lost Mason." Although I'm doing my best to keep my feelings under control, my voice betrays me as I hear the emotion building up in it. "I can't lose her."

Becks shakes her head as if what she's about to say pains her. "Fuck." She closes her eyes. "You really do love her, don't you?"

"I do. I always have." I nod. This particular conversation is making me uncomfortable. I'm not the type of guy to openly share my feelings. But fuck if this girl isn't blessed with the skills of making one talk—something my father would see as something to exploit.

She bites her lip. "Well, don't hate me, but I called her." She shifts nervously. "I . . . I didn't know."

I shake my head and drop my hand. "It's okay; I figured as much." I smile at her, when I suddenly remember the phone call that I received before everything *really* went to shit. I reach in my pocket and pull it out. "I think she called me." I say as I open the missed call log. But the only name that I see is Wes's. I look off to the side and feel my mind starting to spin out of control. "Damn it," I say when the worst possible scenario comes to mind. "It wasn't her." I slide the phone back into my pocket. "You don't think that she's with Luca, do you?"

I can see Becks's hesitation, and it does nothing to stave off my irritation. *If he's there, I'm going to lose my shit,* I silently tell myself.

"Knowing him, I wouldn't doubt it. Luca is nothing, if not predictable, and he's not the type to give her up without a fight," she says in a matter-of-fact tone.

The fuck? How the hell is that supposed to make me feel better? I squeeze my fists and try not to show the effect her words have on me. "Yeah, that's what I'm scared of," I admit. "Well, I better go."

"Hey!" Becks reaches out to me but drops her hands when she can clearly see the frustration written on my face. "I'm sorry. I was wrong about you." She shrugs as if to say she's not good at apologies. "You play the part of an asshole, perfectly. But you're kind of a good guy too. I'm happy she has you."

I tilt my head, sweeping my eyes to her. "Thanks," I say, but I'm still not sure if she means it, or if she's simply fucking with me. "I better go."

She laughs as I walk around the corner and exit the bar. "Take care of my girl, Theo!" she yells. "She's not like me. She's too nice for her own good."

I'm not sure how much time has passed when I pull into Brielle's driveway and throw my truck into park. My whole body is on edge. I planned to take the bike, but it's cold as shit tonight. I run up to the door and lean into its frame, listening for any signs that she may not be alone. I raise my fist to knock, when from the window that's adjacent to the door, I see two figures sitting side by side on the couch. My shoulders tense when I recognize Luca's slouched frame.

I trail my eyes along with her as I watch her stand and move into the kitchen. Her petite frame is hidden under a long

T-shirt and pajama shorts. As much as I want to bust down the door, stride over to Luca, and rip him from the couch, I can't.

She's laughing? I feel my stomach drop out. She takes the bowl and leans over the side of the couch, Luca moving with her, happily.

He says something, and she smiles in response. Whatever it is elicits Luca to lean into her and close the remaining distance between them. Their lips meet, and my skin comes alive as a slow burn heats every inch. That irritating itch to punch something gnaws at my core.

I take a step back and turn around. I reach into my pocket and pull out my phone. My fingers feel numb as I dial and walk back to the truck.

"Hector, yes, I'm sending you an address—Brielle Sutton . . . you've met her once before. Blonde, five foot two. Yes, that girl. I want you and Ramirez on a twenty-four-hour watch until further notice." I pause before opening the driver's side door. I'm thankful to hear that, the two are just around the corner. My eyes flit up to the window. "She'll probably have a Lucas Garrett with her. He's friendly."

I click off the phone and pull out of the driveway. I need to put as much distance as possible between myself and Luca, before I do something I might regret—something she'd never forgive me for.

Besides, I can't protect Brielle in jail.

chapter thirty-six

I finally stop sobbing when I pass out on the couch, my arms clutching a box of tissues and an ice cream spoon. *Sense and Sensibility* is idly playing in the background because, *of course*, I'm a glutton for punishment. This past week has been a series of bad days on top of bad decisions. So I've made the choice to spend the weekend alone.

I keep playing our fight over and over in my head, and I get why he left. It only took seeing him with that hostess for me to think the worst. I just wish Theo could see it from my perspective. Luca isn't a threat. It shouldn't be about choosing between the two of them, when they both mean so much to me. Luca's as close to family as it gets. He's my best friend. Losing him would be like losing a tiny piece of myself. But I love Theo.

We'd been only a few feet away, but I could see it. The walls behind his eyes were already starting to build back up, and I could sense he was hurt as I watched him walk away, hop on his bike, and speed off. I called out to him but he ignored me. I called his phone, but he didn't pick up. I know he probably feels like me not choosing was my choice, but that's not true. Maybe if he had let me talk to Luca, I could have explained it to him without it turning into what it did. But it's too late for that. Theo's gone, and I doubt he's the type of guy who gives second chances.

I wake up to my alarm, and it's six in the evening. Squinting my eyes, I silence it. I feel like crap, and I don't need to look in the mirror to know that my eyes are swollen from crying and my makeup probably looks like something out of a horror movie. But why do I care? I toss my phone back on the coffee table and sit up on the couch.

Out of habit, I sweep my eyes around the room, but I don't know what I expect to find. I know I'm alone. Becks told me this morning, before she left, that she's sleeping at Wes's this weekend, since they're working together and going to Theo's big fight tomorrow night. *But a girl can dream. . . of brown hair, and hazel eyes.*

I run my hands over my face before I push them through my hair, wrapping it in a bun. Yup, tonight's definitely going to be a lazy one. I eye the mint chocolate chip ice cream, which is now more of a soup after I left it sitting on the coffee table. Crap. That was my last pint. I stand up and walk into the kitchen and dump it down the drain. I finish rinsing the bowl, when I hear my phone start to ring; Becks's special ringtone playing loudly.

"Hey B, I just wanted to check in and see how you were doing?" Becks's concerned tone, rings in my ear. I pull the phone back and drop it on my chest, hitting the speaker button as I do. "Are we out of ice cream yet?"

"Hey, friends aren't supposed to judge one another." I roll my eyes. I can practically visualize her pacing around the club's walk-in fridge, brow's crinkled and biting her nails. "But I'm good. How's work?"

"It's fine," she says, drawing her words out in the way she knows I hate. The way that tells me she's about to tell me something that she knows I won't like—kind of like the time she accidentally slept with my English teacher's aide last semester, and then she pretended like it never happened until we bumped into him outside of the Union. The poor guy practically ran from us.

"But . . ." I say, urging her to get on with it. My mind is teeming with all the different possibilities.

"But Theo's here," she begins, and I don't talk because I can tell that there's more. "W- with Katrina."

Wait. What?

Katrina . . .?

"He's with Katrina?" I sit up. My phone flies off my chest and lands at my feet. Picking it up, I ask, "What . . . ugh, what are they doing?" Though I'm not sure I really want to know. An image of a scantily clad Katrina hanging all over him instantly comes to mind.

Should I head up there?

My eyes move down to my pajama shorts and the T-shirt I'm currently wearing, remembering that I'm also not wearing an ounce of makeup, and my hair is in a bun. No. I'm in no shape to compete with Katrina tonight. not that I ever could even if I tried. She's gorgeous and well-traveled—a perfect match for someone like Theo. I'm just . . . me.

"Nothing, really," Becks finally admits. "I've been watching, though, so don't worry. They've just been sitting up there with his dad and another man. Talking."

I feel sick, thinking about the two of them together. Apparently, Theo didn't love me as much as he thought if he's able to move on already. How the hell did I let myself believe that he could actually change? I should have stayed away.

"Thanks, Becks, but you don't have to watch him," I say, trying—but failing—to sound like it doesn't bother me. But lying has never been my strong suit, so I add, "I promise, I'm

fine. Besides, you said it yourself. Theo will always pick Theo.
I don't know what I was thinking."

"Maybe," Becks says, but she's even worse of a liar than
I am. "Oh my God. This bitch!"

"What? What's wrong?"

"Now she's leaning on him, and he's not shoving her
away. That asshole. He's—"

"Becks, I really don't want to know."

I lift the phone to my ear and turn off the speaker. "It's
okay, really." My voice is strained. "But I appreciate you letting
me know. You're a good friend."

"Damn, you're handling this a lot better than I would
be." She half laughs. "If it were me, I'd get my ass up here and
mark my territory. Show the whore who she's really messing
with."

Oh my God. I raise my hand up to my face. "Becks, just
because she and Theo are hanging out doesn't make her a
whore." I shake my head.

"Oh, she's a whore all right." I listen to Becks take in a
quick breath. "A dirty, man-stealing hoe bag with a . . . ugh . . .
hold on one second."

Oh Lord. I laugh to myself. I hear Becks murmuring
something in the background to someone else but it's distant.
She must be holding the phone down, because it sounds like I'm
underwater.

"Ugh . . . I have to run. Apparently, his highness needs
drinks made," she chokes out the words.

"All right, but do me a favor. . ."

"What?"

"Try not to spit in their drinks, please?"

Becks chuckles. "I make no promises."

Hanging up with Becks, the doorbell rings, and secretly I hope it's someone whose heard my silent plea, bringing me more mint chop. I throw the door open and instead I find it's karma slapping me in the face, when I see . . . "Luca? Hey!"

"Hey, Bree!" He walks in the door.

"Ugh, not that I'm mad. But I thought we said tomorrow?"

"We did." Walking over to the coffee table, he grabs the remote and makes himself comfortable on the couch. "Hey! You got anything to eat? I'm starving."

Um . . . "Sure." I'm so confused.

Did Becks send him?

Half an hour later, he's still here. The only explanation he offered was one in the form of a question: *What? I need an excuse to hang out with my best friend?*

"Okay, but this is our last bag of popcorn, so chill out, would ya?" I laugh, tossing the last popped kernel at Luca's head before dumping the new bag in the bowl.

Luca leans over the couch; his arm is extended down the back of it. "No promises, Bree. I'm a growing boy."

I roll my eyes and drop the bag in the trash, grabbing the bowl and moving to settle back on the couch Luca reaches out to take a handful and I swat his arm away.

"This is my bowl," I tease him, raising the popcorn above my head as I lean back over the arm of the couch.

He drops his pillow, the small, square one with daisies, and it falls to the floor. His body brushes up against mine while he reaches for the popcorn; our lips are an inch apart. "We'll see about that."

It's then, somewhere in between the smell of his cologne and the tender way he's watching me, I let myself wonder what it might be like to be with him. Everyone else seems to think we belong together. What if we are? Maybe he's right, and I haven't really given us a chance. For a long time, it's just been the two of us and Becks. Maybe the reason I've been so reluctant to give him up is because, deep down, I know he's the one I should be with. Not Theo.

"Ha." Luca snatches the bowl from my hand, a playful smirk pulling at his lips as he readjusts himself back on his cushion. "Don't worry. I'll share. . . if you're lucky."

I let myself smile, but I'm not sure if it's more forced than real. The sudden shift in my mind makes my head hurt. I lift my eyes and find he's watching me again. His attention lingers in places that it should never be. I reach for my blanket and lay it over my bare legs, my shorts and T-shirt are no longer enough.

"Sorry," he whispers. But he doesn't look away.

Instead, he leans forward and frames my face with his hands. I part my lips to ask what he's doing, when out of nowhere, he crushes his lips against mine. The force of his kiss knocks me back, and I stumble trying to keep up to him. His lips are soft, softer than I'm used to. I close my eyes and try to give in to the moment, if only to see if there is anything. Then I hear Luca moan, and at the sound of it, I squeeze my eyes shut. A part of me, hopes that I can feel something for Luca. But I don't. I feel nothing.

Luca pulls away before I can break the kiss. His body slinks back against the couch. He pushes a hand through his hair. "Sorry, I just . . . I had to."

I nod, feeling a twinge of guilt resonate within my chest. The weight of the kiss settles and casts an uncomfortable heaviness throughout the room. I reach for the controller to start our show. But something Theo said pops into my head, *He loves you.* I hear his voice, and with it, our entire fight flashes across my mind again. I plead to my inner conscience, wishing that I could turn it off. It's no use. I close my eyes, feeling the barrier build between us.

"You okay?" Luca asks. His hand reaches out to rub a small circle across my back.

I pinch the bridge of my nose, when a question appears. And even though I wish I could ignore it, I can't. "Luca, are you in love with me?"

He clears his throat and shifts uncomfortably in his seat. I can see it in his face that I've startled him. "Please, just be honest with me," I beg. My mind prays that he says no.

"You really want to know?" He drops his head. His fingers are mindlessly twisting a single piece of popcorn.

"I do."

"Okay, fine." I watch as he leans forward and sets the bowl down on the table. "Yes. I do I love you."

No. No. No. You can't love me!

It's then that the pain I feel in my chest magnifies a thousand times. "Shit." I pinch my eyes shut.

"Brielle? Are you. . . did you just—"

"Luca, listen to me." I shake my head. "You can't be in love with me."

He arches his brow. "I'm sorry. What?"

"I said—"

"No. I heard you; I just don't understand. Where this is coming from?"

"From nowhere. Everywhere." I shrug my shoulders. My fingers are working my temples as I try to find the words that I know he needs to hear—the truth. "Luca, I . . . I'm in love with, Theo."

"Okay," he groans. "And why are you telling me this?"

Ugh . . . I wasn't expecting that.

"Because you deserve to know the truth."

The air grows thick as I watch him sit there. He sighs as his eyes shift erratically.

"Thanks . . . I guess." His shoulders sag. and his expression is distant. "I mean, I figured as much." He drops his head again. "I kind of, sort of, well, . . . I saw you last weekend. The two of you."

I crinkle my nose while I pull my legs under me to sit up. "Yeah, I know. You came over to say hi."

"No." He rubs the back of his neck. "I . . . um . . . I *saw* you—saw him and what he did to . . . with you. You know, under the—"

"Oh God." I cover my face. *Nope. No. This is not happening! I'm going to kill, Theo.*

"Yeah."

"I'm sorry," I say. My lips press into a thin line as I wish, not for the first time, the couch would open up and swallow me whole—Anything to get away from how awkward this moment has become.

"No. Don't." He scoots toward the edge of the couch. His hands folding over one another continuously. "I don't want your pity."

"Wait. The whole team was with you! They didn't . . . did they—"

"No! God no." He shakes his head. "I mean, we all saw you walk in together. But they were all too busy talking shit about the game to notice *that.*"

I feel a weird form of relief knowing that Luca was the only one to see, when the ability to use my lungs returns to me. I inhale a breath and let it go.

"Luca, I'm sorry—not that I did it." I can see that wasn't what he had been expecting me to say. "But that you had to find out just how close we've become like that."

Theo was right.

I can't have them both. At least, not right now. There's just too much history, and too many emotions to consider. I know that no matter who I choose, someone is going to get hurt. It's not fair for me to shove a new relationship in Luca's face, when I know he'll be struggling. I need to choose.

I stand and begin to make my way toward the bathroom. My mind is already trying to funnel all the ways that tonight could blow up in my face. But I have to try. The one thing I know, without a shadow of a doubt, is that I am not ready to give up the chance to be with Theo.

"Brielle . . . hey! Where are you going?" Luca calls out behind me. I hold my breath as his voice echoes off the walls.

"I'm sorry, but I've got to go!" I yell from the hallway.

"You can't be serious." And just like that, he's on his feet. "Brielle, he's not a good person. What the hell is it going to take for you to see that?"

I brush some powder on my face, then run my mascara over my eyelashes. I eye Becks's black, leather leggings and the matching leather coat. I close the door and slip them on. The leggings fit like an extra skin, but I know that if Becks were here, she would approve. Well, mostly. I bite my lip and stare down at my converse. I need better shoes.

I cross the hall into Becks's room. My eyes immediately locate a pair of black heels with red soles. I eye their height. Okay, I can do this. Becks is always bragging about how these are her lucky shoes. I step into them. Hm . . . I guess we'll see just how lucky they really are.

"What the hell are you wearing?" Luca whines as I walk into the living room. He lets his eyes trail down the length of me as I walk over and grab my purse. "Are you trying to attract the wrong kind of attention?"

Excuse me?

"Luca, that's not what this is about." I head to the door, choosing to ignore him. I know he's hurting. "I don't expect you to understand why I feel the way I do. Hell, I don't even understand it." I shrug, frozen in place, as his face twists in anger. "But if you were truly my friend, and if you truly care about my happiness, then you would understand why I need to leave now. And if not, then . . . well . . . then I guess I'll understand that too."

I open the door, but my feet refuse to move.

"Luca, I don't know what I'll do if I lose you," I whisper from across the room. My fingers grip the door as I keep my eyes focused in front of me. "But I can't let what I have with Theo pass me by because I'm too afraid to take risks. He makes me happy."

I muster up the courage to glance back at him before I head towards my car. On the way, I notice an unmarked car parked out front. Hector and another guy are seated up front. What the . . .? I get in my car and start it, when I feel my phone go off. Pulling it from my pocket, I see a text from Becks.

Enjoy the make-up sex. :)

I knit my brows and quickly type a response.

What?

I watch the tiny dots dance along the screen, until Becks must have given up because she calls me.

"Hey, you two made up yet?" she immediately asks. The cheery tone to her voice makes me smile.

"Becks, what the hell are you talking about?"

"Shit. He must not have made it there yet. I wonder where he's at?"

At the risk of being disappointed, I feel the need to ask, "Theo?"

"Yeah," she says, and I can tell she's smiling. "When he came down, we talked, and then he left, headed your way."

I turn back to see Hector, waiting in his car when I feel the knots in my stomach twist uncomfortably. *Oh no. No. No. No.* Did he see . . .? "Shit, Becks. I think I messed up."

"What? Why? What happened?" she asks, and I hurry, filling her in on the kiss with Luca, and everything since. She gasps, "Oh shit. That has to be it. He must have shown up, saw Luca kiss you, and then stormed off. God Luca is such an ass. I'm surprised Theo didn't kick down the door and kill him right then." She laughs. "What are you going to do?"

"I don't know," I answer her, honestly. Because I don't.

A part of me wishes Theo *had* kicked through the door, because, at least then I'd be able to explain the situation to him. But the fact that he simply left means that seeing Luca and me kissing may have broken whatever final straw he had left. What if I've lost him forever?

I look down at the outfit I'm wearing and strangely the answer appears. "Actually . . . maybe I have one idea."

"Really? What? How are you going to find him if you don't know where he is?"

"I know where he'll be tomorrow."

"Brielle, no. I don't know if that's—"

"It'll be fine." I feel a smile spread across my lips as I get out of the car and make a point to wave at Hector.

The truth is, I don't know what happened—what Theo saw, or didn't see—I only know that Hector is *here*. Which means that even while he's pissed at me, Theo still cares about my safety. I swear, he can be just as bad as my father sometimes. I mean, I don't know why or what must have happened tonight for him to think that I needed the protection. And in this moment, I can't think about that. All I care about is the fact that Theo still cares.

"I've got to go, Becks. But I'll see you tomorrow!"

chapter thirty-seven

THEO

T wo swigs into my bourbon, and I can taste my blood marrying with the subtle notes of caramel. Fuck. I wipe my mouth on my forearm. The beaded remnants of blood streak a line down my arm. I let out a chuckle, well aware of how crazy I must look, and step back into the ring. The sound of my heartbeat pounds behind my ears as I lock eyes with this no-named asshole. It's about damn time. I shake out my hands. Mack finally found someone worthy of my time.

"Fuck. You just don't quit, do you?" My opponent stares wide-eyed at me. "Just stay the fuck down, and I might take it easy on you."

Easy? I almost laugh. *Who said I wanted easy?* I spit, blood splattering at my feet, and roll my shoulders. This is the best kind of medicine you can get without a prescription.

"Easy?" I point a glove at the display board behind us where my name is legible in bold letters. This poor, dumb fuck. He doesn't even know that this fight hasn't even started yet. I'm merely warming up. I could have ended it right from the start, but then . . . where's the fun in that?

"Whatever, man." He shrugs, stepping up to meet me. "It's your funeral."

I fake a punch to his gut, which I know he'll easily be able to dodge, and am met with a knee to the gut. I hit the mat. My hands are flat against the ground. "Ah, come on." I laugh and work my way up to one knee. "Don't start holding back on me now."

I cough. My lungs aching, my ribs burning, and stand. I feel something brush my stomach, so I drop my eyes to my waist. My fingers wrap the bandage barely hanging on and pull it the rest of the way off. I crinkle my nose and toss it aside. I know I should probably stop—knock this asshole on his back. But, fuck it. Unlike these assholes, I don't fight for bragging rights or glory. I fight to see through all the bullshit. To clear my head. I fight to feel the pain.

"Fuck, you're crazy," the guy hedges.

Eh, I guess that's a fair assessment. I've been called worse.

"I- is that a stab wound?"

I nod, and just for fun, I say, "You should see the other guy."

Okay. . . so maybe I like to brag a little bit.

Tired of talking, he slams his fist into my ribs, and I wince. The pain ripples across my chest and knocks the breath out of me. This time when I hit the mat, I don't get up right away. I clutch my abdomen, and I roll off to the far side, coughing and sputtering as I try to catch my breath.

I'm not sure how much time passes, or when I first put two and two together. But eventually, the haze clears, and I'm met with the most brilliant pair of emerald-green eyes. Brielle? No. No, no. It couldn't be. I shake my head, trying to clear my mind, when I see that she is, in fact, here.

What the hell is she doing here? I narrow my eyes in her direction, half choking at the sight of her. Her petite frame slowly makes her way through the crowd until she settles at an empty seat at the bar. Her hair is down, and that outfit . . .

"What the fuc—"

"What? No jokes?" I hear the guy spit out before he rushes over. His fist slams into my cheek. The sound of the blow echoes inside my head. "I guess it's time for a new name to head that board of yours."

Okay. I'm sufficiently warmed up. I crack my neck, raising my hand to brush my fingers across my cheek. The burning sensation I feel tells me that he broke the skin. When the ringing stops, I pull up onto my knees. Damn it. I let out a breath. That was a cheap shot. Bad move, kid. I glare at him for a moment.

I turn my attention back to the bar and catch myself doing a double take. My eyes soak in the scene currently playing out where Brielle is wiggling in her seat as some fucker in a damned suit tries whispering in her ear. *Fucking hell*. I roll my eyes, feeling my blood start to boil. Other than the fact that he chose Brielle to hit on, what kind of sick bastard wears a suit to a place like this?

I tear my eyes away from my girl—I mean, Brielle—as the sound of feet shuffling forces me back into the fight. Again, with the petty, cheap shit? Jesus. This guy is such an asshole. I shake my head as my opponent lunges, swinging and missing. I quickly dodge him and clench my hand into a fist as I make contact with his face—payback for him hitting me when I was distracted. Dick move, kid.

Dick.

Move.

Enough of this bullshit. I sigh. It was fun while it lasted.

I wait until he lunges again. My arms then wrap around his waist, and I flip him onto his back. I bury my hands into him, over and over again, before he has the chance to defend himself. I step off and out of range the moment I see his hand tap and he concedes.

"Good fight, man," I call out to the poor bastard, who's currently heaving back on the mat.

Guess I'll be keeping my title.

I grab my drink, down it, then dip under the ropes. I feel my lips tug to one side. That fight may be over, but bad news for suit guy . . . I still got a couple of demons needing to be absolved tonight.

"Oh, no thank you," I hear Brielle says to the guy.

His perfectly unmarred face is locked on my girl as he stutters trying to come up with a response. The drool practically dripping from this fucker's mouth tells me that he's way out of his league. But, then again, so am I.

Brielle is an angel. Even . . . though . . . *shit.* I lick my lips. My mind loses its train of thought as my eyes follow the curves of her body. I force myself to shut my mouth.

Think, Theo. Think.

Pull your shit together.

I inhale a deep breath. She may be a fucking angel, but there is nothing angelic about the way she looks tonight.

I clear my throat to make myself known. The guy in the suit jerks around.

What the?

I cut my eyes between the two of them. Unfuckin' believable. I almost laugh. It's the fucking porcupine guy—I mean, Blake? The suit somehow makes so much more sense now. This guy's always been a creep.

"Hey, man. Good fight."

I shake my head and laugh, mildly amused, as I turn to Brielle, then back to him. "Care to tell me why you're talking to my girlfriend?"

Wait.

Girlfriend?

What the fu—

"Girlfriend?" The guy arches his brow at the word.

My mind mocks him and his accent. Brielle always did like accents. He looks to Brielle as if waiting for her to explain.

Don't look at her. Look at me, I want to scream.

"Um, no. Space between the words." Brielle sits up and rolls her eyes.

"Right." He reaches back behind him to grab his drink. I watch as he drops his head and moves to slide off the stool. *Fucking pussy.* "I think I'm just going to go." He shoots Brielle a look. "It was great to see you again."

"Bye." She's smiles as I stare after him.

Bye? "The fuck was that, Brielle?" I raise my voice as I watch the asshole join another group of guys by the far wall.

I turn around to the sound of Brielle's heels on the floor as she hops off the stool and starts towards the front door. I barely have time to process the fact that she's leaving before she is already halfway to the door.

The fuck?

I grab a handful of napkins from the bar top and hurry after her as I try to wipe away some of the blood and sweat. Lord knows I'm slowly losing my damn mind. My eyes switch back and forth between the back of her head and the rest of her. Her ass and legs catch the eye of every guy she passes. Fuck, Brielle. I shake my head. She's lethal tonight.

She's almost out the door, when a pair of guys start going at it in front of her. I rush up and throw myself in front of her when I feel something cold splash against my arm. I look back to see Brielle's jacket sleeve is wet. A guy holding an empty pint glass is standing next to her. He moves to touch her, possibly to help her wipe off some of the beer, when the ice forming in my eyes stops him, daring him to touch her.

"It's okay, Theo," she says. Her hand catches mine as she laces her fingers and holds it. "I'm fine. Go. I'm right behind you."

"And take the chance of some drunk asshole grabbing your ass? Yeah, I'd rather not go to jail." I motion for her to keep walking, and thankfully, she doesn't argue. She just shakes her head without talking and walks out.

"Where do you think you're going?" I yell once we're outside, alone in the parking lot. I eye a trash can and quickly toss the napkins in it. Fuck. I'm probably scaring the hell out of her right now. I'd run from me too.

Did she really think I would just let her leave without any sort of explanation? She must have lost her damn mind. And what the hell is she thinking . . . coming to a place like this, dressed like that? And where are Wes and Becks? Shouldn't she be sitting with them?

"Brielle," I call her name, but she ignores me. "Damn it. Will you just talk to me?"

I clasp her wrist and spin her around to face me. She takes a step back and jerks her arm from my grip. "I've told you to stop doing that!"

"Well, if you'd stop walking away from me, I wouldn't have to."

"Me? Walk away from you?" She laughs. "You mean, like how you walked away from me last weekend?"

Damn. This has escalated fast. "The fuck?" I take a step toward her. "I didn't walk away from you. You chose Luca! Something made evidently clear when I saw you kissing him just yesterday!"

"He kissed me!"

I nod. "And I could tell by the way that you kissed him back, you hated it," he says dryly, his words full of sarcasm.

"You made my choice, Theo. Not me."

"What do you want?" I shake my head, not willing to go there with her. "You came here tonight for a reason. What is it?"

She hesitates, her eyes looking everywhere but at me.

"You know what? This is a waste of time," I say, knowing that it will piss her off. But it's the only thing I know to do that will hopefully push her to finally say something. "You won't change my mind. You chose Luca, and—"

"God, you're being a real ass about this." She smiles, but her eyes are blazing. There's nothing humorous about them. "Who the hell are you now? The Theo I knew would have never given me an ultimatum."

Ass?

Did Brielle Sutton just call me an ass?

"It's not as if I didn't want to," I say harshly, because I did want to say something many times, but how could I? What right did I have to ask that of her before, when we couldn't even be together? "You also never fucked that Theo."

I watch her mouth drop as she staggers back a few steps, her feet tripping over those outrageously high heels. Her back hits against the side of her car.

"Wow. No. You're right." She shakes her head. Her fingers are fumbling with her keys. "I don't know what the hell I'm doing anymore." She steps to the side and opens her car door. "I'm sorry; this was a mistake. Goodnight, Theo."

What? "No. Brielle, stop." I reach out and shut her door. "That's not what I meant."

"Then what did you mean? God, just tell me what you want!"

"I've told you what I want. I want you! But I can't be with you, and watch you be with Luca too."

"I don't want Luca. I want you!"

"No." I shake my head. "What you want is the best of both worlds. And it doesn't work like that."

She takes a step toward me and takes hold of my hand. "Oh my God. Luca is just a friend!"

I squint at her, not sure who the fuck she's trying to convince, but I'm not buying it.

"What are you doing here, Brielle?" I cut my eyes behind her. The blue, flashing light of my truck's security system, catches my attention. "Where's is Luca, anyway? I thought y'all had plans?"

"I canceled them."

"You canceled them?"

"Yes. Last night, after I found out you were at the house. I was on my way to see you, but you had come and gone."

"And hedgehog from the bar?"

"Blake? He was there on his own. He just came over to say hi."

Fucking hell.

"Hey." Brielle pulls my face down so that I'm looking at her. I'm fucking fuming, and I know she can see it. "Come back to me."

I step out of her hold, my eyes falling to trail the length of her body, openly.

"To answer your question, I . . . I came here to find you." She picks at her nails. "I didn't expect to find you fighting though. I thought you didn't start until later. I was trying to catch you before. You look like hell."

Not even close. Hell was when my father had too much to drink, came home and beat the absolute shit out of me until he passed out. This was just another asshole at K.O.

"I'm fine. I didn't let him land anything too bad."

"Wait. What? You let him hit you?" she asks, crinkling her nose in that cute way of hers, which makes me want to bend down and kiss the wrinkles away.

"Of course I did. I don't get hit unless I choose to."

She slaps my arm. "What the hell is wrong with you? Why would you want to be hit?"

"You don't want me to answer that." I shake my head. She backs away, slowly, and her back hits the car again. "You scared yet?"

"No. But I wish you wouldn't fight at all."

I groan and push a hand through my hair, my fingers working the sore muscles along the back of my neck. We've been over this. "Can't do that, babe. I told you."

"Right. So. Care to elaborate on what just happened?"

"What? The fight?"

"You do realize that you just called me your girlfriend, right?" she challenges.

I close my eyes. "Space between the words." I decide to use her own words against her. A playful smile spreads along my lips.

"Touché." She drops her eyes to her hands. "Listen, I can't cut Luca out of my life—not completely. Eventually, I hope you'll come to understand that. But you were right, I can't keep pretending that everything is fine. So I choose you. "

Wait. What?

"Explain that sentence."

"The truth is I don't want you to ever feel like I am choosing Luca over you. Because to me, there is no comparison. I love you. Only you."

Oh.

"Brielle." I pause thinking about what it would mean if we were to continue whatever the fuck it is we've been doing. And what it is I could be risking if my father decides to come after me. . . us. "It's not that easy. There's a lot you don't kn—"

"But it is that easy." She smiles, looking up at me. "Do you love me?"

I groan. My mind is racing with all the things we still need to talk about. "Yes, but—"

She raises a finger to my lips. "Theo, please, don't make me beg."

I sigh. The knots in my shoulders twisting. "Of course not. Never." I roll my eyes and kiss her forehead.

I'm so fucked.

I feel her flinch when I wrap my arms around her and pull her closer toward me. "You make me crazy," I tell her. "You know that?"

"At least I'm not stinky."

"Stinky?" I laugh and let her go. "You mean you don't want to jump my bones from all this manliness?"

"Nope. Sorry."

There's that new, feisty attitude, I love.

"Well then. what do you say we get out of here?"

"And get you a shower?"

"Only if you join me."

I smile, hearing her laugh. Then I bend down and press my lips to hers. After what feels like the longest kiss, we run back inside so I can grab my shit from the locker room. It's then that my mind cycles back to something she said. "So . . . um . . . quick question. How pissed was Luca?"

She shakes her head. "What do you mean?"

"You know, when you told him you're choosing me?"

"Oh, my God. Theo!" She playfully swats at my arm, but I catch it and wrap it around her waist. "You're the worst."

"True, but I'm better with you."

chapter thirty-eight

BRIELLE

W e pull out onto the dark road, leaving my car with Mack, and head toward Theo's house. His castle is out in the middle of nowhere. For the most part, I keep my attention outside toward my window, as we pass through endless nothingness, until I feel Theo reach out with his hand and squeeze between my legs. His fingers are so close to a certain area, it makes me tremble.

"I don't know what the hell it is about you in these pants, but fuck. . . it's doing something to me," he says in that raspy voice I love.

I swat at him playfully, tilting my head to the side and laughing. I stare up at the cut along the side of his face and run my finger under it. "Does it hurt?"

He cocks his head sideways and gives me a smug grin. "I'll live."

I nod and pull out my phone to text Becks, but Theo snatches it and pulls at my leg. The force of it carries me across the seat. His fingers trace the seam of my pants that runs along the inside, and he follows it higher up my leg.

"Umm, what are you doing?" I smile, shyly. But deep down, I already know.

He shrugs, slowly tugging at the button on my waistband as I feel it release. His fingers begin teasing the skin just over my thong before he hooks it and pulls it to the side. "I've been waiting to do this all week." He slides a finger deep inside of me, then adds another. "Want to bet on how many times I can make you come tonight?"

I reach for the door and clutch it hard. I can feel my fingers dig into the leather as the pressure in my stomach starts to build. Holy crap. I hear myself suck in a sharp breath. God, I love hearing his dirty talk.

"I want to see how long it takes before you can't handle anymore." His voice is thick with an emotion I can't place.

He pushes his thumb into my wetness and then presses it over my sensitive area. The tiny circular motions move at just the right speed, which keeps me on edge without pushing me over. I wrap my fingers around his bicep and rock into his hands.

"Two can play this game," I say in between breaths.

"Oh yeah?"

"Yes."

Before I can think too much about what I'm doing, I twist onto my knees and lean over the console. My fingers make quick work of his zipper as he lifts his hips for me to work his pants down his thighs a little. His erection tents his boxers, but I pull them down too. I focus on the tiny sounds slipping from his lips as I work my hand over the length of him. He sucks in a quick breath, and I wish we were already back at his house so I could do more.

"Fuck, babe," I hear him growl. "You're too good at this."

I look up and feel my stomach clench when I can see he's fighting with himself—fighting with whether or not he should end this or let me continue. To watch the road or give in to the moment. I feel the road catch under the tires when I look up and see him throw the truck into park. The front of his house looms in the distance.

Before I have time to register what's happening, he's already out of the truck and at my door. His pants and boxers hug his hips and are hanging open. His deep V catches my attention as he pulls the door open and shoves his hands under my ass.

His grip is rough and forceful as he wraps my legs around his torso. I feel his erection rub against my core, and without a thought, I press against it. "Fuck, you're killing me, babe," he groans. He shifts his weight and holds me with one arm. His free hand moves further under my bottom as he pushes two fingers inside of me and begins to thrust in and out.

I rock my head back and moan. My mind suddenly appreciates Theo's need for privacy more than ever. This would definitely turn heads at the monthly HOA meeting had Theo chosen to live in a normal neighborhood. "Theo," I call his name.

"Just hold on, babe. We're almost inside."

I can hear him fumbling with the keys, so I decide to mess with him more—my own form of payback for what he did with me at the restaurant the other night. I kiss him just under his ear and run my tongue along his jaw. "Hurry," I whisper, slipping my hand down between us, like a contortionist, and gripping him. My hand moves up and down in time with his fingers as I kiss the corner of his mouth. "I want—"

"If you finish that sentence, so help me, I'll fuck you on this door."

I stifle a laugh and decide to kiss him instead. "Maybe I'd let you." I bite his lip.

I hear the keys hit the floor seconds before Theo has my back pressed up against the door. The force of it all surprises me but it isn't painful. In fact, I like it. He withdraws his fingers and quickly finds my breasts. His thumb expertly rubs my nipple, making it harden under his touch.

"Are you on the pill?" I faintly hear him mutter in my ear. I suck in a sharp breath as he gently pinches my nipple. "Answer me, Brielle."

"No."

He swirls his thumb around my nipple and pinches it again. *How the hell does this feel so good?*

"I could make you come this way." He pulls back to look at me. But I shake my head.

I know exactly what I want, and to further show him, I roll my hips forward and position myself over the top of his erection. I can feel the tip pressed against me. The feeling of him being so close has my heart racing.

"No more overthinking things tonight. I need this. I want this." I push down on the tip. The instant fullness I feel as I roll my hips up and down the length of him has me calling out his name. Theo sucks in a sharp breath.

"Damn, you're not playing fair."

I lean my head to rest against his chest and feel the deep rise and fall of his breaths. "Do you want me to stop?" I whine at the thought.

"Fuck no." He drops his hand from my breast and grips my waist. The force of it causes me to lean back against the door. My back is arched as Theo begins to thrust inside of me.

At first, he starts out slow, gradually increasing the speed by the minute. Pretty soon, we're both panting when I hear the slight rip of a condom. Theo lifts me high, too high, and I whimper at the loss of him. I was so close. Why did he have to stop?

My mind is only just beginning to let myself question where the condom came from, or how he had managed to finagle it out while slamming into me. When he lowers me back down, each thrust pushes the questions further from my mind.

"Shit, you're so tight." He presses his face into my neck, biting and sucking his way to my lips. "Come for me, baby," He thrusts faster than before.

The feeling of the entire length of him sliding in and out of me pushes me over the edge. My hips buck up, but he holds me down, and I moan his name, threading my fingers in the back of his hair and tugging on it. This is by far my strongest orgasm yet.

"I am so close, " he mumbles against my lips. His words sounding like they're miles away. It doesn't take long though before he joins me. And when he's finished, he rests his head against my chest, my arms wrapping around his neck, lazily. "Well, that was a first." He pulls back and smiles at me. "I've never been unable to make it inside the door."

"You're terrible."

"Oh, I'm terrible?" He arches a brow. "You're the one who decided to throw caution to the wind." He chuckles and brushes his lips against mine. "It's fine. I put the condom on before things got too far. But you need to get on the pill. It feels too damn good without the condom, and I want to feel all of you when I fuck you."

I swallow my gasp and feel my eyes grow wide.

Holy crap, that was hot.

He hesitates a second longer before lifting me and setting me down. My feet brush the ground before I my brain kicks back into gear again. Oh my . . . his staff! "Is . . . is anyone here? Do you think they saw us?"

"No, they have the weekend off." He smiles, removing the condom. "Which is good because there's still a lot I want to do to you."

chapter thirty-nine

I fall out of the shower and clumsily make my way over to the sink. My eyes find the equally spent Theo working to rinse the remaining shampoo from his hair. "I told you to stop biting that damn lip." He chuckles, breathless. The water from the showerhead casts down over his handsome features. How the water is still hot is beyond me. It felt like we were in there for hours.

"Make me."

Our eyes meet through the reflection in the mirror, and for a split second, I wonder if he isn't going to reach out and pull me back in. But thankfully, he hits the water off and starts to dry off. He steps out, and walks up behind me. Reaching his hand out, he runs it down my arm and back up again. His fingers delicately skim the pink marks along the base of my neck, the top of my breasts, and in other *not so obvious* places. A rather pleased grin pulls along his lips.

"I'd ask you to think of whatever kind of food it is that you'd want to eat right now, but Travis isn't here to make it." Theo bends down to kiss my shoulder. "So how does mac 'n' cheese sound?"

I spin around to face him and rise up on my tiptoes, placing a soft kiss on the side of his mouth. "That sounds perfect." My eyes catch the cut lining the top of his cheek. I notice how irritated it is. "This looks bad. Maybe you should call Wil—"

"If I say yes, will you move in with me?" he answers coolly. Using two fingers he tilts my head to the side while bending down to place a series of kisses along my jaw.

I push past him and into the room, motioning to his already forming bruises and the miscellaneous cuts he has all over him. "If I say yes, would you give up fighting? For good?"

"No."

"Then, no." I shrug into one of his shirts. The smell of his cologne and detergent is calming. "I hate seeing you hurt."

"All the more reason you should move in then. With you here, I'll be too preoccupied to even think about fighting."

He wraps the towel around his waist and walks into the room. I lift my eyes toward his crotch and lick my lips. Maybe I should move in if it means getting to see him like this everyday.

I shake my head to clear it. "I can't move in with you, Theo."

"Yes, you can." He lazily rakes his eyes up and down my body. *Oh no,* I think to myself, watching him slowly step toward me. "Let me persuade you."

"No. No, I can't." I back away from him. But it's no use. In one swift motion, he grabs me and throws me down on the bed. "Theo!" I cry out when my own body betrays me, and I hear myself giggling like a schoolgirl. He maneuvers his way on top of me, his fingers tugging at my towel. "What about the mac 'n' cheese?"

"What about it?"

An hour later, Theo asks me if I'm okay, as he leans over the back of the couch and hands me a small white bowl. The plain white shirt he's wearing rises up to reveal the tanned skin of his stomach. "Babe?"

"Huh?"

"I asked if you're okay. You seem pale."

"Yes, sorry," I whisper.

A little while ago, Theo filled me in on some of the details from yesterday—the meeting with his dad, the proposed marriage, and more. My fears of his father's criminal connections were finally realized.

I lift my eyes to meet his. "So, your father is a mobster?"

"Mobster?" He laughs. "That might be a bit of a stretch." He rocks his head from side to side, coming around to sit beside.

It's not like I honestly care about the proper term. Out of everything he's just told me, there's so much more that needs to be explained than that.

"I would say he's a self-made man with underground criminal connections."

I tilt my head. "So, a mobster."

"Sure," he continues. I watch the tiny muscles of his jaw clench as he eyes his bowl. He sets it down on the table in front of us and turns to face me. "I'll understand if you want to walk away. This is a lot more than most people can handle. But if not, if we choose to do this, then you need to know . . . I can't be gentle about what has to be done. Underestimating my father would be a grave mistake. For both of us."

"What does that even mean?" I freeze mid-bite.

"It means that I might have to do things that you're not going to like. Things that are necessary in order to keep you safe."

"Things? What things?" My eyes are burning, but not because I'm concerned for myself. But for him. I can see how much this is affecting him.

"Brielle . . ." He lets his words trail off. "Trust me, it's better if you don't know."

"But isn't that the point?" I shake my head. "For us to be honest with each other? You can lie to whoever you need to, but not to me. Not if this is going to work."

"It may not be that simple." He drops his head.

The two of us sit in a weighted silence as Theo's words hang between us. I lift my hand in an attempt to reach out to him, but catch myself crossing my arms in front of me instead.

"I wish I were stronger so that I could have walked away before things got too far between us," he says. His voice is eerily calm.

"Don't say that."

"Brielle, seriously. Think about it. I'm bad for you."

"I don't care."

"You will if it ends up getting you killed."

"He can't hurt me." I try to reassure him, but I can see his resolve starting to wear thin. "I could tell my father, and we—"

He reaches down with his hand, and with two fingers under my chin, he lifts my face up to his. His minty breath is warm on my lips, right where I want his mouth to be, as he says, "Do you really want to do this? Be with me, I mean?"

I nod, drawing closer to him. "I do."

The words barely leave my mouth before he crashes his lips to mine. His hands settling on either side of my face, and his arms cage me against the couch.

He pulls away, and for a moment, we stare at each other. With our hearts racing, I can feel his energy shift. The air thickens once again. "I'm not the hero here," he whispers. His voice is laden with some unidentifiable emotion. "I've done too many bad things already that can't be forgiven. But I'll do anything to keep you safe.

I see something flicker in his eyes, challenging me to deny what he's just said. His expression is relaxed, but I can tell that he's hurting. I know he still carries some guilt because of Mason, and because he believes that he can't be who I need him to be. But that couldn't be further from the truth. How can he not see that he is everything to me?

I lift my hand and cup his face. My thumb brushes his bottom lip as I stare into those brilliant hazel eyes. "I don't need a hero, Theo. I just need you."

He kisses me then, his mouth closing down on mine. Each kiss is hot and hard as if he's waiting for me to pull away. But I never will. No matter what happens, I'm amazingly unafraid and willing to give him whatever he wants—needs—to prove to him that he deserves to be happy. And that he deserves to be happy . . . with me.

Waking up the next morning, Theo slides his hand under my head and wraps his arm around the back of my neck, dragging my mouth to his. His tongue teases the far corners of my mouth as he pulls my chest to his with one arm. "Say it." He smiles. His teeth capture my bottom lip as he bites it. "Say you'll go with me?"

"I don't know." I push away from him, but he's got me trapped within his viselike grip. My legs wrap the outside of his as he groans into my neck. "Do you really think it's smart to go to the ball and flaunt our relationship in your father's face? After everything?"

"I don't give a fuck about my father."

His tone surprises me.

"All I care about is you, and I know you want to go. Besides, my father may be a man with connections, but he'd never be bold enough to try anything out in the open, especially not in front of Mr. Overshire."

"Right. Katrina's father." Because Katrina's going to be there.

I drag out the words. Squeezing my eyes shut, I bury my face in his shoulder. The sweet smell of the laundry detergent that was used on his shirt wafts me in the face. Dang. Whatever Eliza uses, I need it.

Gently, he pushes my shoulders back until I'm looking at him. "Are you jealous? Of Katrina?" His tone isn't accusing or harsh, but genuinely curious.

"No." I roll my eyes and get up off the bed. My feet carry me towards the bedroom door faster than I can imagine. "Maybe. I don't know. The girl is beautiful," I say over my shoulder as I reach my room.

Whipping around, I bump into his chest. I gasp as he twists me around to face the bed, his hips leveraging my backside from behind. The hard length of his erection presses against my lower back.

"Trust me, babe. You have nothing to worry about," he whispers in my ear. His breath teases my neck as he lifts me and tosses me onto the bed. The color of his eyes darken while his gaze settles between my legs. "You're the one who is beautiful, and I fully intend on showing you exactly how I feel about you."

"Again?" I giggle, feeling the slight puckering of my nipples. The muscles in my stomach begin clenching at the thought. This man is insatiable. I swear. But I'm surprised by the way I'm suddenly aching for the touch that he's holding back.

"I wish—" he smiles brightly, pushing off the bed and walking into his closet—"no, I have a surprise for you. Get dressed, we've got somewhere to be."

chapter forty

BRIELLE

W here are we?" I ask when Theo pulls to a stop outside of a dress shop. He gets out to come around as I scan the store's windows, finding them filled with bridal gowns—each one, bigger than the next. "Um, is there something you want to tell me?" I half laugh as he reaches my door.

"What?" He looks at me questioningly until he turns to see what I'm staring at. "Oh, no." He laughs, his voice full of that playful tone I love. His handsome face brings a smile to my lips. "We're here to buy you a dress for the ball."

"But this is a bridal shop. And it's Sunday."

Theo ignores me and takes my hand. When he opens the door to the shop, two women are inside waiting for us. One is holding flutes filled with champagne, and the other is clutching a measuring tape, clipboard, and a handful of fabric swatches to her chest.

"Is this her? Is this the girl?" They ask simultaneously—although one is a little more excited than the other.

I tilt my head, eyeing the two women standing in front of us. Both are beautiful with annoyingly perfect bodies. Slender but curvy. Young but still mature looking. They walk us over to a small area in the center of the building. Pink-and-cream barrel back chairs and couches, adorned with gold studs and matching pillows, form a circle. I take a seat and am immediately handed a drink by the one named Raven—according to her name tag—before she wanders off to help her

partner, who appears to be a bit mopey. I still haven't had the
opportunity to figure out her name yet.

Raven is beautiful, with long, silky black hair that runs
down her back and caramel-colored skin. She bounces around
the room with enthusiasm that's unmatched by the other girl. I
turn to Theo, who's staring at his phone. The corners of his lips
are turned down as he scrolls the screen, like a man on a
mission.

"Excuse me for a moment." He stands, leaning over to
kiss my forehead, before turning and walking toward the exit.

"Wait, don't . . ." I reach out to pull him back to me but
he's already gone.

I turn back around when I hear someone approaching,
and find the tall blonde, who reminds me of an older, more
sophisticated Katrina standing in front of me. "Stand up,
please." She smiles. My eyes slide down to her name tag, and I
see "Cameron" on the gold plate just above the words "Store
Manager." I stand up as she snatches my arm, walking me to the
small, white platform positioned in the center of the room.
"Let's get your measurements done and you in a dress
before *your boyfriend* returns." Her tone is mocking.

"I can do it!" Raven calls. Her bubbly attitude sets me at
ease as she steps up to the platform.

"Okay." Cameron relinquishes the measuring tape. "I'll
go pull some options. She may be a hard one to fit."

Excuse me?

I feel my eyes grow wide.

Cameron slinks off, out of sight, while Raven hurries,
double-checking each measurement before jotting them down
on the clipboard. "Don't mind Cameron." She rolls her eyes.
Then tucks the sides of her hair back behind her ears so that
they don't fall in her face, as she bends down to measure my

waist. "She's just salty you snagged her dream man." Dream man? I whip my head to the side and lift my arms for Raven to measure my chest. What the hell?

"They know each other?" I decide to ask, hoping my face doesn't give away all the questions running through my mind.

"Oh, yeah." Raven's heels click off the platform as she finishes and moves to a clothing rack, where three dresses hang.

Her fingers skim the first two, then stop when she reaches the third. She pauses, but her eyes are fixed on something in the distance. Turning back to glance at me one last time, she turns and slowly disappears down the hall.

"She apparently dated him back in college!" She yells from somewhere off in the distance. "But he told her he wasn't the dating kind. So they just messed around for a bit until he left her."

I feel my cheeks flare, wondering how long the "until" period actually lasted, while they were simply "messing around." The amount of control it's taking for me not to turn around and walk out the door is draining. Did it end the day before we bumped into each other? Had it been a year since they slept together? A month? Longer? Was he with her while he was with Katrina?

I pinch my eyes shut and try to focus on anything other than the fact that Theo brought me to his ex's—or whatever you'd call her—place of work to buy the gown he wants *me* to wear at the ball *we're* going to together. "Oh my Lord." I whisper, quietly. I'm going to kill him.

"What?" Raven asks. Her bright red lips catch my eyes as she rounds the corner. A heavy, long garment bag is draped over her arms.

"Nothing."

I watch her walk over to the mirrored wall where a lone garment hook sits, fashioned to blend into the mirror seamlessly. She hooks the bag and slowly unzips it, revealing a beautiful floor-length, champagne-colored dress.

"Oh my God." I step down, mindlessly walking toward her, with my mouth agape. "It's beautiful."

"Hell yeah, it is," she says, obviously proud of herself. Her bubbly demeanor, and almost too honest attitude, reminds me of Becks. Only, Becks wouldn't have such a gentle approach. She'd just toss it at me and tell me to put it on, *or else.*

"It's a clear crystal encrusted, spaghetti-strapped chiffon with a plunging neckline and modest train that would totally accentuate your waist perfectly," Raven says.

All I can think is, "Wow." I breathe deeply and bite my lip.

I take another step forward and run my hand down the dress, my fingers tangling with the price tag the moment I reach the banded waist. I twist it around and suddenly feel sick. "Oh wow," I repeat when I see the fifteen-hundred-dollar price stamped in bright red ink. "I could never afford this."

Raven flashes me a small smile, unhooks the dress, and gently leads me by my shoulders to one of the empty dressing rooms. "Why don't you just try it on and think about it." She giggles while giving me a gentle nudge inside. "Then, even if it's a no, at least we can see how beautiful it looks on you."

Half an hour passes of dress after dress. But my heart is still in love with the first one Raven picked out for me. It's perfect—even though my wallet is leaning more towards their clearance aisle on the far wall.

"Did you find one you love?" I spin around after hearing Theo's voice. He's hurrying back inside. His white shirt is soaked along the shoulders.

I see Cameron's reflection in the mirror as she watches Theo move across the room. He walks over to where I'm standing and leans down for a kiss, but I turn away at the last second. Instead, I look back at the navy blue dress hanging on the rack in front of me. It wasn't the prettiest one, but it's affordable and comfy. Plus, Becks has a pair of heels that would go perfectly along with it.

"I think this one will do okay." I answer him.

Just then, Raven rushes up behind us, startling me. "Here you are," she says in a soft voice. I look down and see she's holding a garment bag and a rather large tote in her hands. That proud smile is pulling at her lips. "It's all here, Mr. Wescott." She turns to me. "You're going to look absolutely stunning."

Wait. . .?

"But I haven't even told you which dress I want yet." My eyes are moving along the garment bag, when I see the fifteen-hundred-dollar tag and receipt that have not been so secretly shoved inside the clear lining. "Is that the—"

"Your dress? Yup. It is now." Raven's smile widens. "I knew from the moment you saw yourself, that this was made for you," she coos. She raises her hand to partially cover her mouth as she whispers, "I even threw in the nude Christian Louboutin ankle strap stilettos too."

"Christian. . . Louboutin. . . what?" I shake my head. "Oh no. No, no."

"Is it what you want?"

I jump, almost forgetting that Theo's beside me.

Without looking at him, I say, "It's gorgeous, but it's far too much."

Theo turns back to Raven and shrugs his shoulders. "Well, if you like it, then it's yours." He reaches out to take the items from Raven's arms. He eyes the receipt, which has the total circled in big, bold numbers, and barely bats an eye. "Besides, it's already paid for. Thank you, Raven. You've been very helpful."

I raise a hand to object as he turns around and starts toward the door. Seriously? I groan when he doesn't stop. I look over my shoulder at Raven and thank her for all of her help before I run after him.

"Theo, wait!" I call after him before he manages to step into the street. The sound of the heavy raindrops pelting down on the tin awning makes it hard to hear past a few feet. "I can't let you buy that. It's too much."

He looks down at me and takes a step in my direction. "Are you hungry?"

"Am I . . . what?"

"Are you hungry?"

I rear back. "Seriously?"

"Are. You. Hungry?"

"Um . . . I mean, I guess I could eat." I shake my head, confused as to what my hunger has to do with any of this.

He nods. "Get in the truck, Brielle," he says in a low, demanding voice. His tone makes it clear that there's something else he wants to tell me, but that now isn't the time for it. "We'll talk on the way to lunch."

In the blink of an eye, he's gone, as he steps out into the street and runs through the rain, towards his truck. When I get to the car, Theo is quiet while he waits until I'm buckled and then drives out of the parking lot. I stare out the window, watching the rain beat down. My mind is busying itself, making a list of all the questions I have about his relationship—or whatever he shared— with Cameron.

We hit county road 423, when the rain begins to cover the windshield in sheets, making it hard to see anything. "I'm pulling over." Theo slowly turns into the next parking lot.

I lean forward and try to see if I can make out anything identifiable, but it's pointless. "God, this came out of nowhere." I let myself fall back into my seat and unbuckle the seatbelt.

"What are you doing?" Theo jerks upright as if he thinks I'll leave.

"Nothing" I slide my legs under me, and he relaxes his head against his headrest. "All right, spill," I command.

"Spill what?"

I pull my hand from under my chin and use it to outline the length of him. "This. You. Why you're acting so strange all of a sudden." I purse my lips, feeling annoyed.

If anyone should be upset, it should be me. He should have known that choosing a place his ex works at would have been awkward for me. What the hell does he have to be upset abo—

"I spoke with Luca today."

I'm sorry . . . what? Theo spoke to Luca?

"Luca? Y- you spoke to Luca?" I ask if only to verify that I'm not hearing things. "When?"

"Today. While you were dress shopping." He closes his eyes and pinches the bridge of his nose. This obviously isn't easy for him to talk about, which is why I'm even surprised that he's willing to talk about it. "I. . . uh. . . I called him actually. I wanted to apologize for. . . uh . . . well, for everything."

Oh. I drop my head, my chest tightening. As if reading my mind, he continues, "Yeah," He laughs, sighing as he pushes

a hand through his grown-out, disheveled mess of hair. His
fingers thrum the steering wheel. "He didn't take it so well." He
pauses. "But we ended things okay enough."

"Okay? Enough?"

"Yes, Brielle." He shakes his head. But I am still in
shock. "Do you want a play-by-play or somethi—"

"No, no," I interrupt him, waving him off. "I'm just in
shock is all. I just can't believe you called him."

Theo reaches across the console and takes my hand. His
fingers entwine with mine as he raises my hand to his lips and
kisses it. "Well, it was either make nice with the guy or kill
him." He rasps against the inside of my wrist, playfully biting it.
"Would you have preferred the latter?"

"No." I giggle at the idea because, not for the first time, I
can see the change in him. One thing is for sure. If today has
proved anything, it's that Theo is serious about us—and about
making an effort to be better . . . do better. This realization gives
me hope.

"So," he says. His suddenly somber tone catches me off
guard. "Do you want to talk about it?"

I bite at my lower lip. "About . . . Luca?" I ask not sure
what else he thinks I need to know.

"No." He sucks in a breath as if it pains him to do so.
"About Cameron."

Oh. Her. I press my opposite hand into my palm and
mindlessly knead it. Does their past truly matter? I ask myself.
My mind and heart are torn as to what my response should be.
My heart tells me to forget about it and move on. But my mind
is dying to know.

Thankfully, Theo can tell I'm struggling and is willing to
help. "Before you say anything, I just want to say, please don't
be mad." He cups my face with his hand. "I called Eliza this

morning and asked her to make an appointment. Had I known Cameron worked there, I would have never taken you to that shop. I'm so sorry. I know how awkward that must have been." His thumb runs along my bottom lip, gently tugging the corner free from where I was biting it.

I let myself breathe in more steadily. My heart reels with his every word. "Oh thank God." I let out the breath. "I *was* questioning why you thought to take me there. But I didn't know what to say."

"Oh no. Fuck no." He's smiles. "I wouldn't wish that girl upon my worst enemy."

I roll my eyes, finding that hard to believe. Cameron's beautiful. Other than her blunt mouth and snide glances, how bad could she really be? "I find that hard to believe."

"Trust me, babe. That girl is definitely not my type," he groans, leaning over the console.

My skin prickles at the nearness of him. All of my worries washing away with the rain. "Oh yeah?" I lean closer toward him. "So, then what's your type if not—"

He answers me with a kiss, wrapping his arm that's closest to me around my waist and pulling me onto his lap. I part my lips the moment I feel his hands roaming my body. His fingers trail the bare skin under my shirt. The air is soggy and humid thanks to the rain, causing the tiny hairs along the back of my neck to stick to my skin.

Even through my jeans I can feel Theo's sizable length bulging under me. I rise up onto my knees, trying to work myself into a better position to tease him when my knee slips out from under me. My body falls into the door, my bottom slamming down on the horn.

"Shit." Theo's laughs with me as I collect myself and readjust myself over the top of him. "Are you okay?"

"I'm fine." I continue laughing, pressing my forehead against his shoulder. "Do you think anyone heard?"

I don't realize I'm yelling until Theo says, "Considering the rain has stopped and it looks like we weren't the only ones with the sense enough to pull over, I'm going to go with yes."

I sit up straight and look out the window. An older gentleman and his wife are warily staring back at me. I offer a wave before they start their car and drive off. "Well, great." I slap a hand over my face and cautiously begin to climb back over into my seat.

Theo chuckles. "Well, at least now we can get back to finding a place to eat." He smiles. "Any suggestions?"

I press my seatbelt in until I hear it lock, then look up at him. Those brilliant hazel eyes of his are watching me with a renewed sense of hunger. I smile and lick my lips. My appetite is suddenly craving something more than just . . . food. "I may have one or two."

chapter forty-one

T he rest of the day goes by quickly, and before I know it, it's Monday. I walk into my sociology class, my final class of the day. My mind still pulls me back to my time spent with Theo. The two of us on his couch, in his bed, on the counter, in the shower. It was the perfect weekend, really. He told me about some of his school friends and about how he and Wes met. I even got him to open up some about his father. It was a side of him that I haven't seen in a long time. When he dropped me off at my apartment this morning, it was hard to say goodbye.

Brielle, I hear his voice echo inside my mind. It's more coarse than usual. *Is he getting sick?*

"Brielle! Are you with me?"

"What?" I sit up in my seat. My eyes focus on the professor as he stares blankly at me from the front of the room. Oh God. I offer him a small smile. How embarrassing. "Sorry, were you talking to me?"

"Yes, I asked you a question."

"Right." I nod. "And the answer is . . . um, it's . . ."

The professor crosses his arms in front of him, his expression oddly amused. "Yes?" he urges for me to continue.

Jerk! He knows I have no idea.

"I'm sorry. I . . . um . . . I'm not sure."

He nods. "Then maybe you should keep that mind contained within these four walls rather than letting it drift."

"Yes, sir. I apologize. It won't happen, again."

"I would hope not." He raises his eyebrow and turns back to the rest of the room. His eyes scan the remaining raised hands of his pets, all begging to answer the question I couldn't.

When class is dismissed, I grab my things and shove them into my bag before joining the line of students racing for freedom. As I exit the Language Hall, I see Theo with his bike in the parking lot. I walk a few feet when I hear Luca's familiar laugh drifting from somewhere behind me. I turn around and see him surrounded by a shroud of red hair. The red hair belongs to a girl who has her arms wound around his waist.

I try to make out who it is as a body slams into my side. "Oh sorry," I apologize and step to the side. A small girl with chocolate-brown eyes and perfect curls glares at me as she readjusts herself.

"Watch it, would ya?" she snaps, disappearing a second later.

I turn back toward Luca, surprised when I find that the girl wrapped around his waist is Penny. Her fiery red hair is now pulled back, revealing her features. Her brother, Ethan, stands next to them. The three of them are laughing like old friends.

What the hell?

I scrunch my nose up at the image, when Luca catches me watching. Not wanting to talk, I quickly turn back toward the parking lot and make my way to Theo.

"You look happy." He smiles when he sees me. The hint of warmth in his voice makes my heart swell. His black ripped jeans, black shirt, and fitted black leather jacket hug his lean, muscled body perfectly as he coolly waits next to his bike. "Did you pass an exam or something?"

I roll my eyes and let him pull me into his arms. His hands rest on my backside as I thread my fingers through his hair. "I see you got your hair cut today." I say and quickly brush my lips against his. "It looks nice."

The moment Theo's lips touch mine, my body ignites. I moan into his mouth and am rewarded with an equally eager sound from somewhere deep in his throat. He pulls back when a group of girls pass, snickering as if they've never seen two people kiss before.

"We should probably slow down." He runs his hands over my backside and gives it a gentle squeeze.

Seriously?

"Since when does Theo Wescott, care about what other people think?"

"Since. . . my girlfriend decided to listen to reason and agreed to come to live with me."

"Ah. Nice try." I swat his chest, playfully. "It's not going to happen. I only agreed to weekends. I can't abandon Becks." I smile, watching him groan to himself. "But you're more than welcome to come stay at our place. . . with me."

He seems to think about it for a second, pursing his lips as he stands from his bike. "Will Wes be there?" He folds his fingers around my hand and presses it against his chest. The instant rise in temperature makes me shift uncomfortably.

"Probably," I groan. "I told you, Becks said that he's been staying there almost every night."

He clicks his teeth and drops my hand. "Then, I'll pass."

I take a step towards the campus and notice the bright, green banners blowing in the distance as the wind kicks up. The words "GO MEAN GREEN" are printed boldly for all to see. I drop my eyes down to my wrist and check the time.

"Shoot. We better get going if we plan on making dinner." I tilt my head to the side. Something about the sly expression Theo's wearing tells me that he's purposefully been trying to stall. "What's wrong?"

He shakes his head. "Nothing." Sighing, he throws a leg over his bike. "You sure I can't persuade you into doing anything else?"

"Theo, they're our friends."

"Yeah, but—"

"But . . . what?" I smile and take his hand and climb on behind him.

"But I'd much rather have you all to myself."

The week flies by and Friday evening arrives, much to Theo's dismay, since it's the night before the All Hallows Eve Ball. Eliza finishes preparing some snacks for another impromptu get-together when the call comes in that Becks and Wes have arrived. The fact that Theo agreed for them to stay the night is further proof that he's making an effort to do more things I enjoy. He also knew I'd be sad not having Becks to get ready with, so he invited them Monday, after dinner. The look on Wes's face had surprised Theo more than me.

On one of Theo's random security displays, which he has wired throughout the house, I see Becks and Wes parking. Excited, I run up to the door. As soon as I see Becks, I wrap my arms around my best friend. "I'm so glad you're here." I give her a squeeze.

"Well, of course, I am." She takes another step further inside so that Wes can shut the door behind them. "Your boyfriend, the dictator, didn't give us much of an option." She flashes Theo a playful smirk when he casually strolls into the foyer. "Plus, getting ready for a ball in a castle has been a dream of mine."

"It's not a castle." The boys say in unison.

Becks turns back to Wes, arching her brow up at him in a way I've never seen her do with another guy before. It was a loving look. Had I missed something?

"Uh, huh." She pats his chest. "Don't worry, babe. I still love you." She shakes her head. "You and that small room you call your home."

"Very funny." Wes watches her as she grabs her suitcase and walks further into the house. His ice-blue eyes turning to me next. "Hey, B." He smiles, genuinely. "Lovely as usual."

"Thank you." I smile, returning his gesture. "Well, come on. Let's get y'all settled!"

We all move to head up the stairs, when I feel fingers clasp my wrist. Theo's handsome face twists anxiously as he pulls me to his side. "Tell me again why we agreed to this?"

I pause midstep and watch as the other two make it to the landing of the second floor. "Theo, this was your idea, remember?" I'm trying to keep my voice down.

He rolls his eyes and continues walking up the steps, pulling me along beside him. "Right." He runs a hand over his stubble. My fingers silently ache to do it for him. "Just another one of the many things I do for your happiness."

At that, I let my head fall back, giggling happily as we step up on the landing. "And I love you for it."

"Planning your exit strategy already?" Becks teases Theo but he ignores her.

"So which room is ours?" Wes points to the two doors in front of us, which are the doors to Theo's and my room.

Well, not *my room.*

It's just the one room I use to hang my clothes in. Even though there's plenty of room in Theo's closet for my things, I still feel the need to keep everything separate—in that sense. I didn't want him getting too used to the idea of seeing my things lying around, especially because I'll be living back home with Becks during the week.

It's not that I don't love the idea of living with Theo. It's just, well, I guess a part of me still wonders if I can trust him. I know Theo loves me, but can I trust that he's truly changed? What if he wakes up one day and decides to change his mind about us? It's just . . . it's all too soon. I need more time.

"Neither of these rooms," Theo answers Wes. His harsh tone rips me from my inner thoughts. "Ya'll are staying on the third floor." He tilts his head towards the next set of stairs. "Eliza's prepared the room on the right."

"Oh, I don't mind if they stay in the Rose room." I turn back to Theo and wrap my arms around his waist. "I can ask Eliza where the guest towels are and help them set up—"

"No, that room is not for guests' use." His hands move to my shoulders, his eyes softening as he leans down and kisses me. The kiss is more intimate than I expect from him in front of Becks and Wes. He pulls away, and I can feel the heat flushing my cheeks. "They'll be fine in the room upstairs."

"The room on the right?" Becks can't hide the smile on her face. "How many freaking rooms does this place have? And can I move in?"

We're all shocked when Theo laughs at the comment. "If you think this is big, you should see my father's house." He smiles, moving to the second set of stairs. "Now that's a castle."

Later, Becks and I are eating nachos, when she turns toward me and says, "So, tell me . . . how absolutely insane am I for already using the "L" word with Wes?"

Becks smiles while scraping the opposite side of her chip across my plate. I narrow my eyes at her thievery but decide to let it pass. Eliza *did* have Travis make more nachos than I could ever finish, but still. This queso is delicious.

I raise one finger, asking her to wait a moment as I savor my last bite. The blend of cheeses, roasted tomatoes, and chipotle are making my taste buds dance in delight. I shake my head. "I don't think you're crazy." I carefully peel the top napkin out of the holder and wipe my face. "I think I'm more proud than anything."

"Right! Me too!" She hiccups, reaching for another chip. Her fingers hovering over the top of the plate until she snatches the one I was eyeing. I flash her a look.

"I don't know." She turns her head to the side, her eyes sliding to where Wes and Theo sit idly, playing a video game. "It just feels right. You know?"

As if on cue, Wes throws his controller down, hard, and begins to stumble around his chair. "You got to be fucking kidding me!" he shouts.

Theo, who is still seated, drops his head back and starts laughing. "I thought you said you've gotten better at this, man?" Theo says as a playful smirk presses his lips. "You're terrible."

"Ha. Ha." Wes flips him off. "I went over to capture the flag, but the guy on our team fucking shot me."

"Yeah, because that was our flag you were trying to secure . . . against *our* own team."

I turn back to Becks and shake my head. Wes is definitely wasted.

"Uh, huh. Yeah, he's is a keeper." I smile, trying to stifle a laugh.

"Yeah. Well, maybe not this second." Becks chunks a chip at me over the table. "Bitch. What about you then?" She gives me a lively look. Her eyes narrow. I can tell she's trying to focus on my mouth.

"Me? What about me?"

Becks tilts her head to the side, reaching for her sixth
Claw and downs the last of it. Her next words come out in a
rushed slur. "You know—" she jerks her head back toward the
guys—"about tomorrow. . . about Theo's dad, and everything he
told you? There's no way you can be this fucking calm about
everything."

I nervously, bite my lip when I see her eyes grow wide
with an emotion I can't place. Anger? Worry? Shock? I drop the
chip I've been holding and push the plate away from me, my
appetite now gone. The sound of the ceramic grinding on the
table is strangely distant.

Wasn't I though?

Okay with it all, I mean.

"You know what? Fuck it!" Becks tosses a half-eaten
chip down and stands. Her legs shake as she tries to wrangle
them into submission. "I'm drunk." She brushes her hands
against her jeans. "Talk tomorrow?"

I nod and watch her stumble over to Wes, who barely
seems to notice her as she whispers something in his ear. But
Theo does. He watches her stumble out of the room, then leans
back as if to check on me, mouthing something I can't read—
mostly because I'm on my sixth claw too. But also, because I
can't help smile, seeing him this way.

I shake my head when I see he's about to get up. I would
hate for him to stop playing, when I know he's secretly having
fun. I stand up and make my way over to where he is. My legs,
weaker than I expected. "It's fine. I'll just go take a bath," I say,
earning a half glance from Wes.

"The fuck are you looking at?" Theo groans and shoves
his shoulder. "Watch the fucking screen. You'll probably die a
whole lot less."

I let a smile slip across my face and lean forward to brush my lips against his. "I'll see you soon," I whisper, tasting the slight bitter aftertaste of the beer he's been nursing for the past hour.

"Are you sure?" He quickly reaches out to pull me back down to him. His mouth closes over mine once more. The kiss is fast and rough. The idea of what would come if he were to follow me leaves me breathless, when he finally pulls away. "I can come with you if—"

"No. Really. I'm fine."

He's hesitant to let me leave, but I'm thankful when he does.

I step out into the hall and walk the short distance to my room. Well, the Rose room, I remind myself. My incessant desire to call it mine makes me shudder if I think about why that is for too long. Stripping my shirt, I toss it in the sink. My bottoms and panties quickly follow. I hit the faucet and begin to draw my bath.

Feeling oddly seasonal, I decide to go for the pumpkin spice bath bubbles. The warm aromas are instantly calming as I slink down into the tub. The tips of my toes and my head are the only parts of me that peek out of the bubbles as the rest of my body disappears under the water. I let my head fall back, and my mind relaxes, but too soon I'm consumed by Becks's prying question. The fact that I didn't have an answer for her bothers me.

How do I feel about everything he said?

I bite at the inside of my bottom lip and shut my eyes. I haven't really had a chance to think about it all just yet. Or maybe I have, but I haven't really let it sink in. I was surprised when Theo told me everything he'd done after he left Elm Brook. If I am being honest with myself, it's a side of him that scares me. Not because I think that he would ever hurt me, but because I've seen what it does to him. How quickly he's able to flip that switch and make decisions I'll probably never be able to accept. I also see the guilt he carries everyday because of it.

I know about Katrina, the marriage, and his father's business deal with Mr. Overshire—and what his father threatened if Theo were to mess it up in any way. . . me. But, as strange as it sounds, I don't care. All I care about is Theo and the fact that his walking away from his dad has taken him one step further from becoming the monster of a man his father is.

What happened in the past can't be undone. I drop my head, my mind going back to that night. The gun. The look in Mason's eyes as the sound of the gunshot ripped through the alleyway and tore my world apart. I know everyone believes that I should hate Theo, but I can't. I won't. We all played a part in that night. If I hate anyone it's—

"His father," I whisper to myself, hearing the subtle shake in my voice.

Theo says his father would never think of attempting something in front of the number of people expected to attend tomorrow's ball. But really, even if that weren't the case, I'd still want to go. This is the man who killed my brother, hurt my family . . . hurt Theo. In a way, I hope he tries something. I'd love the chance to expose him. He belongs in jail. Bringing him to justice would bring peace, to not only me but my father, too. My father's sole reason for taking the detective position was in order to hopefully someday bring Mason's killer to justice. I just know it. He was perfectly fine before just being a normal cop.

I hesitate for a moment, letting out a breath I didn't know I was holding, and try to steady myself. My chest aches at the thought, and I turn to face the wall. My mind drifts back to

Theo—his handsome face and the way that I feel about him. The question of how he would feel if his father went to jail pricks at the back of my mind.

"You're beautiful." Theo rips me from my inner thoughts and startles me. I jump so fast that some of the water spills over the side of the tub and pools on the floor.

"Oh God. I'm sorry," I say when I see the mess I've made. I'd like to blame the alcohol but I can't. I giggle to myself. Theo just shakes his head and walks over to crouch down beside the tub.

"Don't worry about it." He laughs with me. His eyes skim the ridge of bubbles overlapping the side before they float up to where I sit, hugging the far corner. The rich green of his eyes is darker under the warm bathroom lights. "Anything I can help you with?"

I feel the corners of my mouth pull as a smile escapes my lips. "Maybe," I say, scooting closer to the side. My hand rises from the tub as the tiny crackles from the bubbles pop against my forearm like rice crispy cereal after milk is poured over them. I run a finger up the length of his arm, leaving a tiny trail of water in its path.

He narrows his eyes, and I can see his mind racing, trying to figure out what I'm doing—only, by the time he does, it's too late. The second my fingers reach his upper bicep, I reach up, wrapping my hands around his arm and pulling him down to me. Water splashes out in waves as he slides into the tub. His shirt and jeans absolutely soaked, but he doesn't care.

Instead, he reaches for a handful of bubbles and presses them to my face.

"Oh, really?" I laugh, splashing him.

"Come here." His hands find the back of my thighs as he hooks them and pulls me onto his lap. His hands squeeze my bottom, the tips of his fingers sliding closer toward my sex with each release.

This playful side of him makes me smile, and I bend down and close the distance between our lips. I feel him push a hand into my hair as he holds me to him. His tongue sweeps across my bottom lip, his arms encircling my waist. "I forgot how fun you are when you're drunk," he breathes against my lips.

"Theo."

"Yes?"

"Stop. Talking," I huff. My words have their intended effect, as Theo's face turns serious, animalistic. My breath catches at the feel of him deepening the kiss, his tongue exploring the far corners of my mouth.

I moan and move my hand to his chest, trying to steady myself. I smooth my hands down his hard-packed stomach and grip the bottom of his shirt, slowly pulling it up and over his head, tossing it to the side where it hits with a loud splat. Yup. Eliza is going to hate me—more than she already does.

Maybe I could offer to help clean it up in the morning?

"Hey. Where did you go?"

"I'm here," I focus on his lips, then suck my bottom lip in between my teeth, biting it. "Take off your pants," I demand and lean down to kiss his neck, sucking lightly.

"Yes, ma'am." He smiles, and without any hesitation, he tilts his hips. My body rises from out of the tub as he unbuttons and slides his pants down his legs, his boxers moving with it.

He lowers me back down. His erection is pressed up behind my backside. I rise slightly and use my hips to maneuver it up and under me. But there's no stopping my hips once I've started. I refuse to wait any longer, and instead, I rock my hips forward on his lap, pinning him beneath me until I feel the tip of his erection line up with my sex. When I do, I sink my hips further into his as I slide down and take the length of him inside of me. The act makes him groan. The tips of his fingers dig into my skin as he moves along with me.

"Fuck." He stops me after a few minutes, his breath ragged as I groan and begin to rub myself against him.

"Don't stop," I beg, and thankfully he obliges.

His hand fists in my hair as he drags my mouth to his. His hips buck forward to meet mine as he repositions me over the top of him. My hands press into the tops of his shoulders, leaving my breasts perfectly positioned for him to take advantage of. His tongue moves down to tease my nipples, as he switches between kissing and sucking.

"You like this?" he moans against my chest.

I nod and pick up the pace. His dirty talk drives me closer to the edge.

"Fuck, you're too good at this." He releases my hair to run both his hands down my back.

His fingers grip my bottom as he begins lifting it up in time with my movements, only to slam me back down on top of him as I roll my hips down his length. He drops his head on the back of the tub and moans. And I love that sound.

"Am I?" I tilt my head down to his chest. "S- so you, l-like t- this?" I say, trying to make it sound sexy and teasing, but my words come out breathy and rushed.

Theo whips his head down and pulls me back. "Say that again," he all but begs.

I pause, concerned that I've said something wrong, but he slowly continues to pump in and out of me. The slow and meticulous thrusts make it hard for me to focus. Leave it to me to try to be sexy and ruin the moment. "I- I said, so you like this?" I repeat.

I watch his eyebrows rise as a smile brushes his swollen lips. "Fuck. Yes. That's hot as shit. I do like it, *and* I love watching you ride me." He's smiling. "And that's a first for me."

"Oh." I almost laugh hearing him say "ride me." That is, until he suddenly jerks his arms around my waist and pulls me to him.

"Hold on," he murmurs against my lips as he stands and steps out of the tub.

I cringe as I imagine the two of us slipping the moment his feet touch the wet floors. But he easily manages to stride out of the bathroom without a single misstep. I cling to him as he walks the short distance to the bed. The second we reach it, he lays me down.

"My turn." He's grinning as he comes down on top of me. His lips meet my neck as he sucks harshly. I know I'll probably wake up to a spot on my neck tomorrow, but in this moment, I couldn't care less.

I push my head back into the mattress and moan as my fingers curl around a handful of the comforter. "Oh God." His fingers move down, as he rubs small circles around the swollen bud between my thighs.

"You know I'm the only one that can make you feel like this," he growls against my skin. His fingers dip down and slide inside my wetness as he circles them around and pumps in and out of me. When I don't say anything, he begins to rub his length against my leg. "Say it, Brielle, say that you're mine. Say it, and I'll fuck you like only I can."

I buck my hips up to meet his hand as he increases the speed, teasing me. "Yes," I moan, feeling my eyes roll back. "I'm y- yours, Theo. O- only yours," I stumble, feeling the pressure beginning to build between my legs. The muscles in my stomach clench.

In an instant, Theo pulls his fingers from me, the loss
making me whimper. But before I have a chance to say
anything, I feel his erection fill me, and the fullness is pure
bliss.

He slides his hands down my legs before pulling them
up to rest on his shoulders as he leans down to thrust deeper
than ever before. "Fuck, I'm close, baby," he whispers after a
few minutes pass. I bite my lip and try to hold on to this
moment. "Come for me, baby. Come with me."

His words are all it takes for me to come completely
undone. My body shudders as I experience the strongest orgasm
I've ever had. I wait until I know he's finished before I slide my
legs off his shoulders and pull him down beside me. My hands
wrap his face as I bring his lips to mine. The passion that we
share is something I used to think I'd never feel after he left and
moved away. And for the first time, I'm thankful that I saved
myself. I can't imagine sharing these moments with anyone else.

"I love you," he says the moment our lips part.

"And I love you."

I pull up to my elbows and sweep my eyes between us
and the bathroom. "Crap."

"What's wrong?" he asks, distracting himself as he runs
his fingers over my stomach.

I cut my eyes to his shirt that's now lying in a huge
puddle of water and the mini flood that's surrounding the tub,
then follow the trail of wet footprints headed in our direction.
"Eliza is going to kill us when she sees this room."

Theo shrugs as if he's thought little of the matter. "Eh,
she's cleaned up worse before."

"Oh," I whisper, a frown taking over my smile.

Of course, she has. I shake my head and push up off the
bed. I pad over to the dresser and pull out the drawer with my

pajamas. My mind chooses to remind me that, whereas Theo may have been my first, I was definitely not his. Even in that brief moment, I find myself stuck, remembering when I watched him and Katrina back in his office at Haze. I could see what they shared. Eliza probably *has* cleaned up worse.

"No, Brielle. I didn't mean it like that," he groans. "Just that, before me, she worked for my father. And I know firsthand some messed up shit that happened there."

I slip a shirt over my head and pull on a pair of my pajama shorts. He loves *me*, I silently tell myself, trying not to let my insecurities ruin our night. I suck in my bottom lip and pad back to the bed. He sees me coming and sits up. His arms wrap my waist the moment I'm close enough for him to reach.

"I'm sorry if I made you think anything else. All of that is in my past. I wish I could explain to you just how different everything with you is, compared to before." He pauses. "All I know is that . . . this . . . what we have, it's real. Don't ever doubt that."

I pull back and let out a breath, wrapping my arms around his neck and leaning my head against his. "Say it."

"Say what, baby?"

"Say that you're mine. Say that you love me, and I'll never doubt it again."

Theo lets out a small laugh, so soft I almost miss it. His arms tighten around my waist, and to ease the tension, I climb up and onto his lap. My knees press on the outside of his thighs.

"I'm yours, Brielle. I've loved you from the moment I met you. . . and I know, I'll love you until the day I die. There's no one else like you anywhere."

chapter forty-two

I wake up, smiling like a fucking idiot as I roll over and see Brielle sleeping next to me. Her beautiful face is completely relaxed as she lays her head on my bicep. Unable to help myself, I reach out and brush a loose strand of hair back from her face. If tonight turns south—if my father even attempts to try anything—I fear what I might do.

The guy's a fucking prick . . . he'd deserve it if it came down to that, but still. After everything I swore to myself that I'd never become—feelings I swore I'd never allow myself to feel—Brielle has taken that and thrown to the wind. If it came down to it, would she forgive me for doing what's necessary to keep her safe? I meant what I said last night that I'm hers. After her, no one else could ever compare. She's ruined me.

Just thinking about her saying that she was mine last night is almost enough to make me come on the fucking spot. This girl continues to surprise me, daily. And her dirty talk . . . damn it, it's hot. I love seeing her become more of that bold, feisty girl I once knew. I hate thinking that she felt like she had to become someone different for everyone else after Mason passed.

If he were still with us, I'd like to think that he'd approve of our relationship—seeing the way that she brings out the best in me. There are some things you just can't fight. If Brielle hadn't come back into my life when she did, I'd hate to think where I would have ended up. I'd be lost, probably preparing to marry Katrina because I wouldn't have a reason to stand up to my father. Or I'd be dead. I sure as hell would not know how good it feels to be loved, or to love someone else as much as I love Brielle.

Reluctantly, I decide to pull my arm out from under her as I roll off the bed and walk into my closet. Someone has to check on the drunkards. I slip a white T-shirt over my head and step into a loose pair of gym shorts and exit the closet. Shit. I may even have time to work in a quick workout too. I peer over to the bed and see that she's still sleeping. I guess all of our activities last night wore her out.

I exit the room and make my way down the stairs. The image of Brielle riding me flashes across my mind and makes my pulse race. The memory of her perfect fucking hips moving in small circles over my cock. Her slim waist and perky breasts. She used my shoulders to support herself, positioning her breasts perfectly in front of my face for me to take full advantage of . . . I could have died and been perfectly happy.

I've always hated it when girls tried to get on top. It's awkward, and they often wind up practically breaking my cock with their fucking erratic movements rather than actually getting me off. But with Brielle, things couldn't be more opposite. Our chemistry is so natural.

I reach the bottom of the stairs and eye Eliza, yelling at Travis in the kitchen. Her hands are waving wildly; I'm almost afraid to get involved, but then she sees me. Damn it. I take a step toward her when I feel my phone buzz in my pocket. The three tiny, heartbeat-like vibrations twist a knot in my chest as my mind latches on to the idea that no news before breakfast could ever mean anything good.

I pull out my phone and raise my hand, requesting Eliza to give me a moment. The screen comes alive in my hand as my deepest fears appear in front of me. A message from an unknown sender with the three words that make my skin itch and my heart clench: It happens tonight.

My eyes slide up from the screen and fall to the worried expression on Eliza's face. "What's wrong?" she asks, but I can barely hear her over the sound of my pulse beating behind my ears.

"Nothing good." I take a step back. "I, um, I need to go speak with Brielle." I turn and walk away. "Please have breakfast ready at eight," I call out behind me as my feet hit the stairs. "Thank you, Eliza."

I spend the morning, trying to convince Brielle to forego the fucking ball, but for some reason, she's now dead set on attending. I roll my eyes. Fucking hell. It'd be a lot easier if I told her why we can't go, but I don't want to scare her until I have a reason to. How is it that we always end up on opposite sides of an argument?

I rub nervously at my jaw. My entire body is on high alert as the time creeps closer to when we're supposed to leave. I turn to Wes, whose idea of prepping involves eating a massive amount of junk food and downing another six-pack of beer. The fuck is it with this guy? How can he be so damn calm all the time?

When seven hits, Wes and I stand at the foot of the stairs as we await our dates to make their grand entrance. Both of us are dressed in our nicest suits. We hear the door crack open, and Becks slinks out in the hall and stands at the top of the landing. Her bright eyes and larger-than-life smile come alive when she spots Wes waiting for her. His dopey-eyed grin, and gelled-down hair make him look younger than usual.

I press my lips into a line and refrain from making a joke about how cheesy they're being. When I catch a glint of gold from the top of the stairs and see Brielle watching me. Her blonde hair is pulled up off her shoulders. The floor-length dress hugs her curves in all the right places and makes her look like she's been frosted with tiny diamonds. She slowly starts to walk down the stairs, cautiously taking one step at a time. Holy shit. I'm in trouble.

I close my mouth, not realizing that it's gone slack, and try to refrain from moving toward her. My arms are longing with the need to wrap her against my body, carry her back up those stairs, and have my way with her. The distance between us right now is hell. I'd give anything to run my hands down her body . . . up and under that dress and make her come as she calls out my name. Instead, I stand here and endure the slow and tortuous time until she's standing in front of me.

"Damn." I reach out, grabbing her waist and pull her to me.

My hands press against her back as I bring my mouth down on top of hers. I can hear Becks and Wes laughing off to the side, but I block them out. When I finally pull away, I keep her close.

"I have a feeling this dress is going to get me in a lot of trouble tonight," I whisper against her lips.

"So, you like it?"

"Oh, I love it."

"Damn, Theo," Wes begins, laughing as he and Becks slowly walk over to join us. "Talk about being pussy whipp—"

"Don't . . . finish . . . that sentence." I offer a warning glance, watching as he makes the notion of zipping his lips.

"Okay, so what the hell now?" Becks steps in front of him and pulls Brielle to her. I loosen my grip but refuse to let her go. The two of them lock arms as they stare impatiently at me.

"I have a car waiting for us outside." After I answer Becks, her eyes grow to the size of large grapes as she rushes to the door and throws it open. A sleek, black Audi A8 L, the extended version, is parked just out front. I turn to Eliza, who's shaking her head as the door slams into the wall. The few art pieces hanging on the wall rattle from the force. "Take the rest of the night off." I smile at her. "Thank you for your help today."

She nods and walks back towards the kitchen.

"Hey," Brielle says. I cut my eyes down and listen as she wraps her hands around my neck. "Everything's going to be okay."

We arrive at the Elm Brook Manor and find the All Hallows Eve Ball is flooded with bodies. Every single one of them are baying to try and get inside.

"Shit." Wes leans forward in his seat and stares out the window. "So much for a small-town event. There's got to be hundreds of people here."

"Yeah, they've been putting this on for years," Becks says, sounding unimpressed. "Brielle and I always go." She cuts her eyes down to her hands. Her fingers folding over one another as she slyly looks up at me. "With Luca."

Of course, you did.

I look out the window as our driver pulls to a stop in front of the Manor. My eyes quickly scan through the sea of people, and I'm thankful when I find that my father is not among them. Feeling pleased, I open the door and step out, reaching for Brielle's hand as she grips the bottom of her dress and steadies herself atop the gravel.

I'm not surprised when I hear some of the people gathered around us gasp at the sheer sight of her. She is beautiful and seeing her in this dress is enough to bring any man to his knees. So I can't blame them. I hold my arm out for her to take, and keep her close as we start walking. I guess there is one good thing that came from Eliza accidentally booking the appointment at Cameron's dress shop.

We make our way up the entry steps as I sweep my eyes around the outside and find it's been completely transformed. The high arched entrance and the stone columns have been decorated with tiny glass-burning lanterns, which cast an eerie glow as you enter the main hall. The rest of the exterior is littered with pumpkins and haystacks.

I remember the field trip that Mason and I had attended here our senior year. The history of this place alone could fill its own textbook—and probably does. No wonder they use it to host the ball.

"This is beautiful," Brielle utters from beside me. Her hands wrap around my bicep as we arrive at the top of the porch. I nod when we reach the front door and are met by a pair of men, passing out masks.

"No, thank you." I close my hand over Brielle's and hurry through the door.

As if tonight isn't stressful enough, now I have to worry about even my enemies being concealed from me. We step inside the Manor, and everything is shrouded in darkness. The only light keeping us all from stumbling around in the pitch-black comes from the low-burning chandeliers, which are fixed with hundreds of candles and carefully hung within the grand ballroom. I lift my eyes up and see the high arched ceilings lined with dark, wooden beams.

This is the perfect place to host a ball.
It's fucking creepy at night.

I can feel the stress starting to knot its way in the back of my neck, as the situation continues to become increasingly harder to control. Who the hell planned this thing? And where—

"Hello, Son," I hear the asshole's voice the second we step into the room. I turn to my side and find him standing tall in his favorite black suit. A gold mask rests atop his face. "Do you like my little contribution to tonight's festivities?" He smiles grimly and points to his mask.

Fuck. I should have known this was his doing. I roll my eyes. "It's a little gaudy for my taste."

I take a step in front of Brielle when I see his eyes slide to my side and rake down the front of her dress. The feral way his eyes pour over her takes everything I have inside of me not to walk over and beat his fucking ass right here and now. "The fuck are you—"

"Theo, I'm thirsty," Brielle says. The sound of her voice pulls me back from the edge. "Come with me, please?" I pause and take a deep breath.

"Well, you heard the girl, Son." My father grins, waving us toward the refreshment table. "Fetch."

I squint, searching the features of his face that I can see for any sign of trickery.

"Hey, man, you ready?" I turn my head to the side as Wes and Becks casually stroll into the room. They, too, have chosen a similar gold mask to wear.

"Yes," I answer when I see my father's stance relent. Wes's shoulders sag as if he's realizing something. "We'll follow you."

"Time to fuck shit up!" Wes shouts excitedly, as he and Becks maneuver their way around us. Brielle and I follow suit.

"Are you okay?" I hear her ask after we make it to the refreshments.

I let my eyes fall to the assortment of foods, while I try to think about how I can answer her without lying. The catered variety of fancy finger foods makes my stomach churn as my nerves rev up, thinking about just how poorly I've thought this all through. I should have just listened to Brielle when she said we shouldn't risk shoving our relationship in my father's fucking face.

"Theo?" Brielle calls to me again. This time she lifts her hand and raises it to my face. "Talk to me."

I search her eyes and feel the undeniable urge to tell her the truth—about the message I received, but then Becks rushes up to us. Her arm hooks into Brielle's as she begins to tug her toward the dance floor.

"Come on Bree. Let's dance!"

"Oh, maybe in a—" she starts, but I shake my head.

"It's fine." I force myself to smile, nodding for her to go and have fun. "Go. I'll be right here."

I watch my girl disappear into the mass of bodies as Wes and I stay off to the side. It works out perfectly, since I intend on keeping my father in my peripherals the entire time we're here.

"Okay. Spill," Wes snaps, catching me off guard. His tone is more harsh than I expected as he steps in front of me, blocking my view of my father.

The fuck?

"Come on, what the hell is going on with you? B's right; something's up."

B? I roll my eyes. Fuck I hate the fact that he feels close enough to have given her a nickname. I'd be jealous if I didn't know that he'd never be dumb enough to try anything, especially because he has Becks now.

"Yeah," I say and sigh, letting my shoulders relax. "It's, um, it's my dad. He threatened Brielle."

"The fuck?" Wes jumps back. His voice rises to the point where he's almost yelling. "Why the hell would he do that?"

I let my head fall back as my mind races with all the reasons why breaking the circle could inadvertently set off something I further can't control. But fuck it. With my father having made a point to approach me so early in the night, it couldn't hurt to have another set of eyes on her.

"Because he's pissed I walked away from the business."

"Holy shit." Wes's mouth drops. "You walked away? Away, away? Like, for good?"

I nod. "Yes."

"Fuck."

"That's about where I'm at." I inhale a deep breath. "Fucked." The idea of asking for help kills me, but Brielle is worth setting aside my pride. "Would you want to help watch her for me?"

"Of course, man." He raises his hand and sets it on my shoulder. "Whatever you need."

"Thanks."

I offer him a small smile just as there's a break in the crowd, and I get a clear shot of Brielle. She and Becks are holding hands, spinning around, dancing, as if no one is watching. Jesus. I drop my head. Seeing her so happy makes me regret not having the strength to walk away. In this world, you always have to watch your back. If you don't, you might never see the monsters that lurk within the shadows. Speaking of monsters . . .

My mind snaps back like a rubber band as I lean around Wes and notice that my father has vanished. Fuck. Fuck. Fuck. Fuck.

"What's wrong?" Wes asks, whipping his head from side to side, viciously, as if he's expecting something to jump out at us.

"He's gone." I feel my chest tighten when I turn my head back to the side, and I can't see Brielle.

"Who?"

"My fucking father!"

I start toward where I last saw Brielle. I hear her before I see her, when she asks, "Who are you looking for?"

At the sound of her voice, I instantly uncoil. I reach out with both arms and pull her to me. "No one. You."

"Okay." Her voice is filled with skepticism. Thankfully, she doesn't pursue it. "Well, good timing then." She smiles. Her hands run down my arms until I feel her fingers lace with mine. "We were just coming to look for y'all."

"Oh no." I shake my head, again. "No, I don't dance."

She takes a step back and pulls on my arm. "Not even for me? Please?"

Fucking hell. "Fine." I run a hand along my jaw, my face betraying me as I feel the corners of my mouth pull into a smile. Damn it. She's lucky I love her so damn much. "One song." I hold up a finger to her and clear my throat, trying to say it in a manner that sounds serious.

"Uh, huh. Sure," she says, already pulling me back into the crowd.

She's facing the opposite way as she leads me toward some unknown place. I tilt my head to the side and decide to take advantage of my time. I let my eyes fall to her ass.

Fuck. I hold my breath.

Maybe I should be more worried about how she looks rather than my fucking father.

"Hey." I stop moving and wait until she turns back. Her expression is confused as she steps closer to me. The roaring music is even louder now that we're in the center of the dance floor. "Where are we goi—" I start to yell, before the music shifts and a slow song takes over the floor. And like a sick joke, most of the crowd dissipates. The only other people left are couples.

I watch Brielle drop my hand as she walks up and wraps her arms around my neck. The feel of her body on me does things to me, and I hesitate to touch her. "Theo, relax," she whispers, her lips grazing my ear and sending a shiver down my spine.

Groaning to myself, I lay my hands on her waist, the tips of my fingers digging into her lower back. "How is this?" I drop my head to hers. An inch is all that separates our lips, when I jerk her closer to me until her body is completely flush with mine. "Is this what you want?"

"It's a start." She giggles in my ear, taking a step back. "But for now, maybe we should leave a little room between us." She turns her head to the side and I follow. The many sets of lingering eyes remind me that we aren't alone.

I feel a small smile spread across my lips, letting the rhythm of the song lead me through the movements. We move in small circles around the room, dancing within pockets of light and dark. A sea of gold masks consumes the space around the dance floor and casts a chilling glare. We've come halfway around, when I see Becks shoot her eyes to the entrance, and nosily, I turn to see what she's staring at.

Ah, fuck.

"What is it?" Brielle asks when she reads my expression.

Twisting around within my arms, she sees him. Luca. The fucking five-foot-ten, brown-headed, blue-eyed bane of my existence. Brielle drops her arms. As if she's wearing a flashing neon sign, his eyes immediately find her. The expression he's wearing nearly makes me feel sorry for him. I know it too well. I lived it. Well, so much for this being a romantic moment. I pinch the gap between my eyes and try not to focus on how his presence is affecting Brielle.

I watch him walk over to the refreshment table, and begin picking at the assortment of finger foods. My mind chooses now, of all times, to dredge up the conversation he and I shared on the phone. The one where he promised to respect our relationship as long as I promised not to break her heart. I inhale a deep breath.

"Go," I say. My voice is as weak as my desire for her to leave me.

"What?"

Brielle turns around to face me. The slight smile she's fighting to hold back challenges my will to be a better man. I lift my hands to her shoulders and gently turn her toward Luca's direction. "Go," I repeat. "It's okay."

I drop my hands, half expecting her to run to him like something out of those sappy movies she loves so much. But she doesn't. Instead, she turns around and throws herself in my arms, and kisses me.

She pulls back with both of her hands holding mine. The bottom of her eyes well up as she takes a step backward before she turns around and makes her way through the crowd of people. I drop my eyes, realizing that I could have waited until after the song was over, so I'm not left standing in the middle of the dance floor.

Alone.

"Holy shit, Theo," Becks says as she and Wes make their way toward me. The two of them are moving as if they're still drunk from last night. "That was epic."

"Thanks," I say, cutting my eyes off to the side when I catch the tailored cut of my father's suit. He sees me watching him and adjusts himself. His steely gaze is unmatched to my own, as I fix my feet toward him. The look of malice is clearly etched across his face, reminding me of who my true enemy is. I take a step.

"Whoa." I stop when I feel Wes's hand reach out and hold me back. "Do you really think that's a good idea?"

I glance down at his hand and he removes it. "No. Probably not, but I have to try." I turn slightly to the side. "Just keep an eye on Brielle for me. I'll be back."

"I will but be careful." He then adds, "This is the devil's territory."

chapter forty-three

THEO

I pinch the bridge of my nose and breathe in, breathe out. I walk the distance to my father and come to a stop in front of him. A few of his "associates" step in between us, as if they're worried I could blow up at any moment. They're wise to assume . . . because I could.

"Ah, Son." The asshole crosses one arm over his chest as the other runs a hand across his salty stubble. "I had a feeling I would see you again. Where is the lovely—"

"Save it," I say, exhausted with the tedious semantics. "Cut the shit, and let's talk."

I listen as he lets out a chuckle, tapping his black patent shoes against the dark hardwood. He lifts his eyes to one of his men before motioning for me to follow him to an empty corner against the far wall. I check Brielle out of the corner of my eye and find her and Luca are still deep in conversation. I inhale another breath, then follow after him.

"You always had a way with words," he says. A thin line of disapproval streaks across his face as he removes his mask. "What can I help you with, Son?" He runs his tongue across his teeth and sets his jaw. "I can only assume this meeting is in result of a certain little message you may have received about your pet?"

"Don't talk about her like that!" I threaten. "Brielle isn't—"

"Oh, but isn't she?" my father growls. The veins in the side of his neck threaten to pop. "I mean, what are we even doing here? You can't seriously be interested in pursuing a life with this girl, can you? You're not necessarily the marrying type."

"And if I am?"

"Please. We both know the Sutton girl will never truly accept who you are."

"Her name is Brielle."

He lets out a breathy laugh. "Come on, we can still salvage this." He extends his hand, pressing it to my shoulder. "Katrina would still take you back; you're a handsome guy."

"You're unbelievable." I shrug his hand away. "Who the fuck are you to speak to who I am? You don't even know me. You never did." I feel my hands curl into fists at my sides. The skin over my knuckles strains as my fingers dig into my palm.

"I care about you, Theo. I just don't accept excuses."

What the fuck did he just say?

Excuses?

That's rich.

I almost laugh when I think back to all the times he fed me one bullshit excuse after the other as he beat me like his own personal punching bag. The fucking bastard.

"You don't care about me. All you care about is building connections and then extorting them." I spit out. He sets his eyes on something in the distance but I ignore it. "The fuck is it with you and the Overshires?" I ask, seeing his brows bunch up in anger. "What does he have over you?"

Within an instant, that cool facade he likes to wear fades and he rushes me. He grabs at my chest and forces me to the wall, waving his finger in my face like the deranged man that he is.

"Listen here, you ungrateful little shit. You should be thanking me," he spits out. The piercing green of his hazel eyes—now faded with age—are fixed on me as he glares in a way that's unsettling. "I gave you a life most kids could only dream of. What? You're going to cry about a few cuts and bruises? Don't be pathetic."

I shove him back as he throws his hands down and adjusts his suit. A family standing next to a group of kids turns their eyes on us, hearing the commotion. He smooths his hair down, his cool facade returning. I watch him smile while one of the ball's attendees passes by. His eyes slide back to me the moment she's far enough away.

"The truth is, you owe me," he says, his tone rising. "Without me, who would you be? Nothing. I made you who you are. Everything you have—" he points to his chest—"is because of me."

"Are you fucking joking? You think I should thank you for what you did?" I nearly jump him at the thought. "I was a child, you sick fuck. And you were an abusive drunk who never learned the meaning of the word 'enough'."

At that, he throws his head back, rubbing a hand over his tired eyes, and down his face. "You know, you're just like your mother—stubborn, selfish, and blind to the bigger picture."

"Well, I guess I'll have to take your word for it," I say, remembering his story about how my mother's love for me made her weak. And in the end, that's what killed her, not the cancer.

"I loved your mother!" he growls, the gravel sound of his voice is almost inaudible. "But she wasn't bred for this life. Her death was inevitable."

Inevitable?

"I'm not here to talk about my mother." I shake my head. His constant need to evade the real issues makes me want to hit something.

I watch as my father tilts his head to the side and squares his shoulders as if readying for a fight. But a commotion behind us tears his eyes away, as I watch the anger dissipate from his face. "No. Not now." He raises his hand, signaling his men to react.

"Theo!" I whip around when I hear Wes call my name. The concerned look etched across his face makes my pulse race while I sweep my eyes behind him and search for Brielle.

"Where is she?"

I take a step toward him, when my father's men block my path. "I promise you, you don't want to do this," I say, and I fucking mean it.

I hear my father tell them that it's okay and they step aside. I grab Wes by the arm and pull him off to the side, my eyes still scanning the room for blonde waves and green eyes. "What happened?" I ask, fearing the worst. My mind suddenly goes to a dark place when I think about the last person I saw her with. "Is it Luca? Did he do something?" I feel myself coming unhinged.

Wes shakes his head, his bloodshot eyes widening by the second.

"What the fuck happ—"

"She's gone," he finally says.

"Gone?" I repeat. "Like she left?"

Wes shakes his head again. His chest rises and falls excessively. Has he been running? "Wes, spit it out. What happened?"

"Luca and Brielle got into a fight, and when he went to leave, we lost Brielle in the crowd," he recites, like he had spent hours rehearsing. "I've looked everywhere, man. Luca's car is still in the lot but she's gone."

The fuck?

"How could she be gone if Luca's car is still here?"

I rack my brain, waiting for something to click. But it doesn't take long as I remember the sliver of a moment my father was distracted.

Damn it. I curse at myself, turning around and making my way back toward him.

"Is there a prob—"

My father starts to say, but before I have a chance to think about it, I rear back and slam my fist into his face. The slew of curse words he tosses my way next comes out in a garbled mess I don't have time for. He raises his hand to his cheek and rolls his jaw, staring at me as if he's never been more proud. I fist my hand into the front of his suit and slam him against the wall, my forearm pressing to his throat. Hard. I can hear his men shuffle behind me, but my father tells them to stay back.

"Where is she?" I try to keep my voice calm even though on the inside, I'm losing my fucking mind.

"Who?" the piece of shit croaks out under my arm.

"Brielle!" I grind my teeth. I refuse to give him what he wants . . . the satisfaction of seeing me break down. "What the fuck have you done with her?"

"Oh," he chokes. "Her."

"Where is she?"

"How should I know? I've been here with you."

I apply more pressure and watch him squirm in pain.

"You know, I could snap your neck," I tell him honestly. The idea of how easy it would be makes me consider showing him. But what would that solve? I inhale a deep breath and shove off him. "I won't ask again."

His grin is both equally terrifying as it is proof that he knows more than he's letting on. "I'd love to help, but sadly, my hands are clean with this one."

I roll my eyes. "Hiring someone to do it for you doesn't make your hands clean. It makes you weak. Who bought her death?" I'm yelling now. The feeling that I may be too late causes the muscles in my body to tense and my heart to race. "Tell me! Keller? Bushkova?" I plead with him. The subtle tremor in my hands is evident as I shove him back to the wall, negating any workable credit I may have held.

Her love made her weak, I hear his words in my mind.

"Neither." He squints as if reading my mind. "I sold it to Hurst."

What?

No.

I stumble back.

My eyes falling to the floor while my mind searches for an answer, as if it could be found in the wood grain of the floor. He wouldn't stoop so low as to call in Hurst. Would he? I run a hand through my hair. My resolve to keep things calm is all but gone now, and I lunge for him.

My fist connects with his jaw again, just as his men grab me from behind. I watch him fall to his knees. "I will kill you for this!" I threaten him. "If anything happens to her, I'll kill you!"

"And I believe you," he says as my back collides with Wes's chest the moment they throw me backward.

"They don't mean . . ." Wes lets his words trail off.

"Graham Hurst. Yes." I nod. "Fuck!" I yell, not caring who's watching.

"But . . . he's . . . sick," Wes says as if I didn't already know. *I trained the guy.* "Didn't you say he raped Dev—"

"Just, shut the fuck up, Wes!" I yell.

I am beyond pissed, not at him but at myself. I should have never left her alone. I close my eyes and let my head fall back. "Wait. That's it!"

"It's pointless to go after her," my father calls from behind his protective bubble of men. "By now, she's probably with that useless brother of hers."

"The fuck did you just say?" Wes yells, but I put my hand on his chest, shaking my head.

"No. Forget him. This is what he wants," I groan, motioning for him to follow me instead. I feel the darkness that's inside me taking over, and my better half steps aside to follow his lead. "Is Becks safe?"

"Yes, she's with her parents," he answers automatically. "We bumped into them and Brielle's, just before I—"

"That's great," I interrupt him, not interested in the details but just that she's safe. "I think I know where Hurst would have taken her," I say as the two of us burst out the front door and sprint around the side of the Manor.

A group of loner teens sees us, taking interest, but none of them makes an effort to move a muscle. They all look high as shit and probably assume we are too. "My senior year, we toured this place," I share with Wes.

"Yeah? And?"

"And if I remember correctly, there's a small shed just on the other side of the guest house," I say as we round the far side of the Manor and notice the exterior light shining from underneath the shed's door, off in the distance. "Multiple shadows," I make a point to tell Wes, as some relief pulses through my veins and fills me with an added strength I'm going to need.

"I'm with you." Wes claps me on the back. "I told you, whatever you need."

The moment we reach the door, I nod.

"Hurst is a strong fighter but he always carries," I warn Wes. "So watch his hands."

I hear Brielle scream. The sound of her voice is all I need to throw the doors open. The fact that she's still alive is enough for me, for now. But I'm wrong.

chapter forty-four

S ilhouettes in the candlelight dance along the floor in an eerie way as a sea of golden masks threaten to swallow me whole. I step around a woman wearing a vintage, navy gown, a double strand of ivory pearls clinging to her neck. I feel the music in every step I take. The steady beat of the bass radiates through my body, dissolving into the hardwood floor through my heels.

I see Luca and drop my train, the heavy crystals sounding like a thick rain as they hit the floor and pool around my feet.

"Holy shit." He nearly drops his plate when he sees me walk up to him. His eyes are moving down my body as I wait for him to realize that I can see him. "Y- you look . . . .y- you are—"

"Thank you." I offer him a small smile, trying not to react in a way that he could misinterpret as anything other than friendly—something I realize isn't as easy as I thought it would be.

I run my eyes over his suit and recognize it as the same one he wore to our school's prom. His father's cut had never fit him then as it does now. The shoulders and arms that were once baggy now hug him perfectly.

"You look handsome," I say after a minute.

As if suddenly remembering something, Luca drops his gaze to his plate and steps to the side. "What are you doing over here?" he asks. The strain in his voice makes my heart sink. I can tell he's hurting.

Out of habit, I reach out and touch his arm. "Luca, please," I beg him. "Can we just move on from this? I can't imagine you not in my life."

He lifts his head to stare at me. The baby blue of his eyes is darker under the soft hue of the candlelight. "Don't do that." He closes his hand over mine, slowly lifting it and setting it back down by my side. The motion surprises me but not as much as the fact that even when he's upset, Luca still remains a gentleman. "You can't say that to me."

Closing my eyes, I turn my head to the side.

"But it's true." I inhale a sharp breath and step toward him. "Just because I'm with Theo doesn't mean that I don't still care about you. You're my best—"

"Don't say that!" The tips of his fingers clench into a fist.

"Say what? That you're my best friend?"

"No." He turns around and sets his plate down on the table behind us. "Don't tell me you care about me."

"What? But I do?"

"Stop, Brielle! Just, stop. You don't mean it like how I mean it."

I hold my breath as I watch the array of emotions flash across his face. "I'm sorry. I didn't mean to—"

"Just . . . leave me . . . leave me alone, okay?" He takes a step backward, turning around and walking off.

"Luca, wait!" I call his name.

My feet are already moving under me as I follow him through the room. The need to check on my friend is more important than anything else.

I watch as he pushes past a family, who glares at him. He then rounds the corner and disappears out the front door.

Crap. I pause when I hit the threshold, dropping my eyes. A foreboding sense washes over me as I work myself up to the idea of taking the next step. Theo's warning from this morning echoes inside my mind and urges me to stop before something bad happens. The hundred or so times I swore that I wouldn't stray swells in my chest, making me doubt myself.

"You got this," I whisper aloud and take a step. Then another. "Luca!" I yell the moment I catch up with him, reaching out and grasping his arm. "Why did you run?"

"Go back inside, Brielle."

"No." I dig my heel into the gravel with the next step.

I watch his shoulders sag as he inhales a rather large breath. As he does so, the back of his jacket gets a slight pull, making me think that he has been working out. He turns around.

"What? What do you want from me?" He throws his arm open wide. The vulnerable expression he's wearing makes my heart contract.

"I just . . ." I pause when I'm not sure what it is I actually want. Forgiveness? For him to say that he'll still be my friend. What?

As if reading my mind, Luca steps closer and takes my hand in his. "If you're wanting me to say that I'll be able to get over this . . . get over you," he almost whispers, "I can't promise that yet. I've waited years for you to wake up and realize what's been in front of you for so long." He closes his eyes. "It's going to take me more than a minute to wrap my head around the idea that this is not going to happen."

"I'm sorry," I say, feeling the bottom of my eyes beginning to well.

Luca raises his hand and brushes a tear that's sliding down my cheek. "Don't be sorry." A slight humor rings behind his words. "I just need time."

"Okay." I nod, then throw my arms around him before he has the chance to react. "Just promise me you'll keep in contact with Becks?" I half laugh, half sob into his shoulder. "Someone has to make sure you're taking care of yourself."

"Do I have to?"

I giggle and pull back to look at him, arching my brow and shaking my head. "Be nice."

He rolls his eyes as if he thinks my request is silly but he's smiling. "Fine. I promise."

"Thank you."

The two of us stand there, staring at one another, for a moment longer before my mind is practically screaming at me to run.

That foreboding sense hits me like a tidal wave, as it crashes over and over until something catches my eye. A tall man in a brown leather jacket and jeans walks up to us, with a gun in his hand. The small, black chunk of metal makes me choke. Images of Mason and his lifeless body invade my mind and dominate the tiny voice that's telling me to run.

"Well, fuck me if Gerald wasn't telling the truth." The man clicks his tongue against the back of his teeth. The sharp features of his face, too angular to be attractive. He's wild looking. "You're gorgeous, baby."

"Hey, man," Luca cautiously takes a step in front of me. His arms reach back to hold me as I grip the sleeve of his jacket. "Put down the gun and let's talk. I have money. I can—"

It's then the man is joined by a group of three others— all of them gangly things in roughed up clothes. "Oh, we have plenty of money, kid. I'm sorry, it's Luca, right?" the man in the leather jacket croaks. His voice is hoarse as if he's ill. He turns back to his men, then cuts his eyes to Luca. "He thought you might be with the girl."

Luca slides his footing back, and I move with him.

"What? What do you want with Brielle?"

"Just to talk." He half closes his eyes, then runs his tongue along his teeth.

"And if she doesn't want to?"

As if on cue, the man bursts out laughing, his mouth gaping as he waves the gun, like he's pointing a finger. "Oh fuck." He laughs. "That's great, kid. I needed a laugh."

I then notice Luca, tilt his head to the side, as he mouths for me to "get ready."

Get ready?

For what?

I sweep my eyes around us, looking for a clue as to what the hell he expects me to be ready for.

"Ha. Yeah, you're welcome." Luca forces himself to laugh. The dry act confuses me. "But I think we should probably head back inside now." He turns, grabbing my arm and pulling me with him. We barely make it a step as two more men walk up and cross their arms in front of their chests. Both of them are standing with their fingers clutched around another chunk of metal. "Shit."

"Oh yeah. I could have told you that trying to run was pointless." The man chuckles to himself. He grits his teeth, like this is the most awkward moment he's ever been in. "Sorry, I thought that was . . . kind of . . . obvious."

I can feel Luca's muscles under his jacket shake as he continues to hold me behind him. He's scared and I am too. The last time any of us were anywhere near a gun, our lives were never the same. All it takes is a second of staring down the barrel of a gun to make you second-guess every decision you've ever made. "I'm sorry, Luca. I should have stayed inside."

chapter forty-five

W hat the hell do you want?" I finally find my voice and am thankful when my words come out stronger than I expected.

The man sucks in a sharp breath as I watch his eyes grow wide. "Well. Well. Well." He shrivels back as if my words have cut him. "We've got a feisty one, guys." He licks his lips. His tongue flicks out in sharp movements and reminds me of a snake. "That's good. I like the ones with a little bite to them."

"We'll scream," Luca threatens.

After the man turns around in a circle, his eyes scanning the parking lot around us, we realize that we're alone.

He raises his gun. "No, I think you're going to do exactly as I say."

"Y- yeah, you're probably right," Luca stutters when the gun is pointed to his face.

"Stop it!" I yell, sprinting out of Luca's hold to a few feet short of the man. "I'll go with you, just let Luca go."

The man seems to think about it for a second, but I can see that it's only an act as he rocks his head back and forth. "Sorry, but no, hot stuff." He slinks closer. His eyes move over my body as if I'm some unknown creature to him. "I'd rather not fight your boyfriend tonight."

My boyfrie—

"Hey, back the fuck up!" I faintly hear Luca shouting in the background, as my body freezes, feeling the man's hands grip my waist.

Using his gun, he slides it up my back. The barrel is perfectly positioned to fire at any moment. "What an exquisite dress," he croaks. The warmth of his breath is hot on my arm as he presses his chest to my back and sniffs my hair. "It's a shame it won't make it through the night with you."

"You're sick." I try to pull away from him.

"Walk," he demands, his hand reaching up to clutch the top of my arm before he pushes me ahead of him.

We stumble through the darkness for a few minutes, raggedly dodging partygoers, who are casually slumped along the entrance steps. When we reach the back of the Manor, there's nothing back here but a distant light off to the left.

Behind me, I can hear Luca yelling, but he's too far away. I know I should be fighting, kicking, screaming, anything. But for some reason, my lips are sealed shut, my body seized in fear. Is this it?

My mind painfully sifts over all the things I never got to do.

Well, at least I won't be dying a virgin.

If my father were here, I'm sure he'd have a lot to say about how I managed to find myself in a situation like this. But I don't have time to think about that.

My heels dig into the soft ground. The image of a floundering fish out of water comes to mind, as I think about how I feel—frenzied and fearful for my life. We're a couple of hundred feet away, when I can finally discern that the light I saw in the distance is actually a spotlight from a small, white, wooden shed that's tucked behind an equally small house.

He pushes me against the wall as he unlatches the door. The gun is pressed to my temple in case I have any idea of running. I'm not stupid enough to think that I would get very far. It's hard to imagine that the shed is even on the same property as the Manor. It's so far away.

"Good girl." He smiles. The yellowish-white of his teeth catches my attention as I try to focus on anything other than the fact that there's a gun being held to my head. He steps back. "Now open it."

I feel my feet drag below me as I hobble to the door. Luca and the others are in tow as I jerk the doors open; a cloud of dust hits me in the face as I do.

"Move," he says in spurts, waving his hand in front of his face.

From the outside, the shed looks freshly remodeled with a new coating of paint. But the inside is as ancient as the equipment it holds. Cobwebs line the ceiling and mostly block out the overhead light. What little light that does make it through flints with tiny bugs that come alive and beat their wings in a disorderly manner.

"Brielle, run!"

I turn in time to see Luca yell as the man in the black shirt, quickly answers him in the form of his fist connecting with his stomach. Luca drops his head, his knees buckling under him. They carry him into the shed.

"Leave him alone!" I shout, running to my friend.

One of the men holding Luca upright spits out, "Back up, bitch." But his elbow is doing little to shove me aside.

It's then, without thinking, I lunge at him. My hands slam against his chest and his arms, and my feet kick at his legs.

"Just leave him alone!"

The man releases his hold and flips his hand back, making contact with my face. The force of it kicks my head back, and I hit the floor, crying out in pain as my teeth cut into the inside of my cheek. The pain comes in hot waves and makes my head spin.

"You bastard!" Luca goes wild then. He turns on the men in a violent approach, his hands connecting with the man's jaw, catching them off guard.

I look down at my hands, which are covered in dust and dirt. Kneeling on the floor, I hold my face. The smell of fertilizer and mold burns my nostrils. I barely have time to worry over the tiny drops of blood falling from my mouth, as the man in the leather jacket comes up behind me and grips my hair. His fingers curl around a bunch of strands as he pulls me to my feet. Searing pain courses through my scalp as the bobby pins are torn until they hang loose.

"Why are you doing this?" My hands move to grab onto his wrists, desperate for some relief. "What do you want from me?"

A voice in the back of my head tells me that I already know.

"Well, precious," he says when we reach a spot not too far away from the others. His hand nearly punches the wall as he slams my head into it. "See, I'm what you might call a bounty hunter." He smiles. His hand with the gun disappears behind his back, only to return with a knife instead. The sleek blade glints under the soft light of the shed. The large serrations cast on it are chipped and show its use. "Only . . . I take more pleasure in my work."

I squirm when he brings the knife to my chest. The tip of the blade glides down my cleavage and doesn't stop. "Spread your legs," he commands, and when I don't, I can hear the hiss slither from his lips. "You can spread them, or I will." He tilts his head. The hilt of the blade digs into my hip.

I focus on Luca so that I don't have to think about what's about to happen, but I see that he's lying on the ground. Four of the men take turns landing kick after kick. Each one sends another splatter of blood spraying against the wall, like some twisted form of art. I can't see his face.

"Please!" I yell when I feel the knife slice through my dress, like butter between my legs. The tip of it catches the inside of my thigh and nicks the skin.

"Look at me."

I turn the other way.

"I said look at me!" He brings the knife up to my neck. The feel of my pulse beating against the cool metal of the blade petrifies me. I pinch my eyes shut and hold my breath. He moves the blade, and I swear I can hear it as it kisses my skin. The quick sting, like that of a paper cut, forces my eyes open as I stare back at him with a blank expression.

He removes the blade.

"Now, where were we?" He bends to the side and spreads the slit in my dress. "Oh, I see you wore lace for me." He sneers, saying, "Too bad this knife will shred those like they were never there."

I press my head to the wall and bite my lip. The sound of subtle rustling comes from the door. A pensive thought crosses my mind.

I glance back to Luca and find his arms are no longer hugging his waist, his hands no longer blocking their blows. "Leave him alone!" I beg.

Luca!

I feel the tip of the blade back on my neck, when the doors creak open with a deafening sound. The man in the leather jacket is suddenly ripped from where he's standing. His body flops to the ground, and then I see a fury of fists skillfully disarming him. I blink my eyes and find Theo fighting the man in a formidable way. They unnervingly move around the room, like an expertly coordinated dance. Each of them takes their turn until Theo lands a spine-chilling blow and the man falls.

Wes comes out from behind Theo, sprinting over to Luca. He shoves two of the guys away from Luca. But his movements aren't as coordinated as Theo's, and before long, he's surrounded. Theo rushes my side.

"Brielle, I'm so sorry, I—" he begins, but I cut him off. Shaking my head, I yell, "Luca!" and I point to him.

I can see his hesitation to leave me cross his face, but thankfully he doesn't argue. Instead, he moves with a quick grace and tears through the guys one by one. I blink hazily as my head aches in an alarming way, but I force myself to go to Luca's side.

"Luca!" I call out to him the moment I reach his body. "Please. Please, don't be dead."

I crouch over him and put my ear to his chest, praying that the pulse I'm hearing is his and not my own. What do I do? I run my eyes over his body, searching for anything that could help relieve some of his pain.

I squeal and throw myself on Luca when a gun is knocked from one of the guy's hands. The handle clashes against the floor, and everyone freezes, waiting to see if it is going to go off. When it doesn't, a collective sigh ushers through the room. I turn to Theo and watch as he nimbly disarms and renders each man unconscious with deft hands.

"Naughty, naughty."

I'm torn from the floor. I hear his voice before I see him.

He clutches my neck with his hand and pulls me in front of his chest. His gun is pressed to my back.

"Hurst, you son of a bitch. Let her go!" Theo yells from across the room. I watch as he takes one of Hurst's men by the head and runs him into the wall. The force knocks the guy out as he falls limp to the floor.

"You know, when I saw the contract, I didn't care how much money your father was offering," the man snickers behind me. The bastard's croak ignites goosebumps to surface along my spine. "No, I took this one for free." He twists the barrel so that it juts into my back "To kill the love of the great Theo Wescott . . . now that's the stuff of legends."

"I'm not going to let that happen," Theo says matter of factly. His stone-clad gaze fastens on Hurst, as he stalks over the men's bodies he's knocked out. "I'll kill you for this!"

"While that may be true—" he pulls me back toward to door—"it still won't help your precious love." I feel his lips graze my ear, as I fight to move away from him. "Tell your brother Mr. Wescott says—"

I fall forward and into Theo's arms as Hurst's hand releases me.

"It's okay. I have you." Theo's hands smooth my hair. I turn to see what's happening when a thick, gargling sound fills the air. "No, babe! Don't look!" Theo warns me but it's too late.

"Oh my God!" I yell when I see the knife embedded in the man's throat. The thick blade buried to the hilt as it jerks, spouting blood. Blood pools around his body. I know without a doubt that he's dead. *Dead . . . wait . . . Luca!* I flip over to my knees and crawl to him.

"An ambulance is on the way," Wes tells me, but I don't acknowledge him.

"Luca!" I shout.

"Brielle, he's going to be—"

"Don't!" I turn on Theo. "Don't say that! That's what you said when Mason was shot and he died." I wipe my nose along my forearm. The blood from my lip mixes with the dust from the floor. "I can't lose Luca too!"

I watch Theo bend down and pick up a gun. He tucks it in the back of his suit. Out of the corner of his eyes, he catches me watching him. Turning to me, he says, "I've never known my father not to have a backup plan." He shrugs his shoulders. "This is mine."

"Very wise, Son."

We all turn our heads to the door, where Theo's father and four other men are standing, grinning like they've got a secret to tell.

"It seems I've highly underestimated you again." He raises a perfectly poised brow. "Now, hand over the girl."

chapter forty-six

S tanding in a hand-tailored, Armani suit, and black Patton shoes. Gerald Wescott radiates a dominance that's unmatched to anyone I've ever seen. Similar to Theo, his masculine jawline is clearly defined, but the roots of his hair and stubble reflect his age, as salt and pepper melt with his natural russet-color.

Like something out of an action movie, Theo reaches for the gun he'd picked up earlier and raises it, pointing it directly at his father. "I think she's fine where she is," he spits out.

The men standing behind his father waste no time in drawing their guns. With their barrels pointed, they all set their sights on Theo.

"Well, Son—" Mr. Wescott steps over Hurst's lanky form as he ignores Theo's threat—"I see you haven't lost your touch." He points to Luca's motionless form. The grin on his face stretches as he stops just shy of Theo. "Although sadly, I think that one is still in need of mercy."

Theo's presses the tip of his gun into his father's jacket. A dry smile pulls at his lips.

"You're going to shoot me? Really? Aren't these daddy issues of yours tiresome yet?"

Theo shakes his head as if to clear his mind. "I don't know." He half laughs "I'm willing to find out if you are."

Mr. Wescott rolls his eyes and turns his shoulder into the gun, knocking Theo back as he steps into the safety of his men. "You know your friend is going to die," he spits over his shoulder, the milky green of his eyes pinning me to the floor.

I wrap an arm over Luca's body and protectively lean into him.

"Serves him right, though, for protecting a dead girl." He shrugs, partially annoyed. "Luckily, there's still time to correct that—yet another reason you should be thanking me, rather than threatening me, Son." He turns to glare at Theo. "It's because of me you've learned how to handle yourself. Learned how to fight. Unlike this pathetic waste of—"

"Theo learned to protect himself because you're an abusive asshole, you deranged lunatic!" I yell, surprising even myself. My head aches as the room spins in a blurred haze. That's what I get for cursing. I rub my temple.

I catch Theo twist to the side. "Brielle, are you—"

"Ah, Brielle—" Theo's dad nods his head as if he knows what I've said is the truth—"I must say, you've pleasantly surprised me over the past month and a half." He motions with his hands around the room. "Never in my life have I witnessed a mere girl cause such a ripple among men and business. It's quite bothersome."

As if on some hidden cue, all of the guns abruptly turn. And for the second time today, my life flashes before my eyes.

"What the fuck?" Wes's voice is shaky and on edge. He steps to my side, doing his best to cover me.

But my eyes are on Theo who hasn't budged, his stance rigid and unnervingly calm.

"Some men are born to protect, while others are meant to kill." Noticing my reaction, his father recites these words, giving meaning to Theo's odd behavior.

"And some only live to die," Theo finishes for him.

I watch Mr. Wescott's expression harden into a thin line as he set his eyes on Theo. "Deaths comes to every man at a certain time and place, but I can assure you, Son that this . . . is not mine."

"We'll see about that."

"You should have heeded the warning—" he continues talking, ignoring Theo's statement—"if this girl means so much to you, as you claim."

I feel my heart contract. "Warning?" I ask. "What warning?"

I watch Theo's hand falter with the gun, and at that moment, one of the men standing behind his father lunges at him.

"Shoot the girl!" His father shouts, as my eyes hold firm onto Theo's face.

Dazed, I watch as Theo sidesteps the man and disarms him. Using the gun's handle, he whips around and slams it into the man's head. The bone-cracking sounds echo through my ears, like a movie's special effects. When the man drops, I see Theo turn and sprint toward me, when the gun goes off, and for a split second, the room and everyone in it are swallowed by a ghostly silence.

"What the hell did you do?" Mr. Wescott turns on his man. A sinister glare contorts his face as he snatches the gun from the closest guy and fires off one shot, instantly killing the man on the far right. "I said, shoot the girl!" he shouts at the man's lifeless body. "Not my son."

"Theo!" I hear a voice screaming that I barely recognize as my own. I drop to my knees and press my hand to his shoulder where a dark red patch is beginning to form over his jacket. "What the hell were you thinking?" I yell at him. The bemused expression he's wearing is already fading from his face.

Theo smiles that devilish grin as he winces in pain. Quietly, he says, "I wasn't."

"This is exactly what I was afraid of," his father's voice pierces the room. "It happened with the Sutton boy, and now it's happening all over again with the girl. You're weak, Son, when they're around. Why can't you see that?"

"Don't you dare talk about my brother!"

Closing his eyes, Theo staggers to his feet. His good arm, clutching the gun. "For a man who claims to care so much about the importance of not seeming weak, last I checked, cowering behind your men isn't a sign of strength."

"Watch it, boy."

"Why? Afraid I'm right?"

Mr. Wescott lets his eyes fall to Theo's wound. "It would hardly be a fair fight even if I were alone."

"Then you have nothing to lose." He jerks his head to the three men still standing behind him. "Send your men away and fight me fairly, Father."

"No."

Theo steps in front of me and squares his shoulder, his expression tight as if he's seeing something for the first time. "You're afraid of something? Someone," he whispers. But his father doesn't move, simply rolling his tongue along the inside of his lip.

"Who's got you so spooked?" Theo asks. "Whoever it is. I won't help you."

A low chuckle wells up in the base of his father's throat as he takes a step in the opposite direction. "Oh you'll help me. You will because now we both have a reason to see Giovanni Russo dead."

Giovanni who?

Theo throws his hands out. "Fuck. That's what this is about? You're insane! That's a suicide mission!"

"Okay, what's going on? Who's Russo? Theo?"

Mr. Wescott pauses next to Hurst, bending down to pick up a piece of dust off the back of his jacket. A mindless gesture. "It won't be if we work together. All you have to do is marry Katrina, gain access to their accounts, and we wouldn't even have to lift a finger. We could pay someone to do it for us." he says plainly.

I feel Wes's hand wrap my wrist as he pulls me back to him. A nauseous feeling stirs in the pit of my stomach. Whatever the hell is going on. Whoever this Russo guy is. It's bad.

"I'm not going to help you. I told you, I'm out!" Theo yells. "What makes you think I won't go to him right now and tell him your plan?"

"What? And implicate yourself for the murder of Alec's man? Please. We both know you're smarter than that." Mr. Wescott grits his teeth, the sound reminding me of fingernails on a chalkboard. "Alec would have you killed on the spot."

In a flash of insanity, Theo raises the gun to his head.

"I won't help you."

"Theo, no!" I reach out to him, but he pushes my hand away. His steely gaze shoots to Wes, the two sharing a silent conversation. Whatever they've communicated to each other, when it's over, Wes has pulled me away.

"Son, put down the gun. We both know you're not going to shoot yourself."

Theo looks as if he's actually contemplating it. His pained expression makes me nervous that he would do it just to prove to his father that he can. But thankfully, he lowers the gun.

"You're right," he groans, his face twisting in anger. He raises the gun up again but stops when it lands on his father. "But I would shoot you. Russo is a reasonable man. If I shoot your—a traitor—surly that would be enough for him to overlook someone so miniscule as Alec's hit man."

"You son of a bitc—"

I watch Theo's fingers tighten around the trigger, when suddenly faint sounds seep through the wooden slats of the shed. A frenzied mass of collective screams reaches us from far away—no doubt, the result from all the gunshots.

Mr. Wescott's man leans out the door, taking a look before saying, "Sir, we need to leave. The police are here, and everyone is fleeing into the parking lot."

My dad! My dad's here! I suddenly realize, and the idea fills me with a sense of hope!

His father tilts his head, staring at Theo. His worn expression seems relieved. "Sorry. It looks like we'll have to continue this little conversation at a later date." He grins, narrowing his eyes.

"I wouldn't count on it."

"Well then, I guess we'll have to see. Won't we?"

I feel my knees buckle underneath me, as Mr. Wescott exits the shed. His men filter out one after the other, behind him, as if one of their colleagues hasn't just died—as if what's just happened hasn't actually happened.

I fall to the floor. My head feels like it's swollen double its normal size.

"Hey, slow down. I think you have a concussion" Theo drops the gun down by Hurst before rushing over to my side. He crouches down, slipping two fingers under my chin as he tilts my head to either side. The pain etched on his face paints a picture of my injuries. "I'm going to kill him." He jerks his hand away and moves to stand up.

"No, don't!" I grab his wrist and slide into his arms, letting him hold me. "He's not worth it. Let the police handle him."

"Brielle, don't you remember what I told you at the batting cages? My father has ties everywhere. I doubt anything will come of this. If it does it won't be from the police."

It hurts to think right now, so I pretend not to hear him.

"Holy shit, you guys." Wes yells from the back of the room.

I squint as I try to think about what Wes is saying, when I see Luca's fingers inch forward as if he were reaching for something.

"Oh my God, Luca!" I cry out, crawling over to him. I grasp his hand and hold it. "We're here, Luca. Stay with us! Where the hell is the ambulance?"

Theo wince as he removes his jacket and tosses it on the floor. The entire sleeve of his dress shirt is wet with blood. Cringing, I look around for something clean I can use to press into the wound.

"I can't believe you let yourself get shot."

"Eh, it's a scratch," he mumbles.

A sharp ringing trills in the background.

Well, that's not a good sign.

I tug at my ear.

"Are you okay, though? I'm worried about you?"

I open my mouth to answer him, when two police officers, guns drawn, swarm the door. "What the hell—" the shorter one starts, his eyes moving around the room. "Holy shit. Everyone just stay where you are. Paramedics are coming."

We nod our heads as more cops arrive.

One by one, we're questioned as the paramedics work to stabilize Luca for his transfer. My father joins us and quickly canvases the scene. After making sure I was okay, his fatherly sentiments are passed over as he works the area like a man on a mission. When I finished giving my statement, I find Theo arguing with one of the paramedics who's trying to look at his wound.

"Get your hands off me," he raises his voice at the man. "I told you, I'm fine. Examine, Brielle."

"But sir," the paramedic urges Theo see reason, "you're bleeding . . . from a gunshot wound . . . she's not."

"Are you fucking—"

"Okay . . . " I slowly step in between the two of them. Theo, as he sees me, slinks back to sit on the steps. "Go ahead and check me, and then Theo would be happy to have you take a look at his shoulder." I turn toward him "Isn't that right, babe?"

"Fine."

The medical exams are quick, and not surprisingly, Theo has to be transferred to the hospital for further care. Sitting on the step next to him as they bring the other ambulance around, I feel nauseous. The once beautiful entrance of the Manor is now littered in blood and random men in uniforms. Hurst's body is laid out on the ground, covered in a sheet, as his men sit idly by, handcuffed and beaten to hell.

The lights from all the cars outside penetrate my eyes like tiny stabs at the back of my head. I close them and think about my brother. How differently tonight could have gone if Theo's dad had succeeded in having me killed. The thought of Mason brings a smile to my lips, and when I open my eyes, I see Theo watching me. His dress shirt is unbuttoned with his arm in a sling, but he's smiling with me.

The second we were alone, he quickly filled me in on the truth behind his father's plan to have me killed. A stupid ruse in order to get him on board to kill, and overthrow, the Dallas crime boss, Giuseppe Russo. Which, now that he knows, Theo says that it makes sense he would want him dead.

Russo had just named his underboss, who would eventually take over in his stead, as none other than Alec Figueroa. Son of the man who despises Theo's father for marrying Theo's mother—his daughter. The second Alec has any sort of power, Gerald Wescott is a dead man. So he figures, take out Russo, take his empire, and eliminate the problem.

But like Theo told his father, going after Russo is a suicide mission. Unfortunately, that leaves us here. Stuck at a crossroad, with two endings in sight. Theo can marry Katrina and join arms with his father. Or he can face Giuseppe Russo and pray he's in a forgiving mood.

"What are we going to do now?" I ask, knowing he'll have an answer.

"I'm not sure. I'll do whatever you want to do, I guess."

I look around the scene and bite my lip. My eyes find Wes, who's holding a very emotional Becks in his arms. It's more emotion than I've seen her show since the night Mason was murdered. A night, much like this one. I watch until I notice they begin loading Luca into the ambulance. He's wearing a neck brace, and they have him connected to multiple small boxes by a bunch of tiny wires.

Whatever I want to do?

I don't want to do any of it.

I want a third option!

I don't want to ever feel like this again.

"I don't want you to marry Katrina, Theo because I'm hoping that someday—not now, but someday, we can. I can't lose you again." I say, fully expecting Theo to come unhinged but he doesn't. He just smiles and reaches out to brush the back of his fingers against my cheek.

"Good. Then we agree because I want to marry you too." He smiles. "I promise I'll fix this. I'll do whatever I have to in order to get out. To be done, for good. But first, I think we need to focus on what happened tonight. And making sure our friends are all right."

My heart contracts for a million different reasons, but for the moment, all I can think about it is . . . "So you want to marry me, huh?" I feel my eyes welling at the sound of it.

"Someday," He says, leaning over to press his lips to mine.

"Excuse me, Sir?" the paramedic who assessed Theo's shoulder interjects. "We're ready to transfer you now."

We stand up and I turn my eyes back to Luca and the ambulance he's in. He has no one to go with him. His parents are out of town.

"Go."

Go?

I turn around, confused by what Theo has just said. He tilts his head toward Luca's door. "Go with him. I'll be fine."

"Wh- what? Are you sure?"

He leans forward and grabs my arm. "Yes."

His lips close over mine as he kisses me. The kiss itself is quick, but I can sense something more behind it—a sense of longing and finality that scares me. It's the kind of kiss you give to someone whom you know you aren't going to see for a while.

"I love you."

With worried eyes, I take a step, but my hand refuses to let go. I'm afraid of what it might mean if I do.

"I love you, too," I whisper, then walk to join Luca in the ambulance, making sure to keep my eyes fastened on Theo until the doors shut, and he disappears.

epilogue

THEO

I love you too . . . I hear the memory of Brielle's words, and that night, echo inside my mind as I lean into the pavement, press my weight over my heels, and stand to my feet.

It's close to midnight and Brielle's probably worried sick since I should have been home hours ago. I was only supposed to swing by and check on Luca, while she studied for her upcoming English exam. But as I stand here—outside *our* flat, in Dallas, I can't seem to get my feet to work long enough for me to make it upstairs.

Never in my life have I felt such pain—such helplessness as I did the night of the All Hallows Eve Ball. From the moment that Wes told me Brielle was missing, every second that followed passed in a manic blur until my father had gone, and Hurst's body sat barely a hundred feet from me.

His blood forever a stain on my hands.

I used to think I knew what it felt like to lose Brielle, but I was wrong. Fuck, was I wrong. Nothing could have prepared me for what I felt hearing Hurst's name leave my father's lips. The instant fear that this time I might not be able to save her, stripped me to my core. And the real fear of who would I become . . . what would I have done . . . if I never got to see my blonde-haired, green-eyed beauty again, has haunted me every day for the past three weeks.

I was just glad that Giuseppe Russo had bigger fish to fry the day I went in to plead my case. Because not only did he grant me a full exoneration for killing Hurst. He released me from having to have anything more to do with them, and their world, for good.

When I told Brielle the news, she nearly fainted. There's just one thing left I had to do . . . my final task before I can truly claim to be the luckiest man alive. Something that until now, the idea wasn't even a possibility. Merely a dream that could never be. My one final task, and the only reason I'm even still standing here, when I should be upstairs with Brielle, making up for time lost.

I need to officially claim Brielle as mine.

But what if she doesn't want me?

Okay, yes, she briefly mentioned the idea on the steps of the manor. But the fact still remains whether or not she could really see a life with me. A future. For real. Crazier things have been said in the wake of a traumatic event, much like the one we experience. But I've been hoping to God that she actually meant it.

When I spoke to Luca today, he all but guaranteed me that she did . . . meant it that is. But it's Luca. And that asshole, although slowly coming around to the idea that I'm not going anywhere, still likes to push my buttons when he can. The only reason I even asked him in the first place is because, while in the hospital, there are some days where he sees her more than I do.

I swear, if he hadn't taken a beating trying to save her, I'd kick his ass for keeping her away from me as much as he does. But as he did, I made the decision not to stand in the way of their friendship anymore.

"Ah, fuck it." I shake my head.

There's no use stalling any longer. I'll only ever know what Brielle wants, if I ever make it up these damn stairs and work up the courage to ask her

I reach into my pocket and finger the velvet box Brielle's ring is in, ready to see it on the girl who's going to wear it for the rest of our lives. *If I get to be so lucky.* Because who I am with her, is who I want to be.

acknowledgements

I am so excited to finally be releasing *With You*. This book has been a work-in-progress for years now, and it wouldn't have been possible without the help of so many people!

Firstly, I'd like to thank all of my #THIELLE shippers. You guys have been here since the beginning, and the amount of support I see daily is still so insane to me. I love each of you so much. Every time I receive a comment or a message on Wattpad or Instagram, it makes my day.

Vince and my mother are next, of course. Your constant support, critics, hours of read-throughs, and laughs truly made this possible. Without it, With You would still be another manuscript left unwritten on my computer. I love you both to the moon and back! I am eternally grateful to the both of you.

I want to thank my amazing editor, Rosanna Aponte, who is the best I could have ever hoped for. Your comments throughout the book always made my day. You have been so helpful and made this such a smooth and quick transition and journey.

Natasha Makensie for her amazing cover, and to Carson Lakey for the excellent proofread and edits. You were with me from the start and I am so thankful for all you did.

To Tori, London, and to all my beta readers; for being amazing friends and supporters. You put up with hours of e-mailing, late-night phone calls, laughs, and so much more. You guys are simply the best!

And, of course . . .

Thank you to my handsome hubby, Jeremy, and my beautiful children, Rhydian and Caelynn; you are the light of my life! Jeremy, you gave me the time to help make my dreams come true, and you put up with my endless hours of writing—even when the craziness ensued. You only complained a little when I kept asking you to read the same paragraphs over and over again. But you were always there for me when I needed the extra push.

about me

Jensen Kristyne is a twenty-something year old mother of two and three fur babies. When she's not reading and writing, she enjoys playing video games with her husband, traveling, and spending time with her family. She and her family live happily in a small town in North Texas where they plan to remain. She began writing on Wattpad, the reading and writing multi-platform for original stories, where With You first took off. You can find Jensen at Jensenkristyne.com, on Instagram, Wattpad, and on You Tube at @authorjensenkristyne!

Lightning Source UK Ltd.
Milton Keynes UK
UKHW010635311221
396440UK00002B/275